TRACY BAACK

LOVE AND OTHER . . .
BOOK ONE

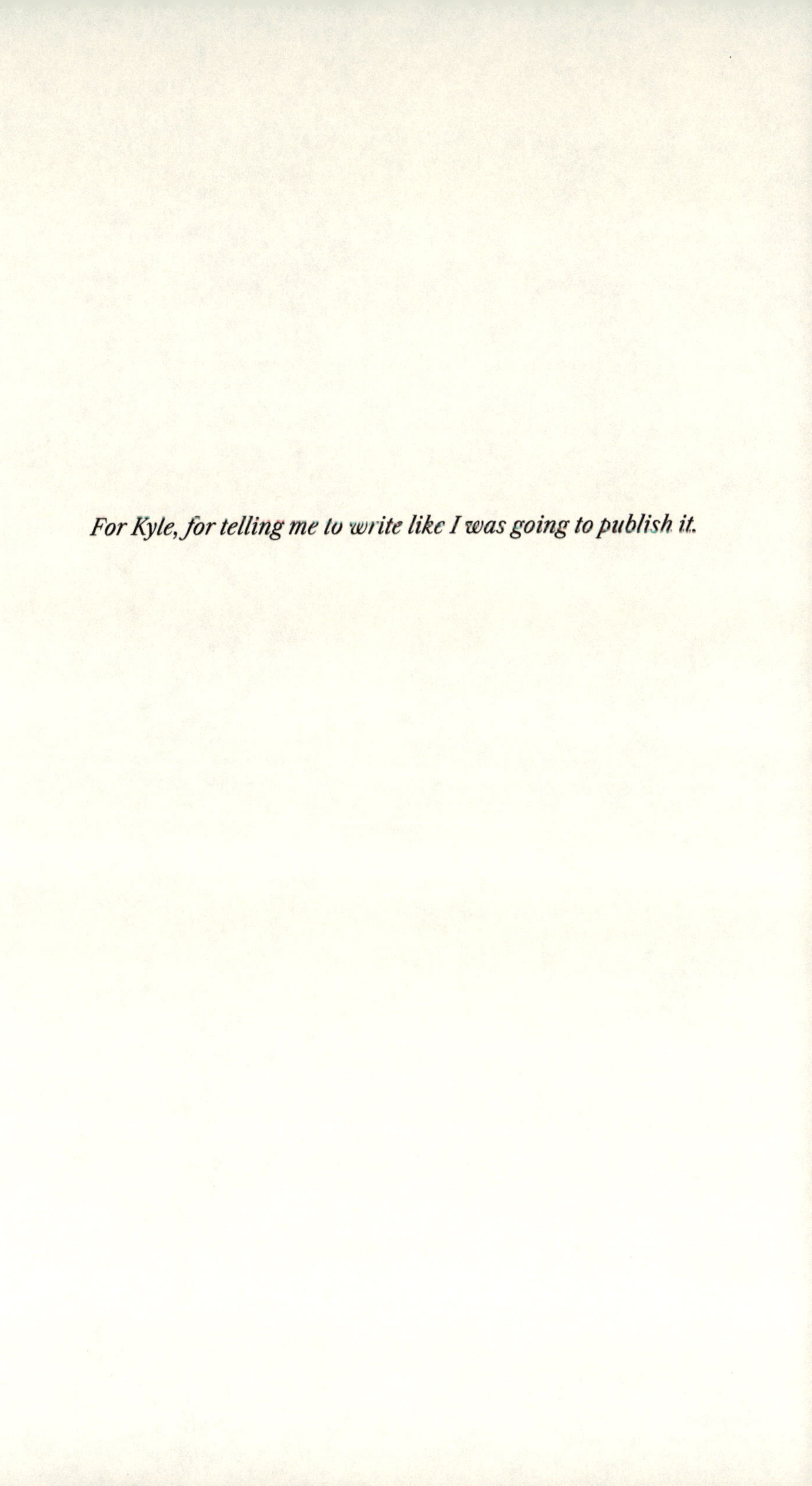

For Kyle, for telling me to write like I was going to publish it.

Author's Note

This story follows a group of college students who are involved with a Christian campus ministry group. If you weren't involved with a similar group, you might scratch your head at a few things in this book. Just roll with me and consider this your insight into a slice of college life you might not have known existed.

If you *were* part of a Christian campus ministry in college (although every group has its own nuances), I hope this story brings back memories and possibly makes you laugh a little. Although I was, of course, inspired by my personal experience, the characters and events in the book are entirely fictional.

This is a closed-door, kisses-only romance.

Content Considerations: Brief mentions of opioid addiction, miscarriage, and child loss among side characters. Contains references to the ramifications of the US withdrawal from Afghanistan.

Chapter One

I squirm as a bead of sweat trickles its way between my shoulder blades down the curve of my spine. My dress is as plastered to my lower back as the fake smile is on my face.

I hate rush week.

The headaches of coordinating outfit colors for each day, memorizing the daily questions, pretending to enjoy the shallow conversations—all to make a favorable impression of our sorority house on eager 18-year-old girls.

"Why did I sign up for this again?" I ask through my teeth as the group of girls we were talking to walks away to the next conversation rotation.

"Oh Lana, because you love the sisterhood, of course!" my best friend, Teegan, bubbles.

Nope. We both know I only signed on to sorority life for the social leadership opportunities that would round out my law school application. I graduated high school with a detailed game plan to achieve my goals, and I've adhered to it nearly to the letter for the past three years.

Teegan, on the other hand, was born for college Greek Life. She's the poster child for FOMO, although she's rarely in danger of missing out since she's usually spearheading the fun. Teegan has thrived in the sorority environment, and our sorority has thrived with her enthusiastic presence. She's been awake early every morning this week, which is saying a lot for someone who loves her beauty sleep. Socializing with large groups of people brings Teegan fully to life. Meanwhile, I've merely endured it all so I could reap the résumé benefits.

I suppose I shouldn't complain too much. After all, this sorority did bring me to my two best friends. Amaya, bestie number two, comes out the side door of the sorority house. Clipboard in hand, she smiles warmly as she directs recruits to their next stations. People are naturally drawn to her commanding presence, a beneficial quality for this week. Amaya's natural afro is pulled into a high ponytail, and the olive-green dress color of the day beautifully accentuates her smooth, caramel skin. When Amaya notices my attention, her dark eyes narrow at me. She points to her frown and changes it to an award-winning smile.

Oops. I re-plaster the smile on my face as I shift my position to try to unplaster my dress from my back. It's Amaya's fault that Teegan and I are stuck on the patio this afternoon. That's what we get for being best friends with the sorority president—voluntold to be on outdoor duty since the interior of our sorority house can't hold everyone.

Teegan's shoulder-length blond hair still looks fantastic despite sitting in the Kansas heat all day. I'd pulled my long, brown tresses into a sleek ponytail, but I'm sure any of the hair that isn't sticking to the sweat on my neck is frizzy by now. I can practically feel the eyeliner melting off my face. Teegan's dewy makeup has stayed intact, her peachy-pink eyeshadow making her blue eyes stand out. She reaches over to wipe a smudge from under my eye before the next group sits down.

Teegan takes the lead with the three girls who joined us for our final rotation of the day. They introduce themselves with smiles, but they look a little shell-shocked. Probably since this is the eightieth conversation group they've had over the past three days. Also, the aforementioned sweat-inducing heat.

When Teegan asks what they've thought about rush week so far, one looks on the verge of tears as she fumbles to come up with a response. I glance at her name tag—Liz. I'll blame the heat for disabling my brain, because I break script. "You know, Liz, recruitment week can get a little overwhelming. I honestly think it's a *little* much."

All three quickly swivel their heads in my direction, eyes wide. They're probably nervous that I'm trying to bait them into saying something negative that could be used to exclude them from our list of candidates.

"I really mean it," I affirm. "I wanted to check into a silent monastery after a week of forced conversations where you're afraid you'll be judged for any slip-up you make."

I see their faces softening. Teegan also makes supportive *mmm-hmm* sounds.

"But I truly believe that God was in control of my recruitment process," I continue, taking a chance bringing up faith before the recruits mentioned it, skirting around rush week conversation rules. "He led me to this house and to the two best friends I never even dreamed I could have."

Teegan puffs up and interjects, "That would be me! Well, one of them, I'm not both best friends."

The girls laugh and look relieved. The glistening in Liz's eyes is clearing up, and her shoulders relax.

"The point is, trust your instincts and trust the process. Take a step back and remember why you decided to join a sorority in the first place. No matter what happens at the end of the week, house or no house, you're going to have new friends who went through this harrowing process with you—and that tends to bond you for life," I say with a genuine smile.

When our time ends, I stand up awkwardly, considering sweat had fused my legs to the chair. "Next time, Teegs, pick a dress for me with more breathable fabric, would you?" Thank goodness I've had Teegan around to pick out all my rush week outfits over the past few years. What would feel like a dentist appointment to me is a trip to the candy store to her.

"There won't be a next time, LaLa. This is our last recruitment week hurrah." Her eyes blink rapidly as she says it, a tiny waver in her voice.

I give Teegan a tight squeeze. "Don't worry, any time you feel the urge, you can pick out color-coordinated outfits for us, okay?"

"Well, I don't exactly know when a lawyer and a special ed teacher would need coordinating outfits, but I appreciate the sentiment," Teegan says as she returns my hug.

Our tender moment is interrupted by Amaya barreling into us, wrapping her arms around us with such gusto that we nearly fall over. She's always been a force to be reckoned with. No doubt she's going to take the business world by storm as she laughs her way through every glass ceiling they throw at her.

"Just think, this is where our bestieship was birthed," Teegan sighs, fighting a losing battle against the tears in her eyes.

"Well, not exactly," Amaya chimes in. "The bid night party on Friday will be the true birthday celebration. No need to get weepy early."

As new freshmen, the three of us wound up in Alpha Omega Pi (or AOPi for short—there's an unwritten rule somewhere that Greek houses must have shortened nicknames). Considering how different we are, I find it interesting that we matched to the same house. I guess it's just evidence of how open-minded AOPi is versus the top two sororities on campus that only seem interested in carbon copies of the current members (family money also doesn't hurt).

As a brand-new AOPi at the bid night house party, I was walking around like a deer in headlights. I wasn't a party girl in high school, so I didn't know how to absorb the rowdy chaos of my first college party until I spotted two other girls standing together who were also clearly not drinking. We made a pact to stick together that night, and we've stuck ever since.

"We can take an emotional trip down memory lane this weekend, but for now we need to get the voting procedure done," Amaya commands. She runs a tight ship, the pro being that our house has finished meetings long before the other sororities every night this week.

"Come on, Beefs, let's get inside," I say to them.

Once we realized we were destined to be best friends freshman year, Teegan started calling us besties, but Amaya shot it down as an overused term of endearment. So Teegan switched to saying "Be Fris" like the first half of a BE-ST FRI-ENDS heart necklace. Apparently two separate syllables are just too much for us, so it got shortened to "Beefs."

Everyone thinks we're total weirdos every time we say it. But we're weirdos who belong to each other, so it's all part of the charm of our friendship.

We loop our arms together and head inside to a blessed blast of cool air. I just need to survive one final Bid Day, and then I can look ahead to the next phase of my life plan: one law school application, coming right up.

————

Bid Day is finally over. And I'm so over all the smiling, hugging, and crying girls everywhere. This is the part of sorority life that I will one hundred percent not miss.

Still, I'm proud of the bid class we got this year. Amaya seems pleased with how the week went and the increasing pool of diverse girls who went through recruitment this year. Townsend seems to be drawing more and more students every year, which is impressive for a mid-sized Division II college in Kansas. It's located in Brooklyn, a city just a few hours west of the Kansas City metro—and yes, we've dubbed ourselves the superior little sister to Brooklyn, New York. We have some decent athletic teams, so it's not surprising that Townsend has been getting a little more attention recently.

I'm certainly grateful I took my parents' advice and gave Townsend a look; I can't imagine what my life would be like if I hadn't landed here. I've grown to love the vibe of Brooklyn, a perfect marriage of a college town and a suburb. The heart of the city is a retail area called Center Square, a central gathering space surrounded by plenty of restaurants, bars, and specialty shops. The Townsend campus is compact and beautiful, with all the limestone buildings and mature trees, and the student body small enough that you're guaranteed to see someone you know while walking to class.

"Come on, Lana, we have to hurry and get changed!" Teegan says, pulling my arm toward the stairs. Our homecoming partner this year, the Alpha Epsilon fraternity, is throwing a joint party tonight to welcome our new members. Frat parties—another thing I won't miss about sorority life. A Friday night watching movies with my Beefs or going out for late-night breakfast food with friends is more my speed than dodging passes from drunk frat guys.

But Teegan and I are serving as designated drivers tonight, and we always keep eagle eyes on the new girls to make sure no one gets taken advantage of at their first party. I know it's important, even though I'd love nothing more than to crawl into bed with fluffy pajamas and Netflix.

After a quick change of clothes and taming my hair into a low ponytail, I drive over to the dorms to pick up a load of freshmen AOPis. Liz and three other girls come down the front steps, and I give them a bright smile and wave. Liz hops in the front seat while the other three pile in the back.

On the drive over, I tell the girls the speech we give freshmen every year: never accept a drink you didn't pour, down a cup of water for every drink you have, designate a buddy and keep an eye out for each other, and don't be afraid to say no to anything that makes you uncomfortable. I'm sure they've already heard these pep talks from their mothers before coming to college, but sometimes it carries more weight coming from a sorority sister.

I also let them know they're welcome to stick with Teegan and me if they get overwhelmed, an offer Liz is quick to take me up on when we arrive. As much as I didn't feel like coming tonight, I'm glad I can be a comfort zone for her. Her gratitude makes the crazy night worth it.

CHAPTER TWO

The next morning, I crack my eye open to check the time. 10:47 a.m.

I prop on one elbow and look at the other beds. Teegan is still fast asleep, eye mask on, and mouth wide open. Amaya is nowhere to be seen, but that's not too surprising considering she skipped out on the party last night. Something about important sorority president business.

Flopping back on my pillow, I cover a huge yawn with my elbow. Teegan and I were supervising underclassmen and driving girls back to the dorms until 3:00 a.m. last night. Or rather, this morning. I consider falling back asleep, but my growling stomach has other plans. Yawning again, I head down to the dining room.

The AOPi house is quieter than usual, but I'm sure a lot of the girls are still sleeping off hangovers or bid week exhaustion (or both). I pop a bagel in the toaster and drink a glass of water as I pour coffee into a mug with some half-and-half.

I start my mellow Taylor Swift playlist and sip my coffee as I wait for my bagel to toast. I mindlessly scroll through Instagram—lots of party photos from last night, different frat houses but same vibes. I'm tapping through Instagram stories when my heart skips a beat and my thumb pauses at the sight of Aaron Adams' blue eyes gazing at me from the screen. I hold down to look more closely at the story he posted. He's with two of his fraternity brothers from Omega Gamma, probably at their house party.

His blond hair looks a little lighter and his skin slightly bronzed after eight weeks at the beach. His muscular frame filling the photo makes it obvious he made time for the gym. I haven't seen Aaron since returning to campus, and I feel a surge of regret at choosing not to spend the summer with him.

Every year, a group of students from Townsend and other Midwest universities spend eight weeks in Florida for an intensive Bible-learning experience hosted by Arrow, the Christian ministry I've been involved with since freshman year. We stay in run-down condos on the beach, living in small groups with an older student as the leader. It's not a bad way to spend the summer, working at jobs in the city on the weekdays and spending the evenings and weekends doing Bible studies or group trainings to grow in our faith.

The first summer, Teegan, Amaya, and I were there as participants in the same small group, and then we got to be small group leaders after sophomore year. This year, Teegan and Amaya were top-tier leaders at Summer Project, in charge of overseeing the small group leaders, as was Aaron. I'd been offered a spot but turned it down to go home to Kansas City over the summer. I know that Kent and Rachel, the head staff members of Arrow, were disappointed with my decision, but I needed to go back home and support my mom.

She's an immigration lawyer and works for the organization that is tasked with resettling refugees on the Kansas side of the KC metro area. With the fall of Afghanistan to the Taliban, they've seen a huge influx of Afghan families needing placement services in addition to the regular arrivals through the refugee resettlement program.

Every time I called home last year, I could hear the stress in my mom's voice. She and her colleagues were all overworked (and underpaid), but they were determined to help these families. Because Congress had yet to pass an Afghan Adjustment Act to provide a pathway to permanency for the Afghan families arriving in the US, many of them needed help with asylum applications and other legal processes to ensure their future safety.

Considering I plan to become an immigration lawyer just like my mom, it was a no-brainer to go back home and help over the summer. Working alongside her gave me experience in the various legal proceedings involved in helping families navigate our complicated immigration system. Mom's connections even provided me the opportunity to spend two weeks in Washington DC with an advocacy group, meeting with legislators about the plight of our Afghan allies.

It was life-altering. And will certainly be a positive thing to include in my application to UC Davis School of Law. So, I didn't *really* regret my decision for a second. But that didn't mean I wasn't having a little bit of FOMO over not being in Florida with all my friends from Arrow, including Aaron.

The toaster pops, so I temporarily turn my phone off to carry my bagel and coffee to a table in the deserted dining room. Once settled, I click to the next photo on Aaron's story. I frown. This time there's a big group crowding around him in a selfie, including several girls—a couple I recognize from Arrow, but others I don't.

Setting my phone down on the table, I take a long drink of my coffee. *Did I make a mistake not going to Summer Project? Did my absence cause Aaron to forget about me?*

I've had a massive crush on Aaron ever since our first Summer Project. I'd noticed him during our freshman year, but after eight weeks of close proximity to his sense of humor, his eagerness to grow in his faith, his outgoing antics, and his radiant smile, I was a total goner.

It just so happened that his flexible post-college options fit perfectly into my well-laid plans for my future. His uncle owns a marketing firm based in Kansas City with remote workers all over the country. Aaron is majoring in business and marketing with a sure-fire job opportunity waiting for him once he graduates. A sure-fire job that could conveniently be done from, say, California.

His pointed attention seemed to indicate that he also had feelings for me. We low-key flirted that first summer and throughout sophomore year. He would DM me random funny reels on Instagram that he thought would make me laugh, and he always made it a point to find me to talk at our weekly Arrow meetings or at the social after parties following the meetings.

It seemed obvious to Teegan, Amaya, and me that Aaron liked me as much as I liked him.

But he never asked me out.

As sophomores, I justified it to myself that we were just young. We had two years of college left and lots of growing to do, so it totally made sense to not start dating yet.

Last year as juniors, we were leading Bible studies of freshmen for Arrow, so we spent even more time together at leaders' meetings. As an added bonus, his fraternity was paired with AOPi as homecoming partners. That meant our houses worked on everything together that fall, including a showcase performance with a skit and dance routine.

It was the only year I signed up to be part of the showcase. Conveniently, Aaron and I wound up as dance partners. Weeks of practice, having an excuse to dance together (even if it was mostly hip hop and swing moves), left me elated.

We killed it at the showcase, and when our routine ended, Aaron spun me around as the crowd cheered. He held me in a tight hug even after setting me down, until it was time to run off the floor. My smile was so wide, I thought my face might break from the strain.

When it came time to announce the winners, our team of AOPis and OGs was huddled together with our fingers crossed. Aaron stood right behind me, his hand loosely resting on my waist. I could feel his breath against my hair as we waited for the first-place announcement.

The announcer called our names, and we were all bear hugging and jumping so enthusiastically that we fell over in a heap. I'll never forget the way Aaron's arms reached out to break my fall and wrap around me in the midst of the chaos.

After the excitement calmed down, Aaron asked if he could drive me back to the AOPi house. This had to be the moment. He was finally going to ask me out on an official date. I even excitedly whispered it to Teegan and Amaya as I explained I wouldn't be riding back with them.

But nope. No declarations of love or date requests. We just talked about the excitement of first place in showcase, our chances of winning homecoming overall, random small talk.

I came home to AOPi that night depressed and confused, swearing to Teegan and Amaya that I was done crushing on Aaron, that it was clearly all in my head and not in his.

While Amaya initially seemed to share my dose of cynicism, Teegan rekindled the hope in my heart. She reasoned that Aaron might be hearing from Kent and the other Arrow leaders that he should hold off starting a relationship until we were closer to graduation. There was an undercurrent in Arrow to focus your time in college on investing in friendships and growing your faith, as opposed to casually dating.

The logic was sound, so I latched back on to my crush and my hopes for a long-term future together. I replaced my misgivings about his lack of clarity with belief in his best intentions, trusting that his shiftiness was due to the environment we were in, not his true feelings.

But now, here we are, seniors. Just nine months away from the start of our futures. So *now* seems like the perfect time to decide if our future is together. Because if we don't start dating ASAP, it's going to be very difficult to stick to my plan of getting married next summer before we move to California.

What if I ruined it? Maybe by not being there this summer, Aaron realized he didn't like me, or there was someone else he liked more.

Ughhh. I rest my forehead on my arm on the table. I can't let my mind catastrophize the situation with Aaron before I've even talked to him. At least I try to convince my brain of such.

I've been so lost in my thoughts that my coffee and bagel are cold. I get a fresh cup and grab a second mug to take to Teegan. Some Beefs time is exactly what I need to break out of this Aaron-induced funk.

Balancing the two coffee mugs in one hand, I turn the door knob to our room. Soft lamplight is on, which means Teegan must be awake. "Morning Sunshine," I whisper as I close the door.

Teegan moans from her bed, where she's at least removed her eye mask. "Ugh, I can tell I'm not a freshman anymore. I'm too old for this."

"Here, ya old lady, I brought you caffeine," I tell Teegan, handing her a mug. "Although with the amount of flavored creamer you use, it might be more sugar than caffeine."

"Bless you," Teegan says. She takes a long sip. "Sugar, caffeine, whatever will get my energy going this morning."

I sit down at my desk, still feeling a little pensive. "What's wrong with you?" Teegan asks before taking another sip. "You look troubled."

That's the thing about having best friends—they know you better than your ability to hide your thoughts. Then again, I never was a good poker player, so I might be easier to read than most.

"Oh, it's nothing really," I begin, picking at my fingernails. "Just scrolling Instagram and saw Aaron surrounded by a bunch of girls at OG's party last night."

Teegan immediately pulls up her phone. A few taps later, she sets it back down and says, "Beef, that's nothing to worry about—just a typical group selfie at a typical frat party. I'm sure it didn't mean anything to Aaron."

"I know, I know, Teegs," I groan. "I'm just a little worried that he may have, you know, moved on or forgotten me since I wasn't at Summer Project. Eight weeks is a long time. Long enough for a college guy's brain to get distracted, anyway." I take another sip of my coffee, looking down at my cup and avoiding Teegan's eyes. I don't like how insecure I sound, but I can't help it.

Teegan moves over to the desk chair next to mine, pulling her knees up to her chest. "Lana, I promise, I don't think you have anything to worry about. Aaron asked about you, like, *so* many times all summer."

"He did?" I ask, my eyes darting up.

"Yes," she confirms. "And did he not like all of your Instagram posts from this past week?"

"He did," I say, looking up with a little more confidence.

Teegan squeezes my shoulder. "Just be patient, LaLa. You'll see Aaron soon, and I'm sure every memory of how incredible and amazing you are will come flooding back. He'll have no choice but to finally snatch you up."

"You're the best, Beef," I tell her. "I'm sorry for being whiny. I want to hear about *your* summer—any gentlemen catch your eye?"

She gives me a sly smile. "Welll, there might be some stories to share. Too bad you'll have to wait till Amaya is back for our group catch-up session."

"What, NO! That's not fair, Teegs, you can't tease me like that!" I exclaim. She just laughs an evil queen cackle.

"Lucky for you, Amaya texted she'll be back in fifteen minutes—just long enough for me to shower and rinse all the nasty frat party out of my hair and for you to sit in torturous suspense," she calls over her shoulder, heading to the bathroom.

I open Aaron's Instagram profile again and look back through his posts from the summer. Every smile, every goofy pose, every look of his crystal blue eyes make my heart beat a little faster.

This is our year, Aaron Adams. I hope you got the memo.

CHAPTER THREE

The first week of classes is always so boring. Syllabi, grading scales, class procedures—I know I should appreciate the slow pitch start to the semester, but it's so hard to focus.

I took the LSAT over the summer and got an admirable score. Between some credits from high school I transferred in and front-loading my first years of college, I arranged it so I'm only taking twelve credit hours this semester. That gives me time to get my law school application turned in early.

At least, that's the theory.

I've decided to use some downtime this week to fill out the bulk of the application, and then hopefully I'll have my personal statement essay finished by mid-September. I'll feel good if I can submit my application to UC Davis by the end of September.

It's risky to put all my eggs in one basket, but I *really* want to attend UC Davis. Maybe I'll consider applying to a couple of other programs, but for the moment, I'm laser-focused on UC Davis early admission.

I made reasonable progress through the packet after classes. My Wednesday afternoon was shot after Amaya roped me into helping her with some projects for our first AOPi chapter meeting, even though I'm not on the leadership board this year. It was worth it though to see her proud, beaming face at the front of our sorority on Wednesday night. She's such a dynamic leader—I can't imagine a single thing going wrong in AOPi this year.

It's now Thursday afternoon, and I'm sitting at my desk alone in our room with a stack of chocolate chip cookies from the dining room, application open on my laptop. My Mindful Mellow Spotify playlist is keeping my brain tuned to the task before me, so I'm making great progress.

Ping.

The text notification sound from my phone summons, and I swipe it open.

AARON

Hey Lana. Feels like it's been forever. Hope I'll see you at Arrow tonight

Aaron texted me. He's thinking about me. He's thinking about seeing me tonight.

I stand up to do a little happy dance.

Okay, I want to let him know I'm excited to see him too without seeming too eager—I don't want to come across needy. I consider for a moment before typing back.

ME

I know, right? Summer was long. I'll be there tonight, so see you then.

I hit send and can immediately see that he's read it. Which means he was waiting on the phone for my response.

Collapsing on my bed, I know I won't be getting any more application questions finished. I shoot a text to our Beefs' group chat.

ME

Aaron just texted saying he hoped to see me tonight

AMAYA

YAS QUEEN!

TEEGAN

<heart eyes emoji> I'm picking out your outfit

I smile at my phone screen. Glancing up at my reflection in the mirror, I decide my day-three dry shampoo is not quite cutting it for my first time seeing Aaron again tonight.

After showering and blow-drying my hair, I'm wrapping chunks around my curling wand when Amaya and Teegan come in the door together.

Teegan beelines it for the closet. "No running shorts and oversized t-shirt for you today, missy."

"But she can't look like she's trying too hard," Amaya jumps in, joining Teegan by the closet. "Don't overdress her—it's still just a weekly Arrow meeting, not a night out."

"I'm just going to wear these cut-off jean shorts and a shirt, chill out," I say with more confidence than I feel. Adrenaline has already taken over as the number-one hormone coursing through my nervous system. My endocrine system is the one that needs to chill out.

"Fine, but make it a cute shirt," Teegan says, pulling a few options out of the closet. She holds up a sleeveless, emerald V-neck blouse. "Here, to make your green eyes pop."

I roll my eyes but accept the hanger from her hand. "We're probably making way too big a deal out of this," I tell them, turning back to the mirror and setting down my curling wand.

"Whatever, you're just telling yourself that because you're totally freaking out," Amaya says matter-of-factly as she exits to the hall bathroom.

I change into my approved shirt and assess my appearance in the mirror. Whatever blend of European blood flows through my family's veins allows me to get a decent tan over the summer that slowly fades during the winter months. However, not being at the beach this summer has left me a shade paler than usual. I'm a very average height at 5'5", my body build also falling right around the fiftieth percentile for a twenty-two-year-old, according to my annual physical this summer. My looks may be more average than extraordinary, but I did spend extra time on my most striking feature—thick, chestnut-brown hair flowing to my lower back.

I'm double-checking my makeup when Amaya calls at me from the hallway. "Stop stressing, Lana. You look great, and tonight is going to be fine. Now let's go before we're late!"

Amaya and I walk over to the student union for the Arrow meeting together. Teegan is picking up freshmen from the dorms, but I have to get to the meeting early because I'm in charge of the welcome team. A handful of us stand out in the lobby to greet students as they arrive, Sharpies at the ready to write name tags. I need to come up with the question of the week to ask—we'll write students' answers to the question below their name, giving people an easy conversation starter.

We arrive at the union and greet the other students and Arrow staff who are there setting up. Amaya heads into the room to place announcement fliers on the chairs, and I open up the box of name tag supplies.

Rachel, the Arrow director's wife, comes over to greet me. She gives me a quick hug and says she missed me this summer before heading into the room to make sure everything is ready to go with the band. I write my name and Washington DC on a label. I've decided the question this week will be, "What was your favorite place you went to over the summer?"

The rest of the girls on the welcome team arrive, and I share the question for the night. Everyone grabs sheets of labels and disperses throughout the lobby to catch all the students coming in from multiple entrances. In a few short minutes, a steady stream of people starts arriving. The lobby buzzes with the excitement of friends greeting each other after summers apart and new introductions being made.

I'm in the middle of writing name tags for a group of girls when, out of the corner of my eye, I see a large group of OG guys coming in the side entrance. My heart beats a little faster, but then I see multiple welcome teamers already poised to write their name tags.

Turning my focus back to the girl in front of me, I write her answer. "That is so cool that you got to go to California with your family," I tell her. "I'm hoping to be there this time next year!" She smiles brightly, and the group heads through the doors to the meeting room.

I feel a tap on my shoulder, and an oh-so-familiar voice asks, "Hey, can I get a name tag?"

Turning with a smile on my face, I look up to see Aaron grinning down at me. He pulls me in for a quick side-hug and asks, "What's the question this week?"

I'm already writing Aaron (and resisting adding a heart) as I tell him, "What was your favorite place you went to this summer?"

"Well, Florida, obviously. I wish that could have been your answer too—we missed you at Summer Project this year," Aaron answers, and I fight back a blush as I smile to myself. He points at my name tag. "DC, huh? I thought you were just staying home for the summer."

Resisting the urge to unload how my summer was so much more than just a summer at home and give him every thrilling detail, I simply respond, "I know, I wish I could have been in two places at once. I was in KC for most of the summer but got to spend a couple of weeks in DC working with an advocacy group. I—"

I'm cut off by one of Aaron's fraternity brothers half-tackling him as the rest of the group comes toward the doors. Aaron is swept up in the current of OG bodies, but he calls back to me, "You'll have to fill me in at After Party!"

Losing the fight against the blush in my cheeks, I wish I could take a quick breather in the bathroom and relive our conversation in my head. But strums of guitar music are welcoming people to the first weekly meeting, so I quickly collect all the supplies from the rest of the team. I stash the box under a table and head in the back door to find where Teegan saved me a seat.

After the first couple of songs, the band introduces the emcee for the year, none other than Bailey Williams. If you picture a stereotypical college sorority girl in your mind, you're picturing Bailey Williams to a T. She's the president of TriAlpha (short for Alpha Alpha Alpha, of course), the self-proclaimed top sorority on campus. She's been a student leader in Arrow along with Amaya, Teegan, and me, and although we all share a common faith, there's still an undercurrent of friction between us. Probably because Amaya is so determined to make AOPi the best it can be, while Bailey is always making low-key jabs about AOPi being a "less-than" sorority from her high-and-mighty roost.

Of course, they picked her as the emcee this year.

Bailey bounces up on stage and grabs the microphone. "Welcome to the first Arrow meeting of the year! We hope your time with us each week points you closer to God and community with each other."

She launches into the list of announcements in her singsong voice, punctuated with wide smiles. Her hair is so flawlessly highlighted that you can't quite pinpoint if she's a blond or a brunette, and it catches the light in all the best ways.

I can't help but smile at the memory of Bailey's face last year when homecoming results were announced and AOPi had knocked TriAlpha off their long-standing first-place position. I know Amaya is gunning for a repeat, although I don't know if that's more about keeping AOPi's positive momentum or rubbing it in Bailey's face.

The band starts playing again, and Bailey exits the stage. I push her out of my mind and focus on the music, then the message given by Kent about making the most of your college years to grow in your faith. It reminds me how extremely grateful I am to have found this community that has helped me deepen my relationship with God so much.

The meeting ends with an announcement that the After Party will be at the bowling alley in the basement of the union. Teegan is the After Party chair this year (because of course she is), and she called ahead to reserve the entire space for Arrow. Cheers go up at the announcement, and everyone starts chatting with friends or heading out the doors.

Teegan turns to me. "So?" She waggles her eyebrows at me.

I smile sheepishly and lean in with a low voice. "Aaron made a point to come over to me to get his name tag. Aaand said we'd catch up more at After Party."

"Let's go then!" Teegan says, pushing me out of the row of seats and motioning for the other AOPis to follow us.

We stop to chat with people a couple of times, but eventually follow the crowd of students heading down the two flights of stairs to the bowling alley. Music is pumping, and black lights accentuate any bit of white or neon. All the bowling lanes are already full, so the AOPis decide to congregate at one of the tables and order pizza from the snack bar.

I'm doing a reasonable job of staying engaged with the conversation among the AOPis, especially trying to get to know some of the freshmen who came, while simultaneously scanning the crowd for Aaron every couple of minutes. I'm hoping to see an opportunity to casually join his conversation group.

Unfortunately, he's deep in a (loud) bowling competition with the OGs and another fraternity—not exactly a great situation to insert myself into without being totally obvious.

With the pizza finished and no bowling lanes opening up, our group decides it's time to head out. My heart sinks a little, but Teegan gives me a knowing look as we're gathering up to leave. She leans over and whispers, "Don't worry, you'll have time soon, LaLa."

I force a weak smile and follow the group of girls toward the exit. At the last second, I look over my shoulder and find Aaron staring straight at me. He grins and holds his hand up in a guy wave, so I give him a small wave back.

Smiling to myself, I turn around and give my full attention back to my sorority sisters. Teegan drives a crew of freshmen to the dorms, and I walk with Amaya and the other upperclassmen to the AOPi house, discussing what we learned from the message at the meeting along the way. Several of the girls are still hyped up with social energy and decide to watch a movie together, but I realize how tired I am and head upstairs instead.

I'm in our room getting ready for bed when Amaya comes in, followed by a tearful Teegan. I immediately jump to my feet. "What's wrong, Teegs?"

She sniffs and then blurts out, "Jake is wrong, that's what!"

I glance quizzically at Amaya, and she saves me from my confusion. "Jake from Nebraska."

Ohhhh right. Jake was one of the student leaders from a Nebraska college at Summer Project. He flirted with Teegan all summer, and they'd kept in touch texting and on social media after returning to school.

"I just opened up Instagram to see Jake with his new *girlfriend*," Teegan moans, practically spitting the final word. She turns her phone to me, and I see a guy who must be Jake with his arm around a smiling redhead. There's a sappy caption about how he's liked her for so long and they're so happy, blah blah blah.

"I guess I was just his distraction to keep himself from openly flirting with the girl he really liked, who was also there," Teegan sniffs. "He never actually liked me at all." She wipes her eyes, and there's a murderous flash in Amaya's. I wouldn't be surprised if she secretly drives up to Nebraska tonight so she can kick him.

Abandoning all hope of early bed, I crush Teegan in a hug. "You know what this calls for, right?"

"Slushies?" Teegan whispers.

"You know it! Get some sweats on, and I'll drive us over," I look meaningfully at Amaya. "You, too. No road trips for you tonight."

She rolls her eyes but agrees. After all, there's no boy drama that a giant Styrofoam cup of frozen sugar can't fix.

We stay up late watching movies on my laptop and drinking every last drop of syrupy goodness. I know I'll be exhausted tomorrow, but for tonight, it's worth it to be there for Teegs, the way she always is for me.

CHAPTER FOUR

On Monday afternoon, I'm walking from the library back to the AOPi house. I decide to call my mom and check in with my family.

Thankfully, she picks up after the second ring. "Hi, my beauty, how are you?"

Just hearing my mom's voice and her favorite term of endearment for me sets everything right in the world. "Hey Mom, I'm doing good. Just finished my first day of real classes with actual homework and heading to the library."

She chuckles. "Just you wait, when you start at UC Davis, they don't waste time the first day on easy syllabus read-throughs. They'll throw you straight into the deep end from day one."

I smile at my mom's confidence in me. It's always "when," not "if," when she talks about me and law school. I fill her in on how things are going in AOPi, classes, and short updates on Amaya and Teegan. She knows how terribly I missed them over the summer.

Mom gives me the rundown on my family, which is mostly all positive. She's still swamped at work, but they're feeling a little more hopeful with the Senate reintroducing an Afghan Adjustment Act. "Hopefully it will get through this time," she says with some exasperation. "We can't keep going at this rate and help all the families who need it."

My twin brothers, Carter and Dean, started eighth grade this year, and unfortunately, Dean didn't have the best of beginnings. "He seems to be getting back on track though," my mom tells me. "Just keep praying for positive influences in his life. He needs to find some friends he connects with who are also making good choices."

Olivia, my fifteen-year-old sister, made the dance team at her high school after years of taking lessons at a dance studio. "Good lord, the drama—I can't handle the drama!" my mom sighs, making me laugh.

We're wrapping up the conversation when my mom asks with a smile in her voice, "So, have you seen your Aaron boy yet this year?" I've shared bits and pieces about Aaron over the years with her, enough for her to know who he is and that my crush hasn't ever gone away.

"Yeah, we got to chat just briefly at the first Arrow meeting on Thursday, but we were both pretty tied up with our groups of friends and didn't get to talk a whole lot," I tell her. "He seemed happy to see me, though."

"Well, of course he was happy to see you, sweetheart. If he has half a brain he'd want to see you every day," she gushes. I hear a knock and a voice in the background, and then she tells me, "I've gotta go, Lana. My next client just arrived a little early."

"That's okay. I love you, Mom."

Later at AOPi, I power up my laptop to get some work done on my UC Davis application. A few minutes later, Teegan barges into the room. "LaLa, a bunch of us are going to a class at the rec. Wanna come with?"

I groan. "Teegs, I'm trying to work on my application! I'm way behind the schedule I made for myself to submit with time to spare before the early admissions deadline. They need to know how serious I am about going there!"

"Look, I know you're like a dog with a bone when it comes to your goals and dreams and plans, the kind of dog who won't let go of the bone even when there's a treat or a car ride or a squirrel running by," Teegan says with exasperation. "But sometimes chasing the squirrel is the more important thing to do."

"The squirrel in this case being?" I question.

"Socializing with your sorority sisters and best friend in the universe. Also, a long, healthy lifespan by way of physical exercise."

She takes the liberty of closing my laptop screen, knowing that I won't turn her down. "Ugh, fine, give me a second to change."

————

The rest of the week passes in a similar blur. Either I forgot how much is crammed into the first weeks of classes—all the extra socializing, impromptu hangouts, Arrow student leaders' kickoff meetings—or I just never had a deadline to finish something important early in the fall before. We're heading to the union for our second Arrow meeting Thursday evening, and I've made zero progress on my application.

However, tonight's Arrow meeting is extra special because Amaya is sharing her faith testimony. She's well-rehearsed and generally self-confident, so I know she's ready. But I also know she's a little nervous, even if she won't admit it. We have a huge group of AOPis sitting in the front two rows to support her.

After the worship songs and announcements, Amaya takes the microphone. She introduces herself and shares about her background growing up in Wichita with a single mom. She never went to church as a child because her mom was always working a second job on weekends. Amaya describes how she struggled to fit in as a young, biracial girl without much supervision, and how she rebelled in high school, hanging out with a crowd her mom didn't approve of but gave her a place to belong.

Amaya pauses for a moment, then continues the story that I already know so well. One of her friends got arrested at the beginning of her senior year of high school, the same day that a classmate randomly invited her to go to church. Amaya felt like it was a sign, so she went. And kept going back.

After a couple of months of reading the Bible on her own, Amaya realized she believed in God, believed all that she was learning. She details the healing that took place in her relationship with her mom, eventually leading to her mom becoming a Christian as well.

She shares about getting involved in Arrow in college so that she could continue growing in her faith. She concludes, "I spent a lot of years looking in the wrong places for somewhere to belong, when God knew I belonged with him all along." Amaya doesn't usually show a lot of emotion in public, but I swear I see a glisten in her eyes as she thanks everyone.

Our AOPi rows erupt in enthusiastic applause, and I give Amaya a short hug as she sits down next to me. "So good! You were amazing, Beef!" I whisper. Growing in my faith alongside Amaya and Teegan has been the greatest part of college. We've grown through Bible studies and small groups, but also by working through obstacles together. Like when Amaya's high school boyfriend broke up with her unexpectedly October of freshman year because she was "too driven." Or when Teegan's parents got divorced at the beginning of our sophomore year, or my current anxiety about Dean's struggles. But facing those challenges together has only deepened our personal faith in addition to our friendship.

After the applause dies down, Kent shares a message about what it means to belong to God and to a community of Christians, just like Amaya introduced. After the last worship song, Bailey takes the stage to give some final reminders, including Arrow's first big social event of the year taking place on Saturday. I totally forgot about Lake Games being this weekend, and I'm tempted to skip it.

After the meeting is over, all the AOPis have planned to go to Amaya's favorite local donut shop to celebrate with her. We're enjoying our specialty donuts and discussing the meeting when I feel a text buzz through on my watch.

AARON

> You at the after party? I don't see you anywhere

I stifle a grin and pull my phone out, discreetly texting under the table.

ME

> Sorry, not there. AOPis out celebrating Amaya

AARON

> Oh yeah. Tell her she did great. Have fun

My heart sighs. One of these days, Aaron and I will have a real conversation. I just hope it's sooner rather than later.

Chapter Five

———

Two days later, Amaya and Teegan are in an AOPi leadership meeting that Amaya just couldn't schedule for a weekday, so I'm driving solo out to the small lake on the outskirts of Brooklyn. Arrow has always hosted Lake Games on Labor Day weekend with relays, obstacle courses, races, and a cookout (college students are suckers for free food). It's a good way to get new students involved, and it's one of the events that student leaders in Arrow never miss.

I almost didn't come.

I know it would have been frowned upon by the Arrow staff to just choose not to be there, and I never would have dreamed of disappointing them in the past, especially considering all they had done to help me grow in my faith and my leadership throughout college. However, after my summer volunteering with Mom and spending time in DC, plus the looming self-imposed deadline for my law school application, I've been reevaluating my scheduling priorities.

But then Aaron texted me to ask if I'd be there. Since we still haven't had a chance to connect, I decided to re-prioritize my schedule *after* this afternoon.

So here I am, ready to bake in the sun and dodge freshman boys in the name of love. Well, maybe not love. Just like. Strong like. Long-standing like.

I notice Aaron giving instructions to a group at one of the relay races, but I stop myself from walking directly to him. I stop to chat with a crowd of freshman, encouraged when I see Liz with the other two girls from my overly-honest rush week conversation. They wound up in different sororities, but I can tell their friendship is going to last a long time as they share about their experiences.

I excuse myself to grab a sports drink from the coolers and stand up to find Aaron smiling at me. "Hey, I was almost worried you weren't coming," he says, grabbing a water bottle.

Buying myself a second to respond as my heart skips a beat, I take a drink. "Yeah, I was thinking about just taking the weekend to get some work done, but I changed my mind at the last minute. Better late than never!" I glance down and see he's wearing a whistle around his neck. "Oh, I forgot that you were one of the leaders in charge this year. Looks like it's a success so far from the size of the crowd!"

Aaron grins, and I can picture the crinkles at the sides of his blue eyes behind his sunglasses. "So far, so good!" he says. "We added a couple of new games this year, and I think they've gone over well."

"Tell me more about your summer!" I pivot.

"It was the best Summer Project ever. We had such a great time," Aaron says with enthusiasm. "Minus the fact that you weren't there, of course. So many funny stories you missed out on. But I'm sure you had a good time at home with your family too. And you still need to tell me about what you did in DC," Aaron says while glancing at the time on his phone. "Hey, I need to go kick off this next race, but I really want to talk more sometime soon."

He grins at me as he backward walks away before turning to the race. Maybe "sometime soon" will finally come—maybe this will be the time he'll finally ask me out for real instead of waltzing around the periphery of our "are we more than friends?" relationship.

Two hours in the blazing sun and zero conversations with Aaron later, I'm beyond done with this event. I start thinking of everything else I could be accomplishing (also, air conditioning). Deciding to call it a day, I try to sneak to the parking lot without drawing attention to the fact that I'm leaving before the event is over. I'm halfway to my car when I hear Aaron yelling my name.

He jogs up. "Leaving already? Aren't you going to stay for Duck Duck Loose?"

The culminating event at Lake Games before the cookout is a race in which a guy and a girl pair up in a two-person kayak to collect giant rubber ducks floating around the lake. The guys paddle while the girls reach out to grab the ducks, of course with the occasional capsize. It sounds totally weird, I know.

Really, it's an excuse for guys and girls to flirt in a social group that kinda sorta mildly discourages flirting.

"Oh, I was going to head back and work on my law school application," I say as nonchalantly as possible, not wanting to seem overeager. Of course, I'd like the chance to flirt with Aaron in a tandem kayak. Would he "accidentally" tip us over so he could casually rescue me from drowning? A girl can dream.

He's looking at me expectantly. "I guess I could maybe stay a little longer."

"Awesome. There are a couple of freshman guys who want to participate but don't have partners. I can pair you up with one of them," Aaron says.

My heart turns into a brick. My brain is working overtime to squelch the burning sensation behind my eyeballs, and I extra regret forgetting my sunglasses. I'm sternly telling my face not to project what I'm feeling to Aaron, but now his brow is furrowing. *Curse you, face that never learned to play poker!*

I pretend to look at the time on my watch.

"You know, I should head out and try to get a little bit done," I manage to squeak out. "You should probably go get the race started because I'm going to just go, um, yeah, just leaving."

Apparently, my words also need to learn to play poker.

I turn away and awkwardly speed walk toward my car. I yank the driver's door open, ready to slam myself inside and possibly unleash a scream.

"Lana?"

I'm startled to see Mateo Alvarez, the shining star athlete of Townsend, standing by the front of my car. Where did he come from? Does he have ninja skills in addition to soccer skills, or was blood rushing so loudly in my ears that I just didn't hear him approach?

"You're not staying for the partner race? I can see people getting into kayaks," Mateo says.

"No, yeah no, I was just leaving. Aaron just asked me if I was staying and I thought he was asking me to do the race with him but he just wanted to pair me up with some freshman guy and really the last thing I want today is to do a relay with some awkward freshman and pretend to have fun so I decided I'm not staying." My eyes go a little wide as I realize how nutty that just sounded. I word-vomited ugly chunks onto one of the smoothest guys involved with Arrow. I just can't stop winning today.

I move to get in my car. Mateo's hand grabs the door before I can close it. He leans down to look at me and says, "Wait—will you be my partner?"

I stare blankly for a moment before a very articulate "Huh?" escapes.

"Stay and do the race with me. As my partner." Mateo gives me a one-sided smile. "Please?"

My mind is trying to figure out how to turn down this pity offer in a dignified way. It's not like Mateo and I aren't friends—we've been attending all the same Arrow weekly meetings and student leader trainings since we were sophomores. But I wouldn't expect him to choose *me* as his partner for the race. I'm sure there are plenty of girls ready and waiting for the chance. As my brain continues scrambling for a response, I feel heat creeping up my neck to my cheeks. I hope Mateo just thinks it's from the sun. "Yeah, okay," suddenly slips out of my mouth. I mentally face-palm myself.

I get out of the car and follow Mateo back to the Lake Games, where the other pairs are lining up for the race. I keep my head down to avoid looking at Aaron, not trusting my dumb face to behave itself. He's already in a kayak and not paying attention anyway.

We don our life jackets and climb into the kayak. I must be hallucinating, because when I glance back at him, Mateo looks awfully pale—almost uncomfortable. Which doesn't make sense because he's a star athlete in super fit condition. Paddling a kayak can't possibly be challenging for him.

The bullhorn signals the start of the race, and all the other pairs take off in a rush with lots of squeals from the girls and splashing by the guys. We push off the shore quickly, but then our kayak noticeably slows, barely gliding forward as Mateo slowly dips the paddle in the lake. *Hmmm, maybe he has a strategy of letting the other kayaks clear out of the way?*

We've made it forward several meters but also mostly veered to one side when I peer back at Mateo again. "Everything okay back there? Is there a secret winning strategy that I should know about? Are we heading for the edges to catch the ducks that other people miss?"

His face is definitely pale now. Deathly white, which is saying a lot for a man of Latino heritage who just spent all summer at the beach. He also seems to be breathing a lot faster than would make sense for the physical effort he has exerted thus far.

"I, um, I've never kayaked before," Mateo says. "I haven't really been on a lake in a long time."

"Really?" I ask, a bit bewildered. "You've never participated in the games? Or come out with your soccer teammates to spend a day on the lake? How have you been at Townsend for three years and never been out on the lake?"

He's breathing shallowly but manages to whisper, "I'm sort of afraid of deep water."

I carefully swivel in my kayak seat so I can face him without tipping us over. Who really cares about rubber ducks anyway? Particularly when your rowing mate is on the verge of a panic attack.

"Hey, it's fine, Mateo," I say calmly. "It's just you and me in a sturdy, non-sinking kayak. I won't do anything to make it tip over, okay?"

He swallows. I'm sure people back on shore are bewildered as to what's going on and why the most popular athlete on campus isn't dominating an athletic competition.

"It's just, when I was young, I was at an aquarium with this older kid in the neighborhood, and, uh, he teased me that one of the really creepy fish was probably caught out of the local lake we always swam in." He closes his eyes and pauses, as if picturing that aquarium fish again. "Ah, ever since then I've just been, well, kinda terrified thinking about what could possibly be swimming below the surface."

"You know what? I don't really like lakes all that much myself," I say quietly, trying to use the soothing voice I heard my mom use with scared clients over the summer. "Hey, just look into my eyes, okay? Don't look down in the water." He slowly opens his eyes and meets my gaze. I take a deep breath and he mimics me. "Keep your eyes on the horizon, and let's paddle back to shore."

His breathing is evening out and color returning to his face. "But the competition—I don't want to disappoint you," he eventually says.

"Mateo, I was literally about to leave," I say with a small laugh. "I honestly don't care. Let's get on solid ground."

He slowly urges the kayak back to shore, away from where the main crowd is standing. We climb out, and I make up excuses to a few curious bystanders. Thankfully, the bullhorn ending the race has sounded, and everyone else is on shore cheering the teams returning to tally up their rubber ducks. No one is even watching as we walk away from the water's edge.

"Thanks for that back there," Mateo says. "I'm sorry I froze up. I didn't realize it would be such a big deal until I got out there and looked down."

"It's really fine, I promise," I reassure him. "Anyway, I think I'm going to duck out of all this chaos."

"Pun intended?" Mateo asks with a small smile. I laugh. "I'll walk you to your car. It's the least I could do after that embarrassment!"

I laugh again and tip my head toward the parking lot. Mateo falls into step beside me. "I heard you got to spend a few weeks in DC this summer advocating for the Afghan Adjustment Act," he says.

My feet skip a step, so caught off guard that he would know that. "Yeah, I did. I don't know that I made much of an impact, but it was a great learning experience."

"Well, every voice helps. It's important legislation that's long overdue," he says matter-of-factly. "I'm glad it was reintroduced to Congress. Hopefully they pass it soon."

I glance over at him out of the corner of my eye. "I, um, I didn't know that you were interested in the AAA," I admit. I see him glance back at me through the corner of his eye. "I just mean, not many people in Arrow really know anything about it."

"My parents emigrated from Guatemala," Mateo shares. "I'm first-generation American-born, so I like to stay at least somewhat informed about immigration issues."

I'm just digesting this surprising information when Mateo one-ups his surprises. "Lana, can I take you to coffee tomorrow afternoon? Maybe Bookafe at two o'clock?"

Now I skip all the steps and come to a standstill. Mateo backtracks until he's beside me, peering down at my blank face. My brain is going to be fired after malfunctioning so epically today. I'm just staring at Mateo, forgetting how to speak or breathe, when he repeats the question. "Lana, I'd like to take you to coffee tomorrow. Bookafe at two? Will you meet me there?"

My thoughts are still confused, but I manage to force out words that sound something like, "Uh yeah, sure, yep, coffee is good. I like coffee."

Half of Mateo's mouth upturns in a smile as he says, "I know you do. I'll see you tomorrow at two."

He opens my car door for me—wait, when did we start walking again and arrive at my car? Also, did I leave it unlocked? I look down at the keys in my hand and realize that at some point I clicked the unlock button without my brain even computing that I was doing it.

I nod once at Mateo and slide into the driver's seat. He smiles one more time before closing the door with a wave. I push the ignition and crank the AC all the way up.

―――――

I leave the parking lot but don't head straight back to AOPi, instead opting to drive around with the air conditioning and my thoughts on full blast.

The cool air returns my brain temperature to normal, and I take a breath. *Surely Mateo just wants to get coffee to talk more about my time in DC and the Afghan Adjustment Act, right?* He brought it up, but then we didn't have a chance to really talk about it since I was eager to leave. It would be great to have a conversation about immigration policy with someone who seems somewhat informed. There aren't very many of those people hanging around Arrow.

With that surprise mentally settled, I'm left to stew over Aaron's surprise rejection. I'm so confused why he would keep sending me signals that he wants to talk, then make me think he wants to be my partner but pair me up with some random freshman instead?

"Make it make sense!" I yell out loud as I park my car outside AOPi and rest my forehead on the steering wheel.

Why does Aaron have to keep playing his cards so close to his chest? How long are we going to keep trudging through these murky super-friends waters?

Is this it? Should I just wash my hands of Aaron?

I sigh out a groan. If there was ever going to be a breaking point in my crush on Aaron . . . this just might be it.

CHAPTER SIX

"I can't believe Amaya and I weren't there to witness this!" Teegan groans as she flops back on the bed next to Amaya.

"There to witness it or to throat punch Aaron?" Amaya questions. I roll my eyes at her.

"Well, that's what you get for volunteering to lead our great sisterhood, oh mighty president and social chair," I tell them. Amaya shrugs and returns to the homecoming responsibilities flowchart she's creating.

"I'm more intrigued by your interaction with Mateo," Teegan says. "Although throat punching Aaron might be intriguing as well."

"I haven't decided whether throat punching is necessary," I admonish them. "I feel so torn—I'm so frustrated with him and tired of second-guessing myself all the time. But also, I've liked Aaron for so long, and we make sense together in the grand scheme of my life goals."

"How romantic," Teegan deadpans.

"You know what I mean!"

"Yes, but back to Mateo," Teegan says.

"Mateo and I are going to talk about immigration policy, Teegs. And I'm excited to talk to someone else who has a personal connection to it. Even though we've been around each other a lot at Arrow stuff and Summer Projects, I didn't know that his parents were immigrants."

Teegan leaps up and opens our shared closet. "What are you doing?" I inquire.

"Even if you're just talking politics, that doesn't mean you don't need a cute outfit to wear tomorrow," she responds.

"Beef, I appreciate your enthusiasm, but I'm just going to wear normal clothes, thanks," I tell her.

Teegan pouts her lower lip. "You're no fun."

———

I park my car in an angled street parking spot. I learned my lesson one embarrassing day freshman year that I am just not meant to parallel park. I may be ready to change the world for under-resourced people, but easing my car into a spot between two other vehicles is not in my skill set, and I prefer to play to my strengths.

I open the familiar faded green door to Bookafe, a local coffee shop in Center Square. Outside of the AOPi house and campus, this is by far the place I've spent the most time in since moving to Brooklyn. With the black walls, floor-to-ceiling bookshelves, the loved-to-perfect-comfort overstuffed chairs, and variety of live plants breathing fresh air into the space, it's the perfect atmosphere to work my way through college classes.

It's the one place I don't even have to wear earbuds—the eclectic playlist streaming through the ceiling speakers combined with the low hum of conversations provides an oddly satisfying soundtrack to concentrate.

The distinct aroma of coffee beans and worn paperbacks floods my nose, calming the nerves I woke up with this morning. *This is just going to be a chance for you to spew all your passion for immigration issues on a willing listener. Relax. In fact, get pumped!*

My self pep talk works, and I smile back at Mateo as I step up next to him in the entry.

"Hey, how are you?" I ask as we fall into line to order.

"Well, aside from the lack of sleep due to nightmares about seaweed zombie fish dragging me down into the depths of a bottomless lake, pretty good," he says with a wry smile and twinkle in his eye.

I burst out laughing. I lower my voice after people turn to look at me. I half-whisper, "I don't know why you asked me to do the race if you know you don't like lakes!"

Mateo smiles and gestures toward the cashier ready to take our order. "It's my treat today—order whatever you want."

"Oh thanks, you didn't have to do that. I appreciate it, though." I turn to the cashier to order. I never need to check the menu here anymore. "I'll have the iced horchata latte, please."

I glance around the coffee shop as Mateo orders, and we move to the end of the counter to wait for our drinks. Bookafe is unusually quiet, probably because it's a Sunday afternoon before a day of no classes. No one is studying today.

"Why don't you go see if the table by the world corner is open, and I'll bring our drinks over?" Mateo suggests.

"Sure," I respond as I head to my favorite spot in my favorite coffee shop. Tucked away from the main seating area, the world corner is literally cornered by two bookcases full of books written by authors from all over the world. I almost majored in English before deciding that social sciences might give me an edge on the immigration law track. Sitting among the words of so many diverse authors has always felt inspiring.

I take a seat and run my finger along the spine of a Salman Rushdie novel. Mateo joins shortly after and hands me my iced latte. I take a sip and instantly feel at home. Something about the horchata flavors takes my mind back to when I was a kid in El Paso, Texas, reveling in all the tastes of Mexico without even realizing how special it was. I close my eyes for a beat as I swallow.

"So, how's the school year starting off for you?" Mateo asks. He takes a drink of his cortado and waits for my answer.

"Oh, fine so far. Rush week was precisely the special torture that it's designed to be." He laughs. "But I think we have a really solid pledge class this year, so the future of AOPi is bright, I suppose."

"Are you the new member educator again this year?" Mateo asks.

"No, between needing solid grades to keep my scholarship plus law school applications, I decided to lighten my load, so no leadership role for me this year," I answer. I take another sip of coffee. "How was your first soccer match?"

"Good, we won both of our two pre-season matches," Mateo says. "Our first division match is this Saturday. We get today off, but we'll be practicing hard all week to get ready. We have a couple of new guys on the team, and I think we're going to play really well together this year."

Mateo quickly turns the conversation back to me, peppering me with one question after another about my plans for the school year, the law school application process, when I'd have to leave to start at UC Davis if (fingers crossed when) I'm accepted.

I'm starting to feel a little thrown off. I sat down expecting to discuss DC and the Afghan Adjustment Act, about where the legislation process is and what effective advocacy looks like. All morning, I had been mentally cataloging interesting talking points from my experiences over the summer. I didn't anticipate so many questions about my personal future steps toward lawyerhood.

He's taking a drink of his cortado when I ask, "Sooo, why did you want to get coffee today?"

"What?" he replies with confused eyebrows as he sets down his cup.

"Why did you ask me to coffee today? Were you wanting to talk about the Afghan Adjustment Act or other immigration issues, or something else?" I eye him over the rim of my cup as I take a drink of my latte.

"I'm sorry, I thought it would be obvious when I asked you yesterday," Mateo says. He clears his throat. "I asked you to coffee because I like you, Lana."

Thankfully, I stop my jaw from dropping to the floor because my mouth is full of a giant gulp of horchata latte, which I promptly start choking on. After an embarrassingly-long coughing fit, I finally sputter out, "I'm sorry, what?"

A smile slowly spreads across Mateo's face. "I. Like. You. Lana."

"Like me?"

"Like you."

Silence.

"Like, LIKE me, like me?"

"Yes."

I don't have extreme heat to blame for the current misfiring happening in my brain or the blush creeping across my cheeks. Bookafe is perfectly well air conditioned.

I probably look slightly psychotic as I openly stare at Mateo's face. He's still smiling at me with patient eyes. He doesn't say anything, as though he can sense that my mind needs a minute to realign the gears.

Finally, after a lineup of facial expressions probably broadcasting all the confusing thoughts running through my head (I really need to prioritize poker lessons), I land on disbelief. "You aren't serious, are you?"

"Completely serious," Mateo says with casual confidence, leaning back in his chair. His eyes stay locked on mine.

"But why?" I ask. "Mateo, this isn't a huge campus. You're the number-one star of the number-one athletic program at Townsend. Everyone knows you. And within the smaller social sphere that is Arrow, you're *the* most popular guy involved."

Mateo raises an eyebrow in silent protest.

"I know, I know, popularity in college is different than the unrelenting beast it is in high school, but there are still hierarchies of social status. And you, sir, are at the very top."

Mateo looks genuinely caught off guard. "Lana, I don't think—"

"Wait, let me finish," I interrupt without even taking a breath. "Literally every single one of the girls from TriAlpha would love to date you. I mean, Bailey Williams might stab my eye out to have the chance to be sitting here with you."

His incredulity softens into what looks alarmingly like amusement.

I pause to collect my thoughts. "The point is you could date any of the gorgeous, popular girls on campus. Why would you pay attention to me?" I ask a bit breathlessly, biting my lip to keep my mind grounded.

Mateo leans forward and looks down at his hands for a moment. I realize I'm holding my breath again.

"I've *been* paying attention to you, Lana," he finally says, peering up through his long, dark eyelashes into my eyes. "For a long time."

Silence.

"Huh?"

He smiles almost wistfully. "Your parents live in Kansas City. You have three younger siblings: twin brothers in eighth grade and a sister in tenth grade. You're studying social science to prepare for law school so you can become an immigration lawyer like your mom—which you'll be amazing at, by the way.

"You ordered an iced latte this afternoon because it's hot out, but as soon as the first leaf changes color to signal your favorite season, you'll switch to flat whites in the afternoons. But you always drink plain brewed coffee in the mornings with just half-and-half, no sugar or flavored creamers. When you're at Creamiery you get the peanut butter cup gelato, but at IceScream you get the coffee ice cream with a brownie mixed in."

I feel my eyes widening in disbelief as he continues.

"You listen to a lot of Taylor Swift and cello music, which is an interesting combination, but you pretty much always have music playing. And you must have taken piano lessons at some point in life because you mindlessly tap melodies with your fingers when you're thinking about something.

"You're always the first one to volunteer to pick up freshmen from the dorms for meetings, and you always talk about the great things Amaya and Teegan or the other girls in AOPi are doing instead of keeping the spotlight on yourself. You signed up for not just one but two early mornings at Summer Project to set up breakfast when no one else wanted to volunteer. And you had great rapport with your coworkers at the outlet mall because you developed authentic friendships with them all summer. I wouldn't be surprised if you still keep in touch with some of them even now."

He pauses to take a deep breath.

"You just . . . genuinely *love* Jesus. And the people around you. Not just the ones that Arrow encourages you to spend time with like your sorority sisters, but also other people, like the ELL students you tutor. You care about helping vulnerable people, not only in your future career but now."

I know for a fact that my mouth is hanging wide open. I'm completely shocked by this (very accurate) list of observations about me.

"Oh, and you constantly complain about sorority life and say you only did it for your law school application, but you secretly love it because it brought you Teegan and Amaya. And you can't imagine the rest of your life without them." He leans back like he just dropped the mic.

His voice lowers as he reiterates, "I've been paying attention, Lana. For a long, long time."

I glance down at the table and see the muffin he offered to share (which I have eaten most of already) is orange chocolate chip, my favorite at Bookafe.

I snap my eyes back up to his and see that he's looking a little nervous. I need to say something.

"Okay," I say quietly. My brain is still working on overdrive, trying to process this conversation. I lightly play the notes to "Moonlight Sonata" on the table with my left hand, trying to work out how to respond.

"So," I begin, "If this is true, if you've liked me for a long time . . ." He nods in affirmation, encouraging me to continue.

I swallow a lump in my throat. "Why are you just now telling me?"

Mateo looks down with a sad smile. He pauses for a beat before answering. "You know, Adams didn't exactly keep it a secret among the guys in Arrow that he had a crush on you."

I feel the blood rush to my face.

"I'm not saying he ever explicitly told guys to stay away from you, but there was always this sense he projected that we should back off because he was going to ask you out," Mateo pauses, fiddling with his coffee cup. "And you, um, it seemed like you probably reciprocated his interest."

I'm for sure crimson by now. Bright Christmas red.

"So I tried to respect that, even though *I* had feelings for you," Mateo concludes.

I move my hands to my lap so I can more aggressively play the piano on my thigh, trying to appear a little less manic. Even though he's already pointed out that he knows I do this.

"Then what changed now?" I ask.

He blows out a breath. "I couldn't stop thinking about you all summer. Being at the Summer Project without you there, it just amplified the difference in my mind between you and the other girls. I mean, they're great, I'm not trying to say anything negative about them. But they mostly just seem to be following the path that Arrow guides you on without exploring other ways to care about people. Meanwhile, you were spending the summer helping your mom with refugees and advocating for immigration legislation in DC, and I found myself thinking about you constantly." Mateo's eyes narrow and his jaw starts working. "So, I was already feeling really conflicted about continuing to hold off on pursuing you, and then at the Lake Games, I saw your face after Adams pulled that stunt and made you feel . . ." He pauses.

Rejected. Tossed aside. Crushed. All the emotions of that moment with Aaron flicker through my mind. Mateo looks into my eyes and nods tersely, as if reading my thoughts.

"Yeah. I decided right there that he'd had his chance—lots of chances—to be honest with you about how he felt, to pursue you the way you deserve to be pursued, and he still hadn't done anything. So I decided I wasn't going to let him stand in the way of me taking my shot anymore."

"Your shot . . . with me?" I squeak, still feeling wildly confused.

"Yes," Mateo says. "Maybe I was doing the right thing giving Adams space, or maybe I was just being a coward, I don't know. But I'm not going to stand back anymore. I understand that I've had time to think about this—about us—and you've just been blindsided, so I'm not asking you to know right away. I'm just asking for the possibility. To get to know you more intentionally, for *you* to get to know *me* more intentionally."

He takes a deep breath and leans forward, his eyes laced with both intensity and insecurity as he asks, "Lana, will you please give me a chance? Let me take you on a clearly-defined date, and then you can decide if you want to continue anything romantic or just be friends."

Somewhere along the way, I apparently stopped breathing because the edges of my vision go a little blurry. I take a deep breath and close my eyes. When I open them, Mateo is anxiously staring into them.

"Okay," I say. "Yes."

Chapter Seven

I open the door to my room, relieved to find that Amaya and Teegan aren't there. They must still be down in the media room watching a movie. I close the door and sink down on my bed.

I'm not sure how to process what just happened with Mateo. My mind isn't sure what thread to grab hold of to start untangling my thoughts and feelings. I pull up Spotify on my phone to turn on some music to help me think.

But which playlist matches the emotions swirling through my body? Moody doesn't feel quite right; this certainly isn't a mindful or magical moment. I finally hit play and repeat on "Hard to Sleep" by Gracie Abrams. The melancholy tone and simple piano melody soothe my chaotic thoughts.

I prop my legs up on the wall above my bed and lay back with my eyes closed. I'm trying to nail down the emotions that I'm experiencing, but nothing is making sense.

I open my eyes as the word hits me.

Startled.

That feeling when something jumps out at you that you aren't expecting—you're not exactly afraid, but your whole body reacts and your heart starts pounding.

Mateo voicing his feelings for me has me experiencing that same sensation. I still feel that heart-thumping adrenaline rush pulsing through my veins. My fingers start playing along with the music on my bedspread next to me, trying to calm my mind down.

How could Mateo have been paying such close attention and I never noticed? Why have I never noticed him like that? How could he have liked me for years and I had no idea?

The song is on its third loop when Teegan and Amaya come through the door together, arguing about the theme for the homecoming float. They take one look at me on the bed and quickly close the door.

"Okay, what happened that's got you listening to your stormy mind music, Lana?" Amaya immediately asks as she takes a seat at her desk chair. "Is it time for a throat punch?"

Teegan moves my hair out of the way and sits down next to my head on the bed. She taps the button to illuminate my phone screen. "Yep, you're on loop—spill it, LaLa," Teegan adds, pausing the music and tossing my phone back down.

I take a deep breath in through my nose and blow it out my mouth.

"It was a date."

"'Scuse me?" Amaya asks.

"With Mateo. It was a date," I repeat, sitting up on the bed to face them. "Or at least, that's what he intended. Mateo Alvarez likes me and wants to take me on an official date."

Teegan literally screams.

I can't help but laugh, despite my jumbled mental state. "Please stop screaming Teegs, I'd rather not alert our entire sorority house."

"What are you talking about?!" Teegan exclaims. "Mateo Alvarez likes you, and you don't want to declare that for the whole campus to hear?"

"Calm down, Teeg," Amaya says, throwing a pen at her. "Back up, Lana, you've gotta give us the whole context of this. No detail left unshared."

I walk back through my entire interaction with Mateo, interrupted frequently by Teegan wanting to know what his facial expression looked like or what I was thinking at any given moment. When I get to the part where he spouted off an absurdly detailed list of observations about me, Teegan sighs "Awww!" as Amaya exclaims, "Shut up!"

I wrap up the story with his earnest request to give him a chance on a real date, and my affirmative answer. Teegan catapults herself at me in a huge hug as Amaya sits back and says, "Well, can't say I was expecting that."

"I know, right?!" I exclaim from around Teegan's head. She releases me and grabs my shoulders.

"Lana, this is the biggest news of our lives," she says solemnly.

I put my hands on her shoulders and reply, "Teegan, it is definitely not, but I appreciate your enthusiastic support."

"So how are you feeling, Beef?" Amaya asks. "I mean, you had your pensive, moody music looping when we arrived, but now that you've rehashed it all, how do you feel?"

I take a moment to really think about it.

"Bewildered, I guess? Like I literally don't know what to think," I say with a shrug. "I don't know, I went to bed last night trying to reconcile my longstanding crush on Aaron with my frustration at his dodginess. Now, I just feel really confused by how caught off guard I am. I mean, never in a thousand years did I see that coming. How could Mateo have liked me this long and I had no clue? How have I not paid more attention to know half as much about him as he does about me?"

Amaya and Teegan share a look. I motion my finger between them and say, "Whoa, what does that mean? What's this look?"

"Lana, you've been completely obsessed with Aaron ever since the beginning of sophomore year," Amaya states with a raised eyebrow.

"Hey! That's not fair," I interject, feeling defensive.

"What Amaya means to say," Teegan jumps in, "is that maybe you didn't notice anything about Mateo because your attention was always on Aaron. And I'm not saying we aren't partially at fault for that," Teegan quickly adds. Placing an arm around my shoulders, she leans her head against mine. "All three of us were constantly analyzing your interactions with Aaron and trying to predict when he was going to make an official move. We were obsessed on your behalf."

"So basically all this time, Mateo has been paying attention to me, but I've been totally ignoring him because all I could see was Aaron." I recap, and Teegan shrugs. I sigh. "Wow, that makes me feel like a jerk."

"You are not a jerk," Amaya says, reaching over to put her hand on mine. "Clearly Mateo doesn't think you're a jerk, or he wouldn't have asked you out. Maybe going on a date with Mateo will be a good thing for your heart."

I bite my lip. "If I'm honest, I feel nervous letting myself even consider dating Mateo. It really felt like Aaron *was* about to make a move forward in our relationship, I mean, aside from his confusing behavior yesterday. I thought it *could* be the breaking point for my crush, but dating Mateo makes it seem much more officially broken."

Amaya looks like she's formulating her words carefully. She's a straight-shooter, and I'm slightly afraid to hear what she's about to say. "Maybe it's time to loosen up on your . . . preoccupation with Aaron. I mean, this isn't the first time we've thought he was on the brink of asking you out."

"Yeah, LaLa, there have been a lot of times over the past two years that Aaron gave all these hints without doing anything concrete," Teegan jumps in. "I think you should give Mateo a real chance," she concludes decisively.

I nudge against her and say, "You're just saying that because you think he's hot."

"I'm not NOT saying that because I think he's totally hot. But I'm mostly saying it because he seems like a great guy who's treating you well. So he deserves a shot," Teegan concludes. "What if he's the squirrel?"

Amaya looks at Teegan like she's grown a third eye. "Don't bother," I say, holding up a hand.

"You said yes to a date, but that doesn't lock you in forever, or lock Aaron out forever. When are you going out with Mateo?" Amaya redirects.

"He said he would text me later tonight to make a plan after checking his practice schedule for the week," I answer. "I feel like I won't be able to concentrate on anything this week until after our date. I'm going to be overanalyzing everything!" I groan and flop back on my bed.

Amaya pulls me up by the wrists and says, "Nu-uh, we've done enough overanalyzing with what's-his-name over the past two years."

I roll my eyes at her.

"That's right," Teegan says, standing up. "We are going to go for a walk around campus and talk about anything and everything except boys."

"This would be a perfect time to get a head start on homecoming planning," Amaya suggests. Teegan and I both roll our eyes now, but we also both know that's exactly what we'll talk about.

———

As promised, Mateo texts me later that night.

Our date will be Friday evening. They have an away game on Saturday, so practice will end by 5:00 Friday. He's picking me up from AOPi at 6:30.

I am freaking out. All night long, I unsuccessfully try to fall asleep, as I keep replaying my two conversations with Mateo this weekend, along with mentally picking back through all of my numerous interactions with Aaron over the past few years.

When the clock rolls to 6:00 a.m., I give up. I quietly get out of bed and put on a fresh t-shirt and shorts in the dark. I stuff my journal and Bible into a small tote and sneak out of the room. I have a feeling my brain won't let up on me until I untangle my thoughts in writing, and I may as well do it while enjoying coffee and a quiet atmosphere.

I can't bring myself to go back to Bookafe today, so I drive to Raelynn's, my second favorite coffee shop in Brooklyn. They have a giant coffee roaster in the shop, so it always smells like heaven, and their drip coffee is the best in town.

I order a bottomless mug and fill it up for the first of many times, adding a splash of half-and-half. Which sends my mind back to Mateo's long list of observations yesterday. I find a seat at a table in the corner and put in my ear buds. Hitting play on Spotify's Maverick City Music Radio playlist, I pull my journal and Bible out of my bag.

Before I start spilling all of my confusion out onto paper, I need to center my thoughts on God, to ask him for help understanding what I'm feeling. I open up to one of my favorite Psalms.

Rest in God alone, my soul, for my hope comes from him. He alone is my rock and my salvation, my stronghold; I will not be shaken. My salvation and glory depend on God, my strong rock. My refuge is in God. Trust in him at all times, you people; pour out your hearts before him. God is our refuge. Psalm 62:5-8.

I take a deep breath and then open my leather journal, which was a gift from my mom for my birthday last month. Sometimes I write down my thoughts about a verse I read, sometimes I write down what I'm praying, and other times my thoughts just come flooding out of my pen onto the pages, which is precisely what happens now.

I don't know what to think. I don't know what to feel. Aaron has been my crush for so long. I've talked with him so often over the past two years, admired him, laughed at his jokes, even danced with him at homecoming showcase. My crush on Aaron has been a central feature of my college experience.

I pause from writing to drink my coffee and think for a minute.

I'm almost afraid to not like Aaron. I'm comfortable liking him. My senses are tuned to find him in a room, I've learned to pick up on his subtle compliments and flirting. I've mastered the art of sending him signals that I like him without coming out and saying it. And I know he could fit with my future.

I sigh.

I've also cried several times over the years because I thought he was going to say something about our relationship but never did. I'd get my hopes up only to end up let down. I came into this year with incredibly high expectations of something finally happening between us now that we're seniors. And I just don't know. On the one hand, Aaron does still seem to be giving me signals that he's interested in me. But he also had a perfect opportunity at Lake Games and didn't take it. What if my hopes for Aaron get let down yet again, and meanwhile I miss out on something different with Mateo?

I drain what's left of my coffee and get up to refill. I need more caffeine before writing another word about Mateo. Settling back into my seat, I pick up my pen and stare at the page. Where to start?

I've never been more surprised by anything in my life than by what Mateo said to me. Not just that he told me he liked me—but the way he told me he liked me. All the evidence he presented of his feelings. That was not a small amount of evidence!! The fact that he has been paying close enough attention to know so much about me is still blowing my mind.

I pause again and try to think back on the past few years of my friendship with Mateo. We were on the student leadership team with Arrow starting sophomore year, so was he noticing things about me already then? Has he really liked me that long without letting on?

We were both group leaders at the Summer Project after sophomore year. I was so dialed in to Aaron that summer, mentally noting his every move and comment in meetings, attempting to nonchalantly sit near to him as often as wasn't obvious. Aaron kept giving me a string of hints that he was interested in dating, so I was convinced heading into junior year that we would become official at some point. But was I getting in my own way of noticing other guys around me because I was too intensely focused on Aaron?

Mateo mentioned breakfast duty that summer, and I suddenly remember that he was the other volunteer one of the mornings. Amaya and I signed up together for Thursdays, but when they still needed another leader to help on Tuesdays, I offered to do it. Mateo and I spent an hour together every Tuesday morning, brewing carafes of coffee and getting breakfast ready for all the participants before everyone left for work. And yes, I always had music playing from my phone. I'd forgotten all the conversations we had that summer about our small groups, the Bible study, the people we met at our jobs.

Another memory hits—we carpooled to work every day that summer along with two other leaders. Mateo worked at a different retail store in the same outlet mall as I did. All that time, I enjoyed our casual friendship, but I was too busy thinking about Aaron to mentally catalog my interactions with Mateo. And I had zero clue that he saw me as anything more. Can I see him as something more?

I pick my pen back up.

Maybe I could like Mateo? It's hard to picture liking someone else other than Aaron. I feel like I don't know Mateo well enough to know if I could LIKE him like him. Then again, that's my own fault because I've been so obsessed with Aaron (I'm not going to admit to Amaya that I used the word obsessed). Mateo proved that we've interacted enough over the years for him to know me, so I just haven't paid enough attention to know him. But now I have a chance—he's asking me for a chance for me to get to know him. It would be dumb not to take that chance, right?

What if taking that chance with Mateo doesn't work out, but it does drive Aaron away? What if I can't break out of my mindset of liking Aaron enough to give Mateo a real shot? What if Mateo changes his mind? Or what if his future isn't compatible with mine??

Similar panicked thoughts continue to appear on the pages of my journal until my hand is cramped. I flip back through the pages I've written, quickly scanning my thought dump for high points that will tell me what to do. But everything is too confused and all over the place to be much help.

I close my eyes and think back over the weekend. Mateo stepping in to be my partner at Lake Games when I was feeling the sting of Aaron's rejection. Not to mention him getting into a kayak with me when he is literally terrified of deep water.

I think about his eyes at Bookafe yesterday. The warmth when he smiled as he told me all of my own favorite things, the hint of fear when he was awaiting my response to his date request. The relief that flooded into them when I said yes.

Calm settles over me as I realize that even if I have no idea how things are going to turn out, at least I know the next step. Going on a date with Mateo is the right move, especially doing so with an open mind. Or open heart, I guess you could say.

I suppose I'll figure the rest out later.

Chapter Eight

After sitting and writing for so long, I need some physical movement to help clear my head. I decide to go for a walk around campus, but first drop my stuff off at AOPi. Teegan is reading her Bible in the living room when I walk through, and she raises her eyebrows at me. "Someone wasn't in our room early this morning. Did someone have trouble sleeping because someone was busy thinking about a very intriguing someone?"

I quickly glance around to make sure no one is listening, then shush her. "Super subtle, Teegs," I call back to her as I head out the side door toward campus.

Teegan wanted to immediately broadcast to all of Townsend that I was going on a date with the most eligible bachelor on campus, but I swore her and Amaya to secrecy. I'm still having a hard time coming to grips with this reality, and I don't need the added pressure of nosy people's judgments of my own eligibility in this situation.

Speaking of judgy people, I walk right into Bailey where the sidewalks from AOPi and TriAlpha converge.

I give her what hopefully passes as a smile. "Sorry about that—just lost in my thoughts." Unfortunately, she's headed the same direction as I am, so we fall into step beside each other. "How are things at TriAlpha going?" I ask. Encouraging her to talk about how awesome her sorority is seems like a good way to avoid her asking me any questions.

"Oh, fantastic," she gushes. "We got the best girls from the pledge class this year, so we're having a great start to the semester." She drones on for another couple of minutes about all the fabulous things about their A+ new pledges, naturally mentioning the heavy influence she had on their selection list. "Girls are already fighting over who will get to be involved in the homecoming events, so I'll have a lot of tough decisions to make when we put teams together."

"Sounds intense," I say, trying to tell her what she seems to want to hear.

"And how is the new AOPi pledge class doing? I hope you'll be able to find enough girls to participate in all of the homecoming competitions," Bailey quips. "If Amaya needs any assistance making sure she doesn't fall behind with the preparations, tell her I am absolutely here to help."

I roll my eyes so hard I give myself a headache. Nothing annoys me more than people backdoor badmouthing my best friends. "Amaya is doing an incredible job. She's the most organized, ambitious person I know, so AOPi is in great hands this year," I counter, trying to sound lighthearted and unaggressive.

Bailey does her signature one eyebrow raise. "Well, I'm sure you'll do fine by AOPi standards. I've got to head this way to the union—big meeting with the OG president to start planning our homecoming showcase routine. See you at Arrow Thursday night!"

Thank goodness Bailey heads the opposite direction from me before I say something I might regret. I take a deep breath and remind myself that I do not hate Bailey. I really don't. But I wouldn't hate it if she maybe stepped in gum on the way to the union.

I pause walking to shoot a text to the Beefs' group message.

ME

Don't worry Amaya, I just talked with Bailey and she has offered her services to help you handle homecoming <eye roll emoji>

AMAYA

smh. Her high opinion of herself knows no bounds

ME

Or maybe it's just her low opinion of us

Lana, are you really positively sure we can't announce your date to the entire campus? It would sure knock Bailey off her high horse to find out Mateo Alvarez asked out an AOPi <praying hands emoji>

NO

sigh

———

On Wednesday afternoon, I'm getting ready for chapter with Teegan when my phone pings with a text. I swipe it open and see Mateo's name in my notifications.

I have a reservation for dinner. Wear something you'll feel comfortable sitting outdoors in. See you at 6:30 Friday

I don't know exactly what my face is saying as I read the text, but Teegan looks over and asks, "Everything okay, Beef?"

"Yes," I tell her. "Mateo just sent me details for our date."

"*Ooo*, why was your face looking so weird then? This is exciting!" She grabs my phone from my hand to read the text from Mateo. "Something comfortable to sit outside. We can work with that."

She immediately starts rummaging through my closet. "That was nice of him to give you wardrobe instructions."

"We still have plenty of time to pick an outfit for Friday, Teegs," I say, pulling her arm away from the closet. "Right now, we have to get ready for chapter, or we'll be late and Amaya will punish us in unsavory ways."

Even as I try to act breezy with Teegan, all through dinner and the chapter meeting, I'm thinking ahead to Friday. *It* was *thoughtful of*

Mateo to let me know how to dress. Where could we be going? I try to think of every place in town with outdoor seating. *Is it going to be somewhere with a fancy patio? Or a casual place in Center Square with high top tables on a wood deck? Super public, where we'll potentially be seen by a lot of Arrow people? What* should *I wear? Will any article of clothing help me feel comfortable on this date?*

After chapter, I sit in our room with my laptop, trying to will myself to concentrate. I had marked in my calendar to be finished with a first draft of the personal statement essay for my law school application by tomorrow. I haven't even started. I really need to focus if I'm going to meet my own deadlines.

Too bad all my focus is being disrupted by Mateo right now.

———

The next day, I'm welcoming people to the Arrow meeting and fearing that everyone would take one look at me and know exactly what's going on in my mind. Mateo and several of his teammates came in a while ago, but they mercifully got name tags from a different welcome team member.

"What superpower would you pick?" I ask the person standing in front of me, writing down their answer. Teleportation is beneath my name, but at this moment, I'd take invisibility.

I'm relieved when the music starts inside the meeting room and I can cease small talk with people. I put the name tag supplies away and duck into the row with the AOPis.

The band plays "Promises" by Maverick City Music, and I close my eyes and try to focus on the lyrics. By the end of the song, my heart feels calmer. We take our seats as a student heads up for the testimony.

I recognize Andrés, one of Mateo's teammates, standing on stage. He introduces himself and says he's going to share the story of how Jesus has changed his life. In contrast to Amaya's polished speech, Andrés is visibly nervous, losing his train of thought a couple of times and saying "um" a lot. But his vulnerability only makes his story more real.

Andrés shares about his difficult upbringing in Miami, living in an area of the city divided by rival gangs. His dad was incarcerated for most of his childhood, and he didn't want to end up the same way. But avoiding the gang life seemed impossible, until a coach for a local soccer nonprofit took notice of Andrés' athletic abilities and got him involved with a team.

The team helped him avoid the full gang experience, but Andrés was still exposed to plenty of violence and drugs. He was always afraid he was just one mistake away from ending up like his father. When he got a scholarship to come join the soccer team at Townsend, he saw it as his way out.

"I arrived last year with a chip on my shoulder," Andrés shares. "I felt like the students I met here couldn't relate with my life. And most of you can't, thank God. But my teammate Mateo kept making this effort to get to know me, to ask me questions, and he was never scared away by any of my answers."

I glance over at where Mateo is sitting in the second row, and see him give Andrés an encouraging smile.

"So when Mateo asked me if I'd want to read the Bible with him, I realized I trusted him as a friend, so I wanted to see what it was about. I started feeling so much more peace in my life. I went home over winter break and saw all these guys around me throwing their lives away, and I knew I didn't want that to be my story." Andrés glances down at Mateo and says, "I came back that next semester and told Mateo I was ready to go all in, that I knew I needed Jesus to save my life. And I've been growing in my faith ever since.

"I guess the point is, if God can change my life, he can change anyone's life," Andrés concludes. "Thanks for letting me share my story."

The whole room claps as Andrés jumps off the stage to rejoin Mateo and the other soccer players, receiving lots of bro hugs and thumps on the back.

My heart starts pounding. I don't even know what the message is about at Arrow. I don't think I hear a single word. I just keep thinking back over Andrés' testimony and the look on Mateo's face as he listened. He obviously cares deeply for Andrés and has invested a lot into their friendship.

Suddenly everyone is standing around me, and I realize the band has started playing the final song. I quickly rise to my feet and go through the motions of singing along. The meeting ends, and the air fills with a mix of conversations and upbeat music pulsing through the speakers.

I watch out of the corner of my eye as the soccer guys congregate around Andrés. My attention snaps less subtly to them when I notice Bailey giving Andrés short congratulatory remarks before turning to Mateo. I have no idea what she's saying, but her body language screams flirtation. My eyes shift to Mateo's face, trying to assess his reaction to Bailey's obvious interest in him. He nods in response to whatever she just said and smiles.

Huh.

I squint a bit as I study his face. It's a very polite smile, but his eyes aren't in it.

That's definitely *not* the same smile he looked at me with.

"Are we going to After Party?" Liz asks me.

"What?" I say, shaking my head to clear my thoughts.

"They said that After Party is at Creamiery," Liz says. "Are we all going?"

"Of course, we are!" Teegan jumps in. "Like I'm going to miss a chance at gelato!"

The girls start walking out the doors, and Teegan leans in toward my ear. "That was quite the testimony, huh? Andrés sure seems like a nice guy, with even nicer friends."

I give her a slight shove as her eyes twinkle mischievously. "Yeah, yeah. Let's go get some gelato."

When we arrive at Creamiery, there's a long line of Arrow students waiting to order. The AOPis are talking around me, but I'm still lost in my thoughts.

"Hey, Lana." Aaron's voice suddenly cuts through the fog.

"Oh, hey, Aaron," I stutter, flustered, as though he could read my mind and know who I was thinking about. We take a step forward as the line moves.

"How are your classes this semester? Do you have a tough schedule?" he asks.

"I'm only taking twelve hours. I wanted to give myself some margin to work on law school stuff. But they're all upper-level courses, so I still have my work cut out for me," I tell him. "What about you? How's your senior year starting off?"

"Same, not too many hours, but more work in each class. Two of my marketing classes are going to have a lot of group projects this semester, which always seem to take more time than individual assignments," Aaron replies as we move up in the line. He gestures at the tubs of gelato in the display case. "What are you going to order? They have this new Almond Joy flavor that totally slaps—you have to try it."

I wrinkle my nose. "Yeah, I hate coconut."

"What?! Aw, it's so good though!" he persists. "You should ask for a sample. You'll love it."

"Um, I guess," I say uncertainly. Aaron asks the employee for a sample and hands me the tiny spoon. I raise the gelato to my mouth and immediately know I won't like it just from the smell. Ugh, the flavor and texture of the coconut shreds are so overpowering, I have to try hard not to gag.

Aaron looks at me expectantly, like there's no way I won't like it. I swallow hard and say, "I mean, it's not my favorite. I'm going to stick with my go-to."

Aaron orders a cup of the Almond Joy, and I ask the next employee for peanut butter cup. As soon as I say the words, I think about how Mateo would have known exactly what I was going to order. Aaron is laughing with a friend waiting for his gelato, and I glance at him out of the corner of my eye.

If I were keeping score, tonight would be a definitive tick on Mateo's side. Aaron may have a few years-long head start, but I'm starting to wonder if he'll be ticking any more boxes.

CHAPTER NINE

Teegan finger-combs her way through the curls in my hair to coax them into loose waves. "I wonder if I should add a bit heavier eyeliner to your makeup look," she questions as she steps back to assess her work. "This is a dinner date after all."

"Leave her alone now, Teeg," Amaya interjects from her observation chair. "She wants to look like herself. The light makeup already looks perfect."

Teegan pouts a little but gives in. I give my completed look a once-over in the full-length mirror. After way too long spent going through my closet, Teegan and I finally decided on a flowy, tiered dress from Anthropologie she found on clearance over the summer. I should fit in regardless of whether we're at an upscale or casual restaurant.

At 6:23 p.m., I head downstairs to wait on the porch. I'm hoping I can race down to Mateo's car and avoid any AOPis seeing me with him. I made Amaya and Teegan promise to stay inside and watch safely from a window so as not to draw attention to my departure. Suffice to say, Teegan is acting like I've ruined Christmas at the moment.

I take a deep breath and open the front door, relieved that no one is hanging around in the entry. Closing the door behind me, I turn around to see Mateo coming up the front walk. He's wearing chino shorts and a blue button-up shirt with the sleeves rolled to his elbows. He pulls his sunglasses off and smiles when he sees me. I glance around quickly (no witnesses) and hurry down the steps toward him.

"You're early," I say.

"Well, Coach is constantly drilling into us that to be on time to practice is to be late, so I guess the habit spills over." His eyes quickly scan down to my toes and back up to my eyes, and I feel the first whisper of a blush forming.

"Wow, you look amazing, Lana."

"Thanks," I say nervously. I'm fumbling to know how to accept compliments from Mateo. Objectively speaking, he's strikingly handsome with bronze skin, tousled black hair, a strong jaw, and deep brown eyes—not to mention his muscular, athletic body build. The perpetual five o'clock shadow along his jaw has to be intentional because it always looks well-kept. I realize he has one dimple on just his right cheek as he smiles at me.

I feel so self-consciously average next to him. Once again, I'm in my head, wondering why he's standing here with me instead of someone like Bailey. I clear my throat and ask, "Am I dressed okay for where we're eating? Where are we going?"

"You're perfect," he says with a smile, gesturing for me to follow. "And that's for me to know and you to find out."

He opens the passenger door of an old blue truck. This isn't a huge, look-at-me truck like a lot of the frat guys drive. It's an unassuming, older Toyota model that looks well taken care of. I climb into the seat, and he closes the door behind me. I smooth my hands across my dress to calm their shaking.

It's fine, you're fine, everything is fine, I chant internally as Mateo gets in and starts the truck. "Ready?" He checks in with me with a quick smile. I nod and try to smile back.

We pull away from the AOPi house, past campus and Center Square. I'm not sure where we're going since we're driving away from most of the retail areas of town. Maybe Mateo knows of a hidden gem of a restaurant.

Mateo makes small talk, asking how my classes are going, and I ask about his soccer practices. We've been driving for about fifteen minutes and made our way to the small highway heading out of the city. I have no idea what our destination could be.

Finally, Mateo pulls into the prairie reserve on the outskirts of Brooklyn, winding through the driving paths until we reach a parking area on a hilltop overlooking the Flint Hills. He backs the truck up to face the view and puts it in park. "We're here!" he says with a mischievous grin. "I told you to dress for dinner outside."

I laugh and open my car door. I've only been out to the reserve a few times, even though I've been at Townsend for over three years now. Looking out at the never-ending rolling views and feeling the breeze blow through my hair relaxes my nerves.

Mateo leads us to the back of the truck where he stashed a picnic basket. He pulls down the tailgate and arranges a thick blanket on it before hopping up to sit with his feet dangling over the edge. I follow suit, settling in next to him.

"Welcome to the Flint Hills Café," Mateo says as he sweeps his hand toward the views. The truck is perfectly angled, so we won't be staring directly into the sun but will be able to appreciate all the colors of the sunset. He sets up a wireless speaker and opens his phone to connect. Ed Sheeran starts streaming through the speaker, and Mateo turns the volume down to a nice background level. I tap my fingers along with the melody, the subconscious movement calming my heart rate.

Mateo hands me a Spindrift from a small cooler and opens the picnic basket. He pulls out two brown-paper wrapped sandwiches that I recognize from Sandy's, a local sandwich shop. He also sets out a bag of ruffled chips and a tub of their famous dip—a secret recipe full of cheese and bacon and I'm convinced some sort of addictive substance that makes it so good.

He hands me my favorite Thai-inspired chicken salad wrap and says, "I'll admit I had to enlist Teegan's help to know what you like to order from Sandy's."

"Mateo, this is incredible," I tell him before taking my first bite. "What did you order?"

He tilts his sandwich toward me. "Classic BLT, but add smoked turkey and chipotle aioli," he says. "It's my favorite, but I like to change it up and try different things from the menu. I'll have to give your wrap a try sometime."

"How did you even get these when they close at three o'clock? It tastes fresh," I ask him, chewing another giant bite.

He looks a bit sheepish and says, "I know Sandy, so I begged her to meet me there tonight to make these two sandwiches. I promised I'd bring the soccer guys in sometime for lunch in return."

I swallow and look into Mateo's eyes. He hasn't said this with any degree of arrogance, just stating a fact. But he pulled those strings for *me*. He planned ahead, making an effort to do something extra special for our date. The fact that we are out in the open air with zero other people around, some of my favorite chill music playing in the background (a song by Piano Guys followed Ed's lead), enjoying one of my favorite meals together—he's done everything right so far to help me relax and feel special on this date.

It makes me realize once again how thoughtful he's been—literally how much thought he has put into this night, into me—and how little thought I've given him leading up to now. I take another bite of my wrap to give my attention to something other than how I still feel like a bit of a jerk.

I need to divert my train of thought, so I ask Mateo how he's feeling about their soccer match tomorrow. They lost some key seniors from last year, but a couple of transfer students came to play with their team because there was a lot of positive buzz about the coach and the program after winning the DII soccer tournament last year.

"It was really awesome hearing Andrés' testimony last night," I tell Mateo. "It's amazing that you've been able to be there for him since his transition here last year."

Mateo swallows a bite of his sandwich, and his face goes soft with emotion. "Yeah, he's an incredible guy. He had a tough past, but I know he's going to go forward to do great things, not just in soccer, but for his life, his family. I'm so proud of him."

"Speaking of family, you said your parents are immigrants from Guatemala—does that mean you speak fluent Spanish?" I ask.

"That depends on your definition of fluent," Mateo says with a chuckle. "If you asked my parents, they'd tell you I have a funny accent when I'm speaking Spanish. And I definitely don't know all the correct grammar, so no writing papers in Spanish for me. But I can carry on conversations with all the native Spanish-speaking players on the team without much effort, so that works to my benefit."

He dips a chip in the addict dip and motions it toward me, "Do you speak any Spanish or other languages?"

"That depends on your definition of speak," I say with a smile, drawing a deep laugh from Mateo. "I actually spent the first ten years of my life in El Paso, so as a kid I knew a little bit of conversational Spanish from friends at school."

"No way! I didn't know you grew up in El Paso," Mateo exclaims. "That's so awesome."

"See, there are things about me you still don't know," I tease, and Mateo winks at me. I'm surprised by the mini flip my heart does in response to that wink.

"I lost most of what I knew once we moved to Kansas City, but I took Spanish one year in high school and then my first semester here. It brought a little bit of it back, but I still can't really have more than a basic conversation."

Mateo asks me about my time in DC over the summer, so I fill him in on everything I did with my mom as well as the advocacy group I worked with in DC. He's tracking with the conversation and the lingo, asking all the right follow-up questions. It's incredibly refreshing to discuss something I'm so passionate about with someone my age who also seems to care and understand the situation.

We continue chatting as we eat, sip our drinks, and listen to the music lightly surrounding us (he seriously nailed it with this playlist). Our conversation is easy, both of us equally listening and talking, with the occasional pause of silence that feels entirely normal.

We've finished the food and are both leaning back on our hands, watching as the sun starts to slip below the hills. The Kansas sky is really putting on a show tonight, pinks and purples dancing together to create a masterpiece. There are just enough clouds to add dimension to the colors and cast bright beams of light through the gaps. We take in the scene in comfortable silence.

Taylor has just started strumming her guitar in the next song on the playlist when Mateo hops down from the tailgate and holds his hand out to me. "Would you care to dance?"

I feel my cheeks flush with color as I look at his sweet smile, his hopeful eyes, his outstretched hand. I nod and put my hand in his, totally not prepared for the pleasant hum of energy that shoots through me when our fingers touch.

I ease off the truck as Mateo steadies me, then he moves his right hand to my shoulder blade and holds out his left. Placing my hand in his, I feel the warmth of the energy moving through my arm and down my back. When Aaron and I danced together in the homecoming exhibition, I remember being so excited to have a reason to touch him, but I can't recall if I felt this same heady buzz. I can't recollect anything about Aaron in this moment as Mateo's sure touch leads me to the music.

Mateo guides me into a twirl out to the side. He spins me back in with a flourish, his hand settling on my waist. "Wow, so suave," I teasingly compliment. "Did you take dance lessons along with all that soccer practice?"

Mateo laughs quietly. "No lessons, just a mom who loved to dance. When my dad or older brother weren't available, I was stuck being her partner." He's smiling softly at the memory, which melts my heart a little. "She says dance is in our DNA, so I guess I'm genetically hardwired for it."

He pulls me the tiniest bit closer, our clasped hands now just inches away from his chest. Without even inhaling deeply, I can detect his distinctly masculine smell, what seems to be a mixture of cedarwood, pine, and maybe a hint of clove? That doesn't mean I don't inhale deeply. Multiple times.

"But I have to admit I never dreamed I'd actually get to dance with you," he says seriously, even though he's smiling to lighten the words. I focus on the sensation of his thumb lightly rubbing the back of my hand, staring at his forearm above his rolled-up sleeve.

My throat has gone dry, so I swallow hard before speaking. "Well, of the two of us, I never even knew it was possible to dream of dancing with you, so I guess I'm still the more surprised one," I say softly, shifting my eyes to his.

Mateo's dark brown eyes are locked on mine with a spark of intensity, and I hold his gaze as my ears tune in to the lyrics of "Timeless."

My mind races even as we sway slowly. *Were we supposed to find this? All along I've been thinking I already found Aaron, but what if I was wrong?*

Heart suddenly pounding, I wonder if Mateo can feel my pulse picking up. We've slowed to barely swaying when Mateo's gaze flickers to my lips for a split second before he closes his eyes. He takes a step back, breathing deeply, and moves to hold both of my hands in front of us.

"Well, I'm going to suggest that we sit back down and enjoy the dessert course of our dinner, because if we keep dancing, I'm going to kiss you, and kissing you is not in my plan for our first date," Mateo says with total honesty.

My face floods with heat, but it's getting dark enough outside that I hope he can't tell.

Mateo clicks a button, and a strand of battery-powered string lights brighten the back of the truck. He helps me back up onto the tailgate and opens the cooler, handing me a small takeout box.

I open it and go still, staring at the contents.

"Tiramisu," I say quietly. I look at Mateo looking at me. "Tiramisu—that's a 'Lana's Favorites' deep cut."

Mateo smiles as he hands me a plastic fork. "I told you. Paying attention."

He pulls a second box from the cooler and adds with a grin, "Don't worry, I'm not going to make you share. That one's all for you."

I throw my head back in a laugh and take a bite. "Well, that's good, because that may very well have been the end of this," I tell him, motioning my fork back and forth between us.

"I'd never take that risk," Mateo says solemnly before taking his first bite. "I haven't had tiramisu before, but I'm officially a fan now."

"I'm a good influence," I giggle.

"No arguments there," he winks. "Okay, while we eat dessert, we each get to ask each other three questions."

"Any question we want?" I ask.

"Yes. The only rule is that you can't repeat the other person's questions," Mateo replies. "Since I've already had time to give it thought, I'll ask first." When I nod my agreement, he continues. "Question one:

what's something about younger Lana that would surprise your friends you met in college?"

Wow, that's a really great conversation starter. Also, there is a *lot* about younger me that would surprise my college friends. I take a bite of tiramisu to buy time to consider what I want to share. I can tell Mateo sees the wheels turning in my head, and I get the feeling that he's going to be prying more of these stories out of me in the future. For now, I settle on a safe but entirely shocking fact.

"When I was in middle school and early high school, I had my own lawn care business," I state.

"No way," Mateo responds with surprise.

"Yes way," I laugh. "When I was in middle school, my parents were trying to balance taking care of me plus my three young siblings along with two demanding careers, so they taught me to mow the lawn to take something off their plate. I realized that being outside—alone, in my own zone, having a break from the noise of my siblings—made me feel calm. Plus, it was satisfying to see the finished product.

"I was a practical kid, and I knew I'd need to save up to buy a car someday—my parents told me that they would match whatever money I had to put toward a car when I turned sixteen. So, I decided there was no reason that boys should have a corner on the lawn care market, not when I could earn money doing something I enjoyed," I finish with a smile.

Mateo is looking at me with open admiration. "That's super impressive," he says. "How many yards were you mowing?"

"By the final summer, I was up to ten lawns," I share, realizing how proud I am of my younger self. "I paid for my first car and got a great tan."

Mateo laughs and waves his hand toward me. "Okay, your turn for a question."

"Wait, give me a second to think," I stall. Mateo looks out at the final traces of the setting sun as I rack my brain. *What do I want to know about him?* I'm starting to feel like I want to know a *lot* about him.

"What's your favorite thing about your family?" I ask. I figure there's a lot you can tell about someone from what they think of their family. Mateo turns to me and smiles as I take a bite of tiramisu.

"Well, joke's on you, because you just asked the question that could keep me talking for hours," he says with a twinkle in his eye. "I should have brought you a second dessert."

I smile at him. "Better get started then! I'll just steal the rest of yours while you're talking."

He jokingly guards his box from me, but then sets it down between us like an open invitation. "My favorite thing about my family . . . I guess if I had to sum it up, I would say it's how we're always there for each other when it counts."

I angle my body toward Mateo, stretch my legs out, and lean against the side of the truck bed, settling in to listen.

"My brother is four years older than me, and my sister just eighteen months older, so we were all close growing up. My parents were really busy running the restaurant they own, my siblings had their activities, and I had soccer, but when it really mattered, we were always there for each other. We couldn't eat dinner together often, but my mom would make us a big breakfast to share before school."

Mateo pauses for a moment, formulating his next thought. "Even as adults now, my family has each other's backs. My sister had a bit of a rough time a couple of years ago," he pauses, voice thick with emotion. He clears his throat before continuing, "But we were all there. My brother flew in from New York, and I went home for the summer."

"Summer after freshman year?" I ask. "The year you didn't go to Summer Project?"

Mateo nods. "We always tackle life together. We're in each other's corner, no questions asked. I love that about my family, and it's how I always want to be," he finishes with conviction.

I digest this personal tidbit of his life he just shared. I'm burning with curiosity to know more about his sister's story, but it seems like something he's protectively guarding, in the best sort of brotherly way. I admire that about him. "How did your family wind up in Michigan?" I ask him.

"Nope, sorry, you have to wait your turn," Mateo says, his joking tone cutting through the serious air and making me laugh. "You'll have to save that for question number two, because now I get to ask mine."

I hold my hands up in surrender.

"Okay, next question," Mateo begins as he copies my position and stretches his legs out next to mine. "Why cello music?"

"Why cello music?"

"Yes, why do you like listening to cello music?" he asks. "I mean, it's a pretty-sounding instrument, but I get the feeling there's a specific reason you like it."

Gosh, this man is so intuitive. Or maybe it's only me he reads like a book?

"Fine, fine, you're right," I say, raising my hands in surrender again. "My dad plays the cello. He's always taught cello and piano lessons—he's the one who taught me to play piano—and he's the reason we moved to Kansas City. He grew up there, and he got a position playing with the Kansas City Symphony. We were living in El Paso at the time, but one of his high school buddies plays for the symphony and told him to come audition for the opening. It was huge for him to get offered the spot."

Mateo nods, subtly encouraging me to keep sharing.

"I grew up hearing him play, and it always relaxed me," I continue. "When I was in high school and got decent at the piano, we even started playing duets sometimes. My mom would come home from a long day at work and ask us to play. She'd just sit there with her eyes closed, listening. I think it helped ground her after hard days advocating for clients," I share.

"Which must be why you like Piano Guys music so much," Mateo guesses.

"Nailed it," I laugh, and Mateo gives a fake bow. "I guess cello music grounds me too. And it makes me feel close to my parents when I'm away, like it transports me back into our living room with them," I finish, suddenly feeling a little emotional thinking about all those days with my parents.

"*And*, it's a pretty-sounding instrument," I say with a wry grin and nudge Mateo's leg with my foot. He glances down at the contact and then smiles back up at me.

"My turn," I declare, hardly pausing before asking, "How did your parents wind up in Michigan? Feel free to take your time because I know that question came out of left field."

Mateo chuckles and says, "That one's easy, although again, it could be a long answer."

I gesture for him to continue. He smiles. "Short version, my parents originally came to the US as asylum seekers."

My face turns serious, because I know that means there's a solemnity to his family's history. Mateo isn't fazed though and continues. "They were granted permanent residence and recently received citizenship, but when they first arrived, they made connections with people who were migrant farmworkers. So, for the first couple of years here, they traveled around the country harvesting crops.

"They were in Hart, Michigan, for the asparagus harvest, and my mom was about twelve weeks pregnant with their first child. One day out in the fields, she started having terrible cramps, and she wound up miscarrying the baby. All these years later, she still gets really sad on the days surrounding the anniversary," Mateo pauses as emotion catches in his voice. I wait patiently for him to continue.

"Miscarriages are unfortunately so common, so it probably had nothing to do with my mom working in the fields. But my dad was convinced that the physical labor was to blame, so he wouldn't let her harvest anymore. She needed something to do so she wasn't alone and grieving all day long, so she started cooking meals to sell to the migrant workers. She's an incredible cook."

Mateo has a wide smile now, clearly proud of his mom. "Pretty soon, locals were wanting to buy her food as well as the workers. One thing led to another, and they opened a restaurant and never left Hart. They're an integral part of the community now—literally everyone in town knows my parents," he finishes with a laugh. "And no one ever goes hungry."

I smile back at him, feeling his love for his family radiating off him. I appreciate how openly Mateo expresses his affection for them, how he wears his emotions on his sleeve. A glance at my watch shows it's already 9:15 p.m. I look over at Mateo and ask, "What time do you have to be on the bus for the match tomorrow? Should we head back so you can get some rest?"

He waves me off and says, "I'm pretty sure I won't be sleeping much tonight regardless of what time I go to bed. You're just trying to get out of answering your final question."

I look down at my hands with a blush at his honesty. It's starting to look like I may not sleep much tonight either.

"Last question: why UC Davis?" Mateo asks. "You live in Kansas, and there are great law schools all over the country, so why California?"

"Well, that's an easy one for me," I tell him. "It's my mom's alma mater. She's originally from southern California, and my grandparents still live there. UC Davis has a great immigration law program. It's always been my dream to go through the same program where my mom got her training; follow in her footsteps, I guess you could say."

Mateo nods. "Your parents sound like great people."

I smile. "They really are. I love them a lot."

"I can tell," Mateo says, smiling back at me. "Alright, final question goes to you."

I pause to mull things over. Talking about going to law school in California has made me wonder where Mateo plans to wind up after college. I'm trying to think of a way to fish for information about his future when I decide to just go the direct route.

"What are you planning to do after you finish at Townsend?"

"I'm not quite so ambitious to be going after a law degree," Mateo says self-deprecatingly. "But I do hope to get my master's degree and become a licensed therapist."

I raise my eyebrows in surprise. "I have to admit I would not have guessed that."

Mateo laughs. "I know, I know, not what you'd expect from a college soccer player, and it wasn't my original major as a freshman. But I've observed the impact that a therapist can have on someone who's struggling, and I've seen the number of kids—especially of immigrant families—who could really benefit from having a professional to talk to."

"Makes sense," I encourage him.

"I haven't decided whether to get a master's in counseling or psychology yet, or where exactly I'm going to apply. I've been fortunate to be here at Townsend on an athletic scholarship, but I don't want to go deep into debt getting my master's. So, I'm hoping to maybe coach soccer somewhere and slowly take online classes toward my degree as I can afford them," Mateo says, looking pointedly at me.

I can practically hear his heart communicating to mine. *I can pursue my next step anywhere. Even California.*

Neither of us says anything—we just sit there looking at each other, the evening breeze rustling my hair as 2Cellos softly swirls from the speaker and the crickets join in to sing around us. There's a touch of magic charging the air that both of us seem reluctant to interrupt.

I finally speak quietly. "Well, I think you'd make a great soccer coach and a great therapist. You're certainly good at observing and listening to people." Mateo just smiles at me in return.

I have a feeling that Mateo wouldn't refuse me anything at this point, so I decide to push my luck. "Can I have one bonus question? You know, since you're such a gentleman?" I ask with a teasing smile.

"Ah, how could I possibly refuse when you phrase it that way?" Mateo responds with a chuckle. "Ask away."

I look in his eyes and consider how to phrase my question. "You've said you liked me for a long time, and you've definitely proved that you were paying attention all the times we hung out with each other at Arrow stuff. I know you said you were giving me space because of Aaron, and I get that. But . . . I guess my question is, why didn't you give me even a hint that you liked me? I had absolutely no clue that you saw me as anything more than a friend. All those Arrow trainings and Tuesday mornings we spent together at Summer Project, why didn't you give any sort of signals?"

Mateo smiles softly, his single dimple showing, then leans his head back against the side of the truck looking up at the sky. After a moment, he looks back at me and says, "I didn't want to lead you on, Lana. Yes, I liked you—a lot—but if I wasn't going to officially pursue a relationship, it didn't seem fair to hint at my feelings."

I ponder his logic—a sharp contrast to Aaron's. "Kind of a risky move though, to blindside me with your feelings and hope I'd say yes to a date?" I assess with raised eyebrows.

He shrugs. "I guess I'd rather take that risk than play with your heart. And I'm willing to take things at your pace as you catch up from the blindsiding," he adds with another soft smile.

I bite my lip and look down at my hands before responding. "That's actually very considerate, Mateo. I'll try to be honest about where I'm at pace-wise going forward."

A grin spreads across Mateo's face as he says, "Does this mean this isn't our last date?"

I laugh. "It's definitely not our last date."

"Well, I suppose that means I can take you home instead of just extending this night into forever then," he jokes with a wink.

I help him pack up the picnic supplies, and he leads me to the passenger door so I can hop in the truck before he turns off the string lights. I have a moment in the total darkness by myself before he comes around to the driver's door. Adrenaline rushes through my body, making my hands shake and giving me the shivers, but it's the greatest sort of rush.

I just had the *best* time with Mateo. I did not see that coming.

Mateo starts the truck and begins driving back toward the highway. I ask if I can connect his phone to continue playing music. I'm not sure how much I trust my conversational abilities right now.

"The truck is faithful but old, so you'll have to use the aux cable," he tells me, fishing his phone out of his pocket. He hands it to me. "The code is three-one-four-seven. Just pull up Spotify."

I type in the number and click the Spotify icon. The music we'd been listening to pops up, and I hit the play button right as I notice that the playlist is titled, "LANA <heart emoji>."

My thumb clicks the screen off as my eyes dart over in the darkness to look at Mateo's profile. His eyes are on the road (the deer in Kansas are a real and present danger), but he starts humming along to Ed Sheeran's song.

Perfect.

Yes, Ed, I do think this night was perfect.

CHAPTER TEN

M ateo pulls up in front of the AOPi house, turning off the truck and coming around to walk me up to the porch. It's 10:00 p.m. on a Friday night, prime time in college world. Thankfully, few girls are home because there's a huge party at ChiSig tonight. I just had an A+ date with Mateo and feel less apprehensive about being seen together, but I'm still grateful to have a private moment to end our evening instead of inquisitive stares and gossip.

I pause with my hand on the doorknob to turn to Mateo in the porch light. His hands are in his pockets, and he's looking down at me with that one-dimpled smile. "Thanks for going out with me tonight, Lana."

I smile back at him and say, "Thank you for asking me. Really, I'm so glad that you asked. I enjoyed tonight a lot. I'll see you sometime next week?" I ask, realizing how intensely I hope to see him again soon.

"Definitely," Mateo says as his smile spreads wider. "I'll text you."

"Okay," I say as I turn the door handle. I take one step through the door but turn back around. "Good luck at your soccer match tomorrow. I hope you wipe the field with the other team," I say with a wry grin.

Mateo laughs and takes a couple of backward steps away from the door. "Thanks, Lana. I'll let you know how we do."

I wave my fingers at him standing there on the porch and slip the door closed. I lean back against it in the dim lighting and take a few breaths with closed eyes.

I don't know what I was expecting, but I wasn't prepared to have such an incredible time with Mateo. Our night together was so easy; the conversation flowed naturally, the silences never awkward. He planned such a perfect date and asked such great questions. All of my insides are giving high-pitched squealing girl energy.

My phone buzzes with a text while I'm still leaning against the door. I glance at the screen and see it's from Mateo.

MATEO

Tonight was even better than I imagined. Already looking forward to our next date, Lana.

Smiling to myself, I head up the stairs, where I know my Beefs will be anxiously waiting. Sure enough, as soon as I open the door, they launch themselves at me with hugs and demands for every detail.

Laughing, I hug Teegan and Amaya back and then push them away. "Give me a second, let me take my shoes off."

"Okay, okay, but at least give me a Taylor song that encapsulates the vibe of the date for our background music," Teegan demands, phone at the ready in her hand.

I blow out a breath with a smile. "'Enchanted,'" I say.

"O. M. G. This is going to be the best story EVER," Teegan squeals as she's running in place. Golden retrievers have nothing on Teegan's energy. Amaya shoves her onto her bed, shushing her as Teegan starts the song on repeat and throws her phone to the side. They're now both sitting, staring in rapt attention.

I take a seat on the bed across from them and fill them in on the evening. They respond with all the appropriate *ooos* and *ahhhs* as I tell them about all the thought that Mateo had put into the details of the date, the magical setting, and the music. Teegan swoons, hand over heart, when I describe dancing together at sunset—but I leave out the part about Mateo confessing to wanting to kiss me. Some details of our time together are for my heart only.

They can't believe Mateo knew that tiramisu was my favorite dessert. "Wait, I didn't even know that," Amaya says with a furrowed brow.

"LaLa picked that at the Valentine's Dessert event that Arrow did our sophomore year," Teegan declares. I blush, realizing that Mateo must have also been paying attention to me that Valentine's Day.

I share the gist of our answers to each other's questions during dessert, trying to convey the vibes of our conversation without sharing every intimate detail. Amaya, not one to be easily won over, is beyond impressed with both Mateo's answers and his thoughtful questions.

"I gotta say, Lana, I have a good feeling about this," Amaya says.

Teegan sits straight up with her hand out in a scout's honor pose. "I swear, Beef, if you don't fall in love with Mateo over this, I am going to on your behalf."

I hit Teegan with a throw pillow, laughing, "Let's not get ahead of ourselves here, Teegs. It was just our first date."

"Well, I say second date because I'm counting coffee as date one, and you're *obviously* going to go out again, so I don't think I'm jumping too far ahead here," Teegan defends herself.

"Lana's right. We need to keep our cool," Amaya inserts, ever the level-headed one. "She still has a lot to get to know about Mateo, not to mention figuring out if their future paths are compatible. And we don't know yet if the Aaron crush has officially fizzled?" She says the final statement more as a question, looking over at me with an eyebrow raised. Teegan immediately turns to gauge my reaction.

There's an awkward charge in the air now, that I know is my responsibility to dispel.

After a minute, I clear my throat. "Look, I honestly don't know what I think about Aaron right now. I'm not even sure *how* to think about it. I crushed on him for like, forever, but . . ." I pause, unsure how to continue.

Teegan eventually wades in slowly, "But, you know, Mateo seems great. Really great. And we *know* he likes you. But Aaron, you know, we don't even really know for sure what he thinks."

"Yeah, Lana, the first person to acknowledge to you that Aaron had a crush on you was Mateo," Amaya says with a hint of sass. "Aaron has never had the guts to shoot straight about your relationship. Mateo is being totally upfront and honest, and I think that's what you deserve," she finishes, crossing her arms.

I'm feeling conflicted, because the dregs of years of feelings for Aaron are rising up wanting to defend him. But also . . . my Beefs aren't wrong.

The refrain of "Enchanted" cycles through the background noise, and I think about the magic I felt on my date with Mateo, the wonder-struck feeling I had on the drive back home.

I bury my head in my hands for a moment, then finally respond. "I know I'm not going to figure this all out tonight. But I promise, I'm going to sort it out."

"Aaand you're going to go on another date with Mateo, right?" Teegan adds hopefully.

"And I'm going to go on another date with Mateo," I reassure her. "I'll cross the what-to-do-with-Aaron bridge when it comes, but no matter what happens with any boys, you two are my for-lifes, okay?"

In bed that night, I'm willing my closed eyes to surrender to sleep, but my mind's eye is bouncing back and forth between Aaron's and Mateo's faces. *Ughhh, how am I supposed to sort through a huge pile of old, clingy feelings alongside this little pile of brand-new, glittery feelings?*

After several minutes, I stop trying to sort through and instead start to replay my favorite parts of tonight's date in my mind.

Mateo's laugh. The soft look on his face when he talked about his family. His profile silhouetted against the setting sun. The warmth that spread through my body when my hand was in his. The intensity in his eyes before he ended our dance. His playfulness and sincerity intermixing our conversation.

I finally drift off into a happy dream.

Chapter Eleven

The dreaming doesn't stop after Friday night. Mateo's dimpled smile infiltrates my daydreams and my actual dreams every night. I force my brain to stay on task during my classes, but any downtime I have is spent reliving my time with Mateo. It's always there, waiting in the background, ready to jump out the moment I let my mind drift.

Mateo texted me Saturday evening to let me know his team won and immediately asked if we could go on another date this week. I said yes. He suggested going on a hike (read: walk through the trees on a dirt path in Kansas) Thursday afternoon because the weather looked promising. I agreed, eager for the opportunity to talk more while having physical movement to focus on.

Tuesday morning, my brain gets sent back into a tailspin when I receive a text from Aaron.

AARON

> Too bad our houses can't be homecoming partners 2 years in a row. Showcase last year was epic

I freeze. I know he can see that I've read his message, so I have to respond.

Two weeks ago, I would have been elated. I would have sent back an entirely over-eager response about how great it was to be dance partners. I would have daydreamed all day long about Aaron and playing out fake possible conversations between us where he would finally officially ask me out.

But now my mind drifts back to Mateo's thumb rubbing the back of my hand, his dark eyes looking into mine like he never wanted to blink.

I finally type up a quick response.

Did I just make it sound like I wasn't involved in homecoming this year because we couldn't be partners again? I mean, maybe that *is* how I would have felt a couple of weeks ago, but that's not what I intended to communicate now.

Frustrated, I throw my phone into my backpack and leave before I'm late to class.

———

My mind struggles to stay focused all day, which is not good because tonight is my first night back doing ELL tutoring. The local school district has an after-school program called "The Hangout" on Tuesdays for middle and high school students at the community center. It's focused on giving at-risk students a place to belong and make positive connections. There are a wide variety of adult volunteers from the Brooklyn community who come to serve as mentors and build relationships with the kids. Some students come just to hang and play ping pong or video games, but others come for homework help or extra tutoring. A few of us work with students who are English Language Learners, and it's been one of the highlights of my time at Townsend.

I hope all three of the girls I worked with last year are there again tonight. And I hope my brain remembers that they're more important than any boy drama going on in my life and appropriately concentrates.

Thankfully, the minute I walk in the community center doors, Sofia launches herself at me. I laugh and hug her back. Sofia was my first "student" when I was a freshman at Townsend and she was a sixth grader. She's essentially fluent in English now and doesn't really need my tutelage anymore, but she's stayed with my group anyway. Sofia was a great help, not only helping translate but also connecting with the two new girls who came last year, Clara and Luisa. All three are freshmen at the high school this year, which could get interesting.

"Lana, I missed you all summer!" Sofia says, arms still wrapped around my neck. She's only a couple of inches shorter than me now, which makes me misty-eyed for some reason.

"Clara and Luisa got pizza and already claimed our old corner table for us," Sofia continues, finally releasing me from her hug. "There's a new girl, Shaista, at school this year who doesn't know much English. Her family came from Afghanistan. We invited her to come be part of our group—I hope that's okay with you."

Now I'm really misty-eyed. "Oh my gosh, it's more than okay, Sofia. I'm so proud of you for including her."

The compliment makes her grin from ear to ear. This is precisely what I love about spending time here.

I get more hugs from Clara and Luisa before introducing myself to Shaista. She's shy, although that could be due to the language barrier and cultural differences. I know from my time with Afghan families this summer that the women were much more reserved until you really got to know them well and were in an environment that felt comfortable to them.

I can tell that Luisa and Clara spent the summer speaking mostly Spanish with their families, because their English is a little rusty at first. I enlist Sofia's help to guide them through a practice conversation while I get Shaista started in the level one workbook. She's able to read Pashto, so we can utilize Google Translate to help us communicate.

I'm not sure it's the most effective lesson ever, but I'm proud of Clara, Luisa, and Sofia for making a concerted effort to include Shaista and her willingness to show up in what must be an intimidating environment. My emotional cup is filled to the brim at the end of the night, even if my brain power is running on empty.

Tuesday evenings are a quick turnaround from my time tutoring to make it back to AOPi for Teegan and I to co-lead our Bible study with the sophomore girls who were in our group last year. Teegan does the bulk of the work preparing to lead, which I'm especially grateful for tonight. We have an encouraging discussion, but by the end of our time, I'm so ready to crash.

When Teegan and I open the door to our room, Amaya is already there, prepping her hair for bed. She waves her phone at me, "Lana, you put a reminder in my phone for me to ask you how your law school essay is coming along." I groan. "I take it that means it's *not* coming along," she says in a stern voice with raised eyebrows.

Teegan jumps to my defense. "Give LaLa a break—she's had a lot going on."

"Hey, I'm not the one who put the reminder in my phone!" Amaya says, rolling her eyes. "When are you going to get to it, Beef?"

I sigh. "Not tonight. I'm so tired I think I could fall asleep standing up. But tomorrow after class, I'm going to get started." Amaya eyes me. "For real."

————

I do not, in fact, get started the next day. Though, I try.

I take my laptop to my favorite place on campus, the huge study room in the library. It's nicknamed the Harry Potter Room because of its resemblance to the Hogwarts dining room with its high ceilings, rows of tables, and giant windows. I hope the change in scenery will help me concentrate so I can make progress on my personal statement.

I open the Word document on my screen and stare at the flashing cursor. *How do I begin explaining why I want to be a lawyer? How do I sum up a long-held dream, the ambition that has guided every decision over the past six years of my life?* The personal statement is supposed to be a "short essay," but I feel like I need to sit down with the admissions reps for an entire afternoon in order to convey why I *need* to go to law school.

With zero words written, I turn on my Mindful Mellow playlist, thinking maybe it will inspire great thoughts to come pouring through my fingertips onto the screen. Lana del Rey croons gently through my earbuds while I stare until my laptop screen blacks out from inactivity.

My phone pings with a text, and I look to see Mateo has sent me a screenshot of the weather forecast for tomorrow afternoon. Partly cloudy with a high of eighty. A gift in a Kansas September. I'm surprised by the rush of serotonin filling my brain as I think about hanging out with Mateo again.

I close my laptop, effectively giving up for the day, and text Mateo instead.

ME

Excited for our hiking date tomorrow afternoon

Three dots immediately start swirling.

MATEO

Not as excited as I am

Chapter Twelve

"Would you at least wear a cute athletic skort?" Teegan pleads with me, frustration in her voice.

"No, Teegs," I state firmly. "We are going on a hike. I am not wearing a skirt. I'm just going to wear shorts and an athletic tank. I do not need to look cute for this."

Teegan groans as I wrap my hair up in a messy bun. She pouts her lower lip. "This is Kansas; it's not even a real hike. You can wear an athletic skirt to walk along a trail."

I can't help but laugh. Dressing me in just the right outfit is one of Teegan's love languages, but I'm not going to be swayed this time. I want to feel comfortable hiking (okay, walking) so my brain can concentrate on my conversation with Mateo today. He's going to pick me up in about ten minutes to drive to a trailhead on the opposite edge of campus.

Lacing up my tennis shoes, I nod and reply, "*Mmhmm*," to all of Teegan's reminders to have fun, forget about Aaron, and remember every detail to report back later.

I'm guessing Mateo might be early again, so I throw my belt bag over my head as I bound down the stairs. Sure enough, he's coming up the walkway as I head out the front door. He somehow manages to look equally as attractive in athletic shorts and a performance tee as he did dressed up nice for our first date.

Mateo smiles and greets me. As he opens the truck door for me, my eyes are drawn to the shift of the muscles in his shoulders, and I'm grateful to be wearing lightweight athletic gear as a flush heats my face.

After starting the truck, Mateo pauses. "Is it okay if we stop by the soccer complex real quick? Coach swears he told us to turn in attendance sheets at practice this morning, but no one remembered. We can't accuse Coach of forgetting, so I need to drop it off."

"Of course, not a problem at all," I reply. Despite the popularity of the home soccer matches among the student body, I haven't ever been to the soccer complex before.

I take a drink from the water bottle Mateo had waiting in the cup holder for me as we pull up to the soccer complex. "You're welcome to come look around if you want," Mateo offers.

I hop out and follow him through the parking lot. We head around to the side of the complex, where the building with the offices and locker rooms sits at one end of the field. I can't go into the locker room, obviously, so I explore as I wait.

Walking down the sideline of the field, I see a few soccer balls apparently forgotten after practice earlier that day. I'm scanning the chalk markings on the grass, imagining the crowds cheering in the stands for Mateo and the team. I gently kick one of the balls onto the edge of the field and run my foot back and forth over its surface.

"Ever been to a match before?" Mateo asks as he jogs up behind me. I shake my head.

"No, but I can imagine how pumped the crowd gets when Townsend wins. With the stands so close to the field, it must get loud. Everyone loves the soccer team here," I say.

Mateo shrugs. "Yeah, I guess so. It is really fun to hear the crowd get going when we're close to shooting on goal."

I stare pensively out at the field. Mateo frowns and asks if I'm okay, and I make a decision.

I turn to face him, the soccer ball still at my feet between us. "You know on our date when you asked me what would surprise my friends about past Lana?"

He nods. "Of course I do."

I give a small smirk. "Well, I told you about my lawn care business, but I could have also told you that I played seven years of competitive soccer."

Without giving him time to process what I said, I kick the ball with my left foot toward the center and take off dribbling down the field. I caught Mateo off guard, but he's much faster than me, so it won't take him long to be hot on my heels.

The familiar rush of streaking down a soccer field with an opponent chasing me takes over my brain and body. I sense Mateo closing in, but I know he won't come after me as aggressively as he would against a real opposing player. I take advantage of him taking it easy on me to juke to one side to escape. I'm just inside the box and pulling my leg back to take my shot when I feel Mateo's arm wrap around my waist as he pulls me off course. The ball slowly rolls to a stop well short of the net.

"Hey! Whistle! Whistle, whistle!" I yell. Mateo is dying laughing as he releases his arm from around me.

"That, sir, was a penalty," I tell him with feigned indignity, poking my finger in his chest.

He just shrugs his shoulder with a smile. "Maybe the penalty was worth it."

I ignore his flirting. "You owe me a penalty kick," I announce as I march to scoop up the ball and place it in position. I point at Mateo and then the goal, commanding him to take the goalie position.

Mateo reluctantly moves in front of the net. "For the record, I haven't played keeper since I was like, eight years old," he says as he crouches and holds his hands out at his sides.

"Well, I haven't shot a PK in almost four years, so we'll call it an even match," I say. My mind immediately transports me back to the fields in Kansas City, hearing my coaches and teammates cheering me on as I stare down the opposing goalkeeper.

I decide to pull out my favorite PK strategy since Mateo doesn't know anything about the way I used to play. Blowing out a deep breath, I glance at both corners of the net before ever so slightly angling my body toward the right side. I'm sprinting toward the ball as Mateo takes my bait and starts a dive to the right, but I take a Jorginho hop and use it to angle my kick to the top left corner instead.

The ball swishes into the back of the net, and I raise my hands in victory as Mateo sits up with his arms on his knees. We both turn our heads at the sound of loud voices.

"Ohhhh, she totally faked you out, bro!" Andrés yells as he walks toward us. Another teammate is doubled over laughing. "Burn, man!"

I can't help but smile as Mateo hops up, defending himself. "Dude, I'm a midfielder! I never claimed to have goalkeeping skills." He's laughing as he gives Andrés a bro hug before mock slapping the back of his head. I start walking toward them, and the three of them meet me halfway.

"Andrés, you know Lana," Mateo says as Andrés gives me a huge grin that clues me in that he probably knows a lot about me from Mateo. "And Lana, this is Chris—he's one of our starting defenders."

Chris reaches out to shake my hand. "That was quite the PK. We always enjoy seeing Alvarez get put in his place," he says with a laugh as he shoves Mateo, who puts him in a headlock in return. This is clearly their typical team dynamic, because all three of them are smiling without a hint of ill will.

"Yeah, well I only learned about two minutes before that impressive display that Lana played competitive soccer her whole life, so I was at a disadvantage," Mateo says as he winks at me. My heart does a much bigger flip flop this time.

I raise my hands up and tilt my head. "Hey, your coach would probably say you're always supposed to be prepared, so I'm just exposing any weak spots." It's crazy how quickly trash talk comes back, even after you've been disengaged for a long time.

Chris and Andrés give Mateo a hard time all over again. When they're done scuffling, Andrés claps Mateo on the back and says, "What would you say to playing a little two v two action?"

Mateo looks over at me and raises one shoulder in question. The exhilaration of being back on the field is still pumping through me, so I nod my head and reply, "Sure!"

"But only if I get Lana as my partner," Mateo quickly adds with a grin. "I'm not going up against her again."

I blush, and he high-fives me as Andrés spells out the rules. "We'll play on one half of the field and take turns attacking the goal. If the ball goes out of bounds or back past the midfield line, the other team takes the ball. First to score five points wins. Cool?"

We all nod, and Mateo loses rock-paper-scissors, so we start on defense. As we jog to position, I hold up a hand and say, "Wait just a sec." I pull the hair ties out of my bun and let the messy waves fall down my back. Flipping my head over, I pull my hair up into a high ponytail and tightly secure it with an extra loop of my hair tie, my signature hairstyle all the years I played.

It always drove new coaches crazy at first—they'd try to insist that I somehow braid my nearly waist-length hair to keep it well-managed so it wouldn't weigh me down or get in my face as I was fighting for the ball. But they all quickly learned that I played my best with my thick mane free-flowing as I maneuvered the field.

Ponytail secure, I jump in place a couple of times and say, "Ready!"

Mateo is openly staring at me with a smile. He asks, "By the way, what position did you play?"

"Striker!" I yell to him as I start jogging toward Chris. "I always sucked at defense!"

Mateo gives a short laugh before quickly closing the distance between him and Andrés, forcing Andrés to pass to Chris. I'm ready for it and bump into him with more of an arm shove than he was probably anticipating. He's thrown off balance just enough that I'm able to boot the ball out of bounds, earning a loud cheer from Mateo.

Hey, a girl has got to use whatever resources she has to her advantage. Even if it's guys taking it easy on her.

Mateo tells me to take the ball to start our offensive at the midfield line. Andrés is standing a few paces back, waiting for me to bring the ball into play. I give the ball a soft kick, keeping my dribble slow and controlled as I watch Andrés moving toward me. I pick up speed as he comes in to fight for the ball. He nearly steals control, but I manage to inside cut the ball and kick a hard left-footed pass over to Mateo on the right side.

As he settles the pass and works his way up the field against Chris, I sprint toward the goal box. I don't think Andrés will expect me to try a header, so when Mateo makes eye contact with me, I give a small upward jerk of my head. He raises his eyebrows right before kicking a perfect cross assist.

My instinct was correct, and Andrés stays grounded instead of jumping to fight for the ball. I offer up a split-second prayer that I haven't forgotten how to do this as I leap up to head the ball into the back of the net.

The joy of this game I once loved so much expands through every cell of my body. Without even thinking about it, my arms raise as though holding a bow and shooting an arrow into the goal—my token score celebration, once upon a time.

I hear Mateo's loud cheer seconds before he whirls me around in celebration. "Yesss, Lana!" he says, then wags his finger at the guys. "Now you see what it's like to be caught off guard by her skills."

Laughing but also winded (this is the most I've sprinted in a while!), I bend down with my hands on my knees, gasping in oxygen as I smile up at Andrés and Chris.

"That's it, we know you're pulling out all the stops. No more going easy," Chris says with a grin.

What follows can only be described as one of the most fun experiences of my entire college career. I'm surprised by how quickly my brain unlocks the closed soccer compartment and unleashes all the muscle memory I have in order to keep up with the guys.

We're equal parts seriously competing, laughing, and trash talking as we go back and forth on the field. Andrés and Chris are up 4–3, and Mateo is fighting Chris to keep the ball to try to tie up the score. He does a lightning-fast pullback to get the ball away from Chris before passing it toward me in the corner of the box.

Andrés is sprinting next to me to try to reach the ball first when we suddenly hear, "Alvarez! Garcia! Garrett! What do you knuckleheads think you're doing?"

We quickly stop short and swivel our bodies to the office building, where Coach Anderson is standing. Looking not too happy.

"Out here goofing off with no cleats, no shin guards, no nothing. One of you idiots is going to wind up rolling an ankle and ruining our season!" Coach yells as the three guys sheepishly hang their heads.

"Sorry Coach, it was my fault," Mateo yells back. "We'll head out right now."

"See you at practice tomorrow—early, for ten extra laps," Coach adds before turning back to the building.

The four of us are out of breath with our hands on our knees or above our heads. I exhale. "Sorry about that, guys."

They look at each other and grin. "Totally worth the extra laps!" Andrés says, as he and Chris give me high fives. "This was awesome. We'll have a rematch after soccer season is over, so you're not too sad about losing."

"Whatever, man. Lana was totally about to score—I could sense it," Mateo says as he throws an arm over my shoulders. I'm grateful that my cheeks are already flushed from running so the guys don't know how much I'm blushing at his touch.

"Sure, sure, you can tell yourself that all you want till you get to prove it!" Chris teases as they wave and head toward the parking lot.

Mateo turns to me. "So, you still want to go out to the trail?"

I shake my head. "Nope, I'd say that counts as sufficient physical exercise for this date." Mateo chuckles as his dimple pops, making me smile. "I have a better idea—let's go get slushies."

———

There's a gas station on the edge of campus that has the mother of all slushie machines. There are ten different flavors, but more importantly, the machine runs on some kind of magic that makes the texture of the slush perfectly smooth without a hint of chunky ice. Similar enchantment keeps the flavor evenly dispersed, so you're never left with a sad pile of barely-flavored ice.

"What the lady wants, she gets," Mateo says, tossing the soccer ball back to the sideline. We head to his truck and drive toward the campus gas station. The weather is not terribly hot, but he cranks up the air anyway. I lean my face toward the vent to try to dry some of the sweat on my forehead. My hair is sticking to the skin on my neck and shoulders, and it's probably three times bigger after running around so much.

I don't even care.

It's a short drive, but the whole way my brain falls back in time to high school, submerged in soccer memories. Amazing wins with my team, heartbreaking losses, the roar of our families and friends cheering us on from their sideline lawn chairs. I've kept a lid on all those memories for the past three years, but it feels good to open it back up and breathe in the nostalgia.

Mateo parks his truck and follows me into the gas station. I head straight to the slushie machine and grab two large cups, handing one to him. He's looking over all the flavors intently, and I elbow him in the side. "Please tell me you've been here for a slushie before."

He gives me a fake grimace. "Only once freshman year. What flavor is better? Cherry Limeade or Blue Raspberry?"

I give an exaggerated sigh. "There's only one correct way to do this." I pull his arm over to the pop machine. "First, you have to get a splash of Vanilla Coke, just enough to give the hint of vanilla," I say as I demonstrate how much.

Heading back over to the slushie machine, I put my cup under the Coke nozzle and begin filling. "Then, you fill it up with Coke slush. No mixing flavors. This right here is perfection." I pop on the lid and stick in a straw.

Mateo looks at me and deadpans, "You know this is the literal opposite of hydration, right?"

"But it's oh-so-good, especially after exercising out in the sun," I say as I take a long sip. "Ahhh, so good."

"Okay, but can I mix in cherry instead of vanilla? I've never really liked Vanilla Coke," Mateo asks as he holds his cup under the Cherry slushie nozzle.

I bat his cup away and say with gravity. "No. Mixing. Slushie. Flavors." He smirks at me, and I make an I'm-watching-you gesture with my fingers. "If you must have cherry instead, at least get a splash of Cherry Coke. I'll try not to take it personally that you don't like vanilla."

"I surrender," he says with a grin as he follows my instructions. We head up to the register to pay, but he stops to grab two cold water bottles first. "At least promise to drink water along with your caffeinated dehydration beverage."

We head out the door, holding our slushie cups and water bottles. As we near the truck, Mateo asks, "What do you say we leave the truck parked here and walk across the street to campus? There's a shaded area with some picnic tables not too far."

I agree, and we stand at the crosswalk waiting for a break in traffic. "Have you tried it yet? Is it the best post-workout drink you've ever tasted?"

Mateo takes a sip. "I'll give you that it tastes great. I'll fight you that it can be classified as a post-workout drink," he quips. We jog across the street before the next wave of cars comes through and walk along the sidewalk to a small alcove with tables outside of the engineering building. There are lots of trees shading the area and a cool breeze blowing, making it the perfect place to sit and relax.

We sit on two benches next to each other around a square table, and I make a show of opening my water bottle and taking a long drink. "See? I'm hydrating."

"I approve," Mateo says before doing the same. He then takes a drink of his slushie before continuing, "So, you're obviously going to have to tell me a little more about that soccer show back there."

I smile down at the table and switch to sipping my slushie. "Yeah, no one at Townsend knows that I used to be so hardcore about soccer. I mean, Teegan and Amaya know that I was on the soccer team in high school, but even they have no idea how competitively I played."

"Or how incredibly skilled you are?" Mateo asks with a raised eyebrow. I blush. "The bow and arrow—was that your signature goal celebration?"

"Starting my sophomore year of high school," I tell him. "I played on our high school team, but in the fall seasons I always played with a club team. It was an ongoing gift from my grandparents on my dad's side, to pay the fees for me to play club soccer. I switched to a new team in a different league sophomore year, and our team name was The Archers. There was an archery range that agreed to sponsor our team if we adopted the name."

Mateo rolls his eyes. "I know exactly how that goes. I once played on a team called The Locomotives, thanks to an auto parts store."

"That definitely makes Archers not seem so bad," I say with a giggle. "In our first game, I scored a goal in minute three, and that's just the celebration that my brain landed on in that moment of adrenaline. My teammates and our sideline went crazy, so it just sort of stuck. Of course, my dad decided to be super embarrassing and started bringing a sign that said 'Bullseye' to hold up every time I scored."

"But you kind of loved it," Mateo says with a mischievous grin.

"You're right, I totally did," I laugh.

He leans in with one elbow propped on the table between us. "So . . . why didn't you keep playing? It sure looked like you had the skill to play for a college team. What made you decide not to?"

I fiddle with my slushie straw for a minute. Eventually, I turn toward him to prop my toes on the edge of his bench. Wrapping my arms around my legs, I rest my chin on my knees while I think.

"I don't know," I start. "Well, that's not true. I *do* know, but sometimes I wonder if my logic was flawed."

Mateo props his head with one hand and just looks at me with those perfect brown eyes, not pushing but just waiting expectantly.

"I had my plan all laid out, knowing exactly what I was going to major in, what activities I would join, what leadership check marks I needed on my résumé to prepare for law school," I finally share. "I knew it was going to take a lot of focus to be prepared to apply at the beginning of my senior year. And I also knew that college athletics takes a lot of time, attention, and dedication, even at the DII or DIII level."

Mateo nods. "You're not wrong there."

"So, even though I had soft offers from a couple of schools, I just shut it down. I decided I was done after my senior year because I had to focus on my long-term future plan. I haven't even touched a soccer ball since the final game of my senior spring season. It's like I just quarantined that area of my life to the past. Even though it used to make me so happy."

Mateo is quiet for a minute, taking in what I'd shared. "And how was it being back out on the field today?" he asks.

I can't stop myself from grinning widely. "Completely amazing. It's like every muscle in my body had just been waiting to be called up to perform again. I don't know that I've had that much fun since coming to Townsend. Thanks so much for letting us play, even if it did result in extra running for you tomorrow. I feel bad about that."

He smiles back at me and says, "I'll gladly run extra laps in the name of you remembering how much fun soccer is."

I take a drink of my slushie and wave toward Mateo. "You've heard my soccer origin story, now you need to tell me yours. What made you get started playing?"

"Well, if we're going to talk origin story, then I guess we'll need to call it *fútbol*, since that's what most of the world calls soccer, including Guatemala." Mateo winks at me. I love the authentic way he pronounces Guatemala. "My dad grew up playing soccer all the time, never on an organized team, but just for fun with the kids on his street. There wasn't any opportunity for him to play seriously, but he always loved the sport."

He's smiling to himself, and I silently soak in how sweet he is every time he talks about his family.

"When my dad had sons living in America, he couldn't wait for us to be able to play 'real *fútbol*,'" he says in an accented voice, I assume mimicking his father. "He was out in the yard teaching my brother Miguel and me soccer drills basically when we started walking. We joined teams as soon as we were old enough.

"When Miguel hit middle school, he decided he wanted to start playing American football with the kids from school. And my dad totally supported him in that. Dad was always cheering him on from the stands, but he couldn't offer much by way of extra coaching since he wasn't very familiar with the sport.

"But I always loved the extra time with my dad kicking the ball around in the backyard, so I stuck with soccer. When my sixth-grade coach told my parents that I might have the natural talent to play in college one day, my dad started working harvest jobs again just to be able to pay the club fees for a better team in a nearby city."

Mateo pauses, lost in the memory. He clears his throat before continuing. "My dad always pushed me to do my best, to constantly improve, but he also always told me how proud he was of me, even when I played poorly. The day I got the offer to play at Townsend was one of the best days of my life, watching my dad cry while we talked to Coach Anderson on speaker. I had an offer to a school closer to home, but Dad had done all sorts of research and was convinced that Coach Anderson was going to be the next great men's soccer coach. So here I am."

My heart is a melted puddle thinking about Mateo with his sweet dad. "Do they ever get to come watch you play?" I ask.

"Sadly, not often. Between the distance and the demands of owning a restaurant, it's hard for them to make it down. But my dad always watches the game tape, and we talk about it after. And they were able to be at the DII tournament last year to see us win. That was unforgettable," Mateo concludes with a wide smile.

"So . . ." Mateo says as he looks down at his hands, fidgeting with his water bottle. I'm not sure I'll ever get used to this naturally confident, popular student athlete acting nervous around me. "We have a home match on Saturday. Would you maybe want to come? You know, if you don't have AOPi stuff going on or anything."

I smile at him when he looks up at my face. "I'd love to come. It's been way too long since I watched a soccer match, especially with someone I care about playing." Mateo grins, and my heart squeezes at the elation on his face.

Glancing down at my watch, I see it's almost 5:00 p.m. "Well, after that unexpected running, I'm going to need to shower before Arrow tonight, so I should probably get back to AOPi," I say reluctantly. In the span of just two dates, I'm learning that time spent with Mateo flies by and never feels like quite enough.

Mateo picks up both of our slushie cups and throws them in the nearby trashcan, tossing his empty water bottle in the recycling bin. He points at my half-full water. "Drink up. I'm holding you hostage till you finish."

I mock roll my eyes and huff, "Such a hydration dictator." Mateo laughs as I exaggeratedly gulp my water and hand him the empty bottle. "Happy?"

"More than you know," Mateo says with a smile, glancing over at me as we start walking back to the car.

I think I'm just going to have to get used to heart flips now.

Chapter Thirteen

The next morning, I smile the whole way to class. I'm in a good mood because the temperature dropped overnight, so the morning air is crisp as I make my way through campus.

I may also be in a good mood because I keep thinking about my soccer "date" with Mateo yesterday.

I still feel invigorated from playing again after such a long time away. I grin to myself thinking about how much fun it was playing together with Mateo, trash-talking Chris and Andrés, and watching the camaraderie of the three of them.

But even beyond the rush of the game, I really enjoyed just sitting and talking with Mateo, hearing more about his life and background, and opening up to him about my own. It felt so . . . natural. Like it was exactly what I should be doing. Maybe what I should have been doing all along.

My phone pings in my hand, and I see a text from my mom asking if I have time to talk today.

I send a message letting her know I'll call after class as I head into the building. I'm half listening to my professor, half mulling over whether to mention Mateo to my mom. Is it too early to do that? I've talked with her in the past about Aaron, so maybe I should bring her up to speed? I don't want it to seem like I'm hiding the fact that I've gone on dates with Mateo from her.

But last night I skipped After Party following the Arrow meeting because I didn't think I could risk trying to carry on a conversation with Aaron while my mind was one hundred percent still immersed in my afternoon with Mateo. My short interaction with Aaron when he sought me out to get a name tag was enough to send my brain into malfunction mode. The more I get to know Mateo, the less I even think about Aaron. But there's still a degree of confusion fog surrounding Aaron in my mind.

After class ends, I have thirty minutes till my next one begins. I find a quiet, deserted bench and pull out my phone to call my mom. She answers on the second ring.

"Hey, Mom! How are you?" I ask. "Everything good at home?"

"Hi, sweetie. I'm good. Trying to get things wrapped up early today so I can make it out in time to go watch Olivia's halftime performance at the football game tonight," she tells me. I know I have her full attention, even though I can sense she's multitasking in her office. Mom's always had that superpower. I think she must have a super brain that can somehow fully engage two tasks at a time.

"Are things with Dean going okay?" I question with a little bit of trepidation.

Mom sighs. "I'm not totally sure, to be honest. Carter has his crew of friends from cross country and track, but Dean is struggling to find his fit. I know he wants some autonomy from Carter, but he mistakes that for meaning he needs to be the opposite of Carter. But at least he's going to school and passing his classes, so I just keep praying that he finds the right niche."

"I don't know what I could do from here, but let me know if you think I could help in any way," I say.

"How are you doing, hon? Any fun plans this weekend?" my mom asks. If there was ever a perfect segue to fill her in on the events of the past couple of weeks, this is it.

"I do have something fun planned," I start slowly. "I'm going to watch the Townsend home soccer match tomorrow."

There's a pause before my mom asks, "Really? What made you decide to go? Not that I don't think you should, because you definitely should, I'm just curious."

I take a deep breath and glance around to make sure no one is listening. "Well . . . there's this . . . um, I'm actually going to the match because of a guy."

"Oh? You mean Aaron? Did he ask you to go?"

"Um, no, it's not Aaron. He still hasn't ever asked me out or anything official like that," I say, fumbling to explain. "There's this other guy from Arrow named Mateo, who's also on the Townsend soccer team. We've been friends the past few years because of Arrow activities and Summer Projects, and, well, apparently he's liked me for a while, and he asked me out on a date a couple of weeks ago."

I'm silent, waiting to see what my mom's response will be. She's never been anything but supportive of me, so I don't know why I'm nervous about how she'll react. But I'm still holding my breath.

"*Hmmm*," my mom finally says. "Well, that's certainly interesting. What's he like? Have you gone on a date already?"

"Mateo is . . ." I look up at the sky, trying to decide how to sum him up. "He's turned out to be pretty amazing. Like, I'm constantly surprised by how much I enjoy being with him, by how sweet and thoughtful he is." I give my mom an extremely abbreviated summary of our conversations at Lake Games and Bookafe, and our first date. I conclude by telling her about playing soccer together yesterday.

There's silence on my mom's end for what feels like a really long time. I finally hear what sounds like a sniffle. "You played soccer again?" she asks, voice laced with emotion.

I grin to myself. "Yeah. It was really amazing."

"I'm clearly going to need to meet this boy. But if he's as sweet as you say, and he got you to do something you love but ignored for such a long time, he already has a stamp of approval in my book," Mom says.

"I've gotta get into class, Mom, but I'm sure you can meet him when you and Dad come visit. I promise I'll keep you updated in the meantime. Tell everyone I love them!"

I hang up and hurry into the building to sit down right as class begins. Relief washes over me. Although I knew my mom would be supportive no matter what, it feels good to hear her so pleased about Mateo. Even if some of that pleasure is due to me opening the door to soccer.

Thinking about soccer reminds me about the match tomorrow, so I slyly pull my phone out under my desk and send a text to Teegan. She's also in a class now, but I can always count on Teegan to check her phone during classes.

ME

Will you go with me to the soccer match tomorrow? I'll feel better having someone to sit with

TEEGAN

Will I go watch Mateo and all his soccer bros running around being all athletic and stuff? Duh yeah

I snicker and cover it up with a cough.

ME

You're so self-sacrificing

TEEGAN

You're lucky to have me. But you're going to have to explain everything since you apparently have harbored a secret knowledge about everything soccer. I used to go to the games freshman year but that was only for the socialization, not the sport

ME

I'm sorry for not telling you about it sooner, but you can't hold it against me forever

TEEGAN

You underestimate my grudge-holding powers. I demand some open swooning over Mateo from you in my presence if I'm ever going to let it go

ME

Sigh. You're impossible

TEEGAN

Impossible not to love, you're so right

ME

<Kiss face emoji>

———

Friday after lunch, my phone dings with a calendar reminder. *Law school app. NO EXCUSES!!!*

The AOPi house is a little more chaotic than usual—several of the freshmen came over after their morning classes to have a reality TV marathon in the movie room. Teegan is trying to get me to join them in the name of sisterhood bonding, but I *must* make progress on my application today if I want to get it submitted this month.

I show Teegan the calendar notification on my phone screen like a trump card. "Fine, fine. Go be a responsible human being," she relents. "You might want to go work someplace else though—Amaya just texted me that she's planning on a power nap this afternoon."

Amaya was up late last night *after* the After Party finalizing some homecoming details and sending out reminders to girls who signed up. I'm so glad I opted out of AOPi leadership this year. But I'm proud of how hard Amaya is working to make AOPi the best version of itself.

Heading out to the parking lot with my backpack, I pause when I see a text from Aaron come through on my watch. I pull out my phone to read the whole message.

My heart starts pounding. Aaron has no idea that I've gone on dates with Mateo. He probably doesn't even know that I've talked to Mateo.

A wave of guilt washes over me, but I shake it out of my system by repeating the mantras Amaya pounded into me when I told her why I skipped After Party. "Aaron has never asked me out. If Aaron feels jealous of me dating Mateo, that's his problem, not mine," she made me repeat over and over until she was convinced I believed it.

I decide to reply to Aaron in the least flirty fashion I can think of. I'll just completely ignore his reference to us dancing together last year.

Aaron sends back a "We Are The Champions" GIF, but I leave it on read and head to my car.

———

I sit down in the driver's seat, about to start the ignition when I see something stuck under my windshield wiper. Opening the door a crack, I half stand and reach around to grab it before sitting back down in the car.

It's a generic letter envelope with Lana scrawled on the outside. I break the seal and pull out a piece of notebook paper, unfolding it to see Mateo's signature at the bottom.

I can't help but smile before I've even read a word.

Lana – I'm writing this after unsuccessfully trying to fall asleep after our dinner date. I feel bad that this isn't a real card, or at least some nice paper, but notebook paper is all I had on hand in the middle of the night. Next time will be better.

I don't even know when I'll give this to you. Probably not right away. I don't want to come on too strong and scare you away because I know that you're still getting used to this, getting used to thinking about us. It's still new for you. But my sister Isabel told me there's a Taylor Swift song about saying how you feel even though the beginning of the relationship is fragile, so maybe you won't mind since you're also a Swiftie. At least I know you like her music. I don't know if being called a Swiftie is a compliment or an insult to you. Please trust I would only ever compliment you.

I'm getting off track here. I just have to tell you that tonight was one of the best nights of my life. I know that probably sounds like an exaggeration. Of course I've had lots of best times with my family, with my soccer teams. But tonight was the longest coming best time. I've thought about what I would do if I had the chance to take you on a date so much over the past couple of years, thought about how I'd feel, what I'd say, what you'd say, how I could make it perfect. And the reality was so much better than anything I'd ever pictured.

You looked so freaking gorgeous. You came walking down the porch steps in that dress with your hair around your shoulders, and I immediately felt like an impostor to be taking you out. And as much as I've admired you over the years, I was still blown away by how much more incredible you are than I even knew. I enjoyed learning more about your life and appreciated how interested you were in hearing about mine.

Maybe I shouldn't have asked you to dance, maybe that was too much for a first date, but between the sunset and the music and you looking so beautiful, I just couldn't help myself. And now I don't regret it because that's an experience I won't stop thinking about for a long time. Maybe ever. I hope not ever.

I guess I should end there or I really will scare you away. And that's the one thing I never want to do.

Mateo

I lean my head back against the headrest and hold the paper to my chest. I'm pretty sure if you held up an x-ray, you'd see my heart growing three sizes like in the classic Grinch cartoon. I immediately reread the letter with a huge, goofy grin on my face that I don't even care to tone down.

"I *really* like Mateo," I whisper to myself at the end. I don't just like the fact that he likes me, although I do appreciate the way he's so open about his feelings, so unafraid to express what he thinks about me. But even more than that, I really like his godly character, his humor, his thoughtfulness, his personality, the way he interacts with and treats other people.

"I really REALLY like him!" I scream in the car, thankful that no one is around to witness this.

I'm about to text him thank you for the note when I decide that's not good enough. Not after he poured his heart out in his letter. I rip a piece of paper out of the notes section of my planner and write Mateo's name at the top.

Mateo – thank you so much for your note. I can't think of a sweeter gesture that anyone has ever done for me. And that's after everything you did on our first date was the sweetest ever.

The song that you're referring to is Delicate. And it's cool that you said all that.

Don't let anyone tell you that the term Swiftie is an insult.

And I'm not scared away. Not even a little.

Can't wait to watch you play tomorrow.

Lana

I fold the paper in half but realize I have no clue where Mateo lives. I assume in an apartment or house with some soccer teammates, but I don't know where. I'm going to need to remedy that asap. For now, I drive toward the soccer complex, hoping they're still at practice.

Luckily, I see Mateo's truck in the parking lot. I leave my car in park, and hurry to tuck my note under Mateo's windshield wiper just like he did mine, then quickly drive away so I don't get caught.

I'm flushed with a rush of happy adrenaline. I smile thinking about him finding the note after practice. I can't decide if I hope no one else is around when he discovers it or if a few teammates are there to razz him over it. I take it back—I definitely hope Andrés or someone else is there to give him grief.

Knowing there's no way I'll be able to concentrate on my personal statement now, I decide to head back to AOPi and just relax with the girls. Watching mind-numbing reality TV will be an easy way to half pay attention and half think about Mateo. Well, let's be honest, probably 90/10 attention in Mateo's favor.

I park but don't head inside until I've reread Mateo's letter twice more. After quietly stashing my backpack in our dark room, I follow the sound of voices giggling and yelling judgments at TV characters down to the movie room. Coming up behind Teegan on the couch, I cover her eyes with my hands. She grabs my wrists and looks up at me in surprise. "I thought you were ditching us to work on your application?"

I shrug my shoulder with a smirk, and she immediately gets up to "go pop more popcorn." Pausing in the empty stairwell, I quietly tell her about finding Mateo's note on my car. I can tell she's about to squeal but clap my hand over her mouth just in time.

"What?!" she whisper yells. "What did he say? Are you going to let me read it?"

I laugh quietly and whisper yell back at her. "*No,* I'm not going to let you read it. But you can rest assured that it was very sweet. And thoughtful. And one of the most romantic gestures I can possibly imagine." I'm goofy grinning again with one hand over my heart.

"Now that's the kind of swooning I was demanding," Teegan says in a normal voice before I shush her. "I officially forgive you for neglecting to tell us about your athletic prowess. But I may not forgive you now for refusing to let me read your love letter. I'll contemplate what your penance will be."

"Beef! It's not a love letter. It was just . . . a nice letter," I tell her, poking her in the side. "And sorry, but you're not guilting me into reading it. Now let's go make some popcorn before the girls wonder what's taking so long."

"Eh, they're in a reality TV trance—they're oblivious to reality right now," Teegan says as she does a happy dance up the stairs.

CHAPTER FOURTEEN

The Townsend soccer match isn't until 4:00 p.m., which means I have all day Saturday to build up equal parts nervous and excited energy. The anticipation of seeing Mateo, plus finally watching soccer again after so long, has me proverbially bouncing off the walls. I don't know if I'll have any sort of interaction with Mateo, but I'm entirely too eager to watch him play. It's killing me to wait all day.

There are several other girls from the sorority going to the match—because we don't have a football team, soccer is *the* sporting event to attend at Townsend. While a lot of DII teams struggle to fill their stands with spectators, Townsend never lacks for fans.

I tell Teegan I want to go on our own and sit separately. It's too much pressure to think about watching Mateo and reliving a soccer match for the first time in forever, while also sitting amidst all my sorority sisters.

We arrive at the soccer field and show our student IDs to get in. There's a whole section of the stands taken up by students, and Teegan and I find a place on the bleachers a few rows up from the front but across the aisle from the main student section.

The teams are clearing the field after warm-ups to stand on the sidelines for the national anthem. The announcer welcomes the opposing team, which is met with loud boos from the Townsend stands, then announces the Townsend Bobcats starting lineup one by one.

"And last but certainly not least, our Bobcats team captain and midfielder, Mateo Alvarez!" The crowd goes wild (particularly all the female voices) as Mateo runs through the tunnel of Townsend players, high-fiving them as he goes. He turns toward the stands, and I realize he's scanning the crowd looking for me.

I know the exact instant his eyes find mine. A huge grin breaks out on his face, popping out that dimple that makes my heart skip a beat every time I see it now. I smile back and give him a small wave with just my fingers, trying not to draw attention to myself.

Teegan elbows me hard in the ribs. "Oh my gosh, Lana, how are you not in a constant state of swooning? That very fine-looking man is positively smitten with you." I'm blushing hard but can't stop smiling. The teams take their positions on the field, and I feel adrenaline coursing through my veins as we wait for the whistle to begin play.

Mateo warned me that the opposing team was some of their toughest competition in the league last year. It's evident as the opponents take the ball on their first offensive run. Mateo falls back to help the defenders, and Chris eventually steals the ball and kicks it upfield to one of our other midfielders.

It's nearing halftime with the score still 0–0. We've had some great shots on goal that have been saved by their keeper, including one beautiful cross from Mateo that looked like it was going to go in but was just tipped out. I've been sitting on my hands the whole time to contain myself from screaming like a crazy person.

During halftime, I try to explain some of the key rules and strategies of soccer to Teegan. "I don't get why they don't just all run to fight for the ball. And why would they kick it back toward their own goal sometimes?" she asks.

"They try to spread out across the field to keep their options open since it can change from offense to defense and back so quickly. Each position has a loose area of the field where they're playing, but they aren't required to stay there," I explain to Teegan's furrowed brow. "Sometimes when we get control of the ball, our players need a second to reset positions and get on the same page for their next attack. That's why they kick it backwards, sometimes even to our own goalie."

Play resumes with Townsend getting the offensive start of the half. We put together a good attack on the goal again but just can't seem to score. The back and forth continues, and I can only imagine how tired Mateo is from covering so much of the field.

There are only two minutes left of regulation before stoppage time kicks in, and our guys are passing well on a great offensive run. I'm on the edge of my seat as Mateo fends off a defender to keep control of the ball heading toward the center of the field. He crosses to Andrés, who's in perfect scoring position, but an opponent is all up in his space. Andrés manages to get a high pass back over to the corner of the box where Mateo is waiting.

I hold my breath with my hands over my mouth as I watch the ball sail toward Mateo, as if in slow motion. He and the guy guarding him both jump for the ball, but Mateo gets the better position and heads the ball toward the goal. The keeper just misses the timing of his dive, and the ball sails over his body into the back of the net.

The Townsend stands erupt as everyone jumps to their feet cheering. Teegan and I bounce up and down as we scream along with the crowd. Mateo and the team come running and celebrating across the field.

After receiving several slaps on the back from teammates, Mateo turns to the stands and finds my eyes. With a one-sided smile, he holds up his hands and shoots an air arrow toward me with a wink before running back out for the kickoff. Teegan is clutching my arm and ruining her vocal cords squealing.

The roar of the crowd has died down, and female voices can be clearly heard from the student section speculating about Mateo's celebration.

"How do you know he's never done that goal celebration before?"

"Trust me, I watch Mateo Alvarez closely every game."

"Well, he obviously aimed it at the crowd. Who was he shooting the arrow to?"

The voices are clamoring over each other, and I can feel Teegan's energy winding up next to me. There's no time to contain her before the proud excitement she's been bottling up the past few weeks boils over and she's yelling, "Right here! Mateo was shooting the arrow to this girl right here!" She's wildly flailing her arm overhead and pointing at me.

I can feel the Christmas red color heating my face again as the crowd of girls turns to look at me, daggers in their eyes. I grab Teegan's arm and hip check her. "Quit it, Teegs!" I command through gritted teeth. I'm certainly not ashamed to be associated with Mateo, but I wasn't mentally prepared for that onslaught of attention.

The flush of embarrassment doesn't leave my cheeks for the remainder of the match, but I still jump and cheer loudly when the final whistle sounds and we've won 1–0. The team celebrates in the middle of the field, and Teegan leans over to say, "Well, I never knew a sports event that ends with a score of one to zero could be so exciting."

I give her an evil eye, but it loses its effect since I'm smiling. The vocal girls across from us shoot parting glares at me as they leave the stands, and I elbow Teegan. "Thanks a lot for that very public outing."

Teegan flips her hair with one hand. "Whatever. You just needed a little nudge out of the nest. I'm nothing if not a good mama eagle."

I laugh and step into the aisle. Mateo catches my eye and winks again, and I grin back at him. When I glance up into the stands, I notice Aaron standing there with some other OGs, looking right at me. I quickly look away and whisper to Teegan, "I think I just saw Aaron."

Walking toward the parking lot, she says, "Lana, Mateo just shot Cupid's arrow at you in front of the entire Townsend student body. Who the heck cares if you saw Aaron?"

"Okay, number one, the entire student body is not here. Number two, it was *not* Cupid's arrow. It was more like inside information from our date. It used to be *my* goal celebration when I played soccer," I correct her.

"Oh-kay, but that just makes it even more sweet than if it was Cupid's arrow, so, point still stands," Teegan says, giving me an admonishing look. My lack of poker face must be projecting the worry I still feel, because Teegan pulls my elbow to stop me. "Lana, all joking aside, I'm serious. It's not your job to worry about what Aaron is thinking at this point. You like Mateo, right?"

Sighing, I confirm. "Yes, I *really* like Mateo."

"You want to continue dating Mateo, right?"

"Yes, Teegs, I definitely want to continue dating Mateo." Just thinking about not going on another date with Mateo makes my stomach churn.

"Then embrace it, LaLa. Let go of worrying about what Aaron thinks, because he has no say over what you do. You don't owe him anything. Be with Mateo without Aaron in your brain," she concludes confidently, tapping my temple.

"You're right, you're right. Thanks Beef," I tell Teegan with a squeeze to the arm.

"Now, I'm starving after all that yelling and jumping. AOPi dinner is over already, so let's go get tacos," Teegan proclaims, unlocking her car.

Embrace it, I tell myself as I click my seatbelt. *Sorry, Aaron, but you're going to need to vacate my mind space now, thank you very much.*

My resolve holds for the next hour as Teegan and I eat tacos and far too many chips, right up until I receive a text message from Aaron.

AARON

> Hey Lana. Did I see you at the soccer game?

I rest my forehead on the table with a groan. "What's wrong?" Teegan asks, and I hold up my phone screen to her. I feel her place a hand on my shoulder, and I shift my face to the side to look at her. "You don't owe him anything, Lana," she says simply.

I sit up straight and nod at Teegan. She dips a chip in salsa, raising an eyebrow at me. I quickly type a response and show it to Teegan for approval, which she gives by way of a small head nod before eating another chip. I hit send.

ME

> Yeah, I was there. It was an incredible match. Go Bobcats!

I can see instantly that Aaron has read it. But no three dots, no response comes through.

Teegan starts babbling away about her practicum experience in a classroom this semester and how adorable all the students are. I'm happy to turn my attention to someone other than Aaron, especially to someone as incredibly supportive as my best friend.

I don't owe you anything. I repeat in my mind as I put my phone away and lean in to listen to Teegan's story. Her passion for helping students have fun learning in different ways is inspiring, even if I don't understand the specific strategies she talks about. Teegan just wants everyone to enjoy life as much as she does.

Later that night when we return to AOPi, I tell Teegan I'm going to grab some water from the kitchen. I pause in the dining room and pull my phone out to text Mateo.

ME

Just got back home. Teegan needed victory tacos after all her hard work cheering. You were incredible!

MATEO

Thanks. Knowing you were in the stands watching made it even better. How did it feel being at a soccer match again?

There he goes, being perfectly considerate again, thinking of my experience and not spotlighting his, even though he just played a heck of a game. I smile to myself as I type a response.

ME

Cloud nine

MATEO

<clapping emoji>

I pause for a moment, looking at the screen. *Embrace it,* I say to myself.

ME

It was great watching soccer again, but watching you play specifically boosted it to cloud nine

MATEO

<heart emoji>

CHAPTER FIFTEEN

Monday morning, I leave the AOPi house with a smile. Mateo and I texted several times yesterday, and I'm feeling more and more confident about how I'm feeling about him. Which is that I like him. A whole lot.

I breathe in the morning air and decide to walk to campus without my ear buds in, a decision I immediately regret when I hear Bailey's voice calling out to me.

She falls into step beside me. "So, Lana," she begins, sounding uncharacteristically unsure. "I heard some interesting rumors about you over the weekend."

Oh boy. Are we really going to middle school gossip this? Undoubtedly, Bailey was one of those popular girls who served as the central power lines for the rumor mill.

Finding no way around it, I simply ask, "What do you mean, Bailey?"

"Well, a couple of the girls from TriAlpha who were at the soccer game claimed they saw you there, and that there seemed to be some sort of flirtation between you and Mateo Alvarez," she says. Then she audibly scoffs, and I work overtime to keep my facial expressions in line. "I told them I didn't know of any such connection, but they insisted."

"I'm not sure why you would care about my romantic life, Bailey," I declare without answering her unspoken question.

That seems to throw Bailey off, and she's scrambling to find a dignified way to get her questions answered. I have to admit it's a little satisfying seeing her fumbling so much when she's usually so socially confident. I struggle not to smile to myself.

"It's always useful to know what dating dynamics are going on with Arrow leaders," Bailey says. "And I'm just being curious as a friend."

I pretend to look at something to my side so I can roll my eyes at her use of the word "friend." My first instinct is to say something snarky back to her, considering how *un*friendly Bailey usually is to me, but then I hear Teegan's voice in my head. *Embrace it.*

"Yes, Bailey, there was flirtation between Mateo and me at the soccer game, because we've gone on a couple of dates."

Bailey's mouth drops open for a moment before she collects herself, but her eyes remain wide. She's silent until we reach the point where our paths diverge toward different buildings.

"Um, wow, how nice for you, Lana," she finally spits out, looking like it physically pained her to do so. "I'm surprised, but, you know, that's very exciting for you. See ya."

She speed walks away, and I can't help but shake my head at her ability to be so condescending in her response to me dating Mateo. As I head into my building for class, I quickly text the Beefs.

ME

Well, Bailey just cornered me into confirming to her that Mateo and I have been dating

AMAYA

Prepare for the entire town of Brooklyn to know about it within a few hours

TEEGAN

I'm here for this gossip train

AMAYA

TEEG

TEEGAN

I'm only jealous that I didn't get to be the engine

ME

<face palm emoji>

Amaya is right. I do need to prepare myself, because the lid has been officially blown off this relationship. Although I'm still a little anxious about how Aaron is going to react, I'm mostly relieved and excited to not feel like I'm keeping my dates with Mateo under wraps anymore.

———

The next afternoon, I'm sitting in the Harry Potter room, laptop open, Mindful Mellow playlist streaming through my ear buds. I've typed and deleted so many beginnings to my personal essay, never making it more than a sentence or two in before deciding I hate the direction I'm going.

I receive a text from Mateo, a welcome distraction from my writer's block.

MATEO

Hey, Coach ended practice early. Where are you right now?

I give a half smile to my phone and take a selfie with the room in the background. I send the photo to him, curious if he'll know the location.

Three dots.

MATEO

Well, this brings up a crucial relationship question. What Hogwarts house would you be in?

ME

Gryffindor, obviously. Where all the cool kids fighting injustice want to be

MATEO

I don't know, I was always fond of Cedric Diggory myself. I think Hufflepuff might be the sleeper of Hogwarts houses

Considering Mateo's patience, loyalty, hard work, and genuine care for others, he'd make a perfect Hufflepuff.

MATEO

I'll be right there

Ten minutes later, Mateo walks through the door, searching the room for me. I catch his eye and wave him over. He sits across the table and asks what I'm working on.

In a low, library-level voice, I tell him, "I'm *supposed* to be working on my personal statement for my law school application. But I don't know where to start. I'm never going to get my application submitted by the end of the week like I was hoping."

"What's the essay about?" Mateo asks, leaning forward. He's oblivious to the number of people casually sneaking glances at us, so I decide to choose oblivion also.

"Why I want to go to law school, pretty much," I answer. "Being an immigration lawyer is the one thing I've wanted for so long that I'm having a hard time condensing my thoughts. It just feels like part of my DNA. How do I explain that?"

Mateo sits back for a moment, thinking. He runs his hand through his hair and rests it on the back of his neck, a thoughtful motion I wouldn't have classified as incredibly attractive until now. He leans closer again and says, "You've seen the shortcomings and challenges of the immigration system your whole life. You've met the real people affected by it. But there are a lot of different ways to help immigrants and refugees, Lana. Immigration attorneys are just one piece of the puzzle. What was the moment you felt in your gut that you had to be *this* part of the solution?"

I sit back in my chair. "I've never thought of it that way before." I think for a minute before recognizing that I know the exact moment.

"I was thirteen. My mom was invited to speak to a class at UC Davis about her experiences with asylum seekers in El Paso and transition to working with refugees in Kansas City. She decided to take me with her for some one-on-one time."

Mateo leans his chin on one hand, listening intently.

"Mom told the story of two families of asylum seekers we knew in El Paso. One family had a daughter, Maria, who was in my class at school. I never knew the specifics of her family's story, I just knew she didn't play at recess at first, that she'd drop to the ground shaking at the sound of a door slamming. That fear seemed to be her baseline emotion.

"My mom was representing the other family in court, pleading their case to receive asylum, but Maria's family didn't have a lawyer. Mom's clients won their case and were granted asylum, but Maria's family apparently wasn't well-organized going into their hearing. The judge denied their request, and they were deported."

I realize I'm crying at the memory when I feel a tear drip off my chin onto my arm. "At the time, I didn't know that Maria's family was deported. All I knew was that my friend was there one day and gone the next. It wasn't until I heard Mom share the story that I understood why Maria had left, that it was because her family didn't have a lawyer helping them present their case."

I swallow hard. "I knew I had to make sure that families who were in danger in their home countries weren't sent back. That's when I knew I had to be *this* part of the solution."

Mateo reaches over and brushes a tear off my cheek with his thumb. "That's what you write about, Lana."

I nod. My mind is suddenly charged with thoughts organizing themselves. My fingers are itching to start typing everything out while the inspiration is flowing.

Sensing my thoughts, Mateo smiles at me and says, "Well, I'll let you get to it. I know you have your ELL tutoring and Bible study tonight, so you better get typing while you have time. Glad I could see you for a few minutes today."

He stands up, but I reach out and grab his hand to stop him from walking away. "I'm glad I got to see you today too, Mateo. And not just because you helped me figure out the answer to my essay," I say with a soft laugh. "I'm just glad to see you."

Mateo slowly grins at me, then promises to text me later with a wink.

Turning to my computer, my essay essentially writes itself as my fingers fly across the keyboard. An hour later, I'm proud of what I've written as I read back through it. I email it to my mom and shoot her a text asking her to look it over.

I pack up my backpack and leave the library feeling a hundred pounds lighter than when I arrived. As I walk back to AOPi, I text Mateo to ask for his email address. I forward the email with my essay to him.

———

The next morning, I wake up to my phone vibrating with a call from my mom. Panicking that something might be wrong, I sneak out of the room and answer in a whisper. "Mom? Is everything okay? What's wrong?"

"Hi, Sleeping Beauty. I was just driving to the office early today and wanted to call you," she answers.

My heart rate is slowly deescalating back to a normal rhythm. "Sheesh you scared me, Mom. I was afraid something had happened."

"I'm sorry honey, I wasn't thinking about what time it was or that it might startle you," she says apologetically. "I just wanted to let you know that I read through your essay this morning, and it was so moving. The admissions team is going to love it, but I loved it even more. I didn't realize how impactful that trip was for you."

"Yeah, I didn't either," I answer as I head downstairs to the living room. "I mean, of course I knew it was impactful, but I hadn't really pieced together that it was *the* defining moment in making me want to become an immigration lawyer until yesterday."

"Really? What made you think of it for the essay then?" my mom asks, right before I hear her honk the horn and mutter something about an incompetent driver. Morning traffic in Kansas City can be a wild ride.

"Actually, Mateo is the one who helped me realize it," I say with a small smile. "I was struggling to know what to write, and he asked me when I knew that being an immigration lawyer was the part of the solution that I had to be."

"Well, another gold star from me then," Mom says with a chipper tone to her voice. "Do you know if he'll be in town the weekend we come to visit in a few weeks?"

"I'll have to find out, Mom. They have an away match that Saturday, but if you're coming in Friday night we might be able to have dinner. When it gets a little closer, I'll ask him about it," I say. "We've gone on a couple of dates, but I'm not sure it's quite to the 'make plans with my parents weeks in advance' stage yet."

I hear the grin in my mom's voice when she responds, "Oh honey, from what you've told me, it sounds like Mateo is far beyond that stage already."

"Mom!" I scold. "That is not helpful! I'm trying not to let my thoughts run wild, okay?!"

"*Mmm-hmm*, whatever you tell yourself," Mom replies. "I just pulled into the parking lot, so I need to head inside. I emailed you back a couple of suggestions to reword in your essay, but otherwise I think it's ready for you to submit."

"Thanks Mom, I appreciate the input," I say. "Have a great day with your clients. Tell everyone hello when you get home later."

"Will do. Love you, sweetie."

"Love you too."

I'm wide awake now, so I grab breakfast before heading upstairs to get dressed. Amaya and Teegan are both up, so I plop down at the desk and power up my laptop to look at my mom's suggestions.

My inbox shows my mom's reply, but also a response from the email I forwarded to Mateo. I click on that first, unable to resist his pull even via email. It's a short response that makes me smile big. *This is so good, Lana. Do you have any weaknesses, or do you just do everything well?*

By the time I've made the few tweaks from my mom, Teegan is back in the room after eating breakfast, so she and Amaya crowd around my laptop to read together. When they get to the end, Teegan wraps her arms around my neck. "Beef, you have such a beautiful love for people. You're going to make the best lawyer."

Amaya stands up and joins our group hug, adding her affirmation. "I agree, and if UC Davis doesn't let you in, then their idiotic admissions department should all be fired."

I laugh, but inside I'm a puddle of gratitude for having found such incredible friends. Now that my essay is complete, my application is ready to submit. It seems fitting to have my two best friends with me when I press send.

I log in to the UC Davis application website and upload my personal statement and other documents. Teegan and Amaya are standing on either side of my chair, and I give a quick glance up to each of them before hitting the submit button.

Smiling at the confirmation screen, I breathe a huge sigh of relief. It may be out of my hands now, but I feel one step closer to my future.

Chapter Sixteen

—————

The rest of the week flies by now that I'm no longer weighed down by the burden of finishing my early admission application. I'll hear back with enough time to apply to other law schools if I don't get accepted, so for now I can fully focus on the fall semester of classes.

Well, classes plus Mateo. And I guess AOPi and Arrow will get some of my attention too.

Unfortunately, aside from a smile across the room at the Arrow meeting, I don't see Mateo throughout the week. They have an away match on Saturday, which they win 2–1. Mateo texts me a rundown of the game play, and I'm itching to watch him play again. Next Saturday's match is at home, and I've already recruited Amaya to attend with me.

The first week of October sends a charge of energy through the AOPi house—we are nothing if not a group of basic college girls obsessed with the fall season. The dining hall gets decorated with pumpkin centerpieces, and everyone pulls out the fall fashion from their wardrobes. With homecoming now just a few weeks away, it also means assigned work hours on the float and yard display, as well as more practices for the showcase performers.

I love the fall frenzy even more so when Mateo asks if we could go to the fall festival together on Friday night. Every first Friday of October, the city of Brooklyn sets up a festival in Center Square with all of the fall essentials—pumpkins, hay bales, music, apple everything, and local businesses with booths to sell their autumn merchandise. It's one of my favorite nights of the entire year, and I'm extra excited to experience it with Mateo this time.

Friday after dinner, I submit myself to Teegan's demand to pick my outfit and do my hair and makeup. The temperature dropped today, so I insist on my outfit including pants instead of a dress, which she initially whines about. By the end of her beauty session, Teegan seems satisfied with my leggings, oversized ribbed tunic, loosely curled hair, and darker-than-usual eye makeup.

As I walk out the front door to greet Mateo, I don't even mind the crowd of girls outside, not-so-subtly staring and whispering. He's smiling as he walks toward me. "Lana, you look incredible, as usual."

I want to return the compliment, considering that Mateo looks nothing less than completely hot in dark jeans and a brick-red Henley shirt, sleeves pulled up to mid-arm. The red of his shirt starkly contrasts his tan complexion and black hair, which looks perfectly tousled tonight. The words stick in my throat, though, because I haven't quite figured out how to feel comfortable complimenting his physical appearance. I mumble something about being glad to see him again.

He opens the passenger door for me, and there's no mistaking the increased volume of girls' voices talking about us. Mateo doesn't seem to mind at all. He simply flashes a dimpled grin at me as he gets in the driver's side and says, "Ready to go revel in your favorite season?"

I laugh. "You have no idea what you're getting yourself into tonight. I'm the manifestation of every stereotype about girls and fall."

"Why do you think I asked you to go with me—I need to experience it through your beautiful eyes," Mateo responds with a chuckle. "I'm happily following wherever you lead tonight."

Center Square is already packed with young families in addition to the college crowd, so we have to park a little far away and walk back toward the action. My heart bursts with delight as we reach the outskirts of the festival and smell the delicious mingling of campfire, pumpkin spice, apple cider, and roasted marshmallows.

I lead Mateo through the heart of the festivities to all my favorite stops. He's all smiles as we peruse local booths, play festival games, enjoy apple cider donuts and hot coffee, and admire the decorative displays. He even suggests pausing to take pictures at some of the photo ops set up around the square. I've always loved this event, but watching Mateo match my enthusiasm in a totally sincere way is making this the greatest fall festival ever.

We're walking to the fire pit to roast marshmallows when Mateo's phone starts ringing. He glances at the screen and says, "Hey, it's my sister. Do you mind if I step away and take this real quick?"

"Of course! I'll just go look at the booths we didn't see on the far side—meet me over there?"

Mateo squeezes my elbow and says thanks right before stepping away and swiping his phone to answer. "Hey, *hermana hermosa*, what's up?" I hear him say before he's out of ear shot, and it makes me smile. I'd love to meet these family members he's clearly so fond of.

I make my way over to the booth of a woman selling handmade jewelry. I'm browsing to see if any pieces inspire as a gift for my mom or Olivia when I feel a hand grab my elbow from behind. Startled, I whirl around to see Aaron standing behind me.

"Oh my gosh, Aaron, you scared me!" I gasp, heart racing.

"I'm sorry. I didn't mean to scare you. Lana, I really need to talk to you. Will you come over here with me for a minute? Please?" he asks, a pleading look in his eye.

My body tenses up, dreading however this conversation is going to go. I nod, though, and follow him through the edge of the festival booths to the entrance of an alley. "What's up?" I ask, trying to sound calmer than I feel.

Aaron has a frenzied energy about him, swinging his arms and shifting his weight back and forth before he finally speaks. "Lana, I just need to know what's going on with you and Alvarez. What are you doing with him?"

I'm a little shocked by Aaron being so forthright and don't respond immediately, not really knowing what to say.

Aaron paces for a few seconds before turning back to face me again. "I just don't understand, Lana. I thought it was obvious that you and I were, you know . . . that we liked each other, and we'd eventually start dating. What are you doing going out with Alvarez?"

I can feel myself shaking as adrenaline pulses through my body. It's not lost on me that six weeks ago, I would have given anything to hear these words from Aaron. But a lot has changed since then. I try to formulate a firm but kind response. "Aaron, yeah, I guess we did like each other, and maybe it did seem obvious. But you never actually said anything. You never did anything. I couldn't know for sure that you really did like me, and that it wasn't all in my head."

Aaron groans and wipes his hand down his face. "Look, I'm sorry I didn't come out and say it, Lana. I've known for a long time that you were who I wanted to end up with after college. I thought I was being super transparent about how I felt about you." He pauses, like what he's said should be the "gotcha" of a winning closing argument.

His eyes look almost wild with panic. I have compassion for how he's feeling, but I'm not persuaded away from my new affection for Mateo. I look down and quietly speak. "I'm sorry, Aaron. I don't really know what to say."

Aaron grabs my hand in both of his. "Lana, if you went out with Mateo to get my attention, to get me to say something and ask you out, it worked, okay? I'm here, I'm being direct, I'm telling you how I feel and that I want to be with you. You made your point."

I narrow my eyes and yank my hand away, the compassion I was feeling for him completely snuffed out. "You did *not* just accuse me of using Mateo to manipulate you into asking me out. How dare you think that I would do that."

He clearly realizes he's said the wrong thing and desperately tries to backtrack. "No, that's not what I meant, I wouldn't think that of you, Lana. I'm sorry, it's just . . . the thought of you dating someone else, that I might have missed my chance when I've been waiting for you for so long just has my head all mixed up."

Now my blood is really hot. Boiling. "*You*, waiting for *me*, for so long? Aaron, I'm the one who's been waiting around on you. I liked you ever since the end of freshman year! You've had two years of chances. *Two years*!" I'm practically yelling now and consciously take a breath to force myself to quiet down, but the heat remains in my voice.

"You strung me along for years, Aaron. I was constantly deciphering what your intentions were, or if you even had any. You flirted and led me on but never did anything. *You* never asked me out. *You* never told me how you felt. *You* had plenty of opportunities but never took any of them. So I'm not apologizing for going out with a guy who was upfront about how he felt about me and is actively pursuing me. A guy I happen to like. A lot."

Aaron's eyes look pained. He strides back and forth with his hands on his hips, but I don't say anything else.

"Okay, it's my fault, I know it's my own fault. I was an idiot for not saying something to you sooner," Aaron says, still pacing like a caged tiger. He lets out a deep breath that turns into more of a growl before pushing the palms of his hands into his eyes. He turns to face me. "Lana, listen. I just need you to know that I'm here, if things don't work out with Alvarez, I'll be right—"

I cut him off before he can finish. "Nope, you're not going to do that, Aaron. I really like Mateo. And I'm going to put one hundred percent of myself into our relationship to make it work. I'm not going to sabotage what I have with Mateo by having a backup option with you in my mind."

"Lana, please—"

"No, Aaron. You and I are just friends. If you want to remain friends, then you can't say things like that anymore. You can't try to make me doubt things with Mateo. You have to accept just being friends, or we need to stay away from each other altogether," I finish, still trembling and breathing hard.

Aaron doesn't say anything, just clenches his jaw and gives a curt nod. He turns to leave the alley, but pauses to say over his shoulder, "Fine, I get it. I'll see you around, Lana."

I'm fighting back tears from sheer emotional exhaustion. I lean against the wall and take a few deep breaths, trying to calm my nervous system. Mateo must be finished talking with his sister by now and looking around for me. My hands are shaking too much to try to take out my phone to see if he's texted me, so I take one more breath before turning right out of the alley back toward the festival.

I've only made it a few feet when I see Mateo standing near the jewelry booth, hands casually in his pockets. *Oh no, I hope he didn't see me with Aaron.* He gives me a soft smile, a new smile I haven't seen before. There's a quiet confidence to it, an easy sweetness that washes warmth over me like a spring sunbeam.

Mateo walks the few feet over and says, "I'm so sorry I had to take a phone call in the middle of our date. Turns out nothing was wrong, Isabel just wanted to chat. But I didn't want to miss it if she needed me."

"Mateo, it's fine, really. I'm glad you want to be there for your sister," I tell him as we start slowly walking back toward the festival center. "Did you still want to go roast marshmallows?" My heart rate is slowly settling back down to normal.

"Of course, it wouldn't be the true fall festival experience if we didn't," he responds with a grin, making me smile. We walk a few paces and then Mateo pauses, turning slightly toward me. "Lana, would it be okay with you if I held your hand?" His deep brown eyes look into mine with such hopefulness that my heart nearly stops.

I smile up at him. "It would be more than okay." He beams back and reaches his right hand down to lace his fingers through mine. I didn't realize how cold my hands were after that intense conversation until my left hand is swallowed up by Mateo's warmth. We walk toward the fire pit, hand in hand, and I abandon all hope of a normalized heart rate.

One of the churches in Brooklyn has a s'mores station set up, so we roast marshmallows while enjoying the warmth of the fire. He tells me a few snippets about Isabel, and it only makes me want to meet her all the more. We head out when things start to wind down. Mateo immediately takes my hand again as we walk back to the truck, and I'm silently swooning the whole way. Teegan will be so pleased.

We drive back to AOPi, discussing our favorite parts of the festival. When Mateo pulls up outside the house, he leaves the car running and shifts toward me rather than getting out. His face looks serious, and I panic again that maybe he saw Aaron leave the alley and got the wrong impression.

"Lana, I wanted to ask you something," he starts. My chest locks up with fear until he reaches down to take my hand, lightly tracing his thumb across the back. "I don't think it's a surprise that I haven't been dating anyone other than you, and as far as I know, you haven't been dating anyone else either," he says, and I give a soft chuckle while shaking my head. He's looking down at our hands when he continues. "Maybe this is silly, but I wanted to officially ask you to date exclusively, to ask if you'd consider being my girlfriend."

I place my other hand on top of his hand sandwiching mine and curl my fingers around his. "I won't just consider it. I'll tell you yes right now," I answer with total confidence.

I want to bottle up the smile Mateo gives me in response and pull it out any time I feel sad or cold or lonely or really just for any reason at all. He squeezes my hands and says, "Well, okay then, Girlfriend. I had a great time at the festival with you tonight. You can officially call me a fall-lover now that I get to spend it with you."

I wish I could find an excuse to continue sitting in the truck with him, holding his hands forever, but I know he has a soccer match tomorrow and needs to get some rest. "Well, Boyfriend, this was my favorite fall festival too. Thanks for humoring me in my obsession. I should head inside now so you can go get some sleep."

Mateo gives my hands one final squeeze before turning off the truck and walking around to my side. Even though it's a short jaunt up to the AOPi house, he still takes my hand, as if unwilling to miss any opportunity to touch me. We're both reluctant to let go and part ways, but a group of girls coming up the steps behind us pops the magic bubble, forcing us to say goodnight.

The second the door closes, I'm ambushed by girls demanding details about Mateo and me, since our relationship is very much out in the open now. I give enough affirmative but vague answers to get them to leave me alone and then head up to our room. It's empty, presumably because Amaya and Teegan are somewhere working on something homecoming-related after returning from the festival. I'm grateful for the quiet, even though I know I'll have to give them a full rundown later.

But for the moment, I lay down on my bed in the silence and soak in the fact that I have a boyfriend. And it's Mateo Alvarez.

I cover my face with a throw pillow and happy scream.

Chapter Seventeen

It was super late by the time I finally went to bed after giving the Beefs a full play-by-play of my evening, including my cringe conversation with Aaron (I'd never seen Amaya so riled up, and trust me, I've seen her riled up plenty of times). Even after going to bed, it took a while to fall asleep since I was running back through every moment with Mateo on repeat. Particularly the feeling of his fingers interlocked with mine.

The clock reads 9:30 a.m. by the time I wake up Saturday morning, immediately smiling again thinking about Mateo's sweet expression when he asked me to be his girlfriend. I've always quietly been a romantic, but I'm still surprised by how giddy I feel.

I reach for my phone and feel it vibrate with a notification. Unlocking it, I see that Mateo sent me a text this morning.

MATEO

> Morning beautiful. Text me when you're up if I can swing by real quick

I sit upright in bed. He knows I'll be at the soccer match tonight, so I'm not sure what would be so urgent. I text him back to give me twenty minutes and rush to throw on leggings and a sweatshirt, then brush my teeth and hair. Slipping out the front door, I close it quietly behind me and sit down on a porch chair to wait for him to arrive. I'm regretting not grabbing a cup of coffee to make sure my brain is fully functional before seeing him.

Mateo's truck pulls up the street a few minutes later with the windows rolled down to let in the cool morning air. He waves at me as I walk down to the curb. He turns off the engine, and I meet him by the driver's door as he opens it. As he steps out of the truck, he hands me a cup of coffee from Raelynn's with a grin. "Thought you might need a morning dose of energy."

I accept the cup and take a sip. He has the coffee to half-and-half ratio perfect. "The Lord bless you," I say with fake piety, making him laugh. "So, what's up?"

His smile falters a little bit. "Ah, I had a favor to ask you. Or not really a favor, just a request, I guess." He runs his hand through his hair and rubs the back of his neck, a subconscious movement I'm catching on to as his equivalent of my fingers playing piano. "I mean, it's okay if you say no or don't want to do it, you might think it's a little silly, and that's totally fine, I won't be upset or anything."

Mateo always has such a humble confidence about him, it's a little bit adorable to see him act so nervous around me. Strike that—it's extremely freaking adorable. I can't help but smile before I put him out of his misery. "Mateo, last night I said yes to being your girlfriend, so there's a pretty high likelihood that I'll say yes to whatever you're trying to ask me."

That makes him grin. "You're right, you did say yes to being my girlfriend." His dimple is killing me right now. "Well, this request is related. On the soccer team, there's this sort of . . . tradition, I guess you could say. If players have a girlfriend, they give one of their old jerseys from a past season's kit to their girlfriend to wear to the soccer matches."

He leans into his truck and comes out holding a soccer jersey with Alvarez stitched above the number fourteen. He smiles a little sheepishly as he looks into my eyes. "I was kind of hoping that maybe you would wear my jersey from last year when you come to the match tonight? But I understand if you don't want to—"

I cut him off by placing my hand on his forearm and taking the jersey from him. "Mateo, I'd be honored to wear your jersey tonight and at any match I'm able to attend." I tuck the jersey under the arm holding my coffee cup so I can take his hand with my free one, making his face light up.

"But I need you to understand something before I wear this. At the last match, I was literally sitting on my hands to keep from wildly yelling throughout the whole game. But no holds barred tonight—I will probably be jumping and screaming my head off, so you have to decide if you want me associated with your name while doing so," I say with a sly smile.

Mateo throws his head back in a laugh. "I'll expect nothing less, Lana. Don't let me down," he teases with a wink. "I've got to go get some homework done before warm-ups later. But after the match tonight, a bunch of the guys from the team and some of their girlfriends are planning to grab some late-night food. Would you want to come with me?"

"I'd love to," I reply. "Where should I meet you after the match?"

Mateo instructs me where to wait with the other players' girl-friends outside the direct entrance to the locker room. He gets back into his truck, and I lean against the open window to tell him goodbye. Mateo reaches up to tuck a stray hair behind my ear with a soft smile, and I feel my cheeks heat up, which only makes him smile bigger. "I'll see you tonight, Lana."

I turn back to the AOPi house and notice an open-mouthed Bailey up the sidewalk, apparently heading out on a run. She startles when she sees me notice her, clamping her mouth shut. She shoves her ear buds in as she takes off jogging down the street without so much as a hello.

Determined to shake her snootiness off, I go inside and head up to our room, where Amaya is out of bed and Teegan is beginning to stir. When I walk in holding a Raelynn's cup, Amaya immediately scolds me. "Are you telling me you got up and went out for coffee without bringing me anything back?"

I give her a little shove and say, "No, I did not go to Raelynn's. This was delivered to me by Mateo, along with his old jersey from last year that he wants me to wear to the match tonight."

Teegan bolts upright in bed. "He what now? You're wearing his name to the soccer game tonight?" I nod and hold it up for her to see. "Ughhh, unfair. I can't come tonight because I have stupid showcase rehearsal! I want to be there to see the look on their huffy little faces when the girls watching the game realize Mateo Alvarez is officially claimed."

I say, "Teegs, don't be ridiculous," at the same time that Amaya says, "I'll take a video."

I roll my eyes at both of them.

Amaya made me promise to do extra hours of pomping on the homecoming float with her today in exchange for accompanying me to the soccer match, so we have plenty of time to catch up just the two of us as we stick squares of tissue paper through chicken wire. She fills me in how her mom is doing, and what companies have caught her eye to apply with after graduation. Amaya's innate drive to succeed has elevated AOPi to the next level, and I have zero doubts that she'll do the same in whatever company has the good sense to snatch her up.

Amaya asks a lot of questions about my family, especially Dean. She knows what it's like to be mixed up with the wrong crowd, so she takes to heart the struggles we're having getting through to him. Seeing where she is now gives me hope for Dean.

My back and my hands are starting to cramp after spending so much time pomping, but I'm grateful for the chance to hang out and talk with Amaya. She's so busy running the world, it can be hard for us to have quality time together.

After dinner, I'm getting dressed in jeans and Mateo's jersey over a long-sleeve shirt when Teegan comes up behind me in the mirror. "Lana, you are drowning in that jersey," she says with disapproval.

"Well, Beef, not sure if you've noticed this, but Mateo is a good six inches taller than me and has significantly larger upper body muscles," I counter sarcastically.

"I have, in fact, noticed these things," Teegan says with a teasing smile, and I elbow her in the ribs. She pulls the jersey tighter around my waist and secures a knot at the base of my back. "Don't worry, you can still see the name and number clearly."

I know it's killing Teegan not to come tonight, so I let her re-curl the waves into my hair and style it in a half-up bun. She adds a little shimmery eyeshadow to my eyes and a small cat eye before humming her approval. "Please take some pictures. Promise me."

Laughing, I pull her into a tight hug. "I promise. Now go do awesome at showcase rehearsal so AOPi can embarrass TriAlpha with how good we are this year."

"Now that's a mission I can get behind."

———

Amaya and I arrive early, but so have a large crowd of students already, probably since the team we're playing tonight beat us last year. We take our seats in the same place that Teegan and I sat last time. The teams are still out on the field doing warm-up drills, so Amaya and I sit and chat while we wait. "I promised Teegan to send her a couple of photos, so let's get a selfie or two before the match starts," I tell Amaya, who pulls out her phone in response.

"Hold on, let me pull your hair to the front of your shoulders so Teegan can admire her handiwork," Amaya says. I smile into the phone as Amaya holds it above our heads, angling down at us.

"Okay, sassy faces," she says as she holds the phone down, angled up at us. Amaya makes a kissy face and I give an open-mouthed smile with my hands framing my chin while looking up away from the screen. "Perfection," Amaya comments as she zooms in on the photo. "Teegan will love this one."

I tilt her phone toward me after she sends the picture to Teegan to examine the photos. In our "sassy" pose, Amaya positioned the camera to get us in the bottom corner with a clear view of a group of girls behind us in the background. A group of girls scowling at the back of my head, or more accurately, my shirt.

"Teegan is having too much of an influence on you," I tell Amaya, giving her major side eye.

"Hey, I'm just following through on my promises," Amaya quips. "Loyalty is a valuable quality in a best friend."

I can't help but laugh as I look back out at the field. The teams are headed to the sidelines, and Mateo finds me quickly in the crowd with a wide grin. I give him a bigger wave this time and settle into the undercurrent of excitement rolling through the crowd. Because of AOPi chapter meetings, I can never attend the Wednesday soccer matches, so I have extra energy built up for this one. Even though Wednesday's match ended in a tie, we're still technically undefeated.

Play begins, and I can tell it's going to be a physical game. Opponents are practically body-checking our guys, but we're not backing down. A few questionable no-calls hint that the refs are going to let a lot of things go, which only ups the physicality of the match.

One of our defenders disrupts the opponents' pass and kicks the ball up field to Mateo, increasing the volume of the Townsend stands. I can already feel my voice starting to go hoarse. The defender on Mateo is shoving like crazy, which makes me want to run out there and kick him. Mateo, however, keeps his cool and control of the ball. He pushes off the defender enough to kick a beautifully arced cross to the box, where one of our forwards is waiting to boot it into the goal.

Amaya and I are on our feet screaming our hearts out along with the rest of the Townsend fans. "That's a goal for Jamar Brown after a perfect assist from Mateo Alvarez!" the announcer yells as the team celebrates together on the field.

At two minutes left till halftime, the opponents are passing down the field toward our goal. I'm jittery with nerves as they get closer and closer to the box, effectively passing around our defenders. Our keeper is poised and ready, but this offensive run is looking too smooth for comfort.

One of their forwards passes to another striker, who sends the ball sailing past our keeper into the net. The student section groans with disappointment, but I'm on my feet yelling in a frustrated voice. "OFFSIDE! He was offside by a mile!!"

The line judge raises the offside flag, and the point is taken off the board for the other team. I clap and cheer along with the crowd as the time runs out for the first half.

Taking my seat next to Amaya, I turn to see her looking at me with both eyebrows raised. "So, you were like, *really* into soccer, weren't you." She says it as more of a statement than a question, and I shrug one shoulder in response.

"I've never seen you so enthusiastic about anything, except maybe law school. If you loved soccer so much, why'd you quit?" Amaya asks.

I consider how to explain my past choice. "I suppose I just saw it as an all-or-nothing thing. It was time to move on to my future career, so I left soccer behind to make way for becoming a lawyer."

Amaya considers this and nods. "That tracks with your personality. You certainly approach things with intensity."

It's an accurate statement. "Yeah, I guess the same intensity I used to play soccer I then channeled into trying to forget soccer. I'm not saying it was the right move, or that I wouldn't go back and change it, but that's how my brain approached it at the time," I conclude.

"Well, Miss Soccer Pro, what the heck does offside mean? You were all worked up but I don't get it at all," Amaya says.

Amaya loves football, so I explain it to her in a way that will track for her. "Okay, pretend the soccer offside rule applies to football. Imagine the quarterback is getting ready to throw a pass to a receiver." Amaya is nodding along; I'm definitely speaking her language now. "If football had the same rules as soccer, then when they're on the opponent's half of the field and the quarterback is throwing the ball, the receiver has to have at least one defender between him and the goal line. After the ball leaves the quarterback's hand, it's okay if the receiver is faster and runs behind the defender to catch the ball and score. But he can't run behind the defenders until *after* the ball is thrown, or he's offside and no touchdown. What counts is when the pass is made, not when it's caught. Does that make sense?"

Amaya nods. "Yep, it does. That rule kinda sucks though."

I laugh. "It does when you're on offense! But it keeps the game more interesting and competitive because a player can't just hang out right next to the goal the whole time. There has to be more strategy and passing that way."

The teams take the field to begin the second half, so we turn our attention back to the match. There's evidently a lot of heated trash talk going on as players start getting more and more chippy.

We're still up 1–0, but the opposing team has the ball on our half of the field. Chris makes an amazing steal and sends the ball to the other side, where Mateo settles the pass. He dribbles straight down the field, juking a defender and making a breakaway toward the box. He shoots hard at the goal, but it's blocked by the keeper. However, the sheer force of the kick ricochets the soccer ball off the keeper's body, and Mateo taps the ball in on the second attempt to score.

I'm jumping, yelling, screaming, and chest bumping with Amaya as Mateo is mobbed by the team celebrating with him. The opposing players are visibly frustrated and upset, understandable since they're now behind 2–0.

The clock is winding down with only a few minutes left, and our players are putting together another good offensive run. Andrés and Mateo are both within the box, fighting defenders for position. A pass is made to Mateo, and he fields it and pivots to either shoot or pass, but a defender runs full speed at him and knocks into him, tripping his legs before he can kick. Mateo rolls to the ground as the Townsend fans are up in arms.

I'm the first to my feet, screaming at the top of my lungs. "Re-fer-REE! Red card, red card!!" Andrés is up in the player's face, who's being held back by a teammate, and Jamar helps Mateo to his feet. Mateo immediately gets between the defender and Andrés, backing him away with an arm across his chest. Finally, the center ref runs over and holds up a yellow card to the offending player, then signals a penalty kick for Mateo.

At this point in the match, it's nearly impossible for the other team to come back to beat or even tie us. But after that flagrant foul, I'm seeing red, and I want Mateo to get a successful PK just to rub it in the defender's face. Hey, I never claimed to be calm or rational about soccer. Or Mateo, at this point.

The goalie crouches at the ready as Mateo positions the ball, but then I swear he looks over his shoulder at the stands, a smile on his face. He takes a few large steps back from the ball, and takes a running approach—right before he Jorginho hops and sends the ball into the net.

Townsend fans erupt, glad to see the opponents put in their place after such a heated match. Amaya and I are high-fiving as Mateo turns and meets my eyes in the stands, grinning and giving a little hop kick right before he's mobbed by teammates. I'm smiling ear-to-ear clapping, and Amaya elbows me in the side. "*Ooo* girl, you've got it bad."

Our team wildly celebrates their decisive victory after the final whistle blows, Mateo at the center of the mosh pit of players. Since I'm staying at the complex to meet Mateo, Amaya and I wait in the stands for the crowd to exit. I explain when a penalty kick is awarded and yellow cards vs. red cards to her. We eventually head down to the parking lot, and I hug her before she gets in her car.

"Thanks for coming with me, Amaya. I know soccer isn't your thing, but I'm glad I had a Beef to watch it with," I tell her.

"Football is definitely more my speed, but I can't deny that was exciting to watch. Or maybe you were just exciting to watch," she says with a smirk. I fake punch her in the arm and walk away smiling.

———

I follow Mateo's directions to the area outside the locker room doors and see three other girls waiting. They're talking and laughing like they know each other already. I feel a little nervous approaching the group, but try to act like I fit in.

One of the girls hears me coming and turns to greet me. "Hey! I'm Linh. You must be Lana. Mateo told my boyfriend, Shawn, that you'd be hanging out."

Her welcome calms my nerves, and the other girls are also smiling, so I step closer. They introduce themselves as Samantha and Reagan, girlfriends of Jorge and Jamar, respectively. They ask how long Mateo and I have been dating, so I tell them just a few weeks.

"And you've already got the girlfriend jersey—Mateo must be serious," Reagan says. "I think Jamar and I had been dating for almost four months before he gave me his jersey to wear!"

I start to blush, but Linh speaks up to rescue me from embarrassment about Mateo by pointing out my screaming at the game. "Didn't I hear you yelling all sorts of stuff at the refs?" she teases.

Embarrassment redirected, I confess my soccer history and enthusiasm, which opens the floodgates of questions. These girls are obviously supportive of their boyfriends but unfamiliar with the rules of soccer. They're listening intently as I explain how they determine if it's a throw-in, corner kick, or goal kick when we hear the locker room doors opening.

The first player to emerge must be Jorge, because Samantha launches herself at him, jumping up with her legs wrapped around his waist. A couple of other guys come out the doors, and then Jamar makes his way over to Reagan. They immediately begin intensely making out. Even Linh, who seemed a little more reserved, is affectionately greeting Shawn with her hands in his hair and his in her back pockets.

I'm starting to panic as I see Mateo come out the door, feeling totally unsure about how to approach him with all these very public displays of affection going on around me. His absurd ability to look unbelievably attractive in Nike joggers and a team hoodie is doing nothing to quell the whirling butterflies.

I don't have to panic for long because Mateo confidently strides over and envelops me in a hug. I wrap my arms around his waist and breathe in his freshly-showered scent with my eyes closed. Mateo holds me in the hug for a long moment before leaning his mouth right next to my ear and speaking in a low voice. "You look super hot wearing my jersey."

My face floods with heat as he pulls back to look at me with a mischievous smile, then he brushes his knuckles across my flushed cheek. "And now you look super adorable."

My brain is nowhere to be found at the moment. I can't come up with two words to string together in response. I'm saved from my brain's hiatus by Jamar's voice calling out, "Yo, Mateo, your girl is the best!"

Mateo releases me but keeps an arm around my shoulders, locking me to his side as he responds. "I obviously know that, but what makes you say so?"

"Reagan just correctly explained the difference between a throw-in and a corner kick," Jamar says with his hands around Reagan's waist. She's beaming at the praise.

"Yeah, not to mention all that accurate grief she gave to the refs," Chris adds with a grin.

All eyes are on me, and Mateo must sense my discomfort at the attention. He pulls me back into his arms with my face buried in his chest and teases his teammates. "Too bad, she's one thousand percent taken, so go find your own soccer expert girlfriends."

Everyone laughs and starts dispersing to vehicles. Mateo smiles down at me as he trails his hand down my arm to take my hand. I shiver head to toe despite the heat still lingering in my face from all the attention—from both Mateo and the crowd.

"We're headed to Mom's Kitchen for late-night breakfast food—that okay with you?" Mateo asks as he leads me toward his truck. "I've never known you to turn it down at After Parties," he adds with a wink.

"People who turn it down have clinical issues, I think," I laugh. "There's nothing breakfast food can't fix."

As we drive across town to the diner, I fangirl over all of Mateo's incredible plays during the match, drawing a pleased smile from him. He confirms that he did indeed hear all my screaming from across the field, and commends me for following through on my threats.

"You've stolen my favorite celebration and my favorite PK strategy, so what do you plan to steal next?" I ask him in a teasing tone. Mateo's eyes are on the road, but the right side of his mouth gently upturns. "Whatever you'll give me, Lana." I smile back at his profile in the dark.

A few of the players have beat us to Mom's Kitchen and pushed several tables together to make room for everyone. Mateo guides me with his hand on the small of my back and pulls out a chair in the middle for me before sitting down. *Sigh.*

The volume level of the diner drastically increases as the table fills and everyone enthusiastically recounts highlights of the night's match. I order decaf, because coffee is an essential component of breakfast food, but I certainly don't need caffeine to add to my energy right now.

The waitress is at the end of the table starting to take food orders, so Mateo leans over to me. "Short stack of pancakes?" he asks with a raised eyebrow. At this point, I shouldn't be surprised when he knows exactly what I'll order at any given place, but I still shake my head in disbelief.

"Do you keep notes of all my favorites on your phone?" I tease. He just taps twice on his temple with a wry smile. "What are you getting?

Please don't tell me you're one of those people who orders egg white health food at ten o'clock at night."

Mateo laughs, and the waitress catches our attention. I order a short stack of pancakes with a toss of my head and side eye at Mateo. "I'll have the strawberry French toast, please," Mateo says, handing the waitress our menus. Phew—crisis averted.

We rejoin the group conversation, and I'm impressed in a new way by Mateo's people skills. He's undoubtedly the leader of the team, with rapport and respect from all the guys, but he's quick to turn conversation around to point out the good plays of other teammates. Mateo also draws me into the discussion easily without making me the center of attention, which I'm grateful for. I could sit here as a fly on the wall just observing Mateo with his friends all night.

Multiple wait staff arrive with trays of food, and I offer Mateo the syrup after drizzling my pancakes. Mateo douses his French toast before giving me a quick wink. "Every good athlete appreciates some post-game sugar," he says before taking a bite.

Despite the arrival of the food, there's no lull in conversation as the group continues in high spirits, alternately praising and razzing each other. I'm starting to cement names with faces of the players that I didn't know before tonight.

When his French toast is finished, Mateo casually places his arm across the back of my chair. I draw in a breath when he reaches over with his left hand to grab mine and pulls it over to rest our hands on his thigh under the table. I never want to lose the tingly sensation that washes through me every time he takes my hand.

All eyes are on Mateo as he recounts a funny story about Andrés from practice this week. Everyone explodes with laughter, and the guys next to Andrés playfully shove him. A shiver runs from my scalp down my neck and back, and I register that Mateo is absentmindedly twirling his fingers through my hair. I look over and study him as he's answering a question from Samantha, and I can't help but smile at the thought that this incredible man is my boyfriend.

I'm piecing together the vibes of the team. If they were a Venn diagram, Mateo would be dead center of the overlap. All these people around the table clearly think the world of Mateo, not just because of his athleticism, but because of his character. And he likes *me*. My brain still has a hard time reconciling that fact, but I just smile as Mateo looks back at me. I angle toward him and lean my right elbow on the table, resting the side of my face against my hand as I hold his gaze.

Mateo gently trails his fingers up and down my hair against my back, and his face turns serious as his eyes flicker with intensity. The rest of the room fades as we wordlessly stare at each other, the look in Mateo's eyes melting me. Forget molten lava—all my internal organs have straight up evaporated into steam.

We're snapped back to reality by the waitress handing out checks. Mateo clears his throat and takes both of ours, instructing the waitress to put both on his card.

Bro hugs and slaps on the back are freely given around the table as everyone stands up, as well as real hugs between the girlfriends, who invite me to sit with them at a match sometime. Mateo leads the charge in returning the tables and chairs to their original set up, then everyone calls out goodnight.

As we walk hand in hand back to the truck, I bite the inside of my lip, trying to decide if now is a good time to make a somewhat serious request. Finally, I clear my throat and timidly question, "Could I ask you to do something?"

Mateo pauses to turn to me and replies, "Lana, you never need to be nervous to ask me anything. I think it's pretty evident that I would do everything for you."

I stop worrying my lip and tell him, "Next weekend, my parents will be in town for some events at AOPi. I know you have an away match on Saturday, but I was wondering if you'd maybe like to join us for dinner or something on Friday night? They'd really like to meet you."

He pulls me to a full stop and into a hug, resting his chin on the top of my head. "I would be honored to meet your parents, Lana. It means a lot that you'd want me to." I breathe out a contented sigh (after a deep inhale of his scent, because what choice do I have). He takes a step back, hands on my elbows. "We should be done with practice by five, so just tell me where and when."

Mateo turns on his Lana playlist in the truck but is quiet on the drive to AOPi, still holding my hand. I'm deep in self-reflection mode as Mateo's thumb traces lines along my wrist. Although I'd obsessively liked Aaron the past two years, he'd never looked at me with such open tenderness that my lungs couldn't find space to inhale. He never made me feel so confident in myself the way Mateo has done since the first day he shared that he liked me. I could never feel sure about anything with Aaron because I never knew what he was thinking. I'm starting to wonder if what started out as a legitimate crush on Aaron snowballed into a crush on having a crush.

It still feels a little implausible that I could go from never thinking of Mateo to constantly thinking of Mateo in just five weeks, yet here I am. And I don't intend to stop.

CHAPTER EIGHTEEN

On Sunday, Teegan and I go out to lunch with a few freshmen AOPis after church, and they're peppering me with questions about my relationship with Mateo. I haven't filled Teegan in on last night yet, but she seems pleased enough with my level of swooning, plus reports from Amaya, to be satisfied with the conversation. Still, as we leave the restaurant, she leans in and whispers, "You realize I need more details than you just fed to the freshmen."

Laughing, I loop my arm through hers. "Promise. How did rehearsal go last night?"

I get a full rundown on the progress they've made on showcase, including her scolding of the guys from Alpha Epsilon who were goofing off instead of taking it seriously. Teegan is sweet and sociable ninety-nine percent of the time, but feisty Teegan lets loose if people start messing with something (or someone) she cares about. Feisty Teegan is terrifying, so I have no doubt that all those boys will be straitlaced at the next rehearsal.

We're walking into the AOPi foyer when the girl on door duty this morning stops me with a huge smile. "Oh Lanaaa," she sing songs. "You had a surprise dropped off by an extremely hot delivery guy while you were gone." She hands me a vibrant bouquet of flowers tied up in brown paper and twine, the signature wrapping of Grow Wild, a local floral and gift shop in Center Square. There's an envelope with my name tucked inside, and I flush and smile as Teegan and the other girls squeal around me.

Teegan acts as a bodyguard, ushering me through the high-pitched calls for me to read the card aloud to everyone. "No comment! No pictures!" she feigns as we sprint up the stairs. Of course, the second we're alone in our room, she's the one demanding for me to read it aloud, which I refuse to do until I've previewed the contents.

I carefully slide my finger under the seal of the gray-blue envelope and find a card with a watercolor design inside. Mateo definitely stepped up his stationary game, even though I loved the notebook paper just as much.

Lana,

Thanks for arguably the best weekend of my life. I'm pretty sure I'm living in a dream, so I'm not going to pinch myself.

Mateo

Apparently Mateo's smolder is just as effective via written words as via his deep brown eyes and dimpled smile, because my insides are once again vaporized. I decide this is a bone I can throw to Teegan, so I surrender the card to her greedy hands.

"You know, we could frame this and post it right here on the wall above the desk," Teegan says. "No, let's post it downstairs in the foyer so that any boy who dares to dream of dating an AOPi knows the standard he needs to live up to." I roll my eyes and grab the card back out of her hand, careful not to crumple it.

"We are not doing that, Beef, but I am going to text him thank you for the flowers and note," I say, pulling out my phone.

"You can't just text him—at least send him a selfie with the flowers!" Teegan urges me.

"Fine, fine," I respond. I hold the flowers up close to my face, give a soft smile, and snap a selfie.

I send the photo and thank you text to Mateo, followed by a second message.

ME

Definitely no pinching allowed

After just a few seconds, I see the text is read and three dots appear.

I'm smiling down at my phone screen when I'm knocked out of my reverie by the sound of Teegan blasting "Lover" through her Bluetooth speaker. She's swaying back and forth, singing along with her hands over her heart, a teasing smile on her face. I shove her onto the bed. "It's much too soon for the L word, Teegan."

She laughs and sits back up. "Lana, if ever there was a magnetic force of a man, he's found you."

———

Wednesday's chapter meeting was extra long as Amaya shared schedule details for our "My VIPs" weekend coming up. AOPi used to host the traditional Mom's Weekend and Dad's Weekend like most Greek houses do, but last year Amaya successfully campaigned to change it to one weekend designed to be more inclusive for all family situations. I'm sure she felt the personal sting of not having a father figure on Dad's Weekend our first two years, and Amaya is an unrelenting force when stung.

My grandparents are holding down the fort with my siblings this weekend so that both of my parents can come. I know they're excited to see me and participate in all of the official AOPi events, but they're not even trying to hide the fact that they're primarily excited about meeting Mateo. My mom has called or texted me about it no less than nineteen times this week already, and it's only Thursday.

I get to the Arrow meeting early to get the name tags ready and make small talk with Rachel. It's evident that she's heard rumors about Mateo and me as she asks me open-ended leading questions, but I don't say anything about him, as Bailey is not-at-all-subtly eavesdropping nearby.

The rush of students begins, and the blood starts pounding in my temples as I see Aaron approaching with some of his fraternity brothers. There are other girls standing nearby available to write name tags, but Aaron makes it a point to come straight over to me. I look down and start slowly writing his name to avoid looking him in the eye.

"Uh, hey Lana, how are you?" Aaron asks, more subdued than normal.

"Fine, yeah, I'm good," I mumble. "You?"

"All right, I guess," he says, and I finally look up from the name tag, trying not to be totally awkward. He's staring intensely at me and asks, "What's the question today?"

"Oh, right," I say. "What will your Halloween costume be this year?"

Aaron is silent for a second before speaking lowly. "Maybe a broken heart?"

I stare at him without breathing for what feels like forever before I finally open my mouth. "Aaron—"

"I know, I know. Don't write that, obviously."

I suspect my look must be attempting murder, because Aaron immediately adds, "I'm sorry, that was out of line. I shouldn't have said that. A friend wouldn't say that."

My eyes drop and study the Sharpie in my hand, still poised above the name tag. Aaron must notice the same thing and says, "Um, a bunch of us OGs are dressing up as Greek gods this year."

I write "Greek god" at the bottom of the name tag and peel it off. It seems like Aaron goes out of his way to make contact with my fingers when he takes the name tag I'm holding out, but I keep my eyes down.

He turns away to go into the room just as Mateo and several of his teammates breach the top of the staircase. At the Arrow meetings since our first date, our only interaction has been smiles from across the room. He's always occupied with the soccer guys and I'm always tied up with the AOPis. But now that we're officially boyfriend/girlfriend, I'm not sure how to play this. I hope Mateo gives me a clear lead to follow.

I shouldn't have been concerned, because of course he does. With his characteristic subtle confidence, Mateo heads straight to me with a smile and gives me a quick hug before asking if I remembered Shawn from the other night.

I smile and reply, "Of course I do. Great to see you, Shawn—is Linh here with you?"

"Nah, she's not here tonight, I'm just checking it out," Shawn responds. "But maybe she'll come with another time."

"Well, let her know that she'd be welcome to sit with me if she wants to come but not sit with a bunch of soccer dudes," I say with a smile as I write his name. "Every week we ask a question and write your answer on your name tag as a conversation starter. The question this week is 'What will your Halloween costume be?'"

The guys all turn to each other mumbling variations of "Halloween? . . . Are you wearing a costume? . . . Are you dressing up?"

Mateo turns to me and asks, "Am I dressing up for Halloween this year?"

I burst out a laugh and tell him, "That is one hundred percent up to you."

He furrows his brow. "But are you?"

Pointing to where my name tag says "Undecided," I shrug and say, "I love fall, but Halloween has never really been my thing." A thought dawns on me, and I gesture at the collective group and say, "But you all should definitely dress up as the guys from *Ted Lasso*. It's the obvious soccer team costume."

There's an outburst of enthusiastic responses. I smile to myself as they start bickering over who would be which character and catch Mateo's eye. "Well, now I know what we'll be doing all night," he says to me with feigned disapproval, making me laugh.

The band starts playing, so I give the guys their name tags with question marks instead of answers. They can fight and sort it all out later. Mateo turns to give me one last smile over his shoulder before heading into the room, his wink shooting a flaming arrow through my heart.

Near the end of Kent's message, I sneak out the back door to head to the restroom. Maybe that 6:00 p.m. coffee wasn't my greatest idea ever. I'm washing my hands at the sink when the door opens and Bailey stands right behind me in the mirror, arms crossed and hip popped. *Here we go.*

"You know, I have it on good authority that Aaron is basically totally depressed ever since he found out about your little dating situation with Mateo," Bailey says, fake concern lacing her voice. I draw in a deep breath through my nose and exhale through my mouth as I turn off the sink.

Pulling out paper towels, I respond without looking at Bailey. "I'm sorry, but I don't think my dating life is any of your business, Bailey." I toss the paper towels in the trash, resisting the urge to clarify that Mateo is, in fact, my boyfriend. Not just a "little dating situation." I turn around to find Bailey totally invading my personal space.

"I don't get it, Lana," she continues. "You already had a perfectly nice, totally cute and popular guy lined up to date you. Did you really need to go after someone else? You and Aaron so *obviously* liked each other, it seems a little *immature* for you to just drop him so suddenly." Her tone and word emphasis has my blood running hot and my rational brain vacating the premises.

"Look, Bailey, I don't understand what you have against me or the other AOPis, and I don't understand why you care about this. My conversations with Aaron and my relationship with Mateo are of zero concern to you, so why don't you just leave me alone?"

I charge out of the bathroom before she can respond, just as students are exiting the meeting room to head home or to the After Party. After partying is a big fat no for me tonight, so I rush down the back staircase to walk straight to AOPi. I send a quick text to the Beefs to let them know I'm bailing, and then I turn on my Christmas piano playlist. I don't have my ear buds with me, but I just hold my phone and hope the muffled music will help me relax as I walk.

I'm a few paces out of the student union when I hear footsteps running behind me in the dark. My pulse quickens until I hear a familiar deep voice call out, "Lana! Wait!" I've never liked my name more than when Mateo says it.

He catches up to me in like two seconds and asks what's wrong. "Are you upset that I hugged you before the meeting? I know we didn't really talk about how we were going to handle being around each other at Arrow stuff, and that's totally my fault, I should have planned ahead and gotten your input."

He's being so sweet and thoughtful, I can't even stand it. I launch myself at him and throw my arms around his neck, face buried in his shoulder. His arms circle my waist as I say, "No, I'm not mad about that at all." He doesn't make a move to let me go, so I stand there until my tiptoes start protesting.

"I just had an unpleasant conversation with someone who's not my favorite person in the world," I say as I take a step back. His face looks concerned with a minor jealous tinge, so to make sure he knows I'm not this affected by talking with Aaron, I shrug one shoulder and add, "Bailey."

Realization dawns on him. "Ah," he says simply. We're both quiet for a second before he asks, "Anything I can help with?"

I shake my head. There's no point in burdening him with Bailey's opinions.

"Well, at least let me walk you back then. I can't let you walk home alone in the dark," Mateo says.

"Are you going to miss the After Party with your teammates, though? Were you planning on going?"

Mateo snorts. "I have a feeling the only after party we'll have tonight is campaigning for who should be which Richmond player for Halloween."

"Yeaaah, sorry about that," I say with a guilty smile.

He takes my hand and winks. "You can make it up to me by detouring to take the long way back to AOPi."

With each day that passes, I'm more convinced that the long way could never be long enough with Mateo.

"P.S., I'm digging the Christmas mood," Mateo teases. I laugh and move to pause the music, but he waves me off to leave it playing as we walk.

The evening is getting cold, so Mateo eventually leads us back to AOPi when he realizes I'm shivering. "I'd offer you my hoodie, but I don't have a t-shirt on underneath," Mateo says apologetically, and I'm extremely grateful for the pitch black so he can't see the color in my cheeks as I'm now fighting back thoughts of shirtless Mateo. Suddenly, I'm not so cold.

At the AOPi front porch, Mateo confirms the time and restaurant for tomorrow night with my parents, then gives me one last lingering hug. He's down the stairs when he turns back and says, "Hey Lana? Don't let Bailey get in your head. I think she generally means well, but she's just jealous of you."

I bark out a laugh. "Yeah no, Bailey Williams is absolutely not jealous of me. Well, maybe other than for the fact that I'm your girlfriend."

Mateo cocks his head and stares at me. "You're beautiful, determined, empathetic, successful, an amazing friend, and you go after what you want. Maybe if I tell you enough times, you'll eventually recognize how uniquely incredible you are, Lana."

My heart explodes with warmth, and I'm in an all-out war with my whole body to not fly down the steps to kiss him. I muster a grateful smile and open the door behind my back as I whisper, "See you tomorrow, Mateo."

CHAPTER NINETEEN

I love my mom. I do.

But this new version of my mom is not someone I've been trained to deal with.

She and my dad arrived in Brooklyn at 4:00 p.m., so we met at Bookafe for afternoon coffee. We've been sitting down with our drinks for exactly twenty-three seconds when she leans in and asks about Mateo like he's some sort of conspiracy theory. My dad rolls his eyes with a smile.

Mom wants to know everything about him: his personality, his interests, his family, his future plans, his soccer prowess—pretty much everything that could be on the Mateo Alvarez Wikipedia page. I try to answer her questions with enough detail to satisfy her without droning on forever, because I really want to hear about how things are going at home.

"Okay, but tell me more about Mateo's—"

"Mom," I cut in. "You're going to meet him at dinner, and you can ask him all the questions you want to then. But for now, I want to hear about how Olivia, Carter, and Dean are doing."

She glances at my dad, and they share some sort of secret conversation in a split-second of eye contact. *Uh-oh.*

Dad clears his throat. "Well, may as well rip the Band-Aid off news from the home front. Dean was suspended from school for two days this week for fighting."

My jaw drops. "What?! Was he hurt? What was he fighting about?"

Mom reassures me, "He's okay, just a bit of a shiner on one eye. We're more concerned about him emotionally. He won't tell us what the fight was about. All he'll say is that the other guy had it coming because of something he said. But he won't say what that was."

I know my mom is trying to put me at ease, but I see the stress on both their faces. I chew the inside of my lip and ask, "Have you considered having him see a therapist?"

"Oh honey, we've tried," my mom says. "The school counselor talked to him about it too, but he refuses. Says therapists are for weaklings. But we keep praying he'll change his mind."

I can tell they're ready to move on in the conversation, so I ask my mom about Samira, one of her Afghan clients from the summer that I became especially close to. She's a single mom who escaped from Afghanistan with her ten-year-old daughter, Zahra, but her thirteen-year-old son, Hassan, had gotten separated from them. Samira chose to leave with Zahra when she had the opportunity, assuming that she would be able to send for Hassan shortly after. Of course, no one had any idea at the time what an impossible nightmare it would turn out to be to get people evacuated from Afghanistan after the final plane departed.

Mom smiles. "She's doing well. She has a stable job, and Zahra is really starting to pick up on English at school. We're still working every possible angle to get Hassan here." She shares updates on some of the other families I worked with over the summer. Dad shares about the students he's teaching in private lessons and jokes about enjoying his freedom before Nutcracker rehearsals begin in earnest.

At 5:45, my mom taps on her watch and says, "We'd best get going to the restaurant. It's almost six o'clock."

Laughing, I tease my mom, "Surely you're not old and hobbling enough that it's going to take you fifteen minutes to walk two doors down."

She brushes me off. "I'm just saying, I'd hate to make a bad impression on Mateo by being late."

My dad jumps in this time. "If everything that Lana has told us about Mateo is true, I have a hard time believing anything we do could give him a bad impression of Lana." But Mom is already walking her coffee mug over to the dirty dish tub, so Dad and I follow suit.

———

Even with my mom purposely walking slower than usual, we make it to the Italian restaurant two doors down in five minutes. We check in at the host stand but say we'll wait for Mateo before sitting down.

We only wait a few minutes before Mateo walks through the door, characteristically early. Another point for him with my parents. He sees me and smiles, crossing the lobby to where we're standing to give me a hug. I slip my right hand into Mateo's left, and say with a proud smile, "Mom, Dad, meet Mateo."

He firmly shakes both of their hands. "Mr. and Mrs. Grant, it's so nice to meet you. Lana has told me such great things about you. I'm excited to get to know you for myself."

Mom pulls him in for a hug and says, "Oh please, call us James and Alexis. And we're equally as eager to get to know you."

The host leads us to a table and passes out menus, which are promptly set aside as Mom dives straight into conversation. She starts off asking Mateo about his time at Townsend and classes this year. Dad interjects to ask several soccer-related questions, wanting to hear how Mateo wound up at Townsend. This naturally leads to my mom grilling him with questions about his family and childhood growing up in Michigan. Mateo answers all of their questions with graciousness and not even a hint of annoyance. I'm smiling to myself at their overzealous curiosity and his charming openness. Also, his hand holding mine under the table.

The waiter returns for a third time asking if we're ready, so we pause the conversation long enough to look at the menus and place an order. The break in my parents' interrogation gives Mateo an opening to ask his own questions about their jobs and backgrounds. He asks my mom about her time in El Paso, which definitively earns him a hundred gold stars in her eyes, because she loves nothing more than to talk about her attorney work at the border.

The conversation continues steadily, and I barely get to add a word in edgewise. I almost feel like a spectator to a dinner between old friends catching up as my parents share about their lives and interests, also inquiring about Mateo's. My dad has droned on about his love for the cello following Mateo's leading questions, and Mateo has enthusiastically shared about inheriting his love of soccer from his father. He adds effusive compliments to my dad for the "Bullseye" sign at my old matches—one hundred gold stars from Dad.

Our food arrives, and my dad says a blessing for our meal and time together. As we unwrap silverware and place napkins in our laps, my mom inquires, "So, Mateo. Lana told us that you liked her for quite a while before you asked her out earlier this year. I'm curious to know when she first caught your eye."

Mateo smiles and sets down his fork. He looks over at me briefly, and I hold my breath because I'm also very curious to know this answer.

"Well, Mrs. Gr—I mean, Alexis—in September of our sophomore year, Lana and I were at a meeting for the student leaders in Arrow. I knew who she was from freshman year, but because I didn't go to the Summer Project that year, I hadn't really gotten to know her very well yet. We broke into small groups to pray for the upcoming school year, and Lana and I were in the same group."

I can picture exactly what Mateo is talking about. We have the same type of meeting for Arrow every fall. I don't remember being in the same group as Mateo that year, but then again, I wouldn't have been paying attention since I was already crushing on Aaron.

Mateo continues, "Everyone in the group was sharing prayer requests about people in their lives who they were trying to be good friends to and share about Jesus with. And everyone was talking about the obvious people around them on campus—people on their dorm floors, or in their fraternities or sororities. The standard groups that students involved with Arrow would be trying to build relationships with."

At this point, Mateo turns to look straight at me. "But Lana here shared about someone else entirely. She had been volunteering as an ELL tutor through the local after-school program, and she desperately wanted to be a positive influence on the middle school girl she was tutoring." He pauses to smile at me, and then turns back to my parents.

"At that moment, I knew that there was something different about Lana, something special. Her love and concern for other people drew outside the typical campus ministry box.

"She caught my eye that day, and she hasn't lost it since," Mateo finishes with a shrug. I think my mom audibly swoons, and my dad just nods his head in approval at Mateo's answer.

I, for one, am rapidly blinking to fend off tears, because I absolutely don't want to start openly crying in the restaurant. Mateo's response was so sincere, so heartfelt—and I had no idea that had been the catalyst to his feelings for me. I'm overcome with affection for him, because he truly saw me for me, for what was close to my heart even all those years ago.

Mateo asks my parents about my siblings, and I over-chew my bite of food, waiting to see how honest they'll be. Apparently, Mateo's winsome willingness to share about his life has opened the door for my parents to speak candidly as well, so they share about their challenges with Dean. Mateo pauses eating and leans in with a furrowed brow as he listens. Genuine concern flickers across his face as I watch his profile, and it only makes my heart swell even more.

"It seems like Dean needs a jolt of some sort to get him off the track he's currently on," my dad shares. "We're just praying the right person at school or in our community crosses paths with him, someone to help him realize he's worth more than the choices he's making right now."

Mateo nods. "It's not my story to share the details, but a couple of years ago my sister had a rough time. Isabel did eventually meet a friend, well, more of a mentor I guess, who latched onto her and wouldn't let go until Isabel believed she could live differently. I'll pray that Dean meets the same kind of person soon."

My parents murmur their appreciation as the waiter comes back to inquire about dessert. We all order decaf coffees, and my parents order a tiramisu to share. I turn toward Mateo, but he's already telling the waiter to bring us two orders of tiramisu. He smiles at me and says, "I know better than to try to make you share."

Dad loudly laughs at that comment, and my mom half-heartedly shushes him as she stifles a giggle. "Now I'm convinced that you really do know my daughter!" my dad says, still chuckling.

Over dessert, Mateo gives my parents a rundown of the team they'll face in tomorrow's match and their chances of repeating their championship performance in the DII tournament. None of my siblings wound up playing soccer, so I can tell my dad is loving the chance to talk about it again. He'd always been so supportive of me playing, and I don't think I realized that when I cut soccer out of my life so abruptly, I was also cutting it out of his. Once again, I'm grateful to Mateo for helping me pull that box out of mental storage.

My mom makes the first move to wind the conversation down when our dessert plates are wiped clean. "It's getting late, and I'm sure you need to get home and rest up before your big match tomorrow. Wouldn't want you losing to a big rival because we kept you out."

My dad pays the bill, and we exit the restaurant into the crisp evening air. My parents and Mateo compete to see who can be more grateful to have met each other. We're parked in opposite directions, so I walk a few paces with Mateo to say goodnight.

He thanks me again for inviting him to meet my parents. "I really enjoyed talking with them." He tucks my hair behind my ear and twirls his fingers through the lengths. "I always enjoy anything with you. I'll miss seeing you tomorrow."

I frown and say, "I know. I'm really sorry I can't come to the match. If it weren't for this AOPi stuff I would totally drive there since it's not far away."

Mateo cuts in, "No, you need to be here this weekend. It's more important for you to spend the time with your parents and your sorority sisters. There will be other soccer matches."

I lean in to give Mateo a hug and tell him, "I'll still expect a full report after the match. And thanks again for coming tonight—I know it meant a lot to my parents to get to meet you for themselves and see how amazing you are." Mateo squeezes me tighter before releasing me to part ways for the night.

Smiling, I walk back over to my parents, who are animatedly recapping our conversation and not being the least bit quiet about their admiration for Mateo. As I approach, my mom whirls around with a grin and exclaims, "So! When can I start planning the wedding?"

"MOM!" I gasp. My dad says, "Now Alexis, I think it's a little too soon to be adding that pressure."

Mom looks indignant. "What? Mateo's future path is compatible with Lana's, and he's clearly over the moon about her." She turns to me. "I know you liked that other boy for so long, but he always made you feel so uncertain of yourself, and I never liked that. It wasn't healthy."

Narrowing my eyes, I tell her, "Mom, you could have said something before if you had concerns. Why'd you let me keep feeding my crush if you thought it wasn't healthy?"

She rolls her eyes. "Please, like any college-aged girl is going to listen to her mom try to convince her not to like a boy."

Touché.

My dad shrugs his shoulders in silent agreement, and Mom continues. "Mateo likes you for who you are, and he brings out the very best in you. You're the happiest and most light-hearted I've seen you in years. It's like he gave you permission to enjoy your passions, to enjoy life. Why wouldn't I want that for my daughter?"

Considering she's making valid points, I surrender the fight.

CHAPTER TWENTY

My parents enjoy the rest of the weekend in Brooklyn, attending AOPi events and catching up with Teegan, Amaya, and their families over dinner together. The parents lament about their babies growing up, and the Beefs roll our eyes at their sentimentality while secretly feeling the same.

Sunday morning, we hug our parents goodbye, and Amaya immediately cracks the proverbial whip to get everyone's noses to the homecoming grindstone. Daily events and competitions this week culminate in the announcement of the winning Greek houses on Saturday before the start of the soccer match.

Teegan and the rest of the showcase performers are off to rehearsal, and Amaya has placed me in charge of the underclassmen pomping our parade float. She's overseeing progress on the yard display since it's the first thing to be judged tomorrow. I'm always amazed by Amaya, but I'm prouder than ever to be her best friend, as she has organized and delegated like a boss. If AOPi doesn't win homecoming, it won't be for lack of whole-hearted effort.

Aside from briefly FaceTiming Sunday evening to hear about their victory on Saturday, I barely get to speak with Mateo all week. It's all-hands-on-deck between classes to make sure everything looks perfect. Teegan leads our team of AOPis and AEs in a commanding showcase performance, dancing and lip-syncing their hearts out to roars of applause from the crowd. I only feel a brief moment of awkwardness watching Aaron perform with the OGs before I firmly kick the echoes of dancing together out of my mind.

By the time the homecoming parade rolls around Friday night, I'm exhausted. The last thing I feel like doing is walking a mile behind our float passing out candy, but I know this is the crown jewel on Amaya's Presidency. So, I let Teegan do my hair and makeup, and I plaster on my rush week fake smile. I encouraged Sofia, Clara, and Luisa to invite Shaista to attend with them, so I'm hopeful to see them along the parade route.

"You knowww," Teegan says in sing song as she applies her eyeliner. "The soccer team has their own float, so at least you'll get to see a certain hot soccer captain at the parade."

Although I roll my eyes at her, I've secretly been banking on the chance of seeing Mateo redeeming the parade exhaustion.

The Greek house pairings are judged by the appearance of the physical float in addition to the level of enthusiasm and school spirit shown by the parade participants. I'm standing next to Liz and some other freshmen girls as Amaya gives the crowd of AOPis and AEs an animated pep talk through a bullhorn. Suddenly, I feel a pinch on my waist.

I turn around to find Mateo grinning at me. He whispers hello and gives me a quick hug before falling back with the rest of the soccer team heading to their float. I'm pretty sure they just get to stand on a trailer and wave to the cheering spectators, as opposed to trying to lead the crowd in organized chants, which is a little bit unfair. Still, I'm smiling as I turn back around to the nudges and hushed squeals of Liz and the other girls around me.

Halfway through the parade, I'm starting to buckle under the torture when I spy Shaista in the crowd along with Sofia and Clara. Luisa isn't with them, but I'm delighted to see Shaista here, smiling widely as she takes in the parade. I catch their attention, and they wave and loudly yell the cheer our group is shouting. I briefly rush over and tell them to meet me outside of Grow Wild at the end of the parade route if they have time.

We finally reach the end of the route, and there's a collective cheer and sigh of relief. People are dispersing to get a late dinner or a head start at the AE house party, and I look around for signs of the soccer team, but I can't find their float. I need to make my way through the crowd if I have any hope of meeting up with my ELL students, so I reluctantly head that way.

The disappointment of missing Mateo fades when I see Sofia, Clara, and Shaista talking as I walk up to the gift shop. They see me coming and give me huge hugs, complimenting me on our house's float.

"It was totally the best one, Lana," Sofia insists.

"Yeah, your team will definitely win," Clara adds. This leads to us trying to explain to Shaista through simple English and hand gestures what a homecoming competition is, which then leads to trying to explain what Greek houses are. America really does have some funny traditions.

I sense Mateo behind me before he even speaks because of the look on the girls' faces. They go from lively conversation to starstruck silence like an F1 driver goes zero to a hundred. I feel Mateo's left arm around my shoulders as he says, "Hey, Lana. Hi there, girls. I'm Mateo."

He holds out his right hand, and they literally giggle like school girls as they take turns exchanging handshakes. I can't really blame them, considering that Mateo's handsome face and dimpled smile make me want to giggle like a school girl too. I introduce each of them, and they are kind enough to go way overboard in talking up how great of a tutor I am. Like, they are *really* trying to sell me to Mateo. He just keeps grinning at me as they go on and on about all my positive qualities, and I fight the urge to burst out laughing.

I love these sweet girls.

Sofia's phone rings, and she answers in Spanish. I assume it's her parents wanting to know where she's disappeared to. She's speaking rapid fire with passionate inflection, and Clara is nodding and giggling intermittently as she listens. Shaista just shrugs at me, and I hold my hands up in an "I have no idea" gesture, making her laugh.

Sofia is oblivious that Mateo is following along with the conversation. He catches her off guard when he interjects in Spanish, evidently demanding her phone because she passes it over to him. He chats for a minute with her parents, and I catch a few words here and there about Townsend and *fútbol* and my name. Sofia and Clara are positively loving their lives right now.

Mateo finishes talking and ends the call, telling Sofia, "You're supposed to meet them outside the taco shop so they can drive you home."

The girls are now *really* starstruck, and gush about how nice it was to meet Mateo. They're saying their goodbyes, but Sofia leans over to me and not-so-quietly says in my ear, "*Chica*, you did not tell us that you had a boyfriend or that he is sooo hot!"

Mateo is fighting back a laugh as he tells Shaista that it was nice to meet her. I playfully shove Sofia and tell her, "It wasn't relevant to our English lessons, you goofball." She gives me one last hug before the three of them head off to meet her parents.

I turn to Mateo with a half-smile and wrap my hands around his waist, angling my neck to look up at his face. "And what exactly was that all about?"

He grins and loops his arms around my back, burying his fingers in my hair. "I guess you'll have to brush up on your Spanish if you want to keep up with conversations."

I stick out my lower lip and give him my best puppy dog eyes, making him chuckle. "I'll never be able to say no to those gorgeous eyes! Sofia was being a little mischievous with her parents, saying they were late meeting up after the parade because they were talking to a hot older guy. I could hear her mom's classic Latina scolding through the phone, so I explained who I was and why we were chatting. And then she naturally had glowing things to say about you being the best influence in Sofia's life, so I agreed with her that you're pretty much the greatest woman who has ever lived."

Mateo has a teasing smile, but I can tell he's also being totally serious. I'm still not the best at receiving compliments, despite how frequently he gives them, so I just smile back and then lean my head against his chest. He rests his chin on the top of my head, still weaving his fingers through my hair against my back.

"I'm really glad you got to meet them. They're such special girls." I feel Mateo nod his head in agreement.

"I can see why you enjoy spending time with them. It was cool to see Sofia and Clara including Shaista."

"I know, right?" I say, pulling back so I can look up at him. "They invited Shaista the first week and have been so kind helping her learn the ropes as she's figuring out school in America and learning English."

Mateo narrows his eyes thoughtfully as he looks at me. "You know that's partially due to your influence, right? You've been that person for them, so they're passing it along to someone else who needs the same belonging."

It warms my heart to think about the chain reaction of acceptance and friendship. I have my mom to credit for my own vision to see the people in need of welcome. I should thank her for that.

We start walking back toward the thinning parade crowd, hand in hand. Mateo offers to give me a ride home, but I have my car here since I'm one of the designated drivers for the party tonight. He looks over at me with concern and says, "Be careful, okay? I've heard stories about homecoming frat parties. Not positive ones."

I squeeze his hand in reassurance. "I will, I promise. It's not my first frat party DD rodeo." I glance over and see his still-furrowed brow. "I'll text you to check in every hour until I get home, okay?"

He looks one part appeased and one part still worried as we arrive on the fringes of the remaining AOPi/AE crowd. Teegan is still here, so she comes over and makes small talk with Mateo for a few minutes before he gives my hand a final squeeze and takes off.

The party at AE is more amped than usual, as everyone is riding high with hopes of a homecoming win tomorrow. We had good showings all week, but you never know what's going to tip the scales in the judges' minds. Still, guys and girls are celebrating as though we've already won, so Amaya, Teegan, and I stay extra aware.

True to my word, I text Mateo occasionally to check in. At midnight, I send him a text:

Hey. Still doing fine. It's getting late though, and you need some sleep before the match. How about I just text you tomorrow morning?

No

I won't sleep till I know you're home safe anyway, so keep checking in

<thumbs up emoji>

I should have just come with you

I snort trying to picture Mateo at a frat party.

You would hate it

I'll try to rally some troops to head home soon so you can get some sleep

Luckily, there's a group of girls who are partied out around 1:00 a.m., so I volunteer to take them back to the dorms. Amaya gives me the okay to head back home after, which I gratefully accept.

Back at AOPi, I park my car and send Mateo a final text to let him know I was home.

Now get some sleep. I'm expecting to scream my heart out at your hat-trick tomorrow

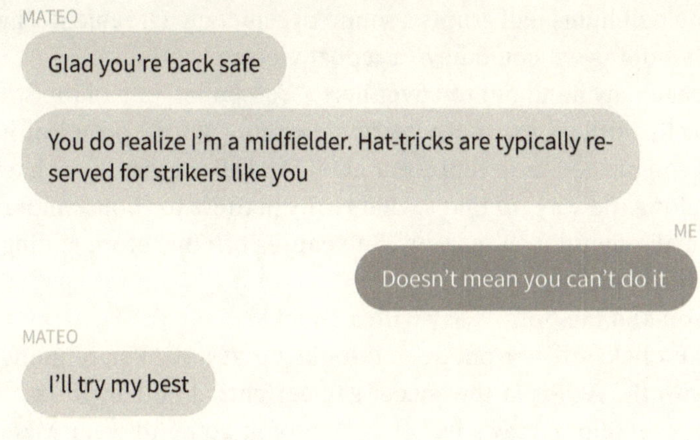

———

Despite our late night, Amaya is awake super early Saturday morning. I hear her moving around the room quietly and attempt to will myself back into dreamland, but I'm thoroughly alert for some reason. Teegan could sleep through a dump truck rolling through the room, so I use the flashlight on my phone to dig a pair of sweats and a hoodie out of my drawer.

Downstairs, the house is the kind of quiet that follows a wild party night. Amaya is already sitting with a cup of coffee at a dining table, scrolling on her phone. I hug her good morning and get my own cup of caffeine before taking the seat across from her.

"Whatcha looking at?" I ask, nodding toward her phone screen.

"Oh, just looking at the other sorority houses' posts of their entries throughout the week. I hate to admit it, but TriAlpha had a really good yard display and float this year. Do you think they had more parade participation than we did?" Amaya asks me.

Amaya and I both appreciate straight-shooting, so I don't beat around the bush or tell her what she'd hope to hear. "Yeah, I think they did, at least judging by the crowd around their float at the start of the parade. I bet Bailey made the new pledges sign blood oaths to attend after Bid Day, and the OGs always have more participation than the other fraternities."

She half hums half grunts a sound of reluctant agreement. "I was really hoping we could have a repeat victory."

I reach my hand out to cover hers. "You pulled out all the stops, Beef. Regardless of whether we win or not, I'm so proud of how well you pushed us to represent AOPi. And all the girls were having fun along the way, so that's what really matters for house morale."

Amaya sighs. "You're right." She pauses briefly before adding, "I just really like to win."

"You and me both," I say with a chuckle.

She clicks off her phone and looks up at me. "You're going to sit with the AOPis at the soccer game, right?" I nod an affirmative response. She narrows her eyes. "Are you going to wear Mateo's jersey or our homecoming shirt?"

I hear the question behind her question—is my relationship with Mateo edging out my relationship with her?

I look her square in the eyes. "I'm wearing my AOPi homecoming shirt and sitting smack dab in the middle of the group today. I might be Mateo's girlfriend, but I was an AOPi and your best friend first. Today is more about celebrating you and our amazing house than it is about Mateo playing soccer, okay?"

Amaya nods acceptance of my answer and stands up. "I think I need to go for a run to work out some of this nervous energy. Wanna come with?"

Running is *not* number one on my wish list for the day, but supporting my best friend certainly is. Teegan remains blissfully snoozing as Amaya and I change in the dark and lace up our tennis shoes. Amaya was right about nervous energy—she's a girl on a mission on our run. I'm struggling to keep up after such a short night of sleep, but there's no way I'll admit defeat.

Back at the house after way too long of a run, Amaya and I are showered and dressed for the day before Teegan rolls out of bed at 9:30 a.m. "About time," I tease as she sleepily rubs her eyes. "At least now I can blow dry my hair in here instead of in the stuffy bathroom."

"Tease away," Teegan yawns. "You're just jealous of my superb sleeping abilities."

I blow my hair dryer in her face, effectively getting her up and moving.

A solid twenty minutes later (cons of having long, super-thick hair), I flip the hair dryer off and check the time on my phone. I see I missed a good morning text from Mateo.

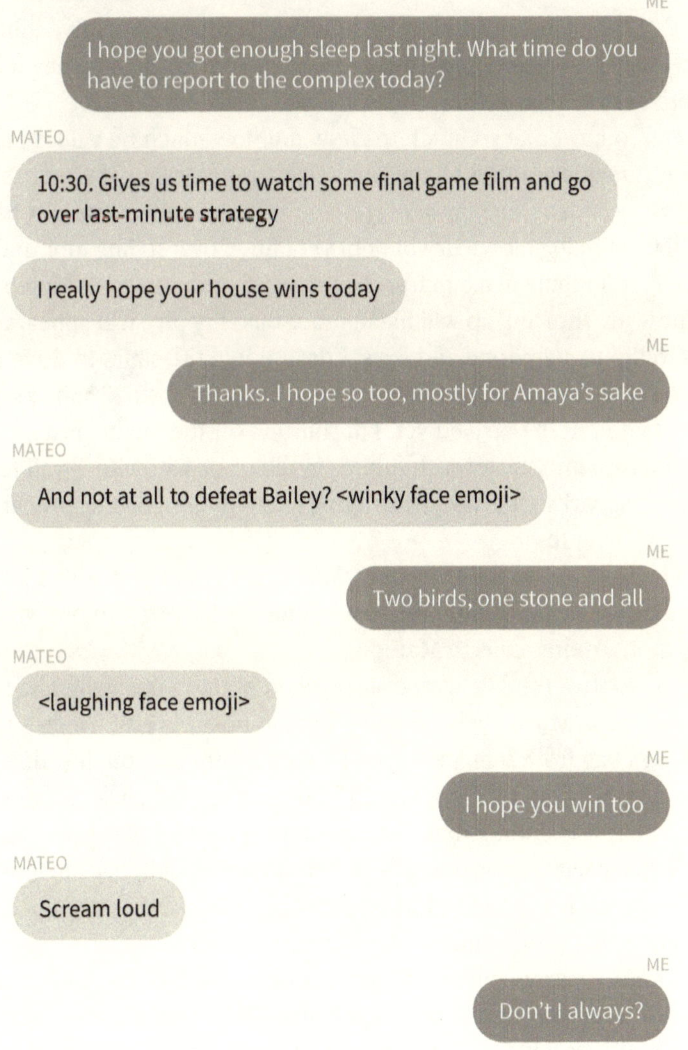

It's 10:09 a.m., and I know that Mateo will be at least five minutes early to the soccer complex. If I leave right now, I might make it over there before he arrives.

Mateo has done so much to show me how much he values me, so many tangible gestures to affirm my significance to him. I want to show the same effort. Glancing at my reflection in the mirror, I see my hair is wild from being blown dry but not yet tamed by a styling tool, and my face is still totally makeup free. Not how I'd prefer to greet Mateo, but I know my showing up will mean more than my physical appearance.

Grabbing my phone and keys, I dash down the stairs to drive over to the soccer complex. I pull into the parking lot at 10:22 a.m., praying that Mateo hasn't arrived yet. I'm shutting off the engine just as I see Mateo turn into the lot with Andrés in the truck with him. I wait to see where he parks, then take a fortifying breath before exiting my car and walking over to his.

They get out of the truck, but Andrés spots me first with a grin as Mateo is reaching behind the seat to pull out his bag. "Yo bro, you got a visitor," Andrés calls to Mateo.

The look of total delighted surprise on Mateo's face when he turns to see me is worth, well, anything I could possibly give. Andrés takes Mateo's bag from him and says, "I'll take this in for you. Just don't be late or we'll all get it from Coach." Mateo slaps his back in thanks as he walks away and then turns to meet me, enveloping me in a hug.

"Lana, what are you doing here?" he says as he pulls back to look me in the eyes. He runs a hand through my hair. "Not that I'm complaining about seeing your beautiful face before the match."

I smile, my arms still loosely hugging his waist. "I just wanted to show up and wish you good luck. At the match I'll be lost in a sea of sorority sisters all wearing matching shirts, so I'll be a little hard to find in the stands."

He brushes his thumb across my cheek and down the side of my neck, sending a shiver through me. "Please, I could spot you anywhere."

I know my cheeks are coloring when his lips curl up in his "I love making you blush because it's adorable" smile, so I give his waist a playful pinch and tell him to get inside so he's not late. He runs his fingers through my hair one last time, then jogs into the office along with the other guys who are just arriving.

Sitting alone in my car, I can't stop smiling. Because Mateo started off so far ahead of me in his confidence about his feelings and our relationship, it feels like he's always being so proactively sweet to me, whereas I'm usually in reactive mode. I feel victorious that I finally got the upper hand in catching Mateo off guard with a display of affection to let him know I'm thinking about him.

A lot.

As in, all the time.

There are *much* worse things to think about.

———

The air is tense with anticipation in the basketball arena. All the Greek houses are crowded into the stands in their pair groupings, awaiting the homecoming results. Most people will walk over to the soccer complex to watch the homecoming match, but first we're all hopefully crossing our fingers to hear the winners announced.

Teegan and I stand on either side of Amaya, arms looped through hers. We all want to win, but Amaya worked her butt off more than anyone to make this a successful homecoming for AOPi. I just hope the judges saw that effort come through.

The president of Greek life at Townsend takes the floor with a microphone and offers generic congratulations to everyone for a great homecoming week. She also talks up our soccer team and their undefeated record ahead of the match, drawing big cheers from the crowd.

"But now, the moment you've all been waiting for," she finally says. "The winning pairing of the Homecoming Championship is . . . Alpha

Alpha Alpha and Omega Gamma!" The TriAlphas and OGs go wild as Amaya slowly deflates next to me. The full standings flash up on the scoreboard screen, with AOPi and AE in second place, edged out by a mere three points.

All around us, people half-heartedly clap for the victors while consoling each other about our great effort and second-place finish. I wrap my arm around Amaya's shoulders and Teegan wraps hers around Amaya's waist. "You still did amazing, Beef," I tell Amaya. "The standard of excellence for AOPi was next-level this year."

Teegan hums affirmation and adds, "Yeah, just sucks that TriAlpha also outdid their high standards this year."

Amaya huffs a small laugh. "It's true—can't control what other houses do or how the judges see things. I am proud of what our house accomplished this year." She pauses, glancing at us on either side. "Still stings though. Especially to stupid TriAlpha."

I put my hands on Amaya's shoulders and look her in the eyes. "Amaya, if you'd rather skip the soccer match and go drown your sorrows in ice cream or slushies or any other form of sugar, Teegan and I will gladly keep you company." Teegan chimes her agreement.

Amaya's eyes soften. "That's really sweet of you, Beef. But I'm not going to make you miss your first-ever homecoming soccer match. Text that man of yours that he'd better make sure they win so at least something good comes out of this day." She pulls me and Teegan into a hug. When Amaya releases us, she gestures at me and says, "I'm serious—get your phone out and text Mateo right now."

Laughing, I pull my phone from my back pocket and see that I already have a text from Mateo a few minutes old.

MATEO

Results yet???

ME

<sad face emoji> We came in second place. TriAlpha edged us out

Mateo sends me a series of Boooo-themed GIFs, making me snort a laugh.

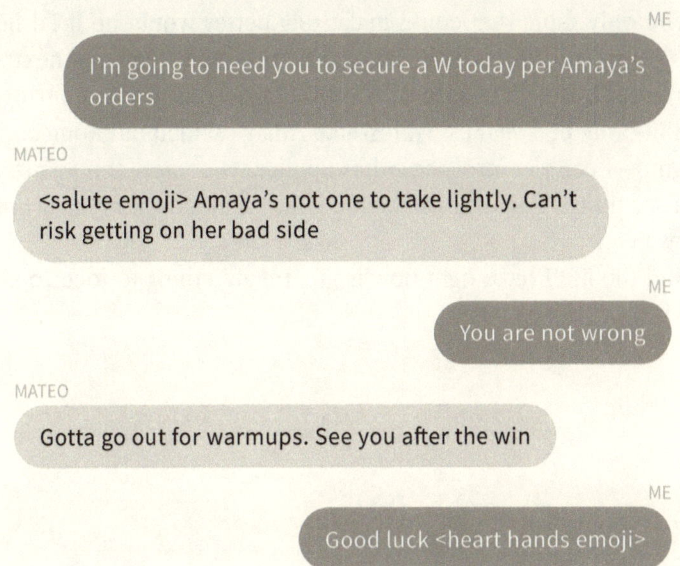

Approximately three hours later, Amaya, Teegan, and I are losing our minds in the middle of the AOPi section as the final whistle signals a 4–3 Bobcat victory. Mateo completed his hat-trick with a third goal in the final minutes of stoppage time to clinch the win, and he's buried under a dogpile of teammates. After each goal he scored, he found my eyes in the crowd with a huge grin. I might have melted if I wasn't crazy cheering every time.

That night, a crowd of AOPis, most of the soccer team, plus Linh, Reagan, and Samantha hang at a local taco shop, reliving the match highlights over chips and salsa. Amaya is sitting across from me, and I'm flanked on either side by Teegan and Mateo (whose fingers are once again entangled in the lengths my hair, giving me constant goosebumps).

A wave of gratitude crashes over me. I have the best friend a girl could ever ask for, times two. I have a boyfriend who makes me feel valued for who I am and totally secure in how he feels about me. I've had an amazing college experience both educationally and socially, finding belonging and connection in Arrow, and yes, I'll admit it, the sorority sisterhood.

The only thing that could make this better would be if I'd heard back from UC Davis about my application and knew my next step was secure. But I've done all that I can on that front, pouring my soul into my personal essay. Just like Amaya said about homecoming judging—I can't control the other applicants or how the admissions staff see things. Focusing on the life I have right now is my only option as I wait.

And the life I have right now isn't a terrible thing to focus on. Not one bit.

CHAPTER TWENTY-ONE

M y *"que sera sera"* attitude lasts exactly two days.

I'm lazily scrolling Instagram as I eat breakfast before class Monday morning when I notice a reel from the #ucdavisschooloflaw hashtag I follow. It's a girl crying and screaming with excitement over being accepted into their early admittance program.

Which means acceptances are starting to go out already. I log in to the website to check my status, but there's no update. Still pending.

I've lost my appetite now, so I throw away the other half of my bagel and trudge upstairs to get my backpack and walk to class early. Maybe a few extra steps among the fall colors will lighten my mood.

Except it's raining when I walk out the side door. Of course it is. Today is the perfect bad-mood cliché.

Putting in an earbud, I queue up my Moody Mellow playlist and grab an umbrella from the basket by the door to walk to campus. Halfway there, my phone rings with a FaceTime notification from Mateo, but I'm too busy wallowing in self-doubt and anxious thoughts to answer. A text pings through a few seconds later, but I don't pause to read it.

What if I don't get in? What if I've planned everything about my life the past six years to get into UC Davis and then they don't want me? What if no law school wants me? What didn't they like about my essay? Were my reference letters not effusive enough? Should I have done something different during college to better round out my résumé?

My mind plagues me with a looping stream-of-consciousness parade of negativity. Even air-playing the piano along with Gracie is doing nothing to calm my thoughts. I arrive early to class and take a seat at the back of the empty room. My professor isn't even here yet. I try to take some deep breaths and blink back the sting behind my eyes.

Eventually, I read my text from Mateo.

MATEO

> Morning, beautiful. Sorry if I interrupted something trying to FaceTime you. Just wanted to say hi before class since I won't see you the next couple of days

I breathe out slowly through my nose. Mateo is just being sweet; he has no idea that I'm upset, or why. My fingers shake as I tap out a response.

ME

> Sorry I didn't answer. Just not in the mood to talk today

Immediate dots.

MATEO

> Are you ok? Is something wrong??

ME

> Saw on Instagram this morning that UC Davis is starting to send out acceptances to the early admittance program. And I haven't received one

> Just panicking that they won't accept me and the last six years of my life have been wasted preparing for something that won't happen

Three dots appear and disappear multiple times before a text finally comes through a couple of minutes later.

MATEO

> They'd be crazy not to want you, Lana. Don't get too worried. It probably takes a long time to get through all the applications. They still have a month to let you know the early admittance decision

I groan. *Ugh, why'd he have to remind me that they have until the end of November to make a decision?* I could be anxiously waiting for another full month.

Clicking off my phone, I lay my head down on the desk. My brain refuses to entertain logic or reason about this right now. Other students trickle in, and when our professor starts his lecture, I sit up and take the most detailed notes of my life. Furiously scribbling every word he says at least keeps my mind occupied.

I go to a kickboxing class at the rec with a couple of sorority sisters before lunch, followed by a long, burning-hot shower. By mid-afternoon, Amaya and Teegan are both back from class for the day.

"Slushies?" I ask pitifully when they walk in the room. They take one look at my wild, air-dried hair and splotchy face, and Teegan immediately grabs her car keys.

Amaya narrows her eyes. "Did Aaron do something?" I shake my head. "Bailey?" Another shake. Amaya's eyes flash with angry concern. "Hold up, Mateo didn't do something, did he??"

"No, no, it's not Mateo," I finally respond as my chin starts quivering. "It's . . . it's UC Davis."

Teegan gasps. "They didn't reject your application, did they?!"

"No, it's still pending. But they accepted someone else!" I moan as I burst into tears.

Three large slushies in hand, Amaya and Teegan listen to me vent all of my panicked thoughts and fears about potential rejection. They wallow with me over sugar and distract me enough to calm my mind a bit. Teegan attempts to cheer me up by doing my hair and makeup before dinner. But as soon as I'm alone, my mind starts spiraling into anxious thoughts again. I probably should have taken them up on their offer to join in a game night several Arrow students were hosting, but I just didn't feel like socializing.

Sitting in bed, I start scrolling through suggested reels on Instagram, trying to divert my mind. A DM notification pops up that Aaron sent me a message. My heart rate spikes, but I open it and see it's a reel of a Golden Retriever playing in a giant pile of leaves.

AARON

Reminded me of you

I watch the reel on loop four times, giggling at the adorableness. Hopefully this is Aaron's peace offering of being friends and not something more. I type back a short reply.

I stare at my phone screen for a minute before responding.

Hoping that Aaron lets it go, I close out of Instagram. Who I'd really like to talk about it with is Mateo. I pull up his name in my text messages, frowning. I'm a little surprised that he didn't try to call again today, or come see me, or at least text me again to check in when he knew I was upset.

It seems uncharacteristic of him when he's always so thoughtful.

My thumb hovers over the call button by his name. I could just call him and talk to him about my day. But he knows that I had a bad morning, that I was upset. Shouldn't *he* be calling *me* to check in? Why isn't he?

This is the first time I've been upset or in a bad mood around him. What if he thinks I'm overreacting and doesn't like it? What if he doesn't like me *anymore? Is he holding out to see if I'll respond to him more rationally? Is that why he hasn't said anything to me today—he's waiting to see if I snap out of it?*

Brow furrowed, I set my phone to the side and burrow into my blankets, pulling a pillow over my head. I just want this day to be over.

———

After a restless night, I wake up with a stormy mind.

I like feeling confident. I *don't* like feeling like I don't know what to do, or how something is going to turn out. I've been so positive about my detailed plan for my future for years now. Everything I did throughout my entire college life was with an assurance that I was checking off each step of the plan.

Being with Mateo shone a spotlight on how unsure I always was about Aaron's feelings and intentions. I didn't even recognize how insecure Aaron was making me feel until Mateo came along. He made me feel so certain of his feelings for me and the relationship we were building.

But with zero new texts or calls from him since I didn't reply to his response yesterday, that confident feeling is faltering.

And I don't like it.

I don't have class until 10:30, but I'm wide awake and pacing the empty room at 7:00. Teegan and Amaya have early classes today, so I'm left to my own devices and identifying with Taylor's panicked thoughts in "Anti-Hero."

Throwing on an AOPi sweatshirt and boots over my joggers, I grab my keys and head to my car before I can change my mind. I drive to the house Mateo shares with three other teammates. When I see his truck still there, I park across the street and pull out my phone.

My hands shake as I stare at my phone, waiting for a reply. *What if he doesn't respond? What if he's over me? What if I've put all of myself into this relationship and he doesn't want it? What if I've put all of myself into my application for UC Davis and they don't want me?*

My breathing is shallow and my eyes stinging as I see the read notification pop up, followed by three bouncing dots.

I exhale a shaky breath and get out of my car, pacing the sidewalk opposite of his house. A couple of minutes later, Mateo comes out the front door, eyes scanning until he sees me.

Dang it, why does he look so attractive this early in the morning? I'm sure I look as crazed as I feel, which is not helping my already bottomed-out confidence as Mateo jogs over to me looking like a magazine cover.

He takes one look at my face and asks, "Lana, what's wrong?" He reaches out to try to catch my hand as I'm pacing past him, but I slip free. My entire body is shaking with a combination of fear, adrenaline, and cold (should have worn a second sweatshirt).

I finally turn to face Mateo. "Did you decide you don't like me when I'm not rational?" I ask, trying to force more confidence in my voice than I feel.

Mateo furrows his eyebrows. "Lana, what are you talking about?"

My chest is tight and my throat feels like it's closing up. I shift my weight back and forth on my feet and furiously play a Concerto with my right hand as I spill out all of my thoughts. "You knew I was really upset yesterday morning, but you didn't do anything to check on me throughout the day. You've only really seen me when I'm happy and poised and determined. Did you decide you don't like me when I'm not?" My voice cracks on my final question, and I cross my arms and pinch above my elbow to stop myself from crying.

Mateo looks stunned and doesn't respond right away. I feel my chin quivering as I stare at his face, so I pinch my arm even harder. *This is it. He's trying to decide how to tell me he's changed his mind.*

Finally, he licks his lips and speaks gently yet firmly. "Lana. Of course, I still like you. I'm sorry, my brain is not fully awake. I'm slow processing all you said, and I'm just confused because I don't know how you could ever doubt that I like you." He reaches out a hand to touch my arm, but I take a step backward, losing my pinching battle as a tear slides down my cheek.

"Then why did you ignore me yesterday?" I barely whisper, not trusting my voice.

Mateo runs a hand through his hair and rubs his neck. "I'm sorry, Lana, I wasn't trying to ignore you. I promise. Please can you believe that?" I sniff but don't say anything, staring at my feet with unfocused eyes.

"I swear I wasn't intentionally ignoring that you were upset. When you didn't respond to my last text, I figured that you agreed with my logic. And then the day was just busy—I had a massive test yesterday afternoon, and Coach thought we were screwing around too much during our morning practice so he added an evening one, and then I had a long conversation with Shawn about what he thinks about God, so it was so late by the time I went to bed that I didn't want to wake you up.

"I say all that not as an excuse—I did know you were upset, and I should have made it a priority to check on you because I care about you. But I tell you that just so you know that I really was busy and not just intentionally ignoring you," Mateo says. This time when he reaches a hand out, I let him touch my shoulder. He puts both hands on my shoulders and bends down to make me look him in the eyes. The tears are actively spilling out of mine now.

Mateo pulls me tightly into his arms, whispering in my ear, "I'm sorry, Lana. I'm sorry I made you feel uncertain about us." My face is buried in his chest, my hands clenched together behind him. He just holds me there as I cry, not saying anything else but just waiting for me.

"I'm terrified that UC Davis won't want me, and you were being all rational and I didn't want to be rational, I just wanted to be upset, and then I was afraid that *you* wouldn't want me when I wasn't rational and I was scared that I scared you away." I'm rambling into his chest, muffled but just loud enough for him to hear.

He squeezes me tighter and then pulls back. Oops, that mascara I was too depressed to remove last night is now smudged all over Mateo's shirt. He wipes tears off my cheeks and tilts my chin up. "Look in my eyes, Lana." I blink and meet his gaze. "I'd never stop liking you because you have emotions. I *like* that you feel things so intensely. I'm sorry that I tried to be logical instead of just listening. This is probably not the last time I'll screw that up. Actually, I can guarantee you that it's not, because I'm always going to want to fix everything for you."

He cups my face with both hands and says softly, "You can't scare me away, Lana. I've liked you for over two years, and I'm not stopping now. You need to believe that."

I nod and lean into his hand, closing my eyes for a second. "I'm sorry—I know I got too in my head and overly worked up and totally blindsided you. I should have just called you yesterday instead of assuming the worst."

Mateo rubs his hands down my arms and takes both of my hands with a smirk. "Well, I blindsided you first at Bookafe, so now we're even."

A small laugh escapes my lips, which feels like an accomplishment after where my mind has been for the past twenty-four hours. I nod my head toward Mateo's chest and say, "Sorry about your shirt."

He glances down and chuckles. "I'll never wash this shirt again."

I let go of his hands and start wiping under my eyes with my hoodie sleeves. "I can only imagine how frightening my raccoon eyes look right now if there's that much mascara on your shirt."

Mateo takes my hands and kisses my knuckles. "You're always beautiful, Lana. Always."

"Yo, Mateo," Shawn's voice pops our personal bubble. "Hate to interrupt, bro, but we gotta leave for practice in twenty."

"Be right there," Mateo calls over his shoulder. "Coach is still punishing us with more conditioning this morning. But I'll call you later today, okay?"

I nod my head. Mateo tucks my hair behind my ear and looks at me with the sweetest smile. I'm crashing down the wave of emotional adrenaline I've been riding, so without thinking, I quickly lean up on my toes and kiss Mateo's cheek. "Thanks for coming out. And for not leaving."

Chapter Twenty-Two

Mateo follows through on his promise, texting me no less than five times throughout the day. At some point during the afternoon, he also managed to slip another watercolor stationary card on my windshield in time for me to find before heading to ELL tutoring. It was short but sweet, reinforcing his feelings for me and that he wasn't leaving. I tuck it into my desk drawer along with the other notes he's given me.

All in all, my mind and heart have settled down, so I'm entirely level-headed by the time I walk into tutoring. Which is good since the girls give me the hardest time ever about not telling them about *"mi novio guapísimo"* for the first twenty minutes. Even though she doesn't understand Spanish, Shaista is starting to come out of her shell and joins the teasing.

After Bible study at AOPi is over, I FaceTime Mateo, per his request. He apologizes profusely again for not understanding what I needed yesterday, and I apologize profusely for overreacting and being unfair to him. It's an apology standoff that ends with a dimpled smile from him that makes me wish I could kiss him through the phone screen.

I start each day logging in to check my application status—always still pending. However, I unfollow the UC Davis hashtag on Instagram because I can't handle seeing any other acceptance videos when my future with them is still a big question mark.

I get an unexpected but welcome distraction from worrying about law school in the form of an email from Elena, one of the directors of the advocacy group I worked with in DC over the summer. They're organizing group video calls for constituents to meet with their legislators to advocate for the Afghan Adjustment Act, and she asks me to help coach the people who sign up and accompany them on their calls. It feels good to have something meaningful to focus attention on while I wait for news from UC Davis. I also love reconnecting with Elena.

Thursday night after the Arrow meeting, we skip out on After Party to celebrate with the soccer team. They officially clinched the regular season title in our conference—unsurprising, with zero losses and only two draws so far. The guys are also still fighting their AFC Richmond costume claims for Halloween, but I'm not at all shocked to find out they unanimously voted Mateo to be Ted Lasso.

The home match on Saturday ends in a 1–1 draw, which is a bummer even though it won't affect their title. Mateo shakes off the disappointment from the match as we walk through Center Square, choosing a place to eat dinner. Afterward, we go to the pop-up costume store to find a Ted Lasso-esque fake mustache for his costume, laughing hysterically in the process.

As much as I love when he plans super special, thoughtful things for us to do, I also love just hanging out doing mundane things together. Mateo himself is the common denominator, with or without the extra romantic gestures.

Halloween night arrives, and I promised Amaya and Teegan that we would stay in and watch not-really-scary movies. But after dinner, I go to Mateo's house to help him finish his costume and take pictures of all the guys transformed into the Greyhounds.

Mateo opens the front door when I arrive, and I do a double take at his clean-shaven face. I guess I knew in the back of my mind that he'd have to shave before rocking the mustache, but I'm still caught off guard. He hugs me tightly, running his hand through my hair like he can't resist. Can't say I object. I breathe in his smell and wish we could just stand here all night instead of parting ways. Alas.

Already dressed in khakis and an AFC Richmond sweater, Mateo leads me to the kitchen table where he has a comb and hair products ready to shape his hair into the Ted Lasso swoop, along with the glorious fake 'stache. He takes a seat in front of me and grins. "Okay, time to work some magic."

I laugh as I pick up the comb, but my metaphorical knees are shaking as I run my fingers through his hair to try to create a faux side part. Mateo has amazing hair, and for as often as he has his fingers buried in my long hair, I've been too timid to reach up and touch his (despite thinking about it—a lot). I rub some pomade on my hands and slowly run my fingers along his scalp and up through the lengths of his hair to swoop and shape it together.

My pulse is picking up steam, and I feel my cheeks warming. Glancing down into Mateo's eyes, I can see by the intensity reflected in his that he's having a similar reaction. I wipe my hands on a towel and give a weak smile. "I think it looks as close as we can get it without cutting your hair," I say as I hand him a mirror.

He softly shakes his head as he takes the mirror and assesses his reflection. Clearing his throat, his voice is still husky as he gives approval. "What do you think, time for the 'stache?" he asks with a wry smile. Giggling, I hold the fake mustache up to his face to see how much I need to trim off to make it the right length.

After cutting a little off each side, I peel off the paper and slowly press the adhesive down along his upper lip. When I stand back to survey the finished product, I burst out laughing.

Mateo grins and looks in the mirror, running his fingers down the sides of his new fake facial hair. He stands up and spins around with his arms out, finishing with a Ted Lasso dance that has me hyperventilating. He finally stops and asks, "Well, what do you think? Is it a good look for me?"

There's still amusement in my eyes as I look up at his face, but I can't resist the magnetic pull to touch him again. I gently brush my fingers along his smooth jaw, causing his expression to sober and his posture to stiffen. "I don't know," I whisper. "I think I miss your usual stubble."

Mateo's darkened eyes reveal an internal war he's fighting as he leans into my touch. He finally closes his eyes for a beat and blows out a breath before kissing my palm and then pulling my hand down, threading his fingers through mine. "Lana, I refuse to let the first time I kiss you be when I'm wearing a ridiculous fake mustache in a house full of my soccer teammates."

He leans his forehead down on my shoulder for a minute before kissing my temple. "And don't worry—the stubble will grow back in a few days," he tells me with a wink. Pretty sure my heart has flipped itself dizzy by now.

A commotion of laughter in the living room must mean that more of the guys have arrived, so we head out to admire everyone's finished looks. Andrés comes charging into the room yelling, "*Fútbol* is life!" with an incredible wig that makes him look just like Dani Rojas. Chris makes a convincing Roy Kent, complete with a well-rehearsed grunt. All the guys lose it over Mateo's Ted appearance, and he takes all the attention in stride without once letting go of my hand.

Once the whole team has arrived, I take a hundred pictures of them before they head to a party and I head back to my movie date with Amaya and Teegan. Mateo gives me a lingering hug by my car, rubbing his hands up and down my back. "I know I'm going to go have fun with my team and you're going to spend some good time with your best friends," he says as he pulls back, "but I'm not going to lie—it's positively killing me to let you get in this car right now."

I smile up at him and run my fingers carefully through his hair and down his jaw one last time. "Go have fun with your team, Ted. And then get to work growing back that stubble." Mateo lightly groans but smiles as I climb into my car.

Driving home, I roll the windows all the way down because I need *all* the cold air right now.

The AOPi house is pretty much deserted as most girls have left for Halloween parties at the various fraternities. Amaya, Teegan, and I decided we wanted to enjoy the quiet night to just chill together. None of us have dared say it out loud yet, but we're all feeling the sober reality that our time together is ticking down.

We have a stash of hot cocoa, candy, and apples with caramel dip ready for a movie marathon. The first movie turns into background noise to our conversation, though, when Teegan asks to see pictures of the soccer team and I fill them in on my interaction with Mateo tonight.

"Ohhh emmm geee," Teegan exclaims as she fans herself. "I cannot even handle how swoon-worthy that is."

"You haven't kissed yet, right?" Amaya asks, and I shake my head in response. "But . . . you want to kiss him, right?"

"If you say no, I'm going to disown you as my Beef," Teegan adds threateningly.

I throw a piece of candy at her. "Of course, I *want* to kiss him. I mean, I like him so much—like, *so* much. And I'm insanely attracted to him."

"Because he's insanely attractive," Teegan interjects, and this time Amaya throws candy at her.

I pop a peanut butter M&M in my mouth and chew slowly, considering how to explain my thoughts. "I think about kissing Mateo pretty much every time I'm with him. But kissing isn't casual to me, you know?" I say. Both Amaya and Teegan nod, helping me feel not crazy. "I guess I want to be pretty certain that there's a long-term future coming with a guy before I kiss him."

Amaya cocks her head to one side. "So, do you see things heading that way with Mateo? I mean, casual isn't a word I'd use to describe you two," she adds with one eyebrow raised.

Teegan's eyes bore through mine waiting for my response. I chew my lip and answer, "Yeah? It's weird because two months ago I was so certain that my future was with Aaron. But after spending the past eight weeks with Mateo," I pause, looking up at the ceiling. "I have a hard time imagining *not* being with him. It makes my chest hurt to even think about it."

Amaya is nodding encouragement, and Teegan is grinning wildly at me, which makes me laugh. "I guess I just have to wait and see if Mateo is on the same page."

Teegan rolls her eyes. "LaLa, we all know that Mateo has been pages ahead of you this whole time. I don't think this is a mystery novel with a twist ending."

Amaya swats at her. "Okay, okay, even if that's the case, Lana still needs to guard her heart a little bit. We can't get ahead of ourselves and her wind up more hurt than she needs to be if there is a twist coming."

I groan and lean my head back, "Let's change the subject now pleeease."

Clearing her throat, Teegan speaks up. "Well, if we're talking about twists, I might have one regarding my own future."

I immediately sit up straight, both Amaya and I staring her down. "What kind of twist?"

Teegan fiddles with her blanket. "Well, I've always planned on becoming a special education teacher—and I really do love all of my classes and field experiences. So it might still be what I do eventually, or maybe even right away, I'm not saying I'm counting it out altogether."

"Spit it out, Beef," Amaya says forcefully.

"Yesterday I met with Kent and Rachel, and they asked me to consider staying here at Townsend and coming on staff with Arrow after I graduate," Teegan explains.

My brain processes her statement for a quick second before I exclaim, "Teegs, that's awesome! You know you'd be amazing on staff!"

Teegan looks a little sheepish and says, "I don't know, I'm a little nervous about it. Of course, I've enjoyed being involved as a student and loved my leadership role at the Summer Project this year. But I'm worried I may not be cut out for a full-time staff position, ya know?"

Amaya face palms at the same time as I huff out an exasperated laugh. Amaya speaks up first. "Girl, please. You practically fill the role of a staff person now. Not to mention you've been an amazing leader here in AOPi. You'll nail it."

I nod my agreement, placing a hand over Teegan's. "Teegs, you love people so much, and you're so kind and caring and just draw people in. Not to mention you're always the life of the party and plan every good social event we ever do. You're a dream staff candidate—it's not surprising at all that Kent and Rachel asked you!"

Teegan's eyes well up as she looks back and forth between us. "You really think so?"

"YES!" Amaya and I simultaneously yell.

"Okay, I haven't officially decided anything yet," she says. "I still need to talk it through with my parents and pray about it. But I feel a lot better about seriously considering it, knowing that you two think I'd be good at it. You know me better than anyone." Her eyes well up again before she whispers, "I don't know what I would have done without you two in college. And I don't know what I'm going to do without you with me every day."

Now all three of us are wiping tears and sniffling noses and hugging each other tightly.

After a few minutes, I sit back and turn to Amaya. "Any life twists from you that we need to know about?"

She scoffs and shakes her head. "Nope. Still planning to take over Kansas City one company at a time," she says with a confident grin. "Just have to figure out where to start."

I don't doubt her for a minute.

Chapter Twenty-Three

The weekend after Halloween, I've already planned to go home to Kansas City. It's my sister's homecoming, so I want to go watch her dance team perform at halftime and see her all dressed up for the dance on Saturday. I've been looking forward to it all semester.

When Friday rolls around, I have mixed feelings: the excitement of going home alongside the reluctance to leave and miss out on spending time with Mateo. We see each other in as many snippets as possible during the week, but between my commitments and his soccer schedule, weekends provide the best opportunity for us to be together.

My mom has big feelings about me driving home before it's dark, so I have to leave mid-afternoon while Mateo is still at practice. Since I won't be able to see him before I go, I decide to pull a page from his book and leave a note on his truck again.

Mateo —

I know I'll see you in just a few days, but I'm still feeling sad to miss out on the soccer match and hanging out with the team or just you or whatever we would do if I was here. I've gotten used to spending every weekend with you, so it sort of feels like I'm entering a twilight zone as I drive away from you. And now I've become the sappy girl saying "I already miss you" before I leave, but it's true . . . I already miss you. Have fun this weekend, but miss me too, ok?

Hugs (as in, literally I want to hug you),

Lana

I slip the card under his windshield wiper at the soccer complex and drive to the gas station to fill up my car. I decide it's worth the bathroom stop halfway to take a slushie on the road. I'm sealing the lid on tight when I hear a familiar voice.

"Lana?" Aaron says as he walks toward me. "I thought that was your car out there."

"Hey, Aaron," I say as I fumble with the straw, trying to get the wrapper off. I bang it too hard and the bottom crumples, so I throw it away and get a new one. Aaron leans his hip against the counter next to me, making me feel even more flustered. *Come on, brain. You've seen Aaron enough times over the past two months that you should be capable of acting like a normal human being.*

"How ya been?" he asks. I look up from my slushie cup and flinch at how close we are to each other. Aaron's arms are crossed, but his upper body is leaning in toward me. My stupid brain chooses to remind me how thrilled I would have been about this close proximity a few months ago, doing nothing to calm down all of my flustered-ness.

But I'm not thrilled now. I take a step backwards and hold my giant slushie cup as a guard between us before answering. "Really good. Enjoying the fall. Still anxiously waiting to hear if I've been accepted to UC Davis. But I'm heading home to KC right now to see my family, so that's good." I take a sip of my slushie since my mouth is suddenly a desert.

"Oh, that's fun," Aaron replies. "Any specific plans? Or just hanging out with your parents and Olivia, Carter, and Dean?"

I shouldn't be surprised by him remembering my siblings' names, considering how much we used to talk. But I still am. "Yeah, it's Olivia's homecoming weekend, so I'll get to see her all dressed up. What about you? Anything fun going on?"

Aaron uncrosses his arms and leans one hand on the counter next to me, the other dropping to his pocket. "Just the usual. Keeping an eye on things at the house party tonight."

I nod. "Yeah, I know how that goes." Because I do—we certainly have a mutual understanding of Greek Life.

"Some of the guys are going to the soccer game tomorrow, but I probably won't," Aaron continues, eyes flickering back and forth between mine. "So, anything else . . . different or new in life?"

I chew on the inside of my lip and shake my head slowly. "Not really. Yeah no, same stuff with class, AOPi, tutoring, Arrow stuff." I pause. "Still dating Mateo, so, ya know, nothing new."

Aaron flinches at the mention of Mateo but quickly recovers a neutral face. I raise my slushie cup like it's the international sign for "I'm going to leave now." Aaron stands upright and says, "Yeah, I should let you hit the road, I guess. Um, I'll walk you out to your car."

"Did you come in to buy something though?" I ask, looking around as I pay for my slushie.

"Oh, yeah, I did, but I don't mind. I'll walk you out and then come back," he says, gesturing toward the door. He pushes it open so I can walk out, following me to my car. I open the door and deposit my slushie cup inside, then stand up to awkwardly wave and say bye.

"Have a good weekend in KC, Lana. Drive safe," he tells me before backing away as I shut myself in the car. I need to pick a playlist for the ride home but don't want to stay here lingering in front of the gas station, so I drive down the street and pull off in another parking lot to pull up my phone.

First, I send a distress signal to the Beef group chat.

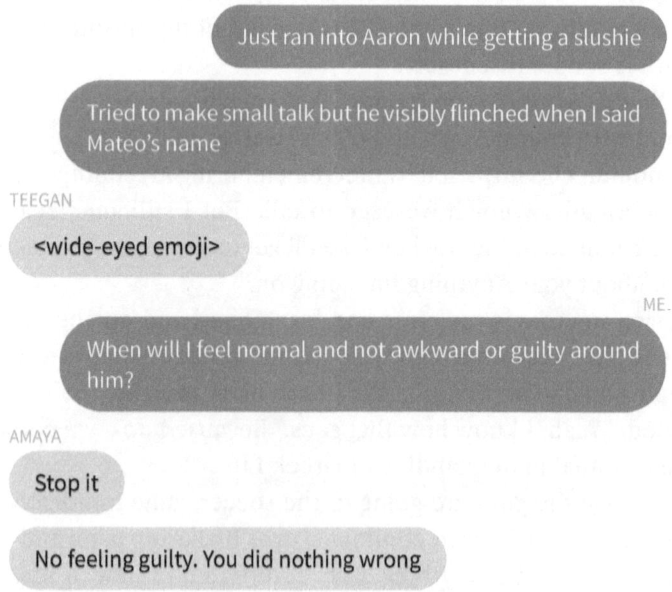

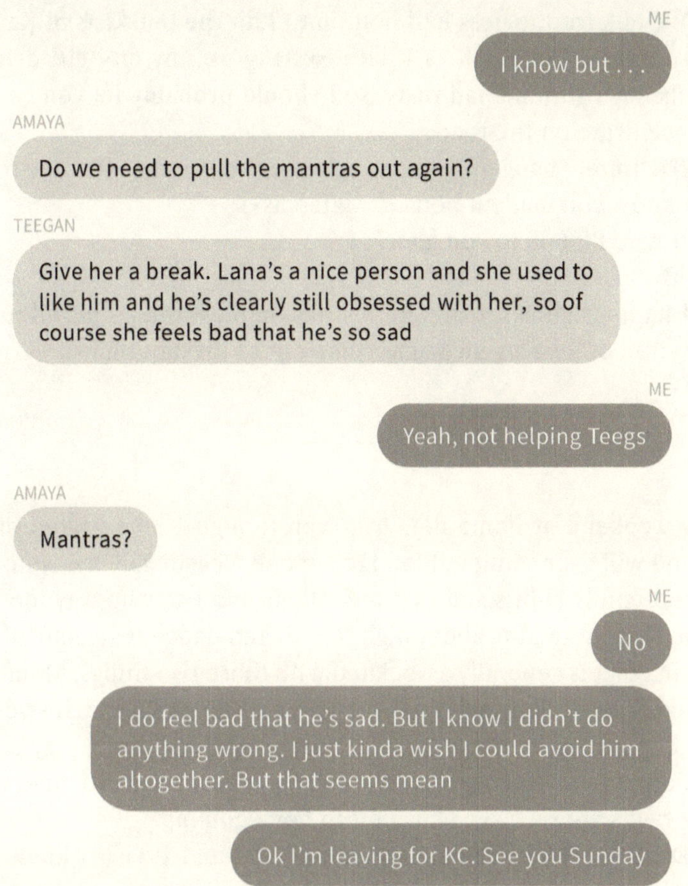

I've just pulled back on the highway after a rest stop halfway home when my phone rings. Smiling at Mateo's name on the screen, I hit the button on my steering wheel to answer the call.

"Hey there!" I say brightly. "Sorry, I'm still in the car driving!"

"Hey you with the fancy Bluetooth car," Mateo teases, making me laugh. "So many wonders of technology at your disposal but you'll still stoop to using a pen and paper."

Giggling, I ask, "So you got my note?"

"Yes. And I'll take the sappiest version of Lana there is, so don't hold back," Mateo says. "I already miss you, too."

We talk for the next half hour until I hit the outskirts of Kansas City traffic. "As much as I hate to hang up, my city girl driving skills have gotten a tad rusty, so I should probably let you go and concentrate on the road."

"Definitely hang up and pay attention to driving. Text me to let me know you made it home?" Mateo asks.

"I will. I'll talk to you later."

"Bye, Lana."

I happy sigh as I hang up. It's the simplest thing, but I'll never get tired of hearing my name come out of his mouth.

———

My weekend at home flies by. Even though I miss Mateo more than I will ever admit out loud to anyone, I easily fall back into the Grant family habits and rhythms. Olivia and I stay up way too late Friday night talking about high school and dance team and all the drama that is generally associated with those two things. Mom and I take a walk Saturday morning to catch up (AKA me answering all her prying questions about Mateo). My dad and I play some cello/piano duets together, and I even get some quality time with the twins after we see Olivia off to homecoming.

Dean is still on the sullen side of life, and I wish I knew the magic words to snap him out of it. I hate feeling powerless to make positive change, especially with someone I care so much about. Still, I convinced him to temporarily abandon his video games to eat junk food watching a movie together Saturday night, so I'll take the small win. I don't know what or who it's going to take to get him on a positive path, so I just pray that God provides whatever needs to happen moving forward.

I listen to my Christmas playlist the whole way back to Brooklyn. We got the tiniest bit of snow flurries for approximately ten minutes this morning, but it's enough to have me fully in the Christmas mood now.

Monday afternoon, I'm sitting in the Harry Potter room at the library working on a paper when a pair of strong, tan arms suddenly surrounds me, and I feel a kiss on the top of my head. I pull my earbuds out and wrap one arm around Mateo's neck, tucking my face right under his chin so I can take a deep inhale of him. I've finally put my finger on where Mateo's scent transports me to—he smells like an open-air spice market in the middle of a Christmas tree farm. I'd like to set up a tent there so I can live among that heady aroma for all eternity.

"I thought I might find you here," Mateo says as he finally releases me and sits down in the chair next to me, pulling my hand into his in one smooth motion. I must not be the only one feeling acute physical touch withdrawal after the weekend apart.

I fill Mateo in on my weekend at home and he recounts the soccer match for me. He offers to walk me back to AOPi before he goes to practice, so I turn to save my progress on my paper. Just before clicking the X on my email tab, my attention snaps to a message in my inbox with the subject "Application status updated."

I freeze. My heart starts pounding, and I turn to Mateo with wide eyes. He looks puzzled and asks, "What is it?" I just point toward my computer screen, and I see his face register the reason for my sudden anxiety.

He takes my hand and says in a low, soothing voice, "Okay, do you want to check it now, or do you want to go back to AOPi and be with Amaya and Teegan before you open it?"

His thoughtfulness calms my nerves enough for me to think clearly. "Yes, that's a good idea. I don't want to open it here in the library," I say as I close my laptop screen. Mateo nods and puts it away in my backpack for me. "But I still want you with me too when I open it."

"Of course," he says with a soft smile. "I'll still walk with you."

I shoot a quick message to the Beef group text.

ME

Help

Meet me on the side porch in ten min. Application status updated

"Okay, Amaya and Teegan will meet us there," I tell Mateo. He holds out his hand to me, which I gratefully accept as we walk out of the library. The familiar feeling of his fingers interlaced with mine is one of the only things grounding my anxious thoughts from taking flight. Mateo takes my phone from me, and seconds later my piano Christmas playlist surrounds us as we walk. My fingers automatically start playing along with Jim Brickman against the back of Mateo's hand, and he just smiles and pulls my hand up to kiss my fingertips.

He doesn't say a word the whole way back to AOPi—just lets me use his hand as my personal keyboard.

We walk up to the side of the AOPi house where Amaya and Teegan are already waiting. Mateo releases my hand as they both lean in to hug me.

"No matter what happens, we're here with you, LaLa," Teegan says.

I sit down at one of the patio tables, so anxious that I'm numb to the cold metal. I open my laptop and click on the application tab that's bookmarked in my browser.

"Hold on, you should call your mom for this too," Amaya says suddenly. Of course I should. I'm so lucky to have these three people in my life who know what's important to me when my mind is too muddled to think clearly. I call my mom on FaceTime, relieved when she answers. I quickly fill her in, and Mateo holds the phone so she can watch.

I close my eyes and inhale slowly. I think all of us are collectively holding our breath, because I don't hear anyone breathing. Finally, I open my eyes and click the mouse to log in with my saved information.

The website takes a second to load, and I desperately reach out and take Mateo's hand with one of mine and Amaya's with the other. I feel Teegan's hand squeeze my shoulder as we all wait.

The screen pops up and everything is a blur except for one word that pops out: Accepted.

A second later, Teegan is screaming and jumping behind me, Amaya is hugging my neck yelling, "You did it, Lana!" and my mom has tears streaming down her face on the phone screen. Mateo's hand squeezes mine tightly, and I don't realize that I'm also crying until he lets go to reach up and wipe a tear off my cheek with a tender smile.

My heart is bursting with joy, and I stand up to jump hug with Amaya and Teegan as Mateo holds my phone so my mom can watch our celebration. I finally take the phone from him to talk to her directly.

The glistening in her eyes and her proud smile feel like a bear hug through the phone screen. "I don't even know the words to tell you how proud I am of you, my beauty. I feel so honored to be your mom." Now the tears are really flowing from my eyes as she continues. "You reached your goal, but I know this is only the beginning of all the amazing things you'll do. You're going to be such a force for good."

My voice cracks as I respond, "Thank you, Mom. You're the reason I'm here. I love you so much."

"I love you too, sweetie. We'll celebrate big next time you're home, but for now, hang up and celebrate with your friends!"

I set the phone down on the table and look up into Mateo's face. I'm surprised to see a sheen in his eyes as he smiles down at me. I reach up to wrap my arms behind his head and bury my face in his neck. He squeezes his arms tight around me and whispers, "I'm so proud of you, Lana. You are incredible."

Teegan and Amaya hug me from behind until I'm the squished middle of a sandwich, making me laugh. When they finally release me, I smile at each of them. "Thanks so much for being here with me. Not just for this moment, but for all the little moments that led up to this moment. I can't believe I get to have the best best friends and the best boyfriend in the world. Every other girl is missing out."

Chapter Twenty-Four

I don't stop smiling the rest of the week. Monday night I FaceTime with my whole family to receive their congratulations. Even Dean smiles and looks happy-ish for me. Tuesday night Mateo surprises me after ELL tutoring to take me out for celebratory tiramisu after arranging for Teegan to lead Bible study without me. I pay the five-hundred-dollar deposit on Wednesday to secure my spot, and Amaya even announces my acceptance at our chapter meeting that night.

My good mood can't even be ruined by Bailey coming up to me at the Arrow meeting to offer her (very shallow) congratulations and condescending advice on how to "survive California life" after growing up in little ol' Kansas.

I even keep my anxious reflexes under control when Aaron comes up to me at After Party. "I heard the rumors that you got accepted to the law school you wanted," he tells me. When I confirm, he says, "Congrats, Lana. I've always known you'd accomplish whatever you set your sights on. There's no stopping you."

"Thanks, Aaron," I say sincerely. "I'm really excited. Are you still planning to work for your uncle's company after you graduate?"

He nods. "Yep, that's the plan. I think I'll take a remote position so I can experience living in another place for a while, though, before settling down back in KC."

I politely small talk a little longer before excusing myself to find the AOPis. That interaction with Aaron wasn't terrible, but I still wish Mateo were here. They have their semifinal match for the conference tournament tomorrow, so they left for Oklahoma today.

Late Friday night, Mateo texts me that they won their match. I immediately FaceTime him, and he answers despite clearly still being in the locker room. I hear the other guys' voices cheering and celebrating as Mateo walks to the edge of the room.

"I can't say I'm surprised you won considering you guys have dominated all season long," I say with a grin. "But congrats anyway! What was the final score?"

Mateo grins back. "Thanks. It was a good match. It was one of those nights where everyone's A-games lined up perfectly. I feel a little sorry for the other team because we beat them 6–0."

I let out a whistle. "Gosh, I wish I had been there to see that!"

"Me too," Mateo says with a dimpled smile. "I've gotten used to you being in the stands—it was weird not to hear you telling off the refs," he adds with a wink.

Laughing, I say, "I can't even try to pretend that's not true. When's the championship?"

"Sunday at three o'clock, so we'll have a light practice tomorrow and watch some film of the other team that won today."

"Well, go celebrate with the guys," I tell him. "Can't wait to hug you when you're back."

When we hang up, I open the map on my phone. It's about a five-hour drive from Brooklyn to the city in Oklahoma where the tournament is being held. Mental gears turning, I send a text to Linh to see if she and the other soccer girlfriends would be up for a road trip for Sunday's match.

LINH

OMG yes. Let's do it. But as a surprise!

ME

We can take my car. Check with the other girls!

———

Sunday morning, I pick up Linh, Reagan, and Samantha, and we drive the five hours to arrive at the tournament stadium just in time for the match. We're all wearing our old jerseys, and Samantha spent the drive making signs for us to hold.

The Townsend section of the stands isn't super full, so we're able to snag a bench on the front row right as warmups are ending and the players get ready for the starting lineup announcements. When Mateo's name is called, I scream at the top of my lungs, and his head whips around my direction at the sound of my voice.

The look of shocked happiness on his face is so worth the ten hours I'll spend in the car today. And then some. I mime shooting an arrow at him, and he catches it against his heart with a wink.

I make up for missing Friday's match by yelling double at the refs today, especially when they totally ignore an opponent blatantly tackling Mateo from behind. It makes me nervous. Missed calls like that often increase the physicality of the match when players think they'll get away with more contact.

A few minutes later, the same player aggressively tackles Mateo before he's reached the ball. The entire Townsend cheering section boos until the ref finally holds up a yellow card. Mateo is still on the ground, holding his left leg. My heart sinks. Soccer players are notorious for their theatrics, but I know Mateo, and he has too much integrity to high-key fake an injury. My hands are over my mouth as I pray he's okay.

Andrés is there, holding a hand out to help Mateo up. Mateo slowly stands and limps around for a few seconds before shaking off the pain and taking a few small hops to test out his leg. He waves a hand to the concerned crowd, eyes finding me to send an unspoken message that he's fine. I finally exhale with relief.

Mateo is awarded a free kick for the foul. With as far back on the field as he is, I'm curious to see if he'll send an assist to a teammate for a header or try to sink a shot.

I don't have to wonder for long as he runs to the ball and sends it sailing behind the keeper into the top right corner of the net. The crowd erupts with cheers as we go up 1–0, and the guys smother Mateo to celebrate on the field.

Multiple mini heart attacks later, we're screaming in the stands and the team is rejoicing in victory on the field. Linh and I hug each other as we jump up and down. "I'm so happy we came!" she yells to me. "Same!" I yell back.

I look up and see Mateo jogging across the field toward the stands. I lock eyes and grin at him. I lean over the edge of the stands when he runs up to pull me into a hug across the barrier. His hands are around my waist, and I hug one arm across his back and clutch the other hand behind his neck as he buries his face in my shoulder.

"You're here," he speaks into my neck before pulling back to look me in the face. He swipes a hand up into my hair, holding on to the back of my head.

"I'm here," I say with a smile. "You were there with me when I got my trophy this week. I couldn't miss watching you get yours today." We just stand there grinning at each other as everyone celebrates around us until a few of the guys come up and jump on Mateo from behind, still riding high on the special adrenaline that comes from a hard-fought victory.

The guys return to the field, and Mateo makes it a point to walk around and shake hands with each of the players from the opposing team. We stay to watch the trophy presentation, but then we hit the road to drive back to Brooklyn before it gets too late.

After dropping the other girls off at their respective houses, I drive back to AOPi. Sitting in my car in the parking lot, I text Mateo to let him know I made it back safely.

MATEO

> Good. On the team bus riding back that way

ME

> Is everyone still hyped up?

Mateo texts me back a photo of Andrés dead asleep against Chris' shoulder, whose mouth is hanging wide open, also sleeping.

I snort.

ME

> <skull emoji>

The three dots start bouncing and continue for a long time. I keep tapping my thumb on the edge of my screen to keep my phone from turning off as I wait for Mateo's message to come through.

Lana. Thank you so much for coming today. That doesn't feel like enough to say. But thank you. Sometimes it really sucks that my parents aren't able to come watch me play, especially in big matches. Looking over and seeing you in the stands, being able to come over and hug you at the end…I can't express how much that meant to me. Thank you for driving down and back to be there for me. I don't deserve you.

Tears spring to my eyes as I read his message. I know how much it meant to have my parents and grandparents on the sidelines back when I played, and that was just high school. Mateo has never let on before how hard it is to have that missing, but it totally makes sense. I'm so glad I decided to get down there today. This amazing man deserves every ounce of effort I have to give.

I'm 100% certain I'm the one who doesn't deserve you. I don't tell you often enough how grateful I am to have you in my life, that you told me how you felt that day at Bookafe and gave me a chance to catch up to you. I'm still a little bewildered why you noticed me, but I'm so thankful that you paid attention even before I did.

I always will, Lana

CHAPTER TWENTY-FIVE

The rest of November rushes by like the Kansas wind blowing the final leaves off the trees. Everyone is starting to buzz with the anticipation of an extended weekend off school for Thanksgiving. I know a lot of people will ditch classes on Monday and Tuesday to just take the full week off, but my studious streak that got me accepted to law school just won't quit, so I'll be one of the few attending every class before heading home Tuesday afternoon.

With the Division II men's soccer tournament looming at the beginning of December, the soccer team still has practice scheduled for the Wednesday morning before Thanksgiving. Coach Anderson asked Mateo and the other captain if they could attend a film-watching strategy session on Friday afternoon. As Mateo phrased it, "Coach's requests are more like expectations." So, even though it means he won't get to fly home for Thanksgiving, Mateo agrees.

When my mom finds out about his situation, she insists that I invite him to join us for Thanksgiving. Mateo gratefully accepts, planning to stay with a teammate who is also from the Kansas City metro. He'll spend the whole day with us on Thursday before driving back to Townsend Friday morning.

My mom is giddy with anticipation, and I half wonder if she called Coach Anderson and asked him to schedule this Friday meeting. If so, I'll need to thank her, because I'm even giddier at the prospect of getting to spend a holiday with Mateo and my family. It certainly feels like a huge step toward the future in our relationship.

I'm attempting to sleep in Wednesday morning, but my mom comes knocking far too early with a long list of preparations I'm supposed to help with. I roll out of my old childhood bed and trudge downstairs in my pajamas, heading straight to the coffee pot.

My dad is sitting at the kitchen counter eating a bowl of cereal as Mom chatters on and on about all the things we need to do to make tomorrow "extra perfect." I look at my dad with a deadpan expression in my eyes, and he just stifles a laugh.

I walk over to where my mom is writing out a to-do list, placing my hand over the pen in hers. "Mom, you have met Mateo. You know that he is kind and gracious and relaxed. You do not need to try hard to impress him tomorrow."

"I have met him, dear," my mom says in a stern tone, "so I know what's at stake. We can't risk losing him!"

My dad bursts out laughing as I face palm and groan. Mom glares at Dad, and he quickly straightens up and turns his laugh into a cough. She is not kidding around.

I play along and help my mom deep clean and prep as much as we can. Olivia is even mildly helpful, enticed by the excitement of finally getting to meet Mateo tomorrow. We order takeout for dinner and sit around the table as Mom rattles off the schedule for tomorrow for the fiftieth time. Mateo will come over in the morning to join us for a casual brunch, we'll get everything prepped and cooking, we'll have time to hang out in the afternoon, and my grandparents will join us for an early dinner at 5:00.

"Ugh, we know, Mom," Dean groans, rolling his eyes.

"You'd better have a more respectful attitude when we have guests tomorrow, young man," my dad tells him with a note of warning in his voice.

Dean looks ready to pick a fight, but I jump in. The last thing I need is Dean going into tomorrow feeling like he's under a microscope. "It's fine, Dad. Mateo has siblings, so he knows how real families act. And he's totally chill—we don't need to roll out the red carpet for him."

My parents let it drop, and Dean sits back with his arms crossed but looking less grumpy.

Despite all my assurances to my family, as I lay in bed that night, all the butterflies in my body wake up and give me anxious energy. I'm not nervous about Mateo being around my family, meeting my siblings and grandparents. I know they'll like him, and I know he'll be so kind to everyone (even Dean) because that's just who he is.

But I can't rein in my thoughts from charging ahead to the future and imagining every family holiday including Mateo in the picture.

Mateo texts me to confirm that he'll be here at 9:00 tomorrow morning.

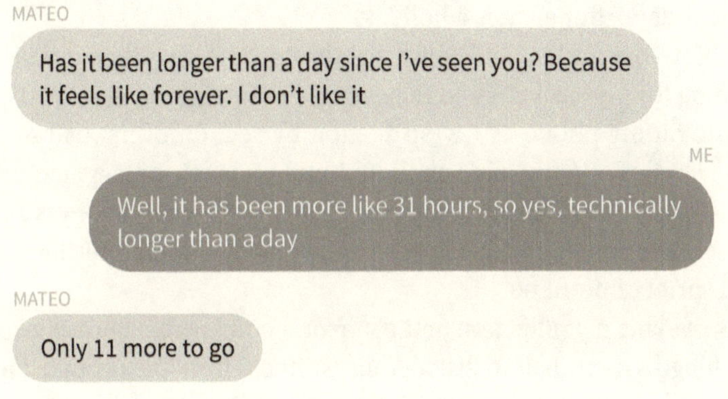

My eyes burst open when my alarm goes off at 7:00 a.m. I'm up and in the shower in a matter of minutes, then head downstairs to get a cup of coffee while my hair air dries. My dad and I sit at the kitchen table, drinking coffee and silently scrolling our phones (although he is more nobly reading the news as opposed to my mindless social media).

I'm about to head upstairs to finish getting ready when my dad stops me. He hugs me tightly and says, "I'm so proud of you, kiddo. I'm going to miss you like crazy when you're in California next year."

"Aw, Dad, don't make me cry right now!" I say as I hug him back. "Let's table that emotion until the spring."

He chuckles and then steps back to study my face. "You know, Lana, your mom may be acting a little . . ."

"Crazed?" I offer with a smile.

"That's one way to put it," he says with a smile in return. "But she means well. You know that we both really like Mateo. And we're really happy to see you so happy. Not just happy about law school, but happy with Mateo. Every parent wants to see that kind of contentment for their kids."

"Thanks, Dad," I respond, giving him another squeeze before heading up to my room.

I may be talking a big game about us not needing to impress Mateo, but that doesn't mean I'm not going to put extra effort into my appearance today. After all, it is a holiday.

I blow-dry my hair and apply slightly more makeup than usual while waiting for my curling wand to heat up. I'm singing along to Christmas music on my phone as I wrap section by section of my hair around the wand. While the curls cool off, I pull on a pair of leggings and an oversized jade-green sweater that I know will make my eyes pop. I tease the curls in my hair into loose waves and add a finishing spray and spritz of perfume.

Surveying my reflection in the mirror, I quickly run a brush through the lengths of my hair to dislodge any stiffness from the product I used. I'm already anticipating Mateo's fingers weaving through my hair, and I get goosebumps just thinking about it.

I head downstairs to help my mom with brunch preparations. I can smell the cinnamon coffee cake already in the oven, an aroma I associate with heaven. We assemble an egg casserole and put it in the oven as we pull the coffee cake out.

Either the smells from the kitchen or my dad woke up my brothers because they're both sitting at the table. Olivia is leaning against the counter, scrolling her phone and trying to act nonchalant. But I can tell she put some extra effort into getting ready today too.

The doorbell rings at 8:55 on the dot, and I smile to myself. *On time is late*, I hear Mateo's smooth, deep voice repeat in my head.

Olivia decides at this moment to drop her cool, casual act and takes off running toward the front door. "Hey!" I call after her as I sprint to catch up. She makes it to the door first but shrieks when I shove her to the side as she's opening it.

Mateo is standing on the porch with an eyebrow raised and smirk on his face as he watches Olivia and I scuffling at the door. I give her a stern look and swipe my disheveled hair out of my face.

"Hey." I smile at Mateo, stepping back so he can come in the door.

Olivia immediately slides in front of me when Mateo steps foot in the foyer. "Hi, I'm Olivia, Lana's very mature younger sister," she says, batting her eyelashes at him. I roll my eyes, but I can't really blame her. I've shown Olivia pictures of Mateo and me together, but nothing can quite prepare a girl to see him in the flesh for the first time.

Mateo is all graciousness as usual, greeting Olivia and giving her a side hug despite holding several things in his hand, including two bouquets of flowers. My parents come up behind us, Mom still in her apron, offering their welcome to Mateo.

Mom goes right in for the hug, and then Mateo hands her one of the bouquets of flowers. "These are for you, Mrs. Grant, for being a welcoming host."

"Oh, you shouldn't have," she says with an appreciative smile. "And you know you're supposed to call me Alexis."

Mateo holds up the second bouquet of flowers. "I hope you might have an extra vase to store these in for the day until Lana's grandparents arrive?"

If Mom wasn't melting already from her own flowers, she certainly is now. Mateo Alvarez, turning women into puddles everywhere he goes.

He then holds up a paper bag. "These are from my mother. She found out you had invited me to join you for Thanksgiving and made a big batch of *polvorosas* to overnight to my teammate's house yesterday. They're a popular Guatemalan shortbread cookie—I'm sure you already have dessert prepared, but she would be honored if you'd add these to the table as a token of her appreciation."

My mom takes the bag from him as she says, "Oh, that is so thoughtful. Please extend our thanks to her."

My dad takes Mateo's coat from him and shakes his hand in greeting, then takes the bag of *polvorosas* from my mom to carry to the kitchen. Mom and Olivia follow him, and I turn to Mateo with a smile. Gosh he looks good, in jeans and a dark gray quarter-zip sweater that accentuates the muscles across his chest and biceps.

"Now my arms are finally open to hug you," he says, pulling me toward him. My head rests against his heart, and I feel him press his face into my hair at the same time his fingers weave their way through against my lower back. I could stand here forever, but I know that Olivia will get snoopy and come back to the foyer if we don't join them in the kitchen soon.

Looking up into Mateo's eyes, I tell him, "I'm sorry you can't be with your family today, but selfishly I'm really, really glad you're here."

He brushes a knuckle across my cheek and says, "Me too. Thanks for inviting me."

I fight every impulse in my body wanting to lean up and kiss him, threading my fingers through his and leading him toward the kitchen instead. I introduce him to the twins, Carter standing up to shake his hand while Dean gives him a small head nod of acknowledgment.

Mom turns down his offer to help with breakfast prep since he's a guest, handing him a cup of coffee instead. Mateo sits down at the table with my dad and the boys, sharing about their recent conference tournament win. I'm cutting up fruit, and Olivia comes to lean her back against the counter facing me. "*He is so freaking hot,*" she mouths silently but exaggeratedly. I give her a playful shove and mouth, "*Behave yourself,*" as I fake point the knife at her. She waggles her eyebrows but doesn't say anything else, returning her attention to texting her friends.

I hear Carter talking about his cross-country team, and Mateo builds him up with admiration for long-distance runners (even though I know as a midfielder he's doing just as much running in a match). I glance over and see Carter beaming, chest puffed up from the praise. Mateo turns to Dean and asks about his interests.

When Dean reluctantly responds that he mostly spends his free time playing video games, Mateo doesn't scoff or drop the subject. Instead, he asks follow-up questions about Dean's favorite games and gaming strategies. Dean sits up a little straighter as he shares more with Mateo's full attention.

"You know," Mateo says, "more and more colleges are starting to have Esports teams. You can even get a scholarship to join if you're good."

Dean sits up *much* straighter as my dad asks, "Esports? What does that mean?"

Mateo explains, "Just like there are teams for athletic sports like soccer or basketball, some colleges are forming teams for video gaming. They practice as a team and engage in competitions just like physical sports athletes."

I've been trying to stay out of the conversation to not disrupt his connection to Dean, but I can't help myself now. "Wait, this is really a thing?" I ask over my shoulder.

Mateo nods. "Yep—in fact, Townsend has a team. There's a guy named Parker in one of my classes who's on it. He told me a little bit about it at the beginning of the semester." He turns back to Dean. "Of course, there are specific games that they focus on, but I recognize some of the ones you said you like."

Dean leans in with more expression on his face than I've seen in a long time. "How do you get on a team?"

"I don't know exactly. I'm sure it varies from college to college," Mateo says. "Obviously you have to be skilled at the games themselves, but Parker talks a lot about teamwork and communication skills. He said he learned to play chess and other games that increased his strategy and pattern analysis skills. So, those would be some practical steps to take."

I can see the wheels turning in Dean's head and a spark in his eyes, sparking hope for him in my heart as well.

Mateo says, "I'd be happy to ask Parker if he'd be willing to connect with you and give you a little inside scoop on the process."

"Yes!" Dean says with uncharacteristic enthusiasm. He seems to remember himself and tones it down a bit before adding, "I mean, if he's okay with it, that would be cool."

Mateo moves on to ask my dad when Nutcracker performances begin, seeming to intuitively sense that less is more with Dean right now. The oven timer beeps, and I look over to see tears in my mom's eyes as she reaches in to pull out the egg casserole.

Conversation over breakfast flows easily. Mateo gives Olivia her time in the spotlight, asking about high school and how homecoming went. Carter is thoughtful and asks Mateo about his family, and even Dean is acting like a fairly approachable human being instead of the prickly version of himself he's been the past couple of years. I reach over to hold Mateo's hand under the table after I'm done eating, smiling to myself as I listen to him engage with my whole family.

———

All the food is prepped to go in the oven at the appropriate times, so my mom sets timers on her phone to remind her when to rotate in each item. With a lull in preparations, we head to the living room with refilled coffee mugs to sit and chat. Mateo takes the love seat, and I sit down next to him, tucking my feet up under me. He places a hand on my knee, and I loop my arm through his with my hand resting on his firm bicep. I'm officially good to go for the afternoon—no need to move for the rest of the day.

Dean requests permission to go to his room to play video games, and my parents agree more readily than they usually do. When Dean asks Carter to play with him, Carter suggests a compromise. "How about we play a game of chess first?" Dean agrees, and I think angels might be singing.

The twins run upstairs, and my mom says to Mateo, "Thank you so much for talking to Dean like that. I sure didn't know anything about these video game teams. But that's the most I've seen him converse with another person in a long time."

She's getting misty-eyed again, but Mateo brushes off the compliment. "It was nothing, no reason to thank me. Most teenage boys don't really want to talk to their parents all that much," he says with a smile.

My mom takes that as a runway to ask more questions about Mateo's family. "Did your family have any Thanksgiving traditions when you were growing up?"

"My mom is all about any reason to share a big meal with loved ones," Mateo replies with a warm grin. "We didn't have any extended family close, but our home was an open door on Thanksgiving to anyone looking for a place to belong. We always had a mash-up of traditional American Thanksgiving side dishes and warm Guatemalan foods like *pepián* or *hilachas* with rice. Trust me, no one ever left our house hungry at the end of the day."

I'm once again struck by the affection in Mateo's face and voice as he talks about his family. I really hope I get to meet them soon.

There's a natural pause in conversation between topics, and Mateo tips his head toward the piano in the corner and says to my dad, "So, Lana told me that you two used to play duets together. Have you played any in a while?"

Olivia rolls her eyes, "Only all summer long while Lana was home. It's all we ever listened to in the evenings."

I aim a throw pillow at her head and hit my target perfectly, earning a classic "La-nuuuh!" whine from her. My mom half-heartedly scolds me while trying not to laugh.

Mateo moves his arm behind my shoulders and angles toward me. "I'd love to hear you and your dad play together if you wouldn't mind."

Heat immediately floods my cheeks, and Mateo gives me that wildly attractive smirk reserved for when he makes me blush, which doesn't help me *not* blush. "Oh, I don't know," I stammer. "It's been a while since I've had any practice."

"Whatever, liar," Olivia rats me out. "You and dad just played again when you were here over homecoming weekend."

The daggers from my eyes aren't working because Olivia just looks at me smugly.

My dad jumps in to further block my way out. "Sure, we can play. Lana, why don't we do the piece we played a lot over the summer? Surely your muscle memory can get you through that one."

"Oh yeah, 'A Thousand Years'," Olivia pipes in again.

"Wait," Mateo interjects, "'A Thousand Years'? Like, the song from *Twilight*?"

I give him an incredulous look. "Do not tell me you were a *Twilight* fan."

He throws his head back in a laugh. "I was not, but my older sister was. She went through a massive *Twilight* phase in high school and subjected my entire family to way more Edward and Bella than any of us ever asked for."

I smile at his response, but my heart is out the starting gate of the Kentucky Derby. I did not mentally prepare myself to play the piano in front of Mateo today, and I particularly did not mentally prepare to play *that* song for Mateo.

The song I poured my heart into all summer long thinking about Aaron. Letting all my angst about how long I had liked him and the uncertainty about what would happen with him flow out through my fingertips in the emotion of the music.

Mom is giving me an empathetic look that communicates she knows exactly what's racing through my head right now. She gives a small nod and says, "Come on, Lana. I'd love to hear you play also. It will be good for you," she adds as her eyes flit to Mateo.

No one else will understand what that comment means, but I'm the only one who needs to hear it.

Mateo, being the sweetest boyfriend on the planet, tries to back-track. "I didn't mean to put you on the spot, Lana. You don't have to play. I don't want to make you uncomfortable."

I look into his eyes—his tender, sweet, captivating eyes—and can't resist. "No, it's okay. We can play." I nod to my dad, who stands up to retrieve his cello, and I move to the piano before I can talk myself out of it.

The music for The Piano Guys' arrangement of "A Thousand Years" is still right there at the top of the stack in the bench. My dad quickly tunes his cello next to me as I glance back through the music to remind myself of the places I made alterations. As much as I'd like to be as good a pianist as Jon Schmidt, I am not even in the same orbit, so there were a few spots I simplified.

"Lana, let's do a quick C scale so I can warm up my fingers," my dad says, but I know he's making this request to give *me* a second to warm up my fingers and chill my nerves. The piano is situated so that Mateo is diagonal to my back, which is good because I'm not sure I could concentrate if I accidentally made eye contact with him. Although, it also means he has a perfect view to watch me play—possibly badly considering how nervous I feel. When I glance at my mom out of the corner of my eye, she gives me an encouraging smile, so I take a deep breath and nod at my dad.

He counts us in, and I press my fingers into the chords of the intro melody until Dad comes in on cue. I'm grateful the music is arranged so that the cello takes center stage for the first verse, giving me some time to block out my worry and settle into the song.

Just like it did this summer, the music draws in my emotions as my fingers move across the keys and I hear the steady, soothing sound of my dad's cello. The arrangement and the lyrics running through my mind grip my heart in a new way.

All summer, my heart cried those lyrics as I played, thinking about how long I had liked Aaron, feeling like I had waited a thousand years, longing for him to pursue me. It sounds super dramatic, but hey, I'm a mildly hopeless romantic.

But today as I'm playing, my heart is stirring with different thoughts—all of them filled with Mateo.

While I was pining for Aaron, Mateo was harboring feelings for me. Did he believe all along that he would find me, that time would lead my heart to his, or did he almost give up hope? I'm so thankful he didn't give up. More importantly, why did it have to take me *this long to find* him? *What's he thinking now?*

The thoughts and emotions overflow my heart, burning behind my eyes as my dad's bow and my fingers fly into the bridge interlude. I force my mind to concentrate on the trickiest part of the arrangement. I make a few mistakes but play forward through them, the number-one rule of duets.

The music winds down to the final seconds of the song until I lightly play the concluding notes. Everything is silent for a few seconds after I lift my hands from the piano till my mom begins softly clapping, soon joined by Olivia and Mateo. I smile at my dad next to me and then swivel on the bench to see Mateo's eyes full of moisture and face full of emotion as he claps.

I think I love you, my mind proclaims as my heart catches at the tender passion in Mateo's gaze as he looks at me.

I'm not really sure how to transition out of our mini performance, but my dad saves me by standing up and giving a flourishing bow, then extending his hand toward me. I giggle and stand up to give a curtsy as my mom praises us. She then further saves me by announcing that we should check on the progress of the turkey and rotate a casserole into the oven.

Everyone follows her to the kitchen, but Mateo pulls my hand to a stop in the hallway. Turning me to face him, he kisses the pads of my fingertips. Voice low and husky, he says, "Lana, that was . . . captivating. You were beautiful." His voice trails off as he leans in toward me, my back against the wall.

For a moment I think (hope?) that Mateo might kiss me. But then I remember that my family is a doorway away. Instead, he cups his left hand on the base of my neck and leans his forehead against mine. "I won't ever forget today, Lana," he whispers.

I reach my hand up and run my fingers along the stubble of his jawline. He pulls his forehead back and turns to kiss the palm of my hand. Drawing in a shaky breath, he takes a step backwards. "We should go see if your mom needs help."

"Yep," I say breathlessly and turn to lead Mateo toward the kitchen, my feet moving on autopilot.

My pulse is silently pounding a steady, *I love you. I love you. I love you.*

Chapter Twenty-Six

The remainder of the afternoon is spent chatting and playing cards amid my mom's choreographed dance with the oven. Mateo even offers to join the twins in their video game for a little bit, as if he needed any other brownie points with my parents.

His absence gives Olivia the opportunity to teasingly wave her phone in front of my face, with a photo she took on the sly of Mateo watching me play the piano. "Olivia Jade!" I whisper yell at her, pulling out her middle name like I'm her parent. I push her into the mudroom for further scolding.

"What were you thinking?! You can't just take pictures of *my* boyfriend without his consent!"

Her face morphs into feigned innocence. "But look at it, Lana. It's *so* sweet. And hot."

I look at the photo more closely. She's not lying. My heart warms and does a little flip flop at the look on Mateo's face.

"He *loves* you," Olivia teases, a little too loudly. I slap my hand over her mouth and give her my best death glare.

"This is inappropriate behavior, young lady. A gross invasion of privacy. You need to delete that photo," I say, crossing my arms.

"I already sent it to my friends group text," Olivia declares. I groan because that one hundred percent tracks with something she'd do. I snatch the phone out of her hands and pull up her text messages. Sure enough, all her besties have sent back responses of fire or dead emojis and fainting GIFs.

"I cannot believe you," I mutter under my breath as I delete the photo from the conversation. As I'm pulling up her photo gallery, she grabs the phone out of my hands and angles away from me. I try to reach over her shoulder to get the phone back, but she holds me off long enough to tap a few buttons.

"There!" she declares. "I deleted it from my phone. I just had to text it to you first." She looks at me with a victorious smirk. My eyes are still narrowed, but no further reprimand crosses my lips. I do want to have that photo.

"You're welcome, sister dear!" she sings as she sashays past me. I can't help but laugh.

The doorbell rings, and I rush to greet my grandparents. I fling open the door and immediately give them hugs around the dishes they're carrying. "Gramma! Grampa! I'm so glad to see you!" One of the gifts of moving to Kansas City was getting to be close to my dad's parents. We live in different parts of the metro, so it's still about a thirty-minute drive between our houses, but they were always present at every special occasion and soccer game.

Olivia and the twins have joined us in the foyer and take turns greeting my grandparents. Dean's uncustomary good-ish mood is still in place, and he gives my grandma a short hug, making her smile. Mom and Dad come to welcome them in and take their dishes and coats.

Mateo is hanging back, so I pull his arm over to introduce him. "Gramma, Grampa, this is my boyfriend Mateo."

"Mr. and Mrs. Grant, I've heard a lot about you from Lana," Mateo says as he shakes my grandpa's hand. Gramma skips the handshake for a hug.

"Young man, we've heard quite the positive earful about you from Lana's mother. And you're even more handsome than she said," my grandma says with a cheeky grin as she pats Mateo's shoulder.

"Gramma!" I squeal, but Mateo just chuckles good-naturedly.

He takes my grandma's hand in both of his and winks at her. "Well, it's obvious that Lana inherited her beauty from both sides of the family." He pivots to me and puts his arm around my shoulders, pulling me to his side.

I loop both arms around his waist and smile up at him. "If you're done charming everyone, we can go in and start eating," I tease.

Everyone moves toward the dining room, but before we follow, Mateo leans down and whispers in my ear. "I'll never be done charming you." His breath against my neck sends a shiver down my spine, which makes him grin.

My grandma has brought her famous cranberry Jello salad and two pies to complete our Thanksgiving spread. Dad prays to bless our meal and give thanks for our time together, and then the delightful chaos of dishes being passed and food being heaped onto plates begins.

We talk about things we're grateful for from the past year. Mateo shares his thankfulness for his soccer team and their successful season, and then adds, "Will you all just think I'm sucking up if I say the highlight of my year was Lana saying yes to a date?" Everyone laughs, and my cheeks turn pink as Mateo winks at me. I notice that Dean half-heartedly rolls his eyes, but a smile is playing at the edge of his lips. Leave it to Mateo to win over even my cranky teenage brother.

As the meal winds down, my mom brews a pot of decaf coffee. Mateo and I clear the plates from the table as my mom unwraps the pies and sets the *polvorosas* from Mateo's mom on a decorative plate. She whispers conspiratorially at us, "Don't tell, but I already sampled one earlier. They're simply divine, Mateo."

"They're one of my favorites. I'll pass along your compliments to my mom."

We linger around the table until my grandma announces that "it's time for these old folks to get to bed." She packages up some *polvorosas* to take home along with the bouquet of flowers from Mateo, leaving the leftover pies with us for tomorrow. We all walk them to the front door to say goodbye, and my grandma whispers in my ear when she hugs me, "He's a keeper, Lana."

"I know, Gramma," I whisper back.

We work collectively to clean up the table, pack up leftovers for the fridge, and load the dishwasher. When we're done, Mateo says he should head back to his teammate's house. "They're being so kind to let me stay with them—I don't want to get back too late." I'm a little disappointed, but considering he's been with us for almost twelve hours today, it does seem fair to let him spend some time with his hosts.

Mateo takes turns telling my family goodbye, giving quick hugs to my mom and Olivia, and shaking hands with my dad and brothers. When he comes to Dean, Mateo pauses to tell him, "I'm going to talk to Parker about the Esports. I'll give him your number if that's okay with your mom and dad." He glances over to my parents, who nod approval.

"I'll walk you out to your truck," I tell Mateo. He turns to put on his coat, and Olivia looks at me and makes kissing faces. I shove her maybe a little too hard, and she bumps into the entryway table, squealing, "Hey!"

I pull Mateo's arm toward the door as I say, "Don't worry about her, such a clumsy girl."

We walk down to where his truck is parked along the street. I'm putting faith in my mother to obstruct Olivia from watching us out the window as we say goodbye. Although, come to think of it, my mom might be the one requiring interference. *Please come through for me, Dad.*

We pause on the sidewalk by the bed of the truck, and I wind my arms around Mateo's waist. "Thank you so much for coming today. It was perfect."

He murmurs agreement, holding me tight against his chest with one hand on my lower back and the other cradling the back of my head. I'm lost in my Christmas tree farm spice market and don't want to go back inside.

Mateo draws back and runs his fingers through my hair, eyes watching as they trail through the entire length before his gaze travels briefly to my lips and then to my eyes. "Lana," he starts, voice gravelly. "I just want to be honest with you. I think about kissing you every single time I see you. I think about it even when I don't see you. Every. Freaking. Day." I glance down briefly, feeling the flush in my cheeks, but look back to meet his gaze. "If I had been following my feelings, I would have kissed you a long time ago."

I smile softly. "Dancing on our first date, right?"

He huffs out a laugh. "Oh Lana, long before that. And countless times since," he pauses, brushing his thumb across my cheek. "But I'm going slow because I want kissing you to be a meaningful progression in our relationship. Kissing isn't just something casual to me."

His words hug my heart with warmth, the same thoughts I'd expressed to Amaya and Teegan. I smile up at him. "We're on the same page, Mateo. And I appreciate you communicating your thoughts so openly."

He smiles back at me and says, "I just didn't want you thinking that I don't want to kiss you. Because I absolutely do. Desperately." I blow out a laugh and look down at my feet before meeting his eyes again. "I never want you wondering how I feel about you, Lana. I'll always be honest with you." Mateo cups my face with both hands, fingers sliding over the sensitive skin at the base of my neck. He leans in and gives me a soft kiss on the cheek before whispering goodnight.

My heart dances a fairy-tale waltz as I head inside. I nibble on another *polvorosa* as I half-heartedly make conversation with my parents. I'm sure they can sense my mind is elsewhere, so they make excuses about being tired and hug me goodnight before heading to their room.

Up in my room, I turn on my Magical Mellow playlist full of mostly ethereal love songs as I remove my makeup and change into pajamas. I cuddle up under a pile of blankets in bed and send a "Happy Thanksgiving!" message to the Beefs group text.

I click to my conversation with Olivia and save the photo of Mateo she sent to me. He's leaning forward with his elbows on his knees, hands clasped together, a slight smile just barely making his dimple show. His feelings for me are on open display all over his face.

Ed Sheeran's voice is quietly singing "Magical," and my fingers tap along with the refrain. I click my phone off and hold it to my chest, closing my eyes. *If this magic isn't what it feels like to be in love, I sure don't know what is.*

The next morning, I wake slowly, in no rush to leave my warm cocoon of blankets. I dart one hand out to grab my phone to check the time. My phone screen reads 9:38 a.m. along with text notification icons. I unlock it and see that Mateo sent me a text at 7:30 this morning.

I smile to myself and sit up, readjusting my blankets around my shoulders. I open my email and see several marketing messages. At first, I don't see anything obviously from Mateo, but then I notice an email from The Piano Guys website with an attachment. I open it to see a digital download of the sheet music to their version of "Perfect" by Ed Sheeran. In the additional notes section of the email is a message from Mateo: *Will you learn this one next?*

Grinning to myself, I immediately download the PDF and send it to my parents' printer. I get out of bed and pull on my slippers and two sweatshirts. Rushing downstairs, I call "Good morning" as I breeze past my parents to retrieve the music from the printer. I flip through the pages. *Sheesh, this is challenging.* I unlock my phone to text Mateo.

Seconds later, the three dots start bouncing.

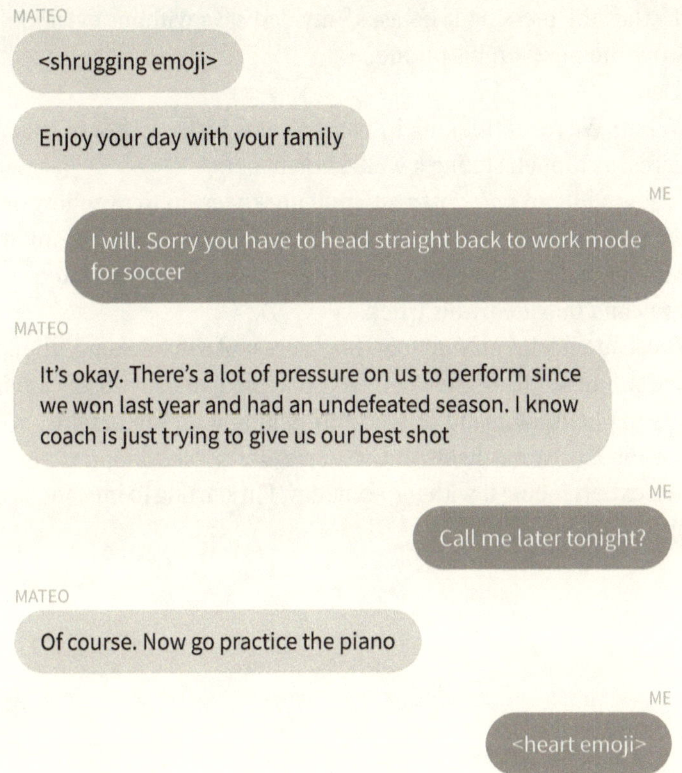

I walk back to the kitchen to get coffee and give my parents a proper morning greeting.

"What on earth were you printing at this time of day?" my mom asks with a mouth full of *polvorosa*.

I laugh. "Healthy breakfast there, Mom." She holds out the container to me with an inviting little shake, and I can't help but reach in and take one for myself. I pour coffee into my favorite Christmas mug and say, "Mateo bought me some new Piano Guys sheet music as an early Christmas gift."

My mom makes a little "*Hmmm*" sound as I sit down at the table between her and Dad. I raise my eyebrows at her, and she says, "It's a very thoughtful gift. From a boy who seems to think very much of you."

I don't even blush, just grin at her comment. "He does, doesn't he?"

"He has my blessing if he asks," my dad says without even looking up from the news on his phone.

"Dad!"

"What? We're all thinking it, Lana. Seems just a matter of time," he declares, as though stating a well-known fact.

I chew a bite of *polvorosa* and pull my knees up to my chest on my chair. Pretending to study the sheet music in front of me, my mind is thinking back to my stolen moments yesterday with Mateo in the hallway and outside by his truck.

Those memories play on loop for the rest of the weekend whenever I have moments to myself between playing games with my siblings, practicing my new piano music, and talking with my parents. We go to see the Christmas lights at the Plaza, and I can't help but imagine Mateo experiencing it with me someday. I'm starting to imagine everything with him.

Chapter Twenty-Seven

B ack at Townsend, campus is buzzing with excitement about the upcoming Division II soccer tournament. I barely get to see Mateo, as Coach Anderson is piling on extra practices, conditioning sessions, and film-watching meetings. I distract myself from missing him by studying for finals, getting quality time with Teegan and Amaya, and doing some follow-up work from the advocacy phone calls I facilitated for Elena.

I'm in the middle of typing a paper for my sociology class when my phone lights up with a text from my mom.

MOM

Check your email for your Christmas gift.

What's the deal with Christmas gift emails this year? I see a forwarded message from an airline. My parents purchased a plane ticket for me to travel to North Carolina to watch the soccer tournament.

Tears spring to my eyes, and I immediately call my mom. "Mom! I can't believe you did that! This is the best gift ever!"

I hear the smile in her voice as she responds. "We felt like it was important for you to be there for Mateo. And it's way too far for you to drive—we would have been worried sick."

"I'm so thankful, Mom. Mateo will be so excited too."

"Well, the gift is half for you and half for him. Ever since he talked with Dean and connected him with that Parker friend, Dean's been a different person. He voluntarily talked to the school counselor to suggest forming an Esports club at the middle school. He's been play- ing chess with Carter and just being all around more pleasant. Mateo even sent me the link to a set of reflex training lights that Parker recommended for us to get Dean for Christmas. Sending you to watch his final soccer matches is the least we could do."

Mateo isn't even here to smolder at me, but my insides are still evaporating from hearing how he's helped my brother. I hang up with my mom and FaceTime Mateo right away to tell him the good news. When he answers, he's clearly running, and good gracious, if he isn't easy on the eyes. Even dressed in warm workout gear, hair poking out from under a beanie, he makes my heart race.

"Oops, did I catch you in the middle of practice?"

"No," he huffs, "just out on a run." He looks away and calls out, "Go ahead, Andrés, I'll catch up with you!" He comes to a stop, breathing deeply. "What's up?"

"I just wanted to tell you about the Christmas gift my parents got me," I say with a smile. He looks slightly confused but plays along. "I have a plane ticket to North Carolina on December eighth."

His face breaks out in a huge grin. "Are you serious? You'll get to be at the tournament?"

I nod and grin back. "Yes! My mom said the gift is just as much for you as it is for me after all you've done to help Dean. I didn't realize you were on a personal contact basis with my mom now," I tease.

He laughs. "I'll take whatever brownie points I can get, especially if it means I get to have you in the stands for the tournament. Lana, this is amazing—you'll get to meet my dad!"

Mateo abandons the rest of his run, and we excitedly talk about the tournament as he walks back to his house (after texting Andrés to meet him there). His limited availability over the next couple of weeks seems like less of a hardship now, knowing that I'll get to be there in person to watch him play.

I alert my professors that I'll miss classes on the eighth, which isn't a huge deal since we'll just be reviewing for finals the following week anyway. Soon, I'm driving home to Kansas City so my parents can drop me off at the airport the following morning.

My flight is on time, and I Uber to the hotel I booked that looked not scary but not too expensive. I text Mateo to let him know I made it, wishing him luck for the match that night. He messages back that his dad's flight was delayed and he'll arrive just in time for the match.

That evening, I arrive at the complex about thirty minutes before the match, scanning the eticket in the family section that Mateo sent me. I'm wearing a sweatshirt with his jersey over the top—thank goodness North Carolina isn't as cold as Kansas right now.

About fifteen minutes later, I hear my name and look up to see a man I'd recognize as Mateo's father even if I wasn't expecting him. I stand up with a smile. "Mr. Alvarez! It's so amazing to meet you!" I hold out my hand, but he steps in and wraps me up in a hug.

"Lana, *que alegria*!" he says, still hugging me tight. "Please, call me Luis, no need to be formal. We hear so much about you, I feel as though I know you already."

We spend the rest of the time before the match happily chatting, then cheer loudly as Mateo and the rest of the team are announced. The ball is kicked off, and I quickly realize I've found the perfect partner to match my screaming energy. My frustrated yells at the refs are echoed in Luis' rapid-fire Spanish shouts. We have plenty of moments to celebrate together as well, as our team closes out the match with a 4-1 victory, meaning we'll head to the final tomorrow.

After the match, Luis and I wait around for Mateo to come out of the locker room, talking like old friends instead of new acquaintances. He tells me more about their restaurant, singing his wife's praises so enthusiastically that I can see why Mateo is so comfortable openly expressing his emotions and his affection for me.

The team starts emerging from the complex doors, and as soon as Mateo spots us, he jogs over and throws his arms around his dad. They stay locked in a tight embrace, having their own conversation in Spanish, and I just stand there trying not to cry at how sweet it is to finally see Mateo with his father.

They pull back to hold each other at arm's length, laughing and conversing at a speed that only Spanish speakers seem capable of achieving. Eventually, I hear my name sprinkled in a couple of times, and they both turn to me, grinning. Mateo steps forward and lifts me off my feet as I congratulate him on the amazing match. Luis is beaming at us and literally clapping with joy, which melts my heart into a warm little puddle.

Mateo sets me down but keeps his hands clasped around my waist. "I still can't believe you're both here. I'm just so happy," he says as he looks back and forth between me and his dad.

"Ay, *tu mamá* is very jealous that I get to meet Lana without her," Luis says with a mischievous grin. He doesn't look to be feeling the slightest bit guilty about that, which makes me laugh. Mateo tucks me to his side and kisses my temple.

"Well, we'll have to find a way to all be together sometime soon so you're not in the doghouse too long," he says to Luis with an equally mischievous smile. "Coach set an early curfew for us tonight to make sure we're well-rested for the final tomorrow. But we can hang out in the hotel lobby for a little bit until then."

Luis is staying at the same hotel as the team, and I feel like he deserves some solo time with Mateo after not seeing him since the summer.

I call for an Uber while they slip into Spanish again, then tell them my plan to head back to my hotel.

"Are you sure, Lana? You can come over to our hotel until curfew," Mateo offers.

"No, you two should go spend some time catching up, and I'm going to go to sleep early," I say, squeezing Mateo's hand. "But I'll see you tomorrow at the match."

Mateo waits with me until my Uber arrives, making sure the license plate matches the info on my app. He wraps his arms around me one more time, whispering "thank you" in my ear before opening the door for me.

———

The next morning, I wake up to a text from an unknown number.

Buenos dias Lana. It is Luis. Mateo sent me your phone number. Would you like to meet for a late breakfast before the match? There is a nice café near the complex.

I smile to myself and check the time. It's 9:15, but the match doesn't start until 1:00, so we have plenty of time.

Buenos dias! That sounds amazing. Tell me the name of the café and I can meet you there at 10.

I quickly shower and freshen up my hair with dry shampoo, carefully applying makeup and putting Mateo's jersey back on over a long-sleeve shirt.

I check my bag in at the front desk to retrieve later tonight before I leave town. My Uber drops me off at the café right at 10:00, and Luis is already there, engaged in lively conversation with the waitress. As I approach the table, he stands up to give me a welcoming hug, then introduces me to our waitress. "Linda, this is Lana, the one I told you about who has captured my son's heart."

I feel the blush warming my cheeks as Linda loudly "*Awwws*" in response. Sliding into the seat across the table, I ask for coffee with cream. A cup of black coffee already sits in front of Luis, and he fills me in on Linda's suggested favorites from the menu.

She sets a mug of coffee and a small pitcher of cream in front of me, pausing to take our orders. Luis and I fall into easy conversation as he asks me more about my family. I'm singing Mateo's praises about how he connected with Dean when our food arrives. Luis asks to bless our meal, so we pause to pray and then dive back into our conversation (and delicious food).

"I'm not surprised that Mateo made that connection with your brother," Luis says as I take a bite of my biscuits and gravy. "He has always had this way with people, of seeing through to their hearts, seeing who they are and loving them." I nod in agreement, because that's completely accurate to what I've seen in Mateo. "My older son, Miguel, he has always been more closed off. Still responsible and hardworking, but he keeps much more inside than Mateo does."

We continue talking about their family, my law school dreams, my childhood in El Paso, flowing easily from one topic to the next over endless cups of coffee. Linda comes over to interrupt us with our check, "Y'all better get on over to the stadium if you're going to the game. It's after twelve already." Surprised at how the time has flown by, I start to pull out my wallet, but Linda holds up a hand to stop me. "Honey, the first thing he told me was that he was taking the check, so save yourself the effort."

I thank Luis for the unexpected kindness, then excuse myself to the restroom before we leave. As we walk out of the café down the street to the sports complex together, Luis says, "Lana, I have an idea, if you will indulge me."

"Of course! What is it?"

"I was thinking, my wife and daughter are so anxious to meet you, and we do not have a Christmas present for Mateo yet. You are already the best gift he has received this year. So I want to make you the Christmas gift for our family. Can I buy a plane ticket so you can come visit us in Michigan before Christmas to surprise Mateo?"

I blink back tears before answering. "Oh my goodness, that is so kind and generous of you. I would love to come and visit, but you certainly don't need to pay for my ticket."

"Ah no, *mija*, I insist. You have made my son so happy these months. And it would mean so much to my wife to meet you for herself. It will honor me to fly you to Michigan," he says with a hand on his chest. "Plus, I don't think I will ever have to buy Mateo another gift again if I bring his heart to see his family," he says with a wink.

"Well, when you put it that way, how could I refuse?" I say, smiling warmly.

Luis looks infinitely pleased at our plan as we find seats in the bleachers. We arrive early so we can sit in the front row, and when Mateo sees us, he motions to his coach and comes jogging over. The bleachers are elevated above the field, but Luis leans down to give Mateo a clap on the back over the edge, wishing him luck.

Mateo turns to me, his deep brown eyes reflecting the afternoon sun and his dimple beckoning me. My heart melts all over again with the intense, open affection in his face as he smiles at me. I lean over the wall of the bleachers to wrap my arms around his neck, squeezing tightly. My hair falls like a curtain around us, and his fingers trace the letters of his last name against my back. I kiss him on the cheek and whisper, "Good luck!" in his ear. When I pull back, he tucks my hair behind my ear with a small smile before running back out to join the team on the sidelines.

The nervous energy from the team fills the stadium. I know how much it would mean to Mateo and all the guys to be repeat champions. Townsend is favored to win, but the opposing team only had one loss during the regular season. It won't be an easy victory.

Both teams play like they have nothing to lose and everything to gain. Each team puts together multiple good shots on goal, but heading into halftime, it's still 0–0. My watch keeps alerting me that my stress level is high and I should take some deep breaths, so I shove it in my pocket.

My anxious energy is reflected in Luis as well. We spend halftime dissecting the play so far, assessing what changes our team will need to make in order to get an advantage. "I think Mateo is going to have to play up farther if we're going to get more pressure on the goal," Luis says, and I agree.

As the second half begins, sure enough, Mateo is playing up closer offensively. He gets a good pass over to Andrés, but the opponents' defender blocks Andrés from getting an open shot, and their goalkeeper sends the ball back down the field.

Thankfully, Chris makes an amazing defensive steal and ricochets the ball off an opponent out of bounds. Our players are able to reset, and Shawn sends a perfect throw-in straight to Jamar, who passes to Andrés in the box. Luis and I clutch each other as we anticipate Andrés' shot on goal, but instead, he makes the extra pass to Mateo in the middle. I hold my breath as Mateo scissor-kicks the ball in the air, sending it sailing past the keeper.

Luis and I are screaming, hugging, jumping, high-fiving, dancing, and every other triumphant action you could think of. Several teammates surround Mateo, miming taking photos of him in celebration. He plays along briefly but is quick to wave them off and embrace all three of the other guys involved in the goal.

Play resumes, and as the clock ticks closer and closer to ninety minutes, the pace of the match is becoming frantic. Our defense breaks up an offensive run by the other team. One of our younger defenders, Alex, kicks the ball back to our goalkeeper, Marc, to give our guys the chance to reset on the field to keep control of the remainder of the time.

What Alex doesn't see until after he's kicked the ball is that Marc is up out of the box, shouting and pointing positions to our offensive players as he reads the defense. The ball rolls behind Marc, and although Chris sprints to save it, he can't make it in time. The ball crosses the goal line.

There's a collective groan among the Townsend fans, and the opposing team roars with excitement as the own goal ties the score. Luis is speaking rapid Spanish to himself, and my hands are clutched against my head. Marc is yelling at Alex, who looks positively miserable. Seconds later, I see Mateo wrap an arm around Alex's shoulders and lean in to speak to him. I don't have to be within earshot to know that Mateo is telling him to shake it off and keep playing hard.

I just want to run out onto the field and give Alex a big hug. And then I want to positively wrap myself around Mateo and kiss him till I can't breathe.

Instead, I settle for a permanent increase in my blood pressure as I watch the final minutes of stoppage time tick off, the score still 1–1. Since the championship can't end in a tie, that means they'll head into penalty kicks to decide the winner.

I look around to see if there are hidden cameras somewhere, because this feels like a sports movie script.

Each team chooses their five players for the shootout, Mateo lining up first for Townsend. I tent my hands over my mouth, heart pounding. He steps back from the ball, then sprints forward to kick the ball into the top left corner of the net, perfectly aiming beyond the keeper's reach. Luis and I cheer and hug each other, but then quickly turn solemn awaiting the other team's first kick. We cheer even louder when Marc successfully blocks their first PK, putting us up one.

Both teams score on their next two PKs, making the score 3–2. My heart plummets when we miss our next shot but the opponents make theirs, evening the score. I feel sick when our fifth player misses as well, and I'm crossing my fingers and praying and holding my breath and closing my eyes hoping the final opponent misses as well to send us into sudden death.

My bubble of hope pops when I hear the loud cheers of opposing fans to my left, and feel Luis' presence deflate next to me. I open my eyes to see the opponents dogpiling their final shooter and our team in varying poses of disappointment.

Mateo's hands are on his hips, his eyes closed and head tilted back toward the sky. My vision blurs with tears as I take in Mateo's defeated stance. *This isn't how the movie script goes,* I think to myself. *He's supposed to win his final match. He's worked so hard. He loves this sport so much. He's the best man on the planet. He's supposed to go out on a high.*

I glance over at Luis, who also has tears in his eyes, and I reach out to give his hand a squeeze. We just stand there, not speaking, both lost in our own sad thoughts as we wait for the Townsend players to exit the field for the locker room.

———

Forty-five minutes later, we move down to the same place we met Mateo coming out of the match yesterday. The mood of the Townsend friends and family standing around is somber as we all process this unexpected disappointment.

One by one, players begin emerging from the locker room doors, met with the comforting sight of their loved ones waiting for them. Mateo makes his way over to us, moving more lethargically than I've ever seen before. My eyes well up with tears again as he leans in to give his dad a long hug. I hear Luis whispering, *"Estoy orgulloso de ti, mijo. Te amo mucho,"* over and over into Mateo's ear. They finally pull back from each other, and Luis pats Mateo's arm firmly before glancing over at me.

Mateo steps toward me and locks his arms around my waist, burying his face in my neck. His fingers aren't even tangling into my hair like they usually do on autopilot—just squeezing my torso like I'm his lifeline. I stand up on my tiptoes to wrap my arms around his neck, wishing I could transfer every cell of positive energy from my body to his. My eyes fill again when I feel moisture from Mateo's eyes slide down my collarbone.

I don't know how long we stand there, but I don't rush to let go. Mateo eventually gives my waist a firmer squeeze before releasing me to swipe the tears away from his eyes. "I'm so glad you're both here," he finally says, voice raw with emotion.

My heart is physically in pain as I watch Mateo's subdued face as he talks with his dad about the team's plans for the remainder of the night. They won't drive back to Brooklyn until tomorrow—they had to leave enough time for press interviews and a celebration if they had won today.

Unfortunately, I have a flight leaving at 8:00 p.m. I wish I could stick around to be here for Mateo, but I need to Uber back to my hotel to pick up my luggage and head to the airport if I'm going to make it on time.

I share my plan, and as we wait for the car, Luis gives me a long hug, expressing how glad he is to get to know me. Mateo is still pensive, so I silently lace my fingers through his without trying to make conversation.

My Uber arrives, and Mateo checks the car against my app, still so thoughtful and protective despite his sadness. I wrap my arms around his waist and lay my head against his chest, listening to his heartbeat for a few seconds. "I'm so sorry it wasn't the happy ending," I whisper.

Mateo sighs, then runs his fingers through my hair as he says, "I'm sad about the match, sad for my team, but this isn't an unhappy ending. I still have plenty to be happy about." He presses his lips to my temple.

"I'll see you back in Brooklyn," I tell him quietly as I slip into the backseat of the car. He nods and closes the door behind me, turning back to his dad.

My parents must have watched the match online, because I have a bunch of messages from my mom about how sad they are for Mateo. What's truly shocking, however, is that I have a text from Dean.

Sorry Lana. Tell Mateo that sucks

I can't help but smile. A six-word text from Dean is quite the show of care.

Exhausted from all the emotion of the day, I fall asleep on the flight back to KC and still feel groggy on the drive home from the airport with my dad. He turns on some cello music, and we ride home in silence.

I fall into bed, but before closing my eyes, I pull out my phone to text Mateo. I know there are no good words to say that are going to make anything feel better, but I need to somehow communicate how much I care for him in the midst of his disappointment.

Made it home safely. Wish there was a way I could make this not a sad day for you. I'm glad I got to meet your dad and watch you play this weekend. I've always loved soccer, but watching you play these past few months has been . . . it's just been the best. Not just because you're amazing at it, but because you're mine. So even though it wasn't the ending we wanted, I'm still grateful to have been there with you

I hit send, not knowing if he'll still be awake or already in bed, especially since he's an hour ahead of me. Three dots start bouncing almost immediately though, making me smile.

Words can't express how glad I am that you came this weekend. Can't lie, losing today totally sucked. But holding you afterward helped me keep things in perspective

Dean specifically asked me to tell you "that sucks" so you have officially won him over to the Mateo fan club <winky face emoji>

MATEO

Speaking of fan clubs, my dad is fighting me for the presidency of yours. He won't stop raving about you. It's legit making my mom furious that she wasn't here

ME

Your dad is precious. I could talk to him all day. It's making more and more sense where you get your magnetism. You both make people feel so important

MATEO

Just wait till you get to meet my mom. She could melt the coldest heart with her kindness. And her food! We'll have to find a way to make it happen

I smile to myself, thinking about the surprise Luis has in store for Mateo.

ME

I hope so

You need to rest. Go to sleep!!

MATEO

I will now. Good night Lana

ME

Night <heart emoji> <heart emoji>

Chapter Twenty-Eight

Eight days later, I'm on another airplane, this time flying north to Grand Rapids, where Mateo's sister, Isabel, will pick me up from the airport. With my parents' enthusiastic support of the trip, Luis and I coordinated dates for me to fly up for a few days. His wife, Rosa, and Isabel are both in on the surprise, but Mateo has no idea.

It was *so* hard to keep a secret from him, especially since we had more free time during finals week to spend together than we had all semester long. It's amazing how much schedules open up when classes and soccer practices are both over.

The plane begins its descent, and thirty minutes later, I'm wheeling my carry-on through the airport, following the ground transportation signs. Isabel got my number from Luis and texted me that she was here, assuring me that she would recognize me instantly from "the zillion photos" Mateo has shown her.

Sure enough, the second I exit the automatic doors, I hear my name called out just before a woman I assume to be Isabel nearly bowls me over in a hug.

Laughing, I hug her back. "The Michigan tourism department should hire you to greet all visitors at the airport," I say as I draw back to look at her. "It's so great to meet you, Isabel."

She shares Mateo's same skin tone and eyes, though hers are a shade darker than his. Her hair falls just to her shoulders, and deep dimples show up in both cheeks with her warm smile.

"Call me Isa. All my family does. I can't believe I'm *finally* getting to meet you! Ay, my mom is *so mad* that I'm seeing you before her, but there's no way she could've left the restaurant today without raising suspicion," Isabel chatters. She loops her arm through mine and leads the way to the parking garage. "I've been hearing about you for so long—I thought I would never meet you in the flesh, and now here we are."

"It's only been a few months," I say with a chuckle, but Isabel immediately waves her free hand at me as if dismissing away my comment.

"*Chica*, no, Mateo has been telling me about you for *years*," she says firmly. "Literally, years. It's about time he finally snatched you away from that dumb other boy."

My cheeks warm. I knew that Mateo had liked me that long, but I had no idea that he openly talked about it with his sister, or that he had explained the situation with Aaron to her. That makes his feelings for me all these years seem that much more real.

Isabel unlocks her car, and I slide my suitcase into the backseat before sitting next to her in the passenger side. "So did you like the playlist we made for your first date?" Isabel asks as she backs out of the parking spot.

"Wait, you made that playlist? Mateo did not mention that," I say with a laugh.

Isabel *tsks*. "Of course, he'd take all the credit. He told me that you listened to chill music, and he knew that you liked Taylor Swift and the cello, but I took it from there. He listened to what I put together and deleted a couple of songs and added a few others, but consider me the DJ of your relationship." Isabel makes a small bowing gesture. I can tell I'm going to have a great time getting to know Isabel. I'm grateful we have this hour drive alone together.

She pulls no punches and jumps right into the deep end as she pulls onto the highway. "So, you really didn't like Mateo before he asked you out? You were just obsessed with that other guy the whole time?"

I groan and bury my face in my hands. "Isa, you couldn't throw me a soft pitch question first?"

She *tsks* again. "Sorry no, *hermana*, you're a soccer player, not softball. We get straight into it," she says with a playful smile as she glances over at me.

"Okay, okay, it's true, Mateo wasn't really on my radar. Like, at all," I admit. I briefly fill her in on how I started to like Aaron at our first

Summer Project and was just kinda stuck on him despite him being so cagey about the status of our relationship. Or lack thereof.

Isabel frowns. "Ayyyy *dios mío*, then it's my fault it took so long for you and Mateo to finally get together. Maybe if he was there that summer you would have noticed him sooner."

Mateo mentioned that he spent that summer at home because Isabel was having a hard time, and as much as I'm dying to know the details, I don't want to make her share if she doesn't want to. "Nothing is your fault Isabel, and we're together now, so it's all turned out okay. It's good that Mateo got to spend that summer here with family."

"He hasn't told you anything about that time, has he," Isabel says, more as a statement than a question. "Of course, he would be too considerate to tell you about my bad choices."

I wait silently as she changes lanes to pass a car. Despite what looks like deep, recent snow, the roads are completely clear. Props to Michigan's winter preparedness.

"I went off to college not really knowing what I wanted to do," Isabel begins. "But my parents were so adamant about wanting us to get a college education, and Miguel was doing so well at Michigan, so I figured I should just go to a community college and get some gen eds out of the way until I decided what I wanted to major in. Unfortunately, the only thing I wound up majoring in was guys. And partying."

Isabel goes on to tell me about the guy she started dating toward the end of her freshman year who eventually introduced her to opioids. She failed out by the end of the fall semester sophomore year and moved in with her boyfriend, despite her parents' pleas to come back home.

"Mateo and I are a year and a half apart in age, but only a grade apart in school, so this was happening during his freshman year at Townsend," Isabel explains. "Right before spring break, I overdosed and almost died—I would have if not for the paramedics responding quickly."

My heart drops. "Isa, that's awful. It must have been terrifying to wake up in the hospital," I say quietly, watching Isabel as she watches the road.

She shrugs one shoulder. "It was awful, but at the same time, it was the best thing that could have happened. It woke me up to the fact that I needed help. Seeing my parents scared that their only daughter was going to die finally snapped me out of it. I went straight to rehab.

"I moved back in with my parents after rehab but kept attending weekly meetings. Mateo coming home that summer to support me meant the world, and hearing about how he had grown in his faith at college opened me up to being interested in going back to church with him. I found the missing piece, the strength outside myself that I needed to stay clean and keep growing. Between Mateo going with me to church, my parents giving me a place to land, a great therapist, and my sponsor at my recovery meetings, I had the support I needed to keep me on track," Isabel concludes.

I'm momentarily speechless, so blown away at the resilience of Mateo's family and all they've faced. "Thanks for trusting me with that part of your story, Isa. I'm sure it must be hard to talk about," I finally say.

"It gets a little easier every time I talk about it, and I know that God can use me sharing my story to help other people," Isa shares. "And now I finally know what I want to do with my future. I'm going back to college so I can become a school counselor. I hope I can use my experience to help high school girls be better prepared and informed to make decisions about their futures."

"That's amazing, Isa!" I exclaim. "When will you start?"

"I'm working as a para-educator in our local school district right now, but I'll start taking night classes next semester and transition full time eventually," she says proudly.

Isabel asks a few questions about my college experience and the law school process. Before I know it, we're slowing *way* down as we pull into the outskirts of Hart. My heart starts pounding with anticipation.

"So, what's the surprise plan here?" I ask.

"Mateo was helping my parents with the Sunday lunch rush, but then Mom was supposed to convince him that they could all go home to take a break mid-afternoon before going back for dinner service. So we'll go surprise them at home, and then we'll all go back to the restaurant tonight. It's closed tomorrow, so you'll have the day to hang out with my parents," Isabel explains. "And I'll come back over after school is out."

I nod as Isabel slows the car and pulls into a driveway. The single-story bungalow is decked out with Christmas lights and a huge wreath on the front door. Excitement rushes through me at the thought of seeing Mateo, especially surprising him.

Isabel tells me to wait for a minute in the car, then bounds up the porch steps to swing open the front door. I hear her yelling, "Hey! *Hermano*! Come help me bring something in from the car! *Apúrate*!"

She returns and leans her head in the driver's door with a merry twinkle in her eye. "Okay, wait till he comes down the steps and then open up the door!"

Seconds later, I see Mateo come out the front door, and my heart is suddenly in my throat. It's only been a few days since I last saw him, but watching him come out of his childhood home, knowing I'm about to spend time with him and his family, has me feeling all sorts of ways.

The fact that he looks incredibly hot in jeans and a fitted long-sleeve tee, with slightly longer than usual stubble is not helping matters.

I see Luis come out on the porch right after Mateo with a wide grin, followed closely by a beautiful woman who has to be Rosa.

"Sheesh, practice a little patience, Isa," Mateo is teasing as he walks toward the car. He jolts to a stop with a look of total shock the moment I stand up out of the car and close the door.

"No way!" he exclaims, glancing at Isabel and then back at his parents, who are all beaming at him. The next moment he's racing toward me and scoops me into his arms, twirling me around as I laugh.

"You're here!" he says as he draws back to look into my eyes. "I can't believe you're here! Am I dreaming? Pinch me," he adds with that dimpled smile.

"Hey, no pinching allowed, remember?" I tease before leaning in to give him another hug. His hands are woven through my hair against my back, clutching me like he'll never let go. "All credit goes to your dad—this was his idea," I say as I tip my head back to smile up at Mateo.

My mention of his dad seems to remind him that we're standing in front of his house with his family. He moves to my side with one arm around my shoulders, and we walk toward the porch. "Apparently, you've already met Isa, and you know my dad," Mateo says as Luis grins and tips his head at me. "But Lana, meet my mom, Rosa. *Mamá*, this is Lana."

Rosa has stepped down to meet us on the walk up to the porch, and she immediately pulls me into a tight embrace. "*El corazón de mi hijo*, finally I meet you," she says with such tenderness that tears spring to my eyes. She pulls back with her hands on my shoulders, looking me over with a soft smile. "You're so beautiful, and so kind, I can already tell," Rosa declares in beautifully accented English as she places a hand on my cheek.

"It's so good to meet you, too," I reply. "Thank you for inviting me into your home at such a busy time before Christmas."

"You are so dear to our Mateo, you are already family, Lana," she asserts. "And your parents welcomed Mateo at Thanksgiving when he couldn't be home with us. That meant so much to this mother's heart."

"My parents loved having him with us, and we loved the *polvorosas* you sent," I gush to her. "In my suitcase, I have a container of home-made peanut brittle my mom made for you."

Rosa smiles widely and gestures toward the front door. "Come in, come in! Let's get out of the cold!" I look back at Mateo in time to see a sheen of moisture in his eyes. Luis steps forward to wrap me up in a hug, then announces he'll carry in my suitcase from Isabel's car. Mateo threads his fingers through mine and leads me up the porch steps into the house.

"It's all making a lot more sense now why my mom was so worried about cleaning the house yesterday," he says with a smirk. "I still can't believe you're here. I'm floored that my dad thought this up and pulled off the surprise."

"Hey, give some credit where credit is due!" Isabel exclaims with a whine as she comes in behind us. She pops her fists on either hip and says, "*Tu novia* wouldn't be standing here if I didn't drive to the airport."

Mateo gives Isabel a teasing noogie on the head, earning an exasperated swat from her, but then he wraps an arm around her in a hug and gives her a brotherly peck on the top of her head. "A million thanks to you, *hermana*. I owe you big time."

Rosa leads me to Isabel's old room to put my suitcase away and take a few minutes to freshen up after traveling. I come out of the bathroom, smiling as I listen to the spirited Spanish conversation coming from the kitchen. I pause in the hallway, hiding to listen to Mateo's voice as he converses with his family, breath catching every time I hear my name. I always love the sound of his voice saying my name, but hearing it in the midst of this conversation with his family makes my heart race.

I make my way into the kitchen, where Isabel is perched on top of the counter with Mateo leaning against it next to her. Luis has his arm around Rosa leaning against the cabinets opposite of them. "Lana! We were just talking about you," Isabel declares exuberantly.

Mateo's face lights up at me, and he raises his arm to welcome me to tuck myself into his side. I lean into him as I laugh. "I'm at a serious disadvantage here being the only one who isn't bilingual."

"Don't worry, everyone's just discussing how much we love you," Isabel assures me, with a wink and mischievous smile in Mateo's direction. Luis stifles a laugh.

Mateo clears his throat and says, "We were talking about the plan for the rest of the day. Would you be okay coming with us to the restaurant for the evening?"

I dance up on my toes and let go of Mateo to clap my hands. "Yes! I've wanted to see the restaurant ever since Mateo told me about it!" I turn to Rosa. "He raves about your cooking, and I've been dying to try it."

Rosa waves me off, but the pleased look on her face shows she appreciates the praise. "Oh, it's nothing too special," she says. "You Americans are more accustomed to Mexican food, so you'll see a lot of familiar things on the menu. But I add my Guatemalan flair wherever I can."

"Mamá, you say that as though your own grandfather wasn't Mexican," Isabel teases. Rosa simply shrugs, and I stifle a laugh.

After standing around chatting a bit more, we make our way to the restaurant. Isabel takes her car so she can drive straight home after, and we take Mateo's truck so we can leave early if I get tired. I appreciate the few minutes alone with Mateo as we make the short drive to "downtown" Hart. There's a small amphitheater overlooking Hart Lake, which Mateo says is used for musical performances throughout the summer. There's a big festival and fireworks show for Fourth of July. Mateo points out other noteworthy places from his upbringing as we drive, and I'm loving getting this deeper glimpse into his life.

We pull up to a brick building on the corner with big windows brightened by multi-color Christmas lights. The sign above the door reads *La Mesa de Familia.* "The Family Table," I read aloud, and Mateo gives me a nod of approval.

Heading inside, I look around and take it all in. Vibrant colors, tantalizing smells, sounds of animated conversations and laughter fill the air. The host stand at the front is painted with a Guatemalan flag, and upbeat Spanish music plays over the speakers.

I grin up at Mateo. "This place is amazing."

He smiles back at me. "*La Mesa* is like the sixth member of our family. Miguel, Isabel, and I all grew up here. We worked every job from waiting tables to washing dishes, cooking to unloading deliveries. This place helped raise us."

Mateo quickly shows me around. Luis and Rosa are already back in the kitchen cooking, and Isabel is waiting tables. Mateo tells me we're on host duty, greeting guests, showing them to their tables, and taking payments at the cash register.

Well, *he's* on duty. I mostly just sit on a stool next to him, admiring how attractive he looks here in his element, chatting with people who have known him his whole life. When it starts to slow down later in the evening, I ask Mateo if it would be okay for me to go watch his mom cook. "She would definitely love to show off for you," he responds with a grin.

I head back to the kitchen, announcing my presence to Rosa. I watch her gracefully move through the kitchen, stirring, frying, and spooning sauces over food on plates to send out to hungry guests. She truly is impressive.

Orders slow to a trickle as the hour grows later, and Rosa starts heaping a little of everything onto a plate for me to taste. Luis takes over preparing the handful of orders that come through as Rosa stands with me, explaining each dish as I take a bite, her smile widening as I moan in pleasure with each one. "Rosa, this is all so delicious. I can't imagine getting to eat like this every day!"

"Now you see why I was out running for soccer all the time—I had to work off all the calories my mom fed me," Mateo's voice says behind me. I turn to see him sauntering into the kitchen. "But make sure you save some room for dessert, because Mamá makes the best *mole de platano* you'll ever eat."

By the time I finish my plate of samples, I'm completely stuffed, but I find room in a second stomach when Rosa presents me with a dish of fried plantains covered in *mole* sauce, sprinkled with cinnamon and sesame seeds. The hint of heat from the chili and the spiciness of the cinnamon balance out the sweetness of the chocolate.

It's to die for. "I want to eat this every day for the rest of my life," I tell Rosa and Mateo as I lick my spoon. Rosa smiles approvingly before moving to clean up the food prep area.

"In the ultimate dessert tournament, *tiramisu* and *mole de platano* are the top two finalists—which will be the winner?" Mateo asks me with a raised eyebrow.

"Ugh, don't make me answer that!"

We stay to help clean up the kitchen and wipe down the tables. Luis and Rosa have a process to close the restaurant until Tuesday, so they send Mateo and me home after I stifle my third yawn. After an early morning getting to the airport and with a belly full of amazing food, I'm ready to doze off.

We walk in the front door, and I lazily stretch my arms above my head as I yawn yet again. Mateo slips his arms around me from behind, pulling my back against his chest and burying his face into my neck. He inhales deeply, then says quietly, "You should go ahead and get some sleep. There's no telling exactly what time my parents will get back home."

Another yawn breaks through at that exact moment, so I nod my head in agreement. "What's the plan tomorrow?"

"The restaurant is closed on Mondays, so we'll all be able to relax and just hang. Isabel will come over for dinner after school is over. I'll get up early to shower in the morning so you can sleep in and then have the bathroom," he says.

Mateo is so thoughtful about literally everything. Here in his hometown, getting to know his family, I'm understanding more and more how he comes by all his incredible-ness.

He tucks my hair behind my ear as he tells me goodnight. I hear Mateo in the kitchen loading the dishwasher as I leave the bathroom in my pajamas. I'm tempted to go back out to talk to him, but my heavy eyelids are telling me to go to bed.

I curl up in Isabel's old bed, feeling cozy under layers of heavy blankets. I laugh when I notice an old *Twilight* poster on the door of the closet. Sleep overtakes me quickly as I close my eyes with a smile.

Chapter Twenty-Nine

I sleep like a rock and wake to the sound of my alarm at 8:00. I gather my toiletry bag and clothes for the day and poke my head out in the hallway. I hear Mateo's hushed voice along with his parents coming from the kitchen, so I turn into the empty bathroom.

There's a towel waiting on the counter. After showering, I put on a pair of jeans and a dark plum sweater, then add some light makeup. I need to let my hair air dry for a little while before blow drying it, or I'll be in here forever with my travel hair dryer.

I enter the kitchen to enthusiastic greetings from Luis and Rosa, who are sitting at the table with Mateo. All three immediately stand up, Luis to pour me a cup of coffee, Rosa to prepare a plate of breakfast, and Mateo to wrap me up in a hug.

We sit down at the table, and Rosa places a plate filled with eggs, black beans, and corn tortillas in front of me. I take a sip of coffee, then fill one of the tortillas to take a bite.

"Yummm." I swallow and turn to Mateo. "When you said you had family breakfasts, you mean you ate like this every morning growing up?"

He grins and nods, squeezing his mother's shoulder. "Sometimes it was fried plantains or potatoes instead of tortillas, but pretty much yes. A home-cooked meal together was always important, right Mamá?"

We spend the morning leisurely drinking coffee. I ask Luis and Rosa about their love story, and they look at each other with lovey-dovey eyes as they take turns sharing perspectives. Luis is constantly touching Rosa—holding her hand, a caress on the shoulder, a quick kiss on her cheek. It's easy to see where Mateo gets his tendency toward physical affection from, and I'm suddenly very grateful to Luis.

After helping clean up the breakfast dishes, I excuse myself to dry and curl my hair before it gets too out of control. I'm halfway done curling when Mateo pokes his head into Isabel's room. "Is it okay if I sit in here with you?" he asks my reflection in the mirror, standing behind me.

I give a wry smile. "Absolutely not, you're supposed to think my hair magically looks good all the time."

Mateo grins back, taking a seat on the edge of the bed next to me. "I grew up with a sister, so I already know that's not true, and you already know that I think you're stunning regardless of whether you've curled your hair or not."

We chat about the plans for the day—making Guatemalan *tamales* for dinner then driving around to look at Christmas lights—as I finish curling. I unplug the curling wand and wait for my hair to cool. When I start to run my fingers through to loosen the curls into waves, Mateo stands up and stops me. "Hold on, this part I can help with. You may have noticed I have a slight obsession with your hair."

I give a soft laugh and answer, "Yes, I did catch on to that."

"Just the consequence of finally being able to run my fingers through it after years of imagining what it would be like." His smile is contemplative as his fingers slowly slide through sections of my hair, breaking up the curls and sending tingles across my scalp.

When he's finished, he wraps his arms around my waist and notches his head in the crook of my neck and shoulder. I grasp onto his arms and lean back into him, just staring at each other in our reflection.

Mateo gently kisses the sensitive skin right by my ear and then whispers, "I'm so glad you're with me. Not just here with me now in Michigan, but here with me in general, always."

It would be so easy to just turn my head and catch his lips. My brain saying no is about to be defeated by my heart saying yes when Rosa calls us from the kitchen. Mateo kisses my knuckles as he takes my hand to lead us from the room.

We spend the rest of the day playing card games, assisting Rosa in making *tamales*, and drinking another full pot of coffee between the four of us. Rosa teaches me how to make *polvorosas*, and Isabel joins us after school just in time to finish off cooking the *tamales*. Mateo FaceTimes Miguel to introduce us virtually, then props the phone up at the table so he can be part of the dinner conversation.

Mateo and I do the dishes while Rosa and Isabel make spiced hot chocolate to accompany the *polvorosas* for our Christmas lights tour. We all pile into the car with warm mugs and Christmas music blaring as we slowly drive around. I'm not mad about the opportunity to sit snuggled close to Mateo. The charm of a small town is extra enchanting during the holidays, with everyone going all-out on lights and yard displays.

When Isabel leaves later that night, she gives me an extra-long hug and whispers to me, "You make me so happy. You make *all* of us so happy because you make Mateo the happiest I've ever seen him. And that's saying something because he's been a happy guy his whole life."

I squeeze her tightly and whisper back, "Feelings mutual."

When I come out to the kitchen Tuesday morning, Mateo informs me that the weather should be warmer today, so he wants to take me on a short hike to see his favorite parts of the lake.

After breakfast, I layer on my thick fleece jacket over my sweater for our hike. Mateo finds an old pair of Isabel's snow boots in the closet, and although they're a half size smaller than I wear, they're not terribly uncomfortable.

We drive slowly through the streets until we reach a small, gravel parking area. "This was one of my favorite spots to come out and explore as a kid," Mateo says as we hop out and head toward a path. "My friends and I would pretend we were adventurers hiking through uncharted woods."

I smile at the thought of him as a carefree, imaginative boy roaming through these woods. "I love Kansas City, but you definitely had some serious outdoorsy perks growing up here!"

As we walk, Mateo points out places of interest or particularly stunning views. We reach a landing that overlooks Hart Lake, fringed in snowy evergreens. It's absolutely breathtaking. I pull out my phone to take a few photos, and then Mateo takes a few selfies of us with the wintry backdrop. I already know what I'll be changing my lock screen to later.

As we take in the view, Mateo asks me about my impressions of his family so far. Although I'd already met his dad, I gush about how adorable it is to see his parents together. "And Isa—oh my, she has so much spunk!" I say, drawing a knowing laugh from Mateo. "But I'm also really impressed by her grit to carve out a new life for herself. On the drive from the airport, she told me about her past struggles with drugs and rehab."

I feel Mateo's hand flinch in mine, and I look over to see his brows furrowed and face darkened. "So, she told you how much of a jerk I was to her?"

I pull Mateo's hand to turn him toward me. "What? No, Mateo, not at all. Isa went on and on about how important you and Miguel were to her, about the difference you made for her that summer you were home."

Mateo runs his hand through his hair and looks off in the distance. "Yeah, but that was after I was awful to her for a long time."

I'm having a hard time computing, my brain malfunctioning trying to imagine Mateo being anything close to a jerk.

"She started struggling with the drugs right before I left for Townsend, and I just thought she was being dumb. And I told her so. I didn't understand anything about addiction at the time. My whole freshman year of college, I would call her up and lecture her about how she was throwing her life away on this guy and disrespecting our parents and all sorts of other condescending things."

Mateo is avoiding eye contact with me as he shares this information, and I don't push it. "It wasn't until she was in the hospital that I finally took time to learn about addiction and what she was struggling with. I learned how to support her better instead of just shaming her. That's why I decided to go home that summer—not only to support her, but to repair my relationship with her.

I reach my hand up to Mateo's cheek, encouraging him to meet my eyes. "You made a mistake, but once you knew better, you did better. And now you guys have an amazing relationship." He gives me a small smile. "And I assume you're both close with Miguel too? At least it seemed like it on the phone last night."

Mateo nods. "Yeah, it's a little harder with him being so far away, but we definitely all work to maintain that connection we formed. We even got matching tattoos that summer to serve as a reminder of our bond no matter where we go in life."

"What? You have a tattoo? How did I not know this?" I ask, totally caught off guard. "What is it?"

"We got tattoos that say '*te amo mucho*,'" Mateo shares. "*Te amo* is written in my mom's handwriting, and *mucho* in my dad's. We all got them in different places—you should ask Isa to see hers on her wrist tonight."

"That is the sweetest thing I've ever heard," I say. "Just when I think you can't possibly be any more perfect, you go and tell me something like that."

Mateo smiles softly at me. "You know I'm not perfect, Lana. I just told you about how terrible I was to my sister a couple of years ago. Not to mention I made the mistake of deferring to another guy and nearly missing out on you," he adds with a teasing pinch to my waist.

"You know what I mean," I counter as I softly punch him on the bicep. "Can I see your tattoo?"

Mateo hesitates a fraction of a second before responding, "Sure." He unzips his jacket and then pulls the bottom of his shirt up to reveal the handwritten tattoo along his bottom left rib. I suck in a breath, taken aback by the simple beauty of the tattoo . . . aaand Mateo's incredibly well-defined abs.

I reach my hand out to trace a finger along the writing, and it's Mateo's turn to suck in a breath. My eyes flicker to his watching me. "That's really beautiful, and really special." I draw my hand back, and Mateo lowers his shirt back down but never breaks eye contact with me. He takes my hand in his and draws circles on my palm with his thumb as the intensity in his eyes sends my heart rate through the roof.

"Lana, I would *really* like to kiss you now. Is that okay with you?" Mateo doesn't move a muscle, waiting for me to answer. Even his thumb on my hand has stilled. My heart is pounding too hard to speak, so I simply nod my head as I hold eye contact with him.

With his left hand still holding mine, he slowly raises his right hand to my face, tracing the line of my forehead down past my ear and through my hair. His thumb comes up to brush down my jawline and across my lips, which part slightly at the contact. All along, his eyes follow the lines his fingers are drawing.

I see the puff of mist from my breath before I realize I'm whispering, "What are you waiting for?"

Mateo's eyes flick back to mine as he cups my face in his hand. "Just making sure I don't forget a single detail."

With that, he leans in and presses his lips gently to mine. I close my eyes to drink in the sensation, my left hand reaching up to loosely clasp his forearm.

Everything I've learned about Mateo's character—everything I've grown to love about him—manifests in the way he kisses me. His tenderness. His honesty and humble confidence. How considerate and thoughtful he is. The open affection that flows from him being so tuned in to his emotions. All of who he is, woven into the tender press of his lips against mine.

Mateo draws back slowly, eyes searching mine. My lips are suddenly whiny and sad, a toddler whose candy was just stolen. I wasn't aware until now that my lips had their own sentient feelings.

I lurch forward and pull his neck back down to me, recapturing his mouth and sliding my fingers through the hair on the back of his head. He responds with a growl deep in his throat and possessively wraps his arms around my waist, tugging me closer to him.

Our first kiss was all of Mateo's tenderness, thoughtfulness, attentiveness. But *this* kiss is all the years of his pent-up longing crashing through his lips to mine, flooding my body with fire. I'm drowning in it, and I never want to break the surface for air.

I've dreamed about kissing Mateo so many times I've lost count. Daydreaming during class, chapter meetings, walking through campus, lying in bed. In my literal dreams at night. In this moment, I'm Dorothy stepping into Oz for the first time. Because my imagination was black and white in comparison to the Technicolor reality of Mateo Alvarez *kissing* me.

He releases me suddenly and takes a step backward. We're breathing heavy, our exhales sending small clouds into the air between us. Mateo gives his head a small shake, as though trying to clear his mind. "Lana, that . . . I just . . . you . . . wow." Mateo trails off as he runs a hand through his hair and rubs his neck. He closes his eyes with a sigh.

"Yeah, same," I finally offer. He opens his eyes and looks at me with a wry smile. That darn dimple is daring me to close the gap between us and pick back up where we left off. But I stay rooted where I am.

Mateo takes a small step toward me and takes both of my hands in his, intertwining our fingers together, tracing my wrist with his thumb. "Lana, I've said I'll always be honest with you, and here's the honest truth: I'm going to have to be really careful about how frequently I kiss you, or eventually I won't be able to control myself to stop."

My cheeks flush at his admission, but if I'm honest with myself, after the heat of that second kiss, I'm in the exact same head space. I give him an encouraging smile. "We're still on the same page, Mateo. Thanks for being honest."

He looks meaningfully in my eyes. "Honesty always, right?"

When I nod, Mateo smiles softly and leans down to brush my lips with the lightest of kisses. "We should probably head back before I start kissing you all over again."

We're quiet as we hike hand in hand back through the snowy scenery to the car. I'm pretty confident Mateo is silent for the same reason I am—we're both replaying every millisecond of those kisses on loop.

With each echo in my mind, my heart screams more and more loudly: *I love you. I love you. I love you.*

———

The rest of the day flies by much too quickly considering my flight home is tomorrow morning. I wish I had planned a longer stay in

Michigan, but I'm also realizing that the longer I stay, the more likely I am to never want to leave Mateo again. At all. Ever.

Later that night, I'm lying in bed wide awake. I had been texting with Amaya and Teegan, filling them in on Mateo and my first kiss. They were both dying for more details, and I promised to give them the full story of my time in Michigan after I return home. But I'm wired after messaging with them, unable to fall asleep. I text Mateo.

ME

Are you asleep?

Instant three dots.

MATEO

Of course not. After experiencing what it's like to kiss you, falling asleep is proving impossible knowing you're on the other side of the wall

I smile as heat floods through me.

ME

I was going to wait till tomorrow morning, but I want to give you your Christmas gift tonight. Meet me out at the Christmas tree?

Seconds later, I hear a quiet knock. I open the door to see Mateo smiling in plaid flannel pants and a white t-shirt, one forearm leaning against the door frame. "I'll do you one better—I'll escort you out to the Christmas tree," he says in a low voice.

It's very, extremely difficult to stop myself from leaning into him and repeating our kiss. I manage to grab his gift from my suitcase and take his offered hand instead.

The twinkling lights of the tree are still glowing in the living room. Rosa likes to leave them on all night long, to keep the Christmas spirit filling the house even while everyone is sleeping.

Mateo takes one look at my pajamas—a matching set of pink pants and button-up top, covered with whimsical Christmas trees—and laughs. "I should have known you would wear Christmas to bed."

I tap my finger against his temple. "You can log it away in your Lana file." He catches my hand and presses a kiss into my palm.

"This isn't fair though—I didn't know you were coming, so I don't have your gift ready," Mateo says with an exaggerated pout.

"You already bought me piano music, which turns out to be the gift that keeps on giving considering how much I'm going to have to practice to get it right!"

We sit on the floor, leaning against the couch in front of the tree. I hand Mateo his present, suddenly nervous. He opens the bag and pulls out one of my old high school soccer jerseys, my last name printed on the back.

I immediately start rambling explanations. "I know it's not the same because it's not like you can wear it or anything, but since you gave me one of your jerseys and since you're the reason I started loving soccer again, it just seemed like—"

Mateo cuts me off by covering my mouth with his, making me lose all sense of time and space. There's just his spice market tree farm scent and the soft lights of the Christmas tree surrounding me as his lips explore mine. Who do I contact about stopping time so I can stay here in this moment, in this kiss, forever?

He brushes his thumb across my cheek as he draws back too soon, smiling softly. "It's perfect, Lana. It's the best gift ever." I smile back at him. "Nope, I take it back, my dad flying you here was the best gift ever. Silver medal to you."

I laugh, then rest my head on his shoulder. He wraps his arm around me, and we sit there staring at the Christmas tree together. Neither of us want the night to end, but we finally part ways and go back to lying wide awake in our separate beds in our separate rooms, daydreaming of each other.

Chapter Thirty

The rest of winter break feels like walking through the clouds. My family and I enjoy all of our favorite traditions of the Christmas season, made even more special this year by the fact that Dean participated without too much grumbling.

My mom has to walk a fine line of being professional versus personal with her clients, but I go visit Samira and Zahra the day after Christmas, taking gifts for Zahra. Samira's English has improved a lot, and she tells me about her laundry job and shows me photos of Hassan celebrating his birthday in Afghanistan.

Mateo and I talk every day, and I get to see Teegan multiple times since her mom lives on the Missouri side of the KC metro. Amaya comes up for a few days to hang out with us, but also to attend a women in business breakfast she somehow secured an invitation to.

We have a blast ringing in the New Year together. I'm sad not to kiss Mateo at midnight, and I can't stop myself from imagining kissing him at this time next year in California.

It might seem crazy to some people, but I know I want to marry Mateo, even though we only started dating in September. We've been in the same orbit much longer. The number of passions we share in common—from soccer to immigration policy, from close family relationships to core friendships, from growing in our faith personally to helping others grow also—we fit together so perfectly.

And the fact that his future is able to align so well with my plans—it all just adds up.

I know I love him, and I suspect he's known he loves me even before I figured things out with us. In my head, I know he's just waiting until he has commitment to back up the words "I love you" before saying them, but it's becoming harder and harder to hold back the phrase each time we talk.

The long stretch of being apart from Mateo is broken up in January by another trip to Washington DC Elena asked if I could come for a few days to help lead some advocacy meetings. A Christian nonprofit focused on welcoming immigrants pulled together women from across the nation who were willing to meet with their Senators in DC to advocate for immigration reform. So many signed up that they needed some extra people with experience to help guide the groups.

Flying back home, I'm feeling tired yet energized from my time there. On my layover in Chicago, I find a somewhat abandoned corner to FaceTime Mateo.

He answers after just two rings, "Hey gorgeous, how are you?"

"Worn out but great," I respond with a smile. I fill him in on my time in DC, explaining the outline of our meetings and detailing the varying responses from different Senators. I love that I can talk about immigration policy and advocacy with him, and he not only understands what I'm saying, but shares a genuine interest.

"Was it good to see the people you worked with over the summer again? Were most of the same people there?" he asks.

"Yes, most everyone was still there. I love spending time around Elena. I feel like I learn a hundred things just listening to her every time she presents," I say. "Plus, she makes me feel like I'm truly doing something meaningful, like I'm empowered to really make a difference."

"Of course you're making a difference, Lana," Mateo responds. "Everywhere you go, you leave behind a trail of people whose lives are better after crossing paths with you. I love being along for the ride."

Blushing at his compliment, I change the subject and ask how his family is doing. We continue chatting until my alarm reminds me to head to the gate for my flight. I promise to text him when I make it home safely and blow him a goodbye kiss into the screen.

"Just one more week till I can kiss you for real again," Mateo says with a one-sided smile and wink.

On board the plane, I twist open the air vent and close my eyes. The short one-hour flight to KC goes by in a snap as I'm lost in memories of kissing Mateo, softly smiling the whole way home.

———

Amaya throws her president weight around to get the three of us into the AOPi house a day before anyone else is allowed back. We capitalize on the quiet, empty house to dance in the dining room, eat way too much junk food for "dinner" in the movie room, and stay up till all hours catching up on our breaks and plans for spring semester while a movie plays as background noise.

Our time is tinged by the bittersweet feeling of knowing how hectic our final semester together will be. Amaya will be extra busy; working every angle on job offers in KC, on top of running AOPi and training the new president for next year.

I have some challenging classes in my final semester, plus my self-imposed schedule of pre-studying for law school. And let's be honest—a decent chunk of my free time will be spent with Mateo.

Although Teegan officially accepted the offer to stay at Townsend on staff with Arrow next year, she'll still be student teaching this semester, which everyone knows is more than a full-time job. Amaya and I put together a "student teaching survival kit" of all of Teegan's favorite candies and snacks, a giant water tumbler, and a mega-sized pack of her favorite individual coffee creamers to keep stashed in her classroom. She somehow manages to happy squeal and cry simultaneously when she opens it, sparking tears in our eyes as well.

So it's no surprise when we're huddled together on the floor of the movie room, sobbing into each other's shoulders in the wee hours of the night.

"I'm just going to miss you so much!" Teegan cries, barely breathing through her tears. "You're both going to move on, but I'll still be here. I hate missing out! And it just won't be the same without you at Townsend!"

Amaya is the first one to snap out of our late-night emotional delirium and talk some sense into us all. "We have to stop. We still have this semester left together, and we're going to make the most of it. And even after we graduate, we are still Beefs—Best Friends Forever. Neither of you are getting rid of me, like, ever."

We blow our noses and wipe our eyes and snuggle up together on our mountain of throw pillows and blankets on the floor. Eventually, we each doze off, and I feel like I won the friendship lottery as I slip off to sleep.

———

The next morning, we sleep until Amaya's alarm goes off at 9:00 a.m. Teegan groans a protest, but Amaya is immediately wide awake and straightening up the movie room. I reluctantly get up to join her, and between the two of us, we eventually get Teegan moving.

We head to Bookafe together to get coffee and pastries before more AOPis start trickling in throughout the day. I text Mateo between helping girls unload their cars, checking in to see when he'll get to town. He drove halfway from Michigan yesterday, so he's aiming to be back in Brooklyn in time for dinner tonight.

Mateo is planning to unload his car and then pick me up for dinner, but I decide to wait at his house. This has everything to do with wanting to surprise him with a sweet gesture and nothing to do with wanting more privacy than the AOPi house affords for Mateo to potentially kiss me in greeting. Scout's honor.

His other roommates aren't arriving till tomorrow, so I get to his house and sit on the folding lawn chair that poses as porch furniture to wait for him to pull up. I'm thankful for the streetlight directly across from their porch piercing the darkness. I curl my hands into the sleeves of my sweatshirt to keep warm, hoping Mateo was accurate on his ETA.

His truck comes down the street a minute later, and I stand up to lean against the porch post as he pulls into the narrow driveway. Mateo smiles as he steps out of the truck, and I rush down the walkway to jump into his waiting arms.

"I missed you," I murmur into his ear, my arms wrapped around his neck.

"*Mmm*, I've been waiting for this," Mateo murmurs back, holding me tightly. He sets my feet down on the ground and draws back to look me in the eyes, threading his fingers through my hair. "And I've really been waiting for this," he adds quietly just before tipping my chin up to meet my lips with his.

I sigh and melt into his kiss, the warmth of his body against mine evaporating the chill of the air around us. We had planned on going to dinner, but my lips have knocked my stomach off the throne. Not even tiramisu or Rosa's cooking could convince me to leave this kiss now.

Far too quickly, Mateo's lips pull back from mine, and he lets out a shaky breath as he leans his forehead against mine, eyes closed. His hands tenderly cradle my face as he opens his eyes and whispers, "I missed you, Lana."

I lean my cheek against his chest, tucking my head under his chin where I fit so perfectly. I feel the shift of the muscles in his shoulders as he rubs his hands up and down my back. I could stand here breathing in his scent all night long. Who needs food? Or sleep? Or shelter? Mateo's arms are perfectly sufficient life support.

My stomach chooses that moment to loudly growl. Traitorous little organ fighting to take back control.

Mateo laughs and says we should go to dinner. He tries to separate himself from me, but I cling on more tightly. "Nope, not hungry," I insist, refusing to release my grasp around him.

Naturally, my stomach growls again, and Mateo pinches my side. "Your stomach says otherwise, Lana. Literally," he says with a wink.

"Finnne," I moan with feigned frustration. Mateo quickly transfers his duffel bag into the house, and we drive to dinner, clasped hands resting on my knee.

We stuff ourselves with pasta and tiramisu as we recap the rest of our winter breaks. We compare schedules for the semester to figure out when we'll have overlapping free time to see each other. I'm still committed to volunteering at The Hangout, because there's no way in the world I would bail on the girls for my final semester here.

"Over break, I found the email for The Hangout director on their website and asked about volunteering there too," Mateo says. My heart skips a beat.

"For real? You're going to start coming on Tuesdays?" I ask, hope and gratefulness and pride welling up in my heart.

"Of course, for real," Mateo answers, smiling. "I'll mostly be in the rec area playing soccer or basketball with the guys, but at least we'll be able to see each other there."

I don't know why exactly, but my eyes fill with tears. I reach my hand over to grab Mateo's across the table. "Why are you always so amazing?" I say with a sniff. Mateo pulls my hand up to press a kiss against my knuckles.

Playfully yet gently, he responds, "Well, you started it."

Chapter Thirty-One

On the day classes resume, I'm looking at my schedule and starting to feel anxious. While I'm grateful that my course load was lighter last fall while I was applying to law school, I'm slightly regretting leaving myself with such an intense schedule for my final semester.

After sitting through two classes of syllabus readings, I walk to my final class of the day, a Theories of Human Communication elective. I'm a few minutes early since my previous class ended before the scheduled time, so I find a seat in the middle of the room and pull out my phone to distract me till the professor arrives.

A few minutes later, I hear my name in a familiar voice. I look up to see Aaron standing in front of me, and I drop my phone in surprise.

Aaron picks my phone up off the floor and hands it to me as he slides into the desk next to mine. "So, Human Communications, huh? I suppose you would be doing a lot of communicating with humans as an immigration lawyer," he says, coming across surprisingly nonchalant compared to our previous recent interactions.

"Yep, you got it. And you're in this class because . . . ?" I ask, much less nonchalantly.

"It's one of the electives offered for business and marketing. I figure marketing is a form of communication, so can't hurt to better understand how people communicate," Aaron explains.

My heart is still pounding, and I hope no one else notices the copious amounts of moisture the sweat glands in my armpits are now producing. I'm bouncing my foot and rehearsing "Perfect" with my right hand on my desk, trying to divert my nervous energy without being obviously awkward.

I'm clearly failing though, evidenced by Aaron turning toward me and reaching his hand over to still my fingers tapping melodies on the desk. My eyes flit over to his, and he clears his throat.

"Listen, Lana, I know I've acted super weird with you and put you in some awkward positions over the past few months, and I'm sorry," he begins in a quiet voice, although we're still the only two students in the classroom. "I feel like I need to just put my cards on the table, since not being clear is what caused me to miss out on us in the first place."

My skin is clammy, and I'm holding my breath as I wait to see where he's going to take this train of thought. Another student comes in the room, and Aaron pauses as she walks past us, but resumes when she takes a seat on the opposite side of the classroom.

"I can't lie, Lana, and say I'm over you, 'cause I'm not. My feelings for you haven't gone away, but I recognize that you're . . . you're with Alvarez, and I do respect that," he continues before clearing his throat again. "Just because I missed out on a relationship with you doesn't mean I want to miss out on your friendship. I really would like to move forward as friends, if that's okay with you. Especially now that we'll have class three days a week together."

He looks at me patiently, his bouncing knee the only tell that he's nervous. I decide if we're going to put cards on the table, I may as well go all in. In a low but firm voice, I begin, "I am okay with that, Aaron. We've known each other for a long time, so I do want to be friends with you, as long as you recognize that being my friend means hearing me talk about Mateo. I care about him a lot, and he's a big part of my life, so you can't act uncomfortable every time I bring him up. Are you okay with that?"

Aaron doesn't answer right away, instead leaning back in his chair and popping his knuckles as his knee continues bouncing. But he eventually turns back toward me. "Okay, yes. I will be—I'll make myself be okay with it, Lana, if it means being your friend again."

A student excuses himself to walk between our desks to sit behind me, giving me a second to close my eyes and exhale.

Aaron leans closer and whispers, "Friends share notes from class, right?" I snort a laugh, and he grins, clearly happy that he successfully lightened the mood. "You were always a better student than me," he adds as he straightens back up when our professor begins her introduction.

Later that night, I'm sitting with Amaya and Teegan at dinner. "So he agreed not to be a weirdo every time you say Mateo's name?" Amaya asks as she twirls fettuccine around her fork, one skeptical eyebrow raised.

I shrug and answer, "So he says. I guess we'll see if he follows through or not."

"I hope he does, for your sake. Otherwise, seeing him in class three times a week on top of Arrow meetings is going to be miserable," Teegan adds.

I pause before concluding, "I hope he does for *his* sake. It doesn't make me feel good about myself that Aaron's still holding on to feelings for me—I really do want him to move on and be happy, as happy as I am with Mateo."

"That's sweet of you, Beef," Teegan says, patting me on the shoulder. "Are you going to tell Mateo about this conversation?"

"I don't think I'm going to tell him about my exact conversation with Aaron, per se," I answer. "I'm not sure planting the thought in his brain that Aaron openly admitted to still having feelings for me is the right move, since I know I don't feel anything for Aaron anymore. But I am going to tell him that we have class together. I don't want to look like I'm hiding the fact that I see Aaron multiple times a week now."

———

Tuesday evening, Mateo picks me up to drive to The Hangout together. It's exhilarating having another excuse to spend time together each week, even if it's mostly just time driving in the car.

We walk into the building, and Mateo's entrance causes quite the stir. He's immediately surrounded by all the middle and high school guys crowding around to greet him and offer condolences on the championship loss. Sofia has edged her way into the center of the group, loudly proclaiming that her mother said to pass along her well wishes to Mateo, posturing as a close acquaintance of his. I roll my eyes but inwardly laugh. This is exactly the spunk that made me fall in love with Sofia years ago.

"Okay, okay, get over here, Sofia, so we can find the other girls." She throws her arms around me in a hug. "Oh, so you're happy to see me too?" I chastise her in jest.

"Can you really blame me for going to Mateo first?" she teases back.

"Point taken," I say with a smile as we head to our usual table. I glance back at Mateo, still surrounded by teenage boys, and grin at him as he winks my way.

Two hours later, I heckle him about his fan club as we walk back to his truck. He opens the door for me but doesn't let go of my hand to let me climb in. "What can I say? Being your boyfriend has really put me on the map," he says with a wry smile.

I giggle and lean forward on my tiptoes to kiss him on the cheek. Immediately, I hear Sofia's enthusiastic voice calling out, "Awww yeah, get it, Lana!"

My head snaps in her direction where she's getting into her older sister's car, along with Clara. My cheeks warm with embarrassment, and I clap my hand to my forehead. "Oh my gosh, I'll never hear the end of it," I moan under my breath.

The next thing I know, Mateo calls out to get Sofia's attention, then firmly plants an arm around my waist before dipping me backward to kiss me full on the lips. Sofia and Clara are screaming, and I hear yells from a couple of the high school boys too.

Mateo stands me back upright and says, "Now you'll really never hear the end of it."

I can feel the Christmas-red color flooding my face down to my neck, which only encourages his smile. I playfully slap him on the chest before getting in the truck and pulling the door shut.

"I cannot believe you," I chide as he gets in the other side.

"What? Just giving them one more reason to keep coming back each week. Hanging out at the program helps keep them out of trouble, right?" Mateo says with a sneaky grin that knows I can't refute his point.

As we drive back to AOPi, he talks about the boys he got to know tonight playing soccer. He pulls up in front of the house, but I stop him from opening the door.

"Hey, I wanted to tell you something real quick," I say. Mateo swivels in his seat to face me, and butterflies suddenly start churning in my stomach. "Um, I just wanted to tell you, well, it's not like a big deal, but I wanted to just . . . let you know . . . that I have a class with Aaron Adams this semester," I stutter out.

A hint of a frown flashes across Mateo's face, and he glances down to my left hand, which is subconsciously playing "Moonlight Sonata" against my knee. I grip tightly onto my knee to make it stop.

"You have a class with Aaron Adams this semester," Mateo restates. I give a slight nod. "So you'll be seeing him every . . . ?"

"Monday, Wednesday, and Friday," I gulp. "I didn't know about it until he showed up in class yesterday."

"He didn't mention anything about it this morning at our Bible study with Kent," Mateo remarks evenly.

"But it's just class, it's not like we're casually hanging out," I add, knowing I'm sounding flustered. "I wanted to be upfront with you, just because of my past, you know—"

"Your past crush on Aaron and his current crush on you, you mean?" Mateo asks, more emotion filling his voice. His hand runs through his hair down to his neck.

"Well, yes. That. But it's not that big of a deal, right?" I ask, a pleading tone now in my voice. Mateo has always been so quietly confident and self-assured—this is not how I expected this conversation to go.

He's silent, lost in his thoughts for a moment, until I reach my hand up to his cheek, tracing the stubble that's grown so familiar. "It's not a big deal, right, Mateo?" I whisper.

Mateo traps my fingers against his cheek with his hand and sighs. "No, it's not. It's not a big deal, Lana. You're right, it's just class."

"Should I not have said anything?" I ask, my voice still a whisper.

"No, I'm glad you did. I'm sorry for responding poorly. I'm glad you told me about it."

"Honesty always, right?" I ask with a little more strength in my voice.

Mateo lowers our hands with a squeeze and nods. "Honesty always," he repeats, although his voice seems to falter.

CHAPTER THIRTY-TWO

Three weeks into the semester, Mateo and I are still trying to find a new rhythm of time together. Although the soccer season is over and he's officially done, he's continuing to work out with the team. No doubt it's hard to quit those habits cold turkey, not to mention the strong relationships he has with his teammates. We see each other every Tuesday and Thursday, and we usually try to go on a date sometime over the weekend. But the more time we spend together, the *more* time I want to spend with him, making my classes and study load rather inconvenient.

I head to the library almost every day after classes, either studying for my courses or working my way through some law school textbooks I purchased early. On a Thursday afternoon, Mateo finds me in the Harry Potter room. I'm alerted to his presence behind me by the spicy tree farm smell flooding my senses right before he places a kiss on my temple.

"What are you reading?" he asks as he sits down next to me.

I look at him sheepishly as I hold up my book. "Literally the dictionary."

Mateo laughs loudly, drawing irritated glares from students studying at nearby tables. He clears his throat and whispers, "Sorry. Was not expecting that response."

I show him the Legal Dictionary that I'm methodically reading and annotating. I'm tempted to feel embarrassed, but Mateo catches me off guard by leaning in to softly kiss my lips. It's crazy how even his gentlest of kisses sends sparks shooting through my body, like the slow, scintillating burn of a sparkler at Fourth of July.

He pulls back with a smile and whispers again. "Your dedication will never cease to amaze me, Lana." I lean forward to give him a quick peck of appreciation on the lips, not even caring if the students at neighboring tables are watching us over their laptops.

"It's nice outside this afternoon," Mateo says. "Would you be up for going for a walk? Or do you need to keep studying?"

"I'm definitely up for a walk. That's enough dictionary for one day," I say with a self-effacing grimace.

I arrange my laptop and books in my backpack, and Mateo throws one strap over his shoulder as he takes my hand. We walk lazily through campus until my phone rings.

"Oh, it's my mom. Let me just see if she needs something quick or if I should call her back later," I say. I tap the button to answer it. "Hey, Mom!"

"Hi, Lana, honey," my mom responds, her voice a bit strained. "What are you up to right now?"

"Just finished studying and now walking through campus with Mateo," I tell her, hoping the strain in her voice isn't related to Dean. He's been doing so well ever since Mateo connected him with Parker.

"Oh, you're with Mateo? Could you give him the phone so I can talk to him for just a minute?" Mom asks, further raising my suspicions.

"Uh, sure," I say, then hold the phone out toward Mateo. "She wants to talk to you?"

Mateo takes the phone with a question in his eyes. He greets my mom, then listens intently. His eyes flick over to me briefly with concern before looking down at the sidewalk. "*Mmmhmm . . .* yeah, I understand . . . yes, of course I will." I can't hear my mom's side of the conversation, but Mateo's short responses aren't sitting well with me.

He hands the phone back to me and takes my hand, so much compassion in his eyes that my blood runs cold. "Mom, what is going on?" I ask into the phone, a slight tremor in my voice.

"Honey, everything is okay with our family. But...there is something terrible that's happened that I need to tell you about," she pauses, and I hear her take a deep breath. "It's Samira's family. We just got word that Hassan, her son who got left behind in Afghanistan...well...he's been killed, Lana."

My heart plummets. I gasp into the phone, "No, that's not true." I look into Mateo's eyes, already brimming with tears as he looks back at me, and I know it *is* true.

"But Mom, you were working so hard to get him here. You were filling out all the papers, you were contacting all the people, doing all the right things so he could get here for Samira. This isn't right." My voice cracks as the tears start overflowing from my eyes.

"I know, honey," my mom says, her own voice thick with emotion. "We were doing everything we could. It's just such an unstable place, and Hassan, he . . . he just got caught in the middle of some fighting and . . . he's gone."

I choke back a sob, and Mateo's free hand starts rubbing circles on my back. "How's Samira? And Zahra? Does she understand what happened?"

"Zahra's been separated from Hassan for so long now, living this different life, that I think she's having a hard time comprehending that he died, that he won't ever be coming back," Mom tells me, causing fresh tears to spill down my cheeks. "And Samira, well, she's gutted, of course. She feels like it's her fault for leaving without him. And she's grieving the fact that she can't even be physically present to put him to rest. She has family members still there who are seeing to his burial, but of course that's not the same."

Another sob breaks out of my throat as my mind submerges in Samira's pain. It's a horrifying reality to lose a child. But to lose a child to such violence, and to not even be able to physically say goodbye? The thought makes me nauseous.

"Honey, I know classes just started, but if you're able to come home this weekend, I'm sure it would mean a lot to Samira and Zahra to see you," my mom says gently.

"Of course. Of course, I'll come, Mom. I'll figure things out and text you when I'm leaving," I respond.

"Okay, be safe, my beauty. I love you so much," my mom's voice breaks on the last word, starting us both crying all over again.

"I love you too, Mom. I'll see you soon," I finally say and end the call.

Immediately I'm wrapped up in Mateo's arms, face buried in his chest as my shoulders shake with sobs. His left hand comes up to hold the back of my head against him, his fingers gently massaging my scalp.

I don't know how long we stand there. I keep pulling back, trying to speak, but my voice always breaks down and I return my face back to Mateo's chest.

Mateo just holds me firmly in his arms as the sobs wracking my body slowly still. I remain pressed against his heart as I finally start to externally process. "It's just so unfair. Samira already lost her husband fighting with the US Army against the Taliban. And now she loses her son because we can't even get him out. The people that helped our country, we can't even get them out to safety. It's so unfair to Samira. To all the Samiras out there."

Tears are streaming down my face again as I step back to look up at Mateo. He swipes both thumbs across my cheeks and asks, "What do you need, Lana? Do you need me to just keep standing here holding you? Do you need me to come up with a plan for you to get home? Whatever you need me to do, I'm here."

Fresh tears spill out of my eyes and trail down to his hands still holding my face. "I can't think straight right now. Can you take over thinking for me?" He nods and kisses a tear from my cheek before pulling me back into his warm embrace. With one hand he pulls out his phone and starts sending text messages as I just cling to him like a life preserver.

A few minutes later, he puts his phone back in his pocket and peers down at me. "Are you good to walk back to AOPi now? Amaya and Teegan are taking care of contacting your professors about missing class tomorrow, and they're packing a bag for you. I texted your mom, and I'm going to drive the four of us in your car to KC once we're all packed, okay?"

My view of Mateo's face blurs as more tears well up. I'm surprised there's any moisture left in me to produce tears, but here we are. "Thank you for taking care of me," I whisper.

————

We walk back to AOPi, where I'm met with more tearful hugs from Amaya and Teegan. Mateo takes my keys and leaves to go pack a bag for himself before coming back to pick us up. My best friends have already taken care of everything for me, which is good because my body feels like a shell with no brainpower controlling it.

Thirty minutes later, we're all sitting quietly in the car, pulling onto the highway out of Brooklyn. Mateo is driving and holding my hand in the passenger side. From the backseat, Teegan takes my phone and cues up Maverick City Music to play over the Bluetooth, filling the heavy silence in the car.

This is so unfair. This is so unfair. This is so unfair. The simple phrase loops on repeat through my mind, filling my body with alternating rushes of grief and rage. I picture the love mixed with sadness on Samira's face as she showed me photos of Hassan over Christmas break. I lean my head back, eyes closed as yet another round of tears wells up.

Teegan reaches a hand up to squeeze my shoulder, and Amaya prays out loud for Samira, Zahra, and their family, as well as for my mom and me. I hear Teegan sniffling behind me, and although my heart is breaking, it's simultaneously bandaged up by this car full of love and support.

My dad immediately opens the front door when we pull into the driveway. I run up the porch steps straight into his arms. "How's Mom?" I whisper as he hugs me.

"You know your mom. She's trying to be strong for everyone, for Samira and Zahra, for you. But she's absolutely crushed," my dad says softly, squeezing me tighter. "She's in the kitchen cleaning the oven or some other unnecessary task to keep her hands occupied."

I walk inside as my dad thanks Amaya, Teegan, and Mateo for coming. Sure enough, Mom's head is buried inside the oven, the racks soaking in the sink. "We're here, Mom," I say, not wanting to startle her. She stands up and faces me, wiping her hands on her apron. She just looks at me for a few seconds before her face crumples, and we cry into each other's shoulders.

Late Sunday afternoon, we're driving back to Brooklyn after a heavy weekend in KC. I'm playing back the time in my mind as I watch the Kansas plains roll past my window. My mom and I spent most of Friday with Samira and Zahra. We returned home Friday night to a spotless house and dinner waiting for us.

Saturday morning, I woke up feeling restless, like I needed to *do* something practical, so I called the industrial laundry company Samira works for to beg them to give her a week of paid leave so she could grieve without worrying about not being able to pay her bills. It was the smallest of victories, but at least I was able to tell her she had the next week off of work.

Samira's family in Afghanistan didn't have strong enough Internet signal to video call her for Hassan's funeral, so they recorded videos and sent them to her later from a stronger Wi-Fi spot. All of us went to her apartment, along with some other Afghan families from the community, to be there for her as she watched them Saturday afternoon. When it became too much for Zahra, I took her to a nearby coffee shop for some hot cocoa and cookies, along with Mateo, Amaya, and Teegan.

We all returned home Saturday evening feeling heavy. We half-heartedly made small talk, but no one was really in the mood to converse much. I excused myself and went outside to call Elena, someone I knew would understand the angst of the situation.

"We have to *do* something, Elena," I told her after summarizing the events. "This shouldn't have happened. Our Afghan allies should have more peace, more certainty and stability by now. Not this."

I know she's likely heard countless heart-rending stories from other Afghan families, but still she empathized with me as I shared. She, of all people, understood my driving need for action.

My exhausted body must have fallen asleep at some point along the drive to Townsend, because I wake to the sensation of Mateo's knuckles brushing against my cheek, his voice quietly calling me out of slumber. I blink slowly, hearing Amaya and Teegan at the trunk unloading our bags.

Tender compassion has taken up permanent residence in Mateo's eyes this weekend, hugging me with comfort every time I look at him. I lean across the console and press a long kiss to his cheek. "Thanks for being with me," I whisper before opening my car door.

Mateo comes around to my side to hand me my keys. He envelops me in his arms and says, "You have Teegs and Amaya here, but I'm on standby. If you need me, just text, and I'll be back to you in minutes, okay?"

I head inside with Teegan and Amaya, turning to wave at Mateo as he drives away in his truck. Because we all missed classes on Friday, we have plenty of work to catch up on. We spread out in our room, laptops open. "Hey Teegs, thanks so much for missing a day of student teaching on such short notice," I tell her once we're settled. "I'm sure that's stressful." She waves me off, reiterating how important I am to her.

I find an email with an attachment in my inbox from Aaron. Clicking it open, I read his message. *Hey Lana, when you missed class Friday I texted Teegan and she filled me in. I took extra good notes and attached them for you. I'm praying for you and your friends. - Aaron*

My eyes sting as I open the attachment and find incredibly detailed notes. That really was a thoughtful gesture. I have so many people in my corner fighting for me and lifting me up. It only makes me more determined than ever to be that person for vulnerable people who need it most.

CHAPTER THIRTY-THREE

I spend a lot of early mornings at Bookafe or Raelynn's when I wake up unable to sleep. I reread Psalm 62 so many times, I have it memorized. My journal fills up with rambling thoughts and lamenting prayers as I try to untangle all of my frustration at Samira's situation.

The cutting pain dulls over time, aided by getting back into routines and a full schedule. I also channel the ache into action, organizing people to call legislators and devoting even more hours to my pre-law school studying. The need to feel like I'm contributing to the cause of justice feels all-encompassing. I reach out to Elena and volunteer to help craft email campaigns each week for constituents to send to Congress about a variety of issues.

I don't tell Shaista about Samira's son, because the last thing she needs is borrowed trauma heaped upon her own. But I do hug her extra tightly each Tuesday evening.

I'm grateful for the routine of weekly Arrow meetings in addition to church to keep me focused on my faith in the midst of discouragement. I arrive early to the first meeting in February on welcome team duty, trying to come up with a lighthearted name tag question.

Peeling labels off and handing them to a group of giggling girls, I glance up and see Aaron heading my way. As apprehensive as I was that first day seeing Aaron in class, it's turned out to be a good thing having class together, I think. He's at least acted less and less awkward each time I've mentioned Mateo in front of him. I'm grateful that we had the forced opportunity to patch things up so we can leave Townsend as friends.

"How's it going, Lana? You all finished with our paper due tomorrow?" Aaron asks, but answers his own question before I can. "Who am I kidding? Of course, you're done already," he concludes with a grin.

"Let me guess, burning the midnight oil tonight?" I tease.

"Guilty as charged," he says. "What's the weekly question?"

"What's your favorite Taylor Swift song?" I reply with a smile.

"Ohhh, you would, Lana," Aaron laughs. "We need to get someone else in charge of the name tag questions!"

"Hey! Rude!" I laugh back. "Just answer the question. You know you have one."

"Okay, okay, 'Blank Space,'" he responds, and I write under his name. He looks at my name tag. "What does YOYOK mean?"

"'You're On Your Own Kid,' from her *Midnights* album," I inform him.

"Well, I guess I know what I'll listen to while burning the midnight oil tonight," Aaron says with a wink. He slaps his name tag to his chest and rejoins the other OGs.

As soon as Aaron steps away, Mateo steps up with Shawn and Linh trailing closely behind. "Hey, Lana," Mateo says, a slight strain in his voice. I notice his eyes dart toward Aaron's back walking into the meeting room.

I quickly lean in to give him a tight hug, mentally channeling reassurance through my embrace. I'm grateful to feel him hug me back, arms encircling me tightly. When he releases me, I smile at Linh and hug her in greeting as well. "So glad you could come again!"

There's lots of laughter and teasing between Shawn and Linh as they try to choose their favorite songs ("Look What You Made Me Do" for Shawn and "The Man" for Linh), but Mateo is uncharacteristically quiet. There's a pit of worry in my stomach as I turn to him, Sharpie poised to write his answer.

"'Timeless,'" he finally answers with a soft smile. I exhale my anxiety as I write his answer, butterflies settling when he leans in to give me a quick peck on the cheek. He whispers in my ear, "But you're never on your own, you know."

As Valentine's Day approaches, I convince Mateo to let me plan our date. I've been so wrapped up in doing anything I can to feel like I'm making a difference following Samira's tragedy that most pockets of my free time have been spent studying or working with Elena, rather than hanging out with Mateo. I want to be the one surprising him with something special for once.

Although Amaya is liberally granting passes to miss chapter meeting on Valentine's Day, I don't feel like fighting the crowds to get restaurant reservations, only to feel rushed to vacate the table in time for the next round of couples.

I also have a little surprise up my sleeve that depends upon daytime hours, so I tell Mateo to plan on me picking him up for an afternoon date at 2:00 p.m.

After a Teegan-directed wardrobe change into a wine-red dress with black tights and boots, I drive to Mateo's house and ring the doorbell at 1:53 p.m. He answers with a grin, looking spectacularly handsome in light jeans and a black button-up shirt rolled up on his forearms. Mateo sharply inhales as he takes in my appearance. He takes my hand to twirl me full-circle, then pulls me close for a brief kiss. "You look absolutely stunning, Lana," he says in a low voice.

I give him a "bouquet" of packets of his favorite pre-workout drink powder arranged in brown paper I got from Grow Wild. "I thought you'd appreciate these more than flowers," I say with a smile. He laughs and kisses me again. "It's perfect," he responds.

We get in my car, and as I pull away from the curb, Mateo reaches over to take my hand. "Okay, I don't know how you do this," I laugh a minute later, releasing his hand to grasp the steering wheel. "I guess my brain isn't capable of paying attention to driving and holding your hand at the same time."

"What can I say? I'm a man of many talents," Mateo jokes.

Truer words were never spoken.

I can tell Mateo is confused when I park in a campus lot and direct him to follow me into one of the buildings. Approaching a service desk,

I exchange my student ID for a key labeled number six, and lead Mateo down a long hallway of doors. I'm infinitely amused by his bewildered expression.

When we reach room six, I unlock it and swing the door open with a flourish, revealing a small, soundproof room with a piano. Realization dawns in his eyes, and he turns to me. "Does this mean what I think it means? You're going to play for me?"

Nodding with a grin, I tell him, "There's no way I was going to play for you in front of an audience at the AOPi house. Lucky for you, the music building has practice rooms available to students, otherwise you'd never hear it!"

Mateo kisses my fingers before releasing my hand, and I pull my "Perfect" sheet music out of my purse and arrange it on the piano, taking a seat on the bench. Mateo leans against the wall watching me, and I suddenly feel self-conscious. After multiple mistakes just a few lines into the music, I cover my face and groan. "I can't play with you standing right there watching me! It's making me flustered!"

He chuckles and moves behind me where I can't see him. "Better?"

I shake out my hands and place them back on the keys. With a deep breath, I start again, still making an occasional misstep but mostly keeping my composure as I focus on the notes. Soon, I'm lost in the flow of the music, like every other time I've practiced this piece.

My concentration is disrupted halfway through the song when Mateo slowly takes a seat on the bench next to me, but I will myself to keep going. As I approach the end of the second chorus, I feel Mateo's gaze on me as his fingers lightly brush the hair on my back. His voice begins to softly sing along, "When I saw you in that dress, looking so beautiful. I don't deserve this, darling, you look perfect tonight."

I'm not sure how, but I manage to make it through the rest of the song without totally flopping. As I lift my hands from the keyboard, I turn to gauge Mateo's reaction. The same intense tenderness fills his eyes as when I played at Thanksgiving, but this time his face is mere inches away from mine.

"Merry Christmas and Happy Valentine's Day," I whisper with a soft smile. Mateo cups my face and gently presses his lips against my smile.

Resting his forehead against mine, he whispers back, "Thank you."

He leans back into our kiss, the gentleness gone as my fingers latch on to his neck and his hands find my waist, pulling me closer to him. I lose myself in his soft lips, his strong fingers against my back, his cinnamint toothpaste taste on my tongue.

My elbow bangs against the piano keys, the sound jarring us apart from each other. I take a deep breath as Mateo runs his hand through his hair, tousling it out of place. Sighing, I reach up to tame it back down and tell him it's time for phase two of our date.

"That's probably good, because phase one is about to get me in trouble. Your lips are off-limits for the rest of the day," he responds with a wry grin, making me blush. His teasing smile spreads across his face as he lightly pinches the blush on my cheeks.

After returning the key, I send a secret text message and drive us to Center Square to find a parking spot. I lead Mateo into Bookafe, where we skip the line and walk back to our table, where a cortado, a flat white, and a giant snickerdoodle cookie are waiting along with a "Reserved" sign.

"Ta da!" I gesture with jazz hands. Mateo smiles as he holds the chair out for me.

"No orange chocolate chip muffin?" he asks.

I shake my head as he sits down. "Nope. Snickerdoodles are your favorite here. You're not the only one who can pay attention."

Mateo looks at me with gratitude, passion, tenderness, and intensity all rolled into one expression, as only he can do. He tucks my hair behind my ear as he tells me, "I'm starting to regret my decision to place your lips off-limits now."

I lean forward to give him a lingering kiss on the cheek. "You never said anything about your cheek," I tease.

We spend the next two hours talking about anything and everything, catching each other up on our families and classes, sharing funny stories about kids from The Hangout, and resisting the urge to kiss each other every minute. He fills me in on Isabel's night class adventures, and I tell him all about the Esports group Dean is getting going at school.

When it's time for me to head home for chapter, Mateo demands my keys. "I'm gonna need you to let me drive so that I can hold your hand as long as possible," he winks at me.

I walk him up to the door of his house, like the proper ending to a date, and he reaches inside to pull out a gift. "I know I told you that you could plan our date today, but there's no way I wasn't getting you a present," he tells me.

Unwrapping the paper, our smiles stare back at me, the photo we took together by Hart Lake printed onto wood. "I love it," I whisper, looking up at Mateo.

"Just making sure you'll never forget our first kiss," he replies with a lopsided smile, dimple daring me to reach up and touch his cheek. I can't resist.

"Like I could ever forget. Think we could temporarily get rid of that off-limits rule?" I ask.

Mateo slowly exhales as his eyes dip to my lips. "Ten seconds probably wouldn't hurt." His mouth follows his eyes, catching my lips in the perfect goodbye kiss. I giggle against his lips when my peripheral vision registers him ticking off the seconds on his fingers. At the count of ten, he reluctantly breaks off.

"Happy Valentine's Day, Lana."

Chapter Thirty-Four

The rest of February flies by. I try to intentionally make more effort to stay present with not only Mateo, but also Teegan and Amaya. It's a challenging tension of wanting to stay focused on my goals while also recognizing that the end of my time at Townsend is rapidly approaching. This sweet season of life will soon be coming to a close, which I avoid thinking about as much as possible.

The week before spring break arrives, and students are split between working extra hard to stay focused and slacking off entirely. I'm clearly one of the former, but Aaron leans more toward the latter, making side comments under his breath in our Human Communications class that I can't help but laugh at.

When Aaron calls me Tuesday afternoon, I assume he has a question about our upcoming quiz on Friday, so I answer as I'm walking out of the library.

"Hey, Aaron, what's up?" I ask.

"Lana, hi. Um, are you done with class for the day?"

"Yep, I'm just leaving the library to head back to AOPi."

"So, there's something that I wanted to talk to you about. Before you head home, could I come meet you, maybe in the outdoor plaza by the library? It will only take me a few minutes to get there," Aaron says.

I hesitate, trying to decide whether to agree. If this was just a question about class, he'd ask over the phone. I have a flashback to the last time Aaron cornered me in the alley at the fall festival, and break out in a cold sweat.

"Lana, please, I only need a few minutes. There's just . . . something I think you should know about."

I agree and hang up the phone. Sitting down on a bench, I hold my backpack on my lap like makeshift armor. My fingers start tapping melodies on the bench next to me as I wait.

Aaron arrives and takes a seat next to me. I cut to the chase. "Alright, tell me what this is about."

He looks out and worries his lip. Now I'm really feeling anxious.

"So, I've been debating all day whether I should say anything or not, but I just really feel like you have the right to know this because it affects you," Aaron begins, angling his body toward mine. "Mateo is looking into playing soccer professionally."

I stare blankly at Aaron as my brain tries to compute. "Huh?"

He blows out a breath before continuing. "Mateo, he's talking to some professional soccer teams about joining after he graduates."

My heart pounds in my ears as I process what he's telling me. I stand up, letting my backpack fall to the ground as I start pacing back and forth.

"What are you saying? Like, he's committed to a team?" I ask.

Aaron stands and holds his hands up. "I don't know all the specifics; he didn't share everything. I just know that he's been pursuing it for a while, that he's hoping to play for a professional team. And I know that you're already committed to going to California, and . . . I assume you were picturing Mateo going there also," Aaron finishes with an awkward cough.

I'm still pacing as my adrenaline builds. "But Mateo hasn't mentioned anything about this. He hasn't said anything about continuing to play soccer," I say out loud, half to myself and half to Aaron.

"I know. That's why I felt like I should tell you. It's something you deserve to know if it could affect your future. I just didn't think it was right for you to continue planning something that might not happen. It didn't seem fair to you," Aaron says.

Why wouldn't Mateo tell me about this? I thought we would be getting engaged, getting married, moving to California together. How could he not tell me he's considering this? My breath grows shallow and rapid. Dots cloud my peripheral vision.

Aaron's hands grasp my elbows, and he turns me to face him. "Lana, take a deep breath. In, out, in, out," he guides my breathing. My vision clears as my breath stabilizes, but my heart still feels like it's in a vice grip.

"Why hasn't he told me?" I whisper.

Aaron shakes his head. "I don't know, Lana, but I'm here for you." His grip on my elbows tightens, and I look up. His blue eyes are fiercely locked on mine, and he takes a half step closer. "I'm . . . I'm still here for you, Lana."

Aaron's words click into place in my mind, and I wrench my arms out of his grip and step backward. "Don't you dare," I hiss as Aaron reaches out to try to take my arm again.

"Lana—"

"NO!" I bark angrily. A girl walking past on a nearby sidewalk jumps, then hurriedly walks away as Aaron closes in to try to contain our conversation.

"Lana, I just want to be here for you as a friend, and, you know, in the future, if you want something different, I want you to know I'm here," Aaron says in a low voice.

I ball up my fist and punch hard against Aaron's chest. "I cannot believe you would drop this bomb on me about Mateo and then try to capitalize on the mess, hoping I'd run to you." My eyes flash with fire as I glare down the caught-with-the-cookie-jar expression on his face. "I've told you multiple times—I don't have feelings for you anymore. We are just friends."

"Okay, okay, I'm sorry, forget I said that," Aaron backpedals.

Grabbing my backpack off the ground, I whirl back around to face him. "We are not friends anymore. Don't try to sit by me in class or talk to me again. Regardless of what happens with me and Mateo, I'm done with you, Aaron."

I stalk off, ignoring his attempts to call me back to let him explain. I'm trembling with anger at Aaron. But as I walk through campus, my anger at Aaron gives way to panic, to confusion, and to anger at Mateo.

How could he not tell me??

Instead of going inside AOPi, I lock myself in my car and sob.

CHAPTER THIRTY-FIVE

J ust a couple of hours later, Mateo is scheduled to pick me up to go to The Hangout together. As upset as I feel, I won't bail on my girls at the last minute. I spend the two hours trying to think of every possible explanation for this being a giant misunderstanding, but I can't construct a convincing argument.

Mateo pulls up in his truck, and I climb inside. *Maybe he'll tell me himself on the drive over,* I think. Inwardly, I feel nauseous, but I fight to keep my composure outwardly.

"So, what did you do today?" I ask as casually as possible. I must be acting weird despite my best attempts, because Mateo glances over and looks at me a little funny. *Darn it, why did I never sign up for those poker lessons??*

"Uh, the usual Tuesday. Bible study, class, worked out and scrimmaged with the team," Mateo answers, flipping on the blinker before turning into the parking lot.

"Oh, nice. You still seem to play a lot with the guys," I respond, leaving what I feel like is an open invitation to explain why he keeps playing soccer so much.

"Yeah, it's been good to keep hanging out with everyone. We should finally schedule that rematch between us and Chris and Andrés," Mateo says with a smile, putting the truck in park.

"Sure, that'd be fun," I respond without much enthusiasm, hopping out of the truck. I'm saved from further conversation by Sofia running up to me in the parking lot exclaiming there's big drama at school to fill me in on. I give a half-hearted wave to Mateo as I follow Sofia inside, grateful for someone else's drama to distract me from my own.

When the program ends, we're back in Mateo's truck driving home. My mind is sprinting circles around variations of the same central question. *Why hasn't he told me anything?*

Mateo parks down the street from the AOPi house in the first open spot. The car is still running when he pivots toward me. "Are you okay, Lana? You're not acting like yourself."

I bark out a laugh. *I'm not acting like myself—yet you can keep acting perfectly normal while hiding something colossal from me,* my brain silently retorts. Aloud, I reply, "Actually, I'm not okay. There's something we need to talk about."

Mateo clicks on the interior light, then looks at me expectantly, waiting for me to speak. Normally, his patience in giving me space to process is comforting, but right now it just makes me more upset.

"When were you planning to tell me that you're going to play professional soccer after graduating?" I ask, while mentally begging for this to all be a big mistake, for Aaron to have been making it up, for it to not be true.

Mateo's eyes widen with shock momentarily, then narrow. "How do you know about that?"

A tiny grenade goes off in my heart, painfully splintering it into a million fragments. *It's true. It's true. Why didn't he tell me?*

I swallow hard. "Well, I guess that confirms it. But you didn't answer my question."

Jaw flexing, Mateo's eyes close for a beat before he looks back at me. "I was planning to tell you when I knew something for certain. It's all still up in the air right now, so I didn't want to worry you if it wasn't going to pan out."

This is really happening. It feels like all the oxygen has been sucked out of the interior of the truck. I open the door and stumble out onto the curb, slamming the door behind me. In a flash, I hear the engine turn off and Mateo's door closing. He's around to my side of the truck, blocking me from walking away in the time it takes me to coordinate my feet to start moving.

"Lana, stop. Listen to me. I was going to talk to you about all of this once I had some concrete information," Mateo says, trying to take my hand. I yank it away.

The thread of logic in his reasoning only serves to feed my frustration, making me dig my heels in further. "You don't think information that potentially impacts my future is something I would want to know about right away?" I throw at him angrily. "Exactly how long have you been pursuing this?"

Mateo purses his lips, and tears sting my eyes. His hesitation is not a good sign.

"Coach Anderson called me about it at the end of winter break," he finally answers, guilt flashing over his face.

"Two months?" I whisper. "You've been planning this for two months?"

"It's not a done deal, Lana!" Mateo says, voice slowly rising with his own frustration. "It was the beginning of an idea when Coach called. He's being recruited by a couple of USL teams as an assistant coach, and if he gets hired, he wanted to make it a condition that I get accepted onto a League Two team this summer and bumped to his team next year if I play well. But nothing is set in stone yet—I don't even know if this is really going to happen."

"When will you know, huh? Exactly how much notice was I going to have that we may be parting ways after graduation?" I demand.

"This was never going to mean we'd be parting ways, Lana. I would have figured things out," Mateo fires back.

"But I don't get to be part of that conversation? I don't get to decide if I want to figure it out? How long till you know, Mateo?"

He draws in a breath and blows it out. "Over spring break I'm traveling to work out with a few teams. I'm hoping to know something definite after that."

This is real. They wouldn't bother to fly him out if they weren't seriously considering him. I watched him play all year, and I know how good he is. He's good enough for this. My stomach heaves as my mind races to process.

"I don't suppose these teams are in Sacramento, are they?"

"No, they're not," Mateo admits. "They're—"

"I don't care where they are," I interrupt. "I just care that apparently you thought I was going to give up everything I've worked for the past six years of my life if we were going to stay together."

"*Lana!* I would never expect you to give up UC Davis. I don't know exactly how we would make things work. I couldn't plan that out until I knew where I might be playing, *if* I would even say yes to playing. But I would never expect you to give up your goals for me." Mateo runs his hand through his hair to his neck. "I can't believe you'd even think that I'm capable of that, after all the ways I've supported you and proved that I believe in you."

I start walking away again because looking at the mix of hurt and frustration in Mateo's eyes is starting to break through my defenses, and I don't want to let go of my anger right now. He quickly cuts in front of me.

"You didn't answer my question either, Lana," Mateo says, eyes narrowing once more. "How did you find out about this?"

Heat springs to my cheeks, and I'm enraged by the embarrassment I feel over finding out from Aaron. Mateo's jaw ticks as he stares me down. "I can't believe this," he mutters.

"Well, I didn't find out from you, and that's the point," I spit out defensively.

"That's not the *only* point here, Lana," Mateo says, rubbing his temples. "I knew I shouldn't have shared about this with our Bible study."

"So you'll share about it with Kent's group but not with your girl-friend, whose life it directly impacts?"

"I just wanted to have some people praying for me to have wisdom to know what to do, Lana. I already explained why I hadn't told you yet," Mateo grits out through his teeth. The muscles in his forearms flex as he clenches his fists. This is the closest thing to angry I've ever seen him. "My gut told me not to risk telling Adams about this, and I should have listened."

"It's your own fault that I found out from Aaron and not from you!" I exclaim, tightly clutching my fury.

"You're defending *him* now? Unbelievable," Mateo shakes his head and rests his hands on his hips. "It wasn't his information to share. But Adams has been a shark circling our relationship since day one, watching for signs of blood. I guess he found his chance."

"This isn't about Aaron. It's about you not being honest with me."

"Aaron made it *also* about him when he inserted himself into our relationship. Are you going to tell me that Adams didn't take this opportunity to conveniently remind you of his feelings for you?" Mateo questions, but it feels more like a declaration.

I fidget back and forth on my feet, right fingers aggressively playing an unknown melody against my left bicep.

Rage, hurt, and sadness weave together in a curtain across Mateo's face. "I knew it," he says quietly, looking down at the ground.

"Okay, yes, he did try to reiterate his feelings for me, but I shut it down, Mateo," I explain, feeling flustered.

Mateo cocks his head to one side as he examines my face. "Are you sure, Lana? You liked him for a long time, long before me. Is that door really closed in your heart, or has this cracked it back open?"

A cold, clammy sweat breaks out across my body, and thick tears fill my eyes. "I can't believe you wouldn't trust me about this," I whisper.

"All it took was one conversation with Adams revealing something I shared in confidence, and you come at me guns blazing," Mateo responds, one eyebrow raised. "I never stood a chance of convincing you that I was trying to do what was best for you by not saying anything yet. He planted that seed of doubt in your mind, and you just latched right onto it instead of trusting me, instead of giving me the benefit of the doubt."

I can barely see his face at this point, and I press the heels of my hands against my eyes to try to stem the flow of tears. "You think I don't trust you, and apparently you don't trust me to handle it if you share about the possibility of your future plans changing. You don't trust me when I say my feelings for Aaron are dead and buried because I only care about you," I say, voice quivering.

Mateo throws up his hands and blows out a frustrated breath. "Yep, great summary. I'm definitely the only person entirely at fault here. Glad to know exactly what you think of me."

Stuffing all my sadness down, I gather up all the inner rage I can muster. "I think we're done, Mateo," I say, voice icy. His eyes are red and glisten with tears, but he doesn't say anything in response. I push past him and start walking down the sidewalk away from AOPi.

"I think we should sleep on this and try to talk tomorrow, Lana, when we've both had time to calm down," Mateo says, jogging after me.

"No, we've said all there is to say," I assert with more resolution than I feel, not bothering to turn around. "We're done talking. We're done."

I hear Mateo's steps pause, and he calls out, "Lana, at least walk back to AOPi. I won't get in your way. You can't walk alone around town after dark."

Pivoting to face him, I scream, "YOU DON'T GET TO DECIDE WHAT I DO WITH MY LIFE!" My chest is heaving and my eyes fill with tears again, so I quickly turn back around so he won't see. "Don't follow me!"

I continue speed-walking down the sidewalk, taking a right on the next street to put some distance between us. I hear the faint sound of a door slamming and truck engine starting. The flash of headlights passes behind me, and I lean over and dry heave.

I quickly survey my surroundings and recognize the next street as one where several professors have houses. Seems like a reasonably safe choice to sit and wallow. I walk down and sit with my back against a tree, hidden from the street.

Oh God. Please let this all be a nightmare. A sob gathers in my chest.
He didn't tell me.
He doesn't trust me.
He let me go.
I cover my face with my hands and weep.

Chapter Thirty-Six

I quietly let myself into the AOPi house shortly after 1:00 a.m. I'm hoping it's late enough that I can sneak through without seeing anyone. Tiptoeing upstairs, I listen outside our bedroom door but am met with silence. Moving quietly through the room, I gather my shower stuff and some pajamas.

It was too cold to sit outside as long as I did, but every time I thought I was done crying a new wave crashed over me. Mateo texted me begging to talk, then begging me to at least let him know I was safe. After the fourth time he called me, I finally texted him back. *I'm safe. Leave me alone.* Then I blocked his number.

I stand in the shower, letting the hot water thaw away the cold and wash away fresh tears. The water temperature is slowly cooling before I finally turn it off.

Burrowing under my covers in bed, I press the heels of my hands to my eyes again. I wish I could erase this day and go back to this morning when I was in love with Mateo, when he was in love with me, when our future was together.

I turn off my alarm when it tries to wake me, covering my head with my blanket. My entire body aches, as if after leaving a gaping hole in my chest, the fragments of my heart slowly sliced jagged paths through every inch of my body. Every attempt to fill my lungs with oxygen feels like a fight against gravity itself.

I am absolutely not going to class today, not going to risk seeing Aaron, not going to risk Mateo finding me. He knows my class schedule, but he can't get to me if I'm holed up in AOPi all day. I'll have to come up with a more solid plan to avoid him long term, but at least for this day I can hide away.

I hear Teegan packing her bag to head to school and Amaya whispering to her. Moments later, Amaya is shaking my shoulder.

"Lana?" she whispers. "You turned off your alarm. Are you going to class?"

"No," I mumble from under the covers.

"Are you sick? Do you need something?" Amaya asks.

I'm silent for a moment, not wanting to answer. Speaking it out loud to someone else makes it truth. Especially speaking it to my best friends.

"Lana?"

"No, I'm not sick. I just . . . Mateo and I broke up."

"WHAT?!" Teegan shrieks as Amaya yanks the covers off my face.

"Explain yourself," Amaya demands.

"You need to get to school, Teegs," I say, trying to postpone.

"I have five minutes," Teegan says. "Explain fast."

Sighing, I sit up in bed and give an extremely abridged version of all that transpired yesterday. Five minutes later, Teegan's eyes are welling up and Amaya's are blazing.

"Are you sure this can't be fixed, Beef?" Teegan asks. "I mean, maybe you just need to talk through it together again when emotions have settled."

I shake my head. "What's there left to talk about? Mateo didn't even trust me enough to tell me about this. He doesn't trust me to not fall for Aaron's scheming. How can I be with someone who doesn't trust me?"

"Not to mention making future plans that would totally disrupt yours without even including you," Amaya huffs out.

Teegan bites her lip. "I have to get to school, but just think about it, LaLa. Maybe you should call him."

"I don't have it in me to rehash all of that again, Teegs. I already blocked his number," I say, pinching my arm to try to stop myself from crying again. "Go before you're late. I don't want to get you in trouble." Teegan reluctantly leaves the room, and Amaya takes my hand and swings her legs up onto the bed next to mine. I lean my head on her shoulder.

"Want to sit in bed watching sad movies together all day? Or listen to angry girl music and eat ice cream?" Amaya offers.

"You're the best, Beef, but no, you need to go to your classes. You already missed a day for me last month, and I'm not going to let you miss for me again."

"All right, but you know I'll be back in minutes if you text me that you need me?" She adds with a squeeze of my hand, "This really sucks, Lana. I'm really sorry."

I squeeze hers back before she stands up to collect her coat and backpack. I head to the restroom, taking extra time to splash water on my face. When I return, there's a cup of coffee and a plate of muffins waiting for me.

I can get through this, I tell myself. *I have the two best friends in the world. I have an amazing family. I have dreams and goals that are within my reach. So what if I no longer have the world's best boyfriend?*

Tears blur my vision at the thought. My own heart doesn't buy my attempt at a poker face.

———

I barely move all day, still buried in my bed by the end of the evening with the *evermore* album on its hundredth loop. Amaya gave me a sick pass to miss chapter, but after the meeting ends, Teegan slips into the room.

"LaLa? You alive in there?" she asks, cautiously approaching.

"I'm in too much pain to be dead, so I guess so," I answer, poking my head out of the mountain of covers.

Teegan is biting her lip as she surveys me. "So, don't be mad, but I talked to Mateo today."

I narrow my eyes at her.

"I'm just trying to look out for you," she says, holding her hands up defensively. "Mateo called me, and he's really sorry, like he feels really,

really terrible. I just wonder if it would be good for both of you to at least try to talk through things. It might not really be as bad as you think it is."

Her comment cuts like a knife. "Not as bad as I think? How could it possibly not be as bad as I think? You weren't there in the conversation, Teegan. Mateo might feel sorry now, but he showed all his cards yesterday. And I'm not interested in reliving that. Don't try to push me, Teegs." My eyes fill again, somehow drawing on an infinite water supply flowing out of my broken heart.

"Okay, I won't. You're my Beef, Lana. I want what's best for you," Teegan reassures me, taking my hand. "I promised Mateo I'd ask you to consider talking, but I'm not going to push you if you don't want to. I swear."

"Please just tell him I don't want to see him. I don't want him showing up here or outside my classes or the library. My heart can't handle it."

Teegan nods, and I suppose I'm grateful that she talked with Mateo solely so she can pass along this message. "Have you told your parents yet?" she asks.

I groan. "No. I'm actively avoiding it." Teegan just gives me a look that I know means I need to stop avoiding it.

I craft a message to my mom.

ME

> Hey Mom. I really don't feel like talking about it, so I'm sending you this message instead of calling, but I just wanted to let you and Dad know that Mateo and I broke up yesterday

Showing my phone to Teegan, she simply raises an eyebrow. Ten seconds after hitting send, it immediately starts ringing. Teegan's look says, "Told you so," without actually saying anything. She leaves the room so I can answer.

Sighing, I hit the green button on my phone. "Mom, I said I didn't feel like talking."

"Lana Renae Grant, you cannot possibly think you could send me that text and I wouldn't call you," Mom responds with a firm voice.

I simply grunt in response.

"You're going to have to explain sooner or later, so may as well be now."

I walk my mom through yesterday's events, attempting to be brief but getting roped into longer answers by her many follow-up questions.

"Hmm," she finally says, after we've exhausted the play-by-play of my conversations.

"Mom, I'm going to be home in just a few days for spring break. I'm worn out, and I just really don't want to talk about this anymore. Can you please just hold off sharing your many thoughts until I'm home?" I plead.

"All right, honey. You know I love you," she responds.

"I know. Love you too."

Chapter Thirty-Seven

I return to class on Thursday but choose not to go to the library or to the Arrow meeting that night. On Friday, I purposely arrive later than usual to my Human Communications class so I can choose a desk far away from Aaron. I finish the quiz as quickly as possible and leave without giving him the chance to talk to me. I've also blocked his number and social media accounts, determined to act as though I don't know him at all.

Lana from a year ago would never have been able to believe it.

Classes finished, I pack my suitcase and say goodbye to Teegan and Amaya for break. When I arrive at my car in the parking lot, my breath catches.

Under my windshield wiper is a stack of three notes with my name in Mateo's handwriting. I swallow hard and pull them out, staring at them in my hands as I sit behind the steering wheel. Shaking, I stuff them in the glove box without reading them.

They haunt me on the three-hour drive home, silently calling out to me. Images of Mateo's dimple, his warm brown eyes, his strong arms, and his sweet lips dance through my thoughts. Memories of all the tender, thoughtful ways he pursued me fight against the anger in my mind.

When I pull into my parents' driveway, I turn the car off and reach a trembling hand toward the glove box. Suddenly, the image of Mateo's narrowed eyes and clenched fists flashes through my mind, and I snatch my hand back. *I can't. I just can't.*

My parents are approaching my car, so I open the door and stand up. They both hug me without saying anything. "Can we not talk tonight?"

I ask quietly in my mom's embrace. I feel her nod, and my dad grabs my suitcase from the trunk.

Inside, it's obvious my siblings have no idea how to treat this Mateo-less version of Lana. Olivia gives me a hug and declares, "I hate that you had to give up such a hot guy, but girl power. Solidarity."

I huff a laugh. "Um, thanks for that, sis."

Carter gives me an awkward hug, which really isn't too odd for a middle school boy anyway. Dean leans in for the world's fastest hug, then tells me, "I'm sorry, Lana. I'll stop texting with Parker if you want me to, you know, since he's Mateo's friend."

It's the sweetest thing I could imagine Dean saying, and I pull him in for a forced real hug. "No way. You don't have to do that. Keep talking to Parker and working on that Esports future." He's visibly relieved to be released from both my hug and the obligation to cut ties with Parker on my behalf.

We have popcorn and watch a comedy as a family that night, and I'm thankful for a reason to half-heartedly laugh.

My free pass to not talk expires quickly, however. When I sit down with coffee and a muffin the next morning, my mom is raring to go. She begins by having me recount my conversations with Aaron and Mateo again, probably listening for any discrepancies. Sometimes having a lawyer for a mom kinda sucks.

Mom pours us fresh cups of coffee, and I can see her mental wheels turning. She sits back down across from me, and I brace myself. "Lana, I want you to think this through before you answer. Are you really sure you want to abandon the love you had with Mateo just because there might be some complications in the plan you had mapped out?"

I'm silent, partially because she told me to think before answering and partially because I don't know how to answer. I take a long drink of coffee, begging the caffeine to knock the gears of my brain into working order.

"You're oversimplifying this, Mom," I finally begin. "Of course, I don't *want* to give up what I had with Mateo. But what kind of love doesn't trust the person you're with to tell them you're considering something that might land you in opposite corners of the country for the next three years? What kind of love plans a major move like that behind your back for two months?"

She holds up a hand. "I'm not disagreeing with you that he should have told you sooner. He should have included you in the conversation. But I do understand his hesitance to bring it up, to worry you about the future if it wasn't even going to materialize." She takes a sip of coffee. "But even if it does materialize, you could still find a way forward together."

"A way forward together? What way forward is there other than *me* giving up *my* dream that I've been working toward for so long? The dream I've achieved?" I shoot back, feeling my anger and defenses rising again. "I never would have guessed you would be the one telling me to give up my dreams for a boy."

Mom sighs. "Oh Lana. I'm not saying to give up your dreams for a boy. But when you have someone important in your life, someone you want to *keep* in your life, sometimes you have to consider more than just *your* plans."

She pauses. "You've always been my driven one, holding so doggedly to your goals that you throw off anything getting in your way. It's an admirable quality. But . . . it does have its shortcomings as well. Like potentially missing out on other blessings or opportunities God might have for you because they don't fit into the box of what you've already decided."

She pauses again before continuing. "I guess I'm just saying that it's okay for your dreams to evolve, or to have more than one dream at the same time. It seems like you need to hear that you have permission."

I fidget with the handle of my coffee mug, unable to make eye contact or respond. If I'm honest, my mom's words landed a blow like a strong right hook. But I'm not sure that I want to be honest right now. I'm not sure that I want to consider that I might have been wrong to react the way I did with Mateo.

I deflect instead. "But what about him not trusting me about Aaron?" I question without addressing my mom's admonition. "If he can't believe me when I say that I have no interest in Aaron, how can we have a solid relationship?"

"You're right, trust is essential in a healthy relationship," Mom concedes. I know she's not surrendering though. "But put yourself in his shoes, Lana. He knows you had a crush on Aaron for years while he had a crush on you. And suddenly you're listening to Aaron calling Mateo's intentions into question, defending the man who's been vying for your affection. If the roles were reversed, don't you think you'd be feeling just a little insecure?"

I'm silent once more, stung by her honesty.

She stands up and kisses me on the top of my head before walking through the kitchen. She pauses before the hallway and turns back. "I know Mateo always came across as so confident and self-assured, but I also saw the way he looked at you. Like you were the greatest treasure ever discovered on earth. Any man in his right mind would get a little frantic if someone threatened to steal that treasure from him. I'm not saying you *should* get back together with Mateo. I'm just saying that maybe you're expecting a little too much level-headedness from a man who is hopelessly in love with you."

———

My mom is merciful enough to not bring up Mateo again while I'm home. She must have sworn the rest of my family into silence as well, because no one so much as mentions Townsend. I visit Samira and Zahra on Sunday, go shopping with Olivia on Monday, play video games with Dean, join Carter on runs, and generally do anything and everything I can to avoid thinking about Mateo. Or about how much I miss him. Or about how many times I reach for my phone to text him about something and then remember it all.

On Thursday, I'm walking around the neighborhood when I get a phone call from Elena. After general greetings, she says, "Lana, I have an opportunity to talk to you about, and I need you to hear me out before you write me off."

"Okaaay, that's a weird statement, Elena," I respond with a laugh. "I promise not to shut you down."

"My assistant is leaving to take a job as a staffer for a Senator. She's wrapping things up over the next month and then will be moving on," Elena explains. "This is a pivotal time to mobilize people to advocate for immigration reform as legislators are campaigning for election season. They need to hear what their constituents care about. So I need an assistant who's both knowledgeable and passionate about these issues so we don't lose steam. Lana, you're my number one choice."

She pauses to let me absorb this information.

"You mean, you want me to come work with you? Like, in DC?" I clarify, mind spinning.

"Yes, I want you to come to DC to work with me for a year. You already have experience, and you clearly have the personal drive to see progress made. You're the perfect fit, Lana. I know you've already been accepted to UC Davis, and this would mean deferring law school for a year, but you'd be making a huge difference. Plus, the University of Maryland Francis King Carey School of Law just up the road in Baltimore has a great Immigration Clinic, and their Chacón Center for Immigrant Justice would let you be involved volunteering even if you're not enrolled as a student. So, you would still keep your foot in the door to pursue law school, all while gaining even more valuable experience," Elena concludes. She obviously thought through every facet before presenting this idea to me.

"Wow, Elena, I'm so honored that you would want me to work with you," I eventually respond. "I . . . I'm just going to need to think about this before I make a decision."

"Of course. I know this is a huge curve ball to your plans, Lana. But I had to try to snag you while I have the chance," Elena says, a smile in her voice. "Look up the Chacón Center, give it some thought, and let me know any questions you have."

I promise to do so and hang up.

My sense of control and confidence over my future is faltering, and I'm not a fan of the feeling. "God, were my carefully-laid plans really so terrible that you had to completely torpedo them all?" I question out loud.

Chapter Thirty-Eight

B ack home, I shut myself in my room and pull up the website for the Chacón Center, reading everything I can find about it. I have to admit it's appealing, right up my alley. I go down the rabbit hole of reading their news articles and social media posts for hours.

I corner my parents in the kitchen after dinner. I explain my offer from Elena, everything I learned from my online sleuthing, and a long list of pros and cons I've mentally detailed already.

They listen quietly, sometimes interjecting clarifying questions, but mostly just absorbing my rambling thoughts. When I finally take a breath and sit down from my pacing, I look back and forth between them.

"Well, what do you think about it, honey?" my mom asks.

"I don't know what I think about it. I want to know what *you* think about it," I counter.

My dad answers first. "It sounds like a really incredible opportunity. Not the kind of thing most fresh college graduates get offered to them."

Mom hums her agreement. "It does add a year onto your timeline of becoming a lawyer. But it's certainly not a wasted year. There's a lot of potential for valuable experience."

I chew the inside of my cheek. "But I'd lose the deposit I've made to UC Davis. Not to mention probably losing my spot there forever. I can't imagine they'd look kindly upon offering me early acceptance only for me to defer."

"True," my mom says, nodding. "This might close the door on UC Davis. But not the door on law school. There are a lot of good immigration law programs, Lana."

"I know that in theory, I guess," I say. "I mean, I've always known UC Davis wasn't the only program out there. But it was . . . the *one*, you know? The one you attended, the one that sparked my interest in immigration law in the first place, the one I've dreamed of forever and fought so hard to get accepted to."

My parents simply nod along, giving me space to continue externally processing.

"Working with Elena for a year would seriously be a dream. But I already had a dream—one that I've actually achieved. How do I know if I'm supposed to give that up?"

Mom simply shrugs her shoulder as my dad says, "We can't answer that for you, Lana. You've got to open your mind up to any possibility. It might be UC Davis in the fall. But if it's this opportunity with Elena, don't shut it down just because you've already sacrificed so much on the path to California. Take some time to think about what you *really* want."

———

After a sleepless night, I wake up early and drive to a local coffee shop. I do my best thinking sitting by a window drinking bottomless coffee and journaling my feelings.

Is it really okay to let go of UC Davis? To let go of a dream, a goal I poured so much of my life into?

I think about all the things I threw aside in the name of reaching my goals—soccer, any social or leadership opportunity that didn't fit my check boxes, and . . . Mateo. Tears prick my eyes again.

Do I double down on my original dream because I put so much into achieving it? Or is it okay to open myself up to something different, even if it derails my plan?

And possibly the most agonizing thought to stare in the mirror: *Would changing my plan mean admitting that I was wrong to push Mateo away?*

My heartache can't even handle posing that question to myself, so I mentally lock it up and move on to more pro/con lists.

Several hours and a massive hand cramp later, I'm feeling on the verge of peace about a decision. I drive to a nearby park and go for a long walk in the fresh air and sunshine, appreciating the hints of spring popping up through the soil in the flowerbeds.

I return to an empty house since my siblings are all with friends today. I wander the quiet rooms, my feet eventually carrying me to the living room to stand in front of the piano. I slowly take a seat on the bench and run my fingertips over the keys.

A copy of the sheet music to "Perfect" still sits on the piano, causing my shoulders to droop in a fresh wave of sadness. I stack the papers and store them safely out of sight inside the bench. Returning my fingers to the keys, the slow, mournful melody of "Moonlight Sonata" fills the room. Every pensive thought in my mind and conflicted emotion in my heart melt their way into the piano keys, taking on a melancholy beauty in the music.

I sleep peacefully that night, not waking up a single time until 10:00 a.m. Saturday morning. My parents have moved from the kitchen to the living room, so I take my coffee in to join them.

"I'm going to do it. I'm going to accept Elena's offer," I declare.

"You feel good about it?" my dad asks.

"I guess so?" Dad quirks an eyebrow at my response. "I mean, yes, as good as I can feel about throwing away my greatest life goal." Now they both quirk eyebrows at me.

"I know, that was overly dramatic," I sigh. "I'm still working on getting that permission to change dreams advice to sink in. But after all my research, all my lists, all my thinking and praying and agonizing over it, I realized that passing up this opportunity from Elena just to stick to my original plan isn't what I really want. I want to go to DC. I want to make a difference there for people like Samira."

My mom smiles. "I'm happy for you, my beauty. You're going to do amazing things in DC."

I smile back. "I'm not giving up on law school forever. But one extra year won't ruin my whole future."

After eating some breakfast, I call Elena. She's over the moon that I've accepted and promises to get information to me soon about my job description and living in the greater DC area. I craft an email to

UC Davis explaining my decision and officially withdrawing from the program. My stomach sinks just a little as my mouse hovers over the send button. *Am I really sure I want to do this?* I question myself. But my mom's words echo in my mind: *It's okay for your dreams to evolve.*

I click send.

Chapter Thirty-Nine

B ack at the AOPi house Sunday night, I fill Amaya and Teegan in on the sharp pivot in my plans.

"Wow," Amaya speaks first. "I guess I'm a little shocked that anything would change your mind about UC Davis. Honestly, I'm shocked that you could change your mind about anything you'd set it on. But it sounds like an incredible opportunity. A perfect job description for you, if there ever was one."

Teegan gives me a big hug. "I'm super excited for you, Beef. And so proud of you." As she sits back down, I can read on her face that she's debating whether or not to say something.

"Just spit it out, Teegs. What else do you want to say?"

She still hesitates, but then says, "I guess I just wonder where this leaves things with Mateo?"

I bury my head in my hands. "Ugh, I don't know." I look back up to meet her sad eyes. "I mean, yes, I have realized that I need to be more flexible with my plans. But that doesn't change the fact that Mateo didn't tell me about his opportunity. And I also can't erase the mental picture of the distrust in his eyes when he questioned me about Aaron. I don't know how to get past that."

It's a mental picture I replay every time those niggling doubts about whether I was wrong to push Mateo away start to creep in. It's the only way I can hold onto my resolve to *keep* pushing him away when the little voice deep inside me starts yelling about how much I want him back.

Teegan's face is downcast, but she shrugs. Amaya throws an arm around my shoulders and asks me to tell them more about the Chacón

Center. Grateful for the change in subject, I launch into a summary of my research, fighting not to let Teegan's misgivings water those seeds of doubt about keeping Mateo at arm's length.

It's a battle I'm too scared to lose.

———

Although I feel completely confident in my decision to work for Elena, I wake up Monday morning overwhelmed with dread. I wish I could finish my classes remotely and avoid the Townsend campus forever. Except, not really, because I'm not ready to leave Amaya and Teegan yet. If only I could create a bubble around me to keep Mateo and Aaron away, I could move through campus without anxiety.

Outside the door to my Human Communications class, I pause and give a compelling mental pep talk. I hunch into myself and enter the room with my eyes down, choosing a seat in the back corner. I listen to the professor and take detailed notes, careful not to look around the room or participate in the discussion and risk inviting interaction with Aaron. Beelining it out of the room, I hurry back to AOPi and feel I've created a successful game plan for avoiding Aaron in class.

Now I just have to draw up a plan for The Hangout. And Arrow meetings. And generally being out in public on campus or in town.

Ugh.

Tuesday afternoon, I'm pacing my room, trying to decide what to do about The Hangout. Go, and risk Mateo being there? Or not go, and give up one of the precious few weeks I have left with Sofia, Shaista, and the other girls?

I decide to risk it and walk down to my car, only to see a bright paper under the windshield wiper again. I approach like the note is a scorpion that might sting me.

I won't go to The Hangout. It was your place first is written on the front of the folded paper, along with an arrow at the bottom indicating there's more inside. I add the note to the pile in my glove box without opening it, breathing a sigh of relief that I can at least go to the program confidently knowing I won't see Mateo. My sigh quickly falls into a groan as I realize that all the middle and high school guys who have grown accustomed to Mateo's presence there will be disappointed. Guilt starts to gnaw on my armored heart.

No! That isn't my fault. It's Mateo's fault. He can feel guilty.

I push away the nagging feelings as I drive to the program and go inside to find the girls. There are a lot of murmurs with Mateo's name when I enter solo, and I'm mentally scrambling to come up with an explanation that doesn't include me tipping my breakup cards to a room full of teenagers.

The program director tells a group of the guys that Mateo had a new commitment come up, and he wouldn't be free on Tuesdays any longer. There are a lot of disappointed faces, and the guilty feelings start to overpower my justifying self-talk. Sofia asks me about it, but I shrug it off and change the subject.

Arrow meetings are the final hurdle. I contact Rachel and ask to pass off my welcome team duties, using my busy schedule as an excuse, even though there's a slim-to-none chance that she hasn't heard about our breakup via Kent. She graciously doesn't call me out on my fib.

Without the requirement to arrive early, I purposely come late and slip in the back, where Amaya saved a seat for me. I half-heartedly sing along with the worship songs and keep my eyes glued to Kent as he shares a message about trusting God with our unknowns. When the band starts the final song, I whisper thanks to Amaya and sneak out the back before the meeting officially ends, successfully avoiding interaction with anyone.

Walking home alone, I take a deep breath. *I did it. I made it through the week.*

I've always been good at coming up with solid plans. And now I have a strategy to survive the rest of my time at Townsend. *Keep your head down. Straight in, straight out. Minimize interaction. Rinse and repeat.*

CHAPTER FORTY

M y rinse-and-repeat plan turns out to be effective but depressing.

Time at AOPi with Teegan and Amaya is my safe haven, my lifeline, my only bright spot over the next two weeks. They express their concern about how little I'm eating, how infrequently I'm washing my hair, how disengaged I am from anything outside of class or the sorority house. But aside from Teegan's unacceptable suggestion of talking to Mateo to at least patch things over, they don't have any alternative solutions to my pared down existence.

Rinse and repeat.

The stack of unread notes in my glove box grows each time I drive anywhere. It's unfair that a pile of paper can weigh like a ton of bricks on your heart.

I mask my voice with optimism when I talk with my mom, focusing on my excitement about my upcoming year in DC and conversations I have with Elena, or our mutual encouragement with how well Dean is doing now. We just avoid acknowledging the role Mateo played in that storyline. Mom always reminds me that she's praying for wisdom and peace for me, and I lie to myself that she only means about DC and not about any other aspect of my life.

It's Friday, April fifth, when my failsafe plan fails. I notice that Aaron is missing from Human Communications, which is a pleasant opportunity to participate in the class discussion for once. My guard is down, which is my fatal mistake.

I walk out of the building straight into Aaron. It's a surprise ambush.

"Lana, you can try to walk away, but we have to talk," he insists as I skirt my way around him. He matches my pace, and I seriously consider making a run for it.

"Look, you have to listen to what I have to say this one time, and then I will never talk to you again, okay?" he says as he steps in front of me to block my path.

I audibly groan my frustration but stop walking. I cross my arms and put on my best if-looks-could-kill expression, silently waiting for him to speak.

"Lana, I'm sorry. I'm really, truly sorry for how terrible I was to you," Aaron begins. "I never had any right to your affection because I never made a clear move to ask you out. And I never should have tried to sabotage your relationship with Mateo, which is exactly what I did."

Shocked by his honesty and apology, I allow my expression to soften slightly but remain silent.

"Maybe Mateo should have told you about the soccer opportunity sooner, but maybe he had valid reasons he didn't. Either way, it wasn't my place to tell you, especially since I was motivated to tell you because I hoped you would break up and I'd have another shot. I've talked about it—a lot—with Kent, and I know how wrong I was. I'm not even going to try to give you excuses because it was inexcusable. I'm genuinely sorry for the pain it's caused you. And Mateo." He pauses, searching my face for any kind of response.

I finally relent. "Thank you for apologizing so honestly. I . . . I do forgive you, even if I'm furious with you for doing it and still don't want to be friends anymore."

Aaron holds his hands up and shakes his head. "I have zero expectation of us being friends. You gave me that chance, and I screwed it up. I know I don't deserve another chance, so I'll leave you alone after today. But I did want to apologize." I nod in response but cast my gaze down to the ground as he continues, "And . . . I did want to tell you that I also talked about it with Mateo."

My eyes shoot daggers back up to his.

"I apologized to him too, asked for his forgiveness for getting in the way and driving a wedge between you two. The blame for you guys breaking up is all on me."

I blow out a breath. "Aaron, I do appreciate you taking responsibility for your actions. But Mateo made his own choices and assumptions too."

"I know, but . . . Lana, I really do think he'd go back in time and change things if he could. The guy is a total wreck. You both are. I told Mateo the biggest reason I regret everything I did is because I really do care about you. And I feel terrible that I did something that's made you such a shell of yourself."

Tears burn my eyes, but I try to blink them back. Aaron keeps a respectful distance, but there's genuine concern on his face.

"I never thought I would be the one saying this, but I think you need to talk to Mateo," he says. "I don't know if you can fix things or not, but at least talk. Blame all this on me, not on him. Because you deserve to not be miserable. You deserve to be the confident, joyful woman that you were before I wrecked things between you two."

I clear my throat but still don't trust my brain or my vocal cords to respond.

"Please just tell me you'll think about it?" Aaron pleads. "I swear this is the last time I'll try to talk to you, Lana. I really am sorry—sorry that I ruined our friendship on top of everything. Just . . . think about what I've said, okay?"

I nod and whisper, "I will."

Aaron nods back, then takes a few steps toward me. He slows as he walks past me, his voice low when he says, "Goodbye, Lana."

"Goodbye."

CHAPTER FORTY-ONE

That evening, I download Aaron's conversation with Amaya and Teegan over extra-large slushies on the floor of our room. When I finish, they're stunned into silence, which is quite the accomplishment for these two.

"I . . . wow," is all Amaya can say.

"Yep," I respond as I drain the final dregs from my giant cup.

"So, are you going to?" Teegan hesitantly asks.

"Am I going to . . . ?"

"Talk to Mateo."

"I don't knowwww," I groan, slumping to the ground and covering my face with a pillow. "What do you think?" I ask my two best friends, peeking my eyes above the pillow.

Amaya and Teegan glance back and forth at each other, both seeming reluctant to be the first to speak.

Teegan finally draws first blood. "I mean . . . Aaron did make some compelling points."

My eyes bore into Amaya's. "Look, Lana, I'm not going to tell you that you need to take Mateo back," she begins, calculating her response. "But as much as I want to throat punch Aaron for everything he's done, I do agree with him that you've been a shell of yourself. And as your best friends, it's hard for us to watch. Especially when you *were* so happy with Mateo."

Teegan jumps back in. "LaLa, you've grown a lot in your flexibility and willingness to change plans recently. Maybe Mateo deserves to see that."

I give Teegan a blank stare, trying to recall my "stay-mad-at-Mateo" mental picture to loop again.

Then my bubbly, sweet best friend splashes ice water over my attempt. "And maybe you need to think back through if what Mateo said and did is really as unforgivable as you keep convincing yourself it was."

"Ouch, Teegs," I wince. Even Amaya looks a little shocked by Teegan's straightforward statement.

Teegan's eyes glisten with unshed tears. "He's *it* for you, Lana. Mateo brought out all your best qualities because he saw *you*—Lana Grant, intensely-focused justice crusader with the biggest heart for vulnerable people. He wanted your dreams for you—I think he would have done anything to help you chase them down." She pauses, voice choked with emotion. "You don't have to limp through life miserable knowing you've been cut off from your person."

Amaya and I just stare at her.

"Yes, he messed up. We all know that. *He* knows that. But don't throw away the chance to have something so special just because you won't admit that you were wrong too." Teegan wipes her eyes and gives her head a shake. "I love you, Lana, and I'll be in your corner no matter what. But you still have a chance to put these pieces back together, and I just . . . please don't be too stubborn to miss it."

———

I shower and let Teegan curl my hair while we watch a movie together. Even though I'm just going to sleep, it seems like a healing step to practice basic hygiene. I also want to assure Teegan I'm not mad after her honest comments.

Sleep proves hard to come by, and I wake early again Saturday morning. I quietly dress in leggings and an AOPi sweatshirt, grabbing my bag with my Bible and journal.

When I get to my car, there's no note on my windshield. A wave of disappointment trickles through me as I drive to Bookafe and order a bottomless coffee. Out of habit, I make my way to my favorite table in the world corner. I open my journal, but no words flow from my pen. I look to the bookshelf next to me and run my finger over the same Salman Rushdie novel from the day Mateo revealed his feelings for me at this table.

The memory floods over me, and I close my eyes as the burning sensation of drowning squeezes my lungs. I was so caught off guard by his declaration that day that I didn't even fully appreciate how thoughtful and sweet every word was, but now they waltz their way back through my thoughts. I sit in silence for hours, halfheartedly picking at a chocolate chip orange muffin and letting my coffee go cold as I stare at the empty pages of my journal.

When the tables around me start to fill with conversation, I pack up and leave, not quite sure what to do next. As I drive out of Center Square, I pass the plaza where the fall festival is held, dredging up more memories of Mateo: his total delight in celebrating my favorite season with me, the fiery sparks shooting through my arm when we held hands for the first time, his adorable nervousness when he asked me to be his girlfriend.

My subconscious has apparently turned into a glutton for punishment, because I find myself pulling into the parking lot of the soccer complex. I stare at the field where I rediscovered my love for soccer, where we played together, where I watched Mateo play. *He was so talented. He* is *so talented. He deserves to keep playing,* my thoughts betray, stinging my heart and eyes with guilt. I was so cruelly self-centered that I didn't even consider that this was a dream he deserved.

I contemplate driving to Mateo's house to crack open the door to conversation.

Instead, I keep driving and driving, out of the Brooklyn city limits. I arrive at the prairie reserve and put my car in park, looking out at the rolling hills where spring green is fully overtaking the brown of winter.

After queuing up my Moody Mellow playlist, I pocket my phone as I get out of the car and put in one ear bud. I start meandering down the path, too slow and aimless to label it hiking or even walking. Pausing frequently to stare out at the sky, I eventually find myself approaching the parking area where Mateo and I had our first real date.

My breath starts to catch, but I speed walk through till I'm back on the hiking path. I fight the urge to look back to the very spot I first found myself starting to fall for Mateo. My brain chooses this moment to tune in to the music playing in my ear, just in time to hear Taylor sing, *"I miss your tan skin, your sweet smile, so good to me, so right."*

"I don't need your commiseration right now, Taylor!" I yell out loud, yanking the ear bud out. I pause on the trail and half sit against a rock, eyes filling with tears.

I press the heels of my hands against my eyes, trying to stem the flow. But I can't silence the voice that's been pounding with increasing volume on the door of my heart all morning. *You're being too stubborn to admit you've made a massive mistake!*

Staring out at the horizon, I take in the beams of sunlight cutting their way through the thick, puffy white clouds filling in the sky. I focus on the sounds of birds calling to each other, the sensation of the breeze cooling my skin and swirling through my hair.

I *have* made a massive mistake.

I'm overwhelmed by the compelling urge to find Mateo, to explain to him how I've realized I need to be open to change, to not cement my plans all the time. I need to tell him I'm sorry for being so quick to leave him behind when I perceived him as a threat to my goals. I need to tell him that I trust him. That I *love* him.

With determination in my step, I begin walking back the way I came. When I reach the space of our first date, I stare down at the ground and bite my cheek to fight against the tears in my eyes. *I've been such an idiot.*

"Lana?"

I jump. My heart knows my name in that voice. It starts beating wildly even before I look up to see Mateo standing in front of me.

"I'm sorry if I startled you," he says apologetically. My eyes take him in, feeding information to my brain to process. He's wearing his favorite pair of Nike joggers and a Townsend Soccer hoodie, looking athletic and attractive as per usual. But there are dark circles under his eyes, and the stubble along his chin is more unkempt than usual, creeping down his neck in a disheveled way.

The information my mind latches onto, though, is the hollow, haunted look in his eyes. My body physically hurts seeing those dark brown eyes, usually so full of joy and warmth, looking so drained.

"I . . . I know you haven't wanted to see me, Lana," Mateo begins. "Teegan communicated your request, and I've tried to honor that. After the hundredth or so text message left unread, I accepted the fact that you'd blocked my number. I assumed my unanswered notes meant you didn't want to talk. I've tried to imagine you confidently moving forward, working toward your dreams like you always do, even if that meant without me. Tried to will myself to let you move on."

I try to swallow the huge lump in my throat, but it refuses to budge.

"I'm sorry for intruding today, but . . ." he pauses and looks down at the ground, clearing his throat. "Aaron talked to me this week and apologized for everything that he did. And he told me that he hates himself for doing something that made you so miserable. That he can't stand to see how depressed and closed off you've been.

"So I decided I needed to try, just try, to talk to you so you could at least have some peace. I've been practicing what I'd say for a couple of days, trying to get it right. When you weren't at AOPi, I drove all over town to each of your favorite spots, hoping to find you. Rubbing salt in the wound," he says with a pained look. "I saw your car parked here, and, well, here I am."

I still haven't said anything, but I haven't stopped him either, hoping that's enough permission for him to keep talking since my brain and vocal cords can't seem to coordinate.

"I just . . . I'm so sorry, Lana," he hangs his head, and I see him fighting back tears. "Hindsight is 20/20, and I know that I should have told you about the professional soccer opportunity the first day Coach Anderson called. I should have included you. It was unfair of me to go so far down an alternate path without even talking to you about it, even if I thought I was protecting you. I'd go back for a do-over in a heartbeat," he says, regret dripping from his voice.

"And I'm sorry for doubting you about Aaron. I should have just trusted you. I *do* trust you. When we were at the fall festival, I over-heard your conversation with Aaron in the alley." My heart hiccups at his admission as he continues. "I heard you tell him that you didn't like him anymore, that he wouldn't be your backup option because you were all-in on our relationship."

He pauses with a sad smile. "I heard you say it, and that's what gave me the confidence to ask you to be official." His eyes water again as he says, "But I let doubts get in the way, insecurities about your old feelings for him needle their way back in when you started seeing each other regularly this semester. It was obvious his feelings for you never faded, and I just got so in my head over whether I might lose you to him.

"It's not an excuse. I shouldn't have reacted the way I did about Adams telling you my plans. I'm so ashamed of how I treated you that night," he says in a choked voice. I can barely see through the tears in my eyes, but I know he's fighting them as well as he stares at the ground, jaw flexing, hands buried in the pocket of his hoodie.

"Lana, I need you to know that I love you. That before . . . before I ruined everything between us, I was going to . . ." He draws a shuddered breath in as he stares at his hands, which are fidgeting with a velvet ring box. My eyes widen.

"I was going to ask you for forever. I bought this. I had a whole plan, but then—" His voice breaks off, the tears pouring unhindered out of his eyes.

My heart implodes all over again, and I bring my hand up to stifle a sob from escaping.

"I'm so sorry I ruined it, Lana," Mateo continues, his pained eyes meeting mine. "I can't go back and change it, as much as I wish I could. And I can't expect you not to date other people. But, know that I won't be. Because I've loved you for such a long—" His voice breaks again as he swipes at his eyes. "I've loved you for such a long time, I don't think I can ever stop. So I'll be holding out hope that I can find my way back to you someday, no matter how long it may take."

Waves of tears make their way down my cheeks, dripping onto my sweatshirt, my hair sticking to the wet streaks as the breeze whirls it around me. I wipe my face with the sleeves of my sweatshirt, taking a deep breath.

"You don't have to say anything back, Lana," Mateo says sadly. He quietly adds, "I just needed you to know."

I take in the sight of this man I grew to love so much, standing in front of me in so much pain. Pain I had caused by my stubborn refusal to let go of *my* plans or to admit that I overreacted. *I don't want to lose him,* my heart screams, finally kicking my brain into gear.

Mateo turns to leave, and I take a step forward. "Wait, Mateo. Please don't go."

He turns back to me, a pinprick of cautious hope in his eyes.

"You weren't the only one who ruined our relationship, Mateo. I did too. Probably more than you did. I felt so threatened at the prospect of losing control of the future I had mapped out that I totally overreacted and lashed out at you. I'm sorry. I'm sorry for looking at you as a threat to my future instead of as a gift. You've always been a gift. I'm sorry for pushing you away that night, and then pushing you further and further instead of admitting that I shouldn't have done it in the first place.

"You should be playing soccer—you *deserve* to keep playing soccer," I tell him with a watery smile. "I was such a brat to not even acknowledge how incredible it was that you had the opportunity to go pro. I'm sorry I was so selfish. The truth is, I miss watching you play soccer."

I take another deep breath.

"I miss the way you smile at me, that teasing, satisfied smile you get every time you make me blush. I miss you constantly weaving your fingers through my hair," I continue, pausing to sniff and wipe my cheeks again. "I miss talking to you about everything. I miss watching the way you make people feel important—the boys at The Hangout, my family, your family, the guys on your soccer team, literally everyone you interact with," I say with a small laugh. "I miss the safe feeling of your arms around me. I miss the pattern of your heartbeat. I miss the way you kiss me, with so much tenderness and passion that they shouldn't even be able to coexist in the same kiss."

Mateo isn't even trying to wipe the tears from his face as he watches me, listening patiently like he always does. I take a steadying breath to try to stem the heaving sobs in my chest. "I miss *you*, Mateo. I've been slowly dying inside since I walked away from you, but I was too stubborn to admit it. But I love you. I love you, and I want forever with you."

In a heartbeat, Mateo has closed the gap between us, pulling me into a kiss that feels like every dream in the universe coming true. But just as quickly, he lets go and takes a step back.

"Wait, Lana, before you decide you want to be together, you deserve to know the whole situation," he says, holding both my hands between us. "Coach Anderson got hired by Lincoln United, and I accepted a spot on one of the League Two teams that they draw from. If I play well this summer, I'll likely get bumped to his team next year. I can't be in California, but I'm willing to figure out a way for us to still be together, to do *anything* to be with you. But you deserve the choice. You're not giving up your dream—I won't let you."

My heart swells with pride. *He did it. He made it pro.* I throw my arms around his neck and tell him, "I'm so proud of you, Mateo." I feel moisture against my neck where his face is buried. I pull back, taking his hands again. "You deserve this. I'm so happy for you."

He smiles at me, that dimple taking me in all over again. "Thank you, Lana. That means a lot." His smile falters. "But Virginia is pretty far away from California."

The gears in my mind suddenly start firing on all cylinders. "Wait, Virginia? What part of Virginia?"

Mateo looks at me quizzically. "Pretty far north, in Leesburg. Basically the northeast outskirts of Washington DC."

My heart stops, so full of joy it can't even contract. I feel a smile spread across my face and see Mateo's confusion in response. I reach my hand up to his chin, tracing the stubble on his jawline with my fingers.

"Mateo, I'm not going to UC Davis next year," I whisper.

He grabs my hand from his cheek and holds it against his chest. "What are you talking about, Lana? You're in, you worked so hard to get there, and you're already accepted. Why would you not go?"

I smile up at him. "Because I'm moving to DC instead. I'm deferring law school for a year and going to work as Elena's assistant."

Mateo's eyes widen in surprise, and I feel his heart pounding against my hand. He's looking at me like it's too good to be true. "We'll be in the same place?"

"Same place. But even if we weren't, I'd still want forever with you," I say before leaning up on my tiptoes to continue the kiss he interrupted.

For a perfect, time-stopping moment, everything is right in my world. Mateo's hands are woven through my hair, cradling my head. Spice market Christmas tree farm smell surrounds me as his lips declare his love over and over to mine.

He breaks the magic again, untangling me from his embrace against my whined protests. "Wait just one minute, Lana," he says with a laugh as he pries my arms off his waist. He reaches out a hand to stop me when I try to step back to him. "You. Stay here."

And then he's down on his knee, velvet box in hand, love shining in his eyes as he looks up at me. "Lana, I love you. I've loved you for years, and I'm going to love you more every year for the rest of our lives. Will you marry me?"

I don't even bother to look at the ring, because all I can see is the moisture gathered in Mateo's sweet eyes as he smiles at me. I lean down to place my hands on his cheeks as I answer, "Yes! Forever yes. I love you, Mateo."

He stands up and crushes me against his chest, my happy tears soaking into his hoodie. He lets go just enough to slip the ring onto my finger, which I barely glance at because I'm so enamored by the man in front of me. My fiancé. How in the world did I ever convince myself that I could live without him? I want both dreams.

Mateo pulls out his phone and pushes a few buttons until a familiar song starts playing. "Would you care to dance?" he asks with a grin. I laugh as he twirls me around and then settles me close in his arms, our hands tucked under his chin, his other hand softly caressing the lengths of my hair.

I rest my head against his heart, smiling.

I found a love, for me.

Epilogue

Four years later . . .

"Lana Alvarez, *magna cum laude*."

Wild cheers and applause break out as I walk across the stage to accept my diploma and shake hands with the Dean of the University of Maryland Francis King Carey School of Law. I turn to face my fan club and hold the diploma aloft, a grin filling my face.

Mateo is clapping most exuberantly of all, his tender eyes full of tears. My dad is next to him with Mom by his side, cheering through her own tears, looking about as proud as I've ever seen her.

I know I should exit the stage in a timely manner, but I can't help but take in all the faces—*my* faces—in the crowd. Of course, my siblings are there too, along with Mateo's parents, Miguel, and Isabel with her husband. Amaya is whistling, and Teegan jumps up and down next to her fiancé. Samira and Zahra stand between my mom and Elena, beaming up at me. Several friends we've made over the past few years here in DC round out the group, all cheering me on.

I still shake my head sometimes at teenage Lana and her certainty over her future. She held that perfect plan in a toddler-hiding-candy death grip. Bless her heart. I'm still grateful for her determination, even if learning to let go a little is what got me here on *this* stage, in this specific community.

The DC area has become a third home to Mateo and me. He killed it that first summer playing for the League Two team and was enthusiastically welcomed by Coach Anderson to Lincoln United. We got married in Brooklyn that October, the stunning colors of my favorite season providing the perfect wedding backdrop at the prairie reserve.

I'm not sure who cried more—Mateo, my mom, or Luis. They were all fiercely vying for a first-place finish.

We found the perfect spot to live just north of the DC metro, halfway between Mateo's soccer complex and the University of Maryland in Baltimore. After a year working with Elena on Capitol Hill and volunteering with the Chacón Center, I was accepted to the law program for the immigration clinic. Despite years of being a dedicated student, it was the hardest I ever had to work. I never would have made it through without Mateo encouraging me every time I had a bad day.

For my part, I was loudly cheering as frequently as I could as Mateo played as a substitute for Lincoln United. I think the referees came to recognize (and dread) the sound of my voice. Mateo also reached out to the director of the soccer program that Andrés was involved with in Miami, leaning on his expertise to start a similar nonprofit soccer club for disadvantaged youth in DC. Mateo really liked playing soccer, but he *loved* interacting with those kids and watching them heal, grow, and just have fun being kids. I jumped in to help with skills training for the girls' teams any time I had the chance.

After suffering a torn Achilles tendon in his third season with Lincoln, Mateo decided to retire from professional soccer rather than work his way back to playing condition. He swore he was totally content to focus on finishing his master's degree and running the nonprofit instead of continuing to play (aside from the co-ed rec team we joined together).

Between the soccer club and the community we've built here, I have a hard time picturing us moving away from DC anytime soon. Then again, I've learned my lesson about holding on too tightly to my plans for the future. What I do know is that Mateo is my forever, regardless of where we wind up geographically.

And that's the perfect forever for me.

Bonus

————————

Are you curious to hear Mateo's point of view?
Scan the code to read some bonus chapters from his perspective!

Continue following The Beefs' journey by reading Teegan's story next
in *Love and Other Chances.*
Scan the code:

Acknowledgments

Wow, sitting down to write the acknowledgments for my first novel is not an easy assignment. It feels like I should thank every significant person in my life up till now, but that's not very realistic. I'll keep things relevant to this particular debut novel journey.

Kyle, I am the luckiest. If you hadn't responded with enthusiasm and support that date night when I sheepishly confessed that I had started writing a romance novel, this book literally wouldn't exist. Thanks for always being proud of me even when I was hesitant to admit out loud that I wrote this thing. The first fictional man I wrote had to be a supportive and wonderful people magnet because that's exactly who you are. I love you, babe.

Mandy B., thanks for being the very first person to read this book. I was TERRIFIED asking you to test read it. But you were so gracious and encouraging and enthusiastic. I literally took a screenshot of your message with the things you loved about the book, and I read it every time I was feeling scared to take a step toward publishing this for real.

Thank you to my next alpha reader, Diana W., for giving me incredible feedback to make the characters even better. Also, for being the one to reel me back into the world of reading contemporary romance in the first place!

To my bestest gals, Amity, Amy, Diana, Haley, Jen, Lani, Leah, and Megan—you are the best hype squad EVER!!! Thanks for being so pumped and excited and wanting to know every detail when I took the coward's way out and told you via text message that I wrote a book because I was too chicken to ever say the words out loud during Bible study. Thanks for supporting me in this adventure in ways that I can't even know yet as of this writing. You make me feel like a million bucks. You're my people, and I will probably get teary-eyed every time I read these words I'm writing here for all of time, because I'm so grateful to have found you.

Addyson, thanks for making sure my college lingo and Spanish tidbits weren't too far off, and for being so excited about my book and talking it up to all your friends. And thank you for going to the greatest university ever. I'm so proud to be your aunt.

Lauren, Parker, and Sierra at Author's Best Friend, THANK YOU for helping me figure out how the heck to publish a book. Lauren, your manuscript critique helped me round out my characters and gave me encouragement to keep going. Parker, the book cover—WOW I love it! And Sierra, thanks for helping me with all the technical tasks and answering all of my frantic dumb questions.

To my line editor/proofreader, Sarah Lemcke, thank you for helping me polish and fine tune my manuscript. And thanks for all the random laughs from your side comments during editing crunch time!

To Manhappiness, for being such a perfectly wonderful city that you inspired my fictitious setting.

Thanks to the people who contributed to this book's content without knowing they did. To Allie and Kelsey for the inspiration of the "Beefs" nickname. And to the random DII men's soccer teams I stalked on Instagram to get a semi-realistic-ish storyline for the Townsend Bobcats—thanks for posting about your seasons for your fans and random aspiring authors.

A special thank you to Bri Stensrud for inspiring the role of Elena's character. Can I be the president of your fan club?? You've influenced my life more than you could ever understand. Check out Bri's book Start With Welcome and go follow Women of Welcome on Instagram at @womenofwelcome right now!

Deepest gratitude from the bottom of my aching heart to the Afghan families I've had the privilege of getting to know, whose lived experiences inspired the fictionalized events Samira's character faced: You've given us so much, and you deserve far more than we've given you in return.

Finally, I'd be remiss not to thank You, Jesus, the center of my everything. You created me exactly the way I am, with a mind constantly hovering around stories and love, with an affinity for writing words. I boxed those things up for a long time as unworthy pursuits, but now I'm embracing the fullness of how You wired me. We love because You first loved us.

Also by Tracy Baack

Love and Other . . . Series:

Love and Other Goals
Love and Other Chances
Love and Other Distractions

Christmas in Noel Series:

Saved by Noel
Joy to Noel

Kansas City Crowns Series:

Home Safe

Find them here:

Click here or scan the QR code:

ABOUT THE AUTHOR

Tracy Baack connects with readers through relatable romance. She enjoys writing character-driven contemporary romance novels with so much character depth and development, you just might think they're real people. Her books are always closed-door but full of heart-melting swoon, and they end happily ever after (after a little dose of angst).

Tracy lives with her husband and four children in the suburbs of Kansas City, Kansas, where she loves supporting indie bookstores. Her primary love language is sending the perfect GIF for any moment.

Tracy is the author of *Love and Other Goals*, *Love and Other Chances*, *Love and Other Distractions*, *Home Safe*, *Saved by Noel*, and *Joy to Noel* (with more on the way because she just might be a writing addict).

Connect with Tracy on Instagram at @authortracybaack or through her website www.tracybaack.com.